Wilder West:
The Collected Tales of K.D. West
Volume II

Stillpoint/Eros

All sexual encounters in this work occur between — and among — consenting adults aged 18 and above.

Cover art: *Passion* by Ashley Harrigan (flickr.com)
Used through a Creative Commons license.

Cover and Book design: David Kudler / StillpointDigitalPress.com

Print ISBN: 978-1-938808-30-2

Ebook ISBN: 978-1-938808-31-9

10 9 8 6 5 4 3 2 1 0 PROOF

StillpointEros.com

Stillpoint/Eros

Contents:

Wilder West

The Visitor Saga

In the first installment in this series, The Visitor, *Lea flew to Atlanta for a job interview. Her best friend Kirsten's brother Sean offered to let Lea sleep on his couch — Sean, whom Lea had lusted after for years. When she arrived, she found that she was being hosted by not one hunky firefighter but two: Sean and his roommate Andy.*

When someone visited her pull-out couch that night, Lea didn't know which of the men treated her to a pair of the most mind-scrambling fucks she'd ever experienced — but honestly, she couldn't find it in herself to care.

It wasn't until the next day, of course, after she'd gotten the job, that Lea realized that she'd had not one but two visitors to her bed the night before. And so as she celebrated her impending move to Georgia with them that night, she decided they should all celebrate together. And so they did.

The Visitor Comes Home

Lea was back in an airplane bathroom; her legs were down this time, and her panties were up; she was done using the facilities, and masturbation was the last thing on her mind — and the last thing that her body could handle.

Sean and Andy had made very sure that she'd had *all* that she could handle over the last three days. And nights.

Well, *more* than she could handle, which she wouldn't have thought possible. She wouldn't be walking straight for days. Probably wouldn't be able to touch herself for weeks. Well. Till the next day, anyway. Well. Okay. Until that night. If she were careful.

Not that she would be complaining any time soon.

But what she wasn't sure how to handle was how to explain any or all of this to her best friend and roommate, Kirsten — Sean's sister. Lea couldn't think of a good way to approach the fact that not only had Lea finally, *finally* bedded Kirsten's older brother, whom Lea'd crushed on and lusted after since the two women were still in college, but that they'd frolicked with *Sean's* roommate. Who, like Sean, was a tall, broad-shouldered, Southern firefighter. A wet dream on legs.

And that was quite outside the difficulty of letting Lea's best friend know that she would be leaving San Francisco at the end of the month, leaving Kirsten without a roommate.

It was overwhelming to feel so excited and *satisfied* at the same time as Lea felt nervous and *sore*.

The bell rang and the captain's voice rang out. "We've got some turbulence ahead. Please take your seats and buckle your seat belts. We'll try to keep this as smooth and as entertaining as possible."

Thanks, *thought Lea.* Will you come home with me?

When Lea texted *Landed!* from the airport and didn't get a text back, she figured that Kirsten was at work; the Union Square store looked askance at pulling out your phone on the sales floor. Still, it would have been nice.

So Lea sent the same text to Sean and Andy and was gratified to receive *great miss u* from Andy and *WHEN ARE YOU COMING BACK????* from Sean. She was grinning from her head to her aching hamstrings as she boarded the BART train and texted back *Can't wait to come back there and burn down the REST of Dixie!*

Her two Georgia boys informed her that would never happen, not even if she brought Sherman and his whole army.

She informed them — as her bus approached her stop — that the only army she planned on encountering when she came back to Atlanta was the two of them, and she had every hope that the South would rise again. And again.

Which they solemnly promised her it would.

Backpack on her back, Lea was giggling — *giggling!* — as she made her way up to her floor, fished out her keys, and threw open the door to the crowded one-bedroom that she shared with Kirsten.

The apartment was small. Lea and Kirsten had learned to deal with this. They'd lived together before, were (mostly) compatible and (mostly) in sync, and so they'd learned how to avoid being walked in on — or being the one who walked in.

Obviously, the lesson hadn't stuck, because the sight that greeted Lea upon returning from her odyssey was her best friend, head thrown back in ecstasy, her blonde mane trailing along the length of the kitchen table, her legs wrapped over a pair of very fine, very feminine shoulders.

"*SORRY!*" shouted Lea before her brain could point out to her that she could simply have closed the door and come back later.

Kirsten's blue eyes — the same ridiculous, washed-denim blue as her brother's — flew open, as did Kirsten's mouth. The woman who was pleasuring Kirsten looked up into Kirsten's face, and then spun around on her knees and screamed, covering her body and bolting through the door to the apartment's miniscule bathroom, which she shut with a bang.

Kirsten and Lea stared at each other.

"I… I…" spluttered Kirsten.

"Sorry, I'll come back, oh, god, I'm so sorry!"

"No, Lea, wait," soft, long, Georgia vowels called out.

Head whirling, Lea turned to the front door, took a breath and closed it. "You, um, want to put some clothes on?"

Behind Lea, Kirsten chuckled. "Kinda late for that."

Lea turned and tried to return her friend's grin. Given how awkward Kirsten's smile looked and how brightly Kirsten was blushing from head to mid-thigh, Lea figured she was doing a pretty good job of approximating it.

"Um," Kirsten began, then shook her head and chuckled. "Thought you were coming back tomorrow."

"Nope."

"Guess not."

The friends both laughed, and Lea felt her heart begin to descend from her throat when she made out a quiet, sustained sniffle from the bathroom.

Kirsten grimaced and went over to the bathroom door. "Hey, Gianna, sweety? You want your clothes?"

"Please." The voice from behind the door was very small and very moist.

Lea picked up the skirt, top, and undies at her feet that looked nothing like anything she'd ever seen Kirsten wear and raised an eyebrow at her friend.

Kirsten shrugged and took the clothes, turning to the bathroom door and knocking. "Here y'are, sweetie." She passed the clothes through.

Lea found herself staring at her friend's naked back, at the freckles that were so much like the ones she'd been staring at — licking — just that morning. She shook her head, trying to clear it.

The bathroom door opened. Gianna turned out to be a very petite woman. She shuffled out, her eyes downcast.

Kirsten turned to Lea, tits high, as if they were meeting at a formal ball. "Gianna, I've told you about my friend Lea. Lea..." Kirsten's eyes widened slightly. "This is my... my girlfriend Gianna."

Lea and Gianna both glanced at Kirsten before looking at each other.

"Nice to meet you," said Lea.

"Pleasure," said Gianna, almost managing a smile before her dark skin darkened several shades. "Call me, K. Bye," she murmured to Kirsten, kissing the blonde on the lips very briefly before disappearing out the door.

Lea finally dropped her backpack to the floor.

"Welcome home?" Kirsten flashed a dazzling, off-center smile.

"Thanks. Kirsten? Girlfriend?"

"Uh, yeah." The blush that had begun finally to recede on Kirsten's fair skin came roaring back.

"I mean," Lea said, "that's great, but... Wow. Since when?"

"'Bout a month." When she noticed Lea's shocked expression, Kirsten shrugged. "Well, honey, you've been a bit pre-occupied with the whole job search. And... Anyway. Yeah."

"So, girls?"

"Yup."

"Did you just —?"

"Oh, gawd, no. She's not the first or anything."

"*Really?*"

Blushing fully now, Kirsten turned and walked into their kitchen. "Um, naw. Remember Billy?"

"The guy with the thing for handcuffs?"

"Yeah, but, see, um, more of a Billie-with-an-i-e than a Billy-with-a-y." Kirsten grabbed a bottle of Pinot Gris out of the fridge and poured two large water glasses full.

"Oh." Fuck. That had been… Just after college! No wonder Kirsten had never brought him — her — over. "Why didn't you ever *say* anything?"

Kirsten's shoulder's slumped. "Some of us don't come from liberal San Fran families, sweetie." She handed Lea one glass of wine and sipped at the other.

"Kirsten…"

"Yeah, well, see, also, see, I mean I've always liked guys too, but see, I've known I've liked girls a long time, only I didn't actually think that was anything I could, you know, do something about until college."

"So? You could have told me!"

Kirsten favored Lea with a miserable smirk. "Sweetie. You're my best friend. And that's why I couldn't."

Lea just stared at Kirsten.

"Gawd, Lea, don't…" Kirsten looked away, took a drink, and put down the glass. "I couldn't tell you, sweetie, 'cause, you know, besides being my roommate and my BFF and all that shit, you have a cute fucking ass and I had a huge fucking crush on you that confused the shit out of me, okay?"

"Uh. Okay?" Lea tried to consider whether any of this upset her or weirded her out. Nope. Well, it did made Kirsten's whole obsession with helping Lea choose her underwear seem a bit less benign. But other than that… nope.

"And I still love you, but no, not like *that*. I mean, I figured out real quick you were just about the straightest girl on God's green earth, so I haven't been lusting after you all these years, which I didn't want you to have to think about, which is another reason why I didn't tell you, okay?"

Lea clicked her glass to her friend's. "Okay, K. I got it. I'm sorry."

Kirsten laughed. "*Sorry?* What the hell for?"

"That you didn't feel like you could just tell me."

"Aw, honey, I probably should have long ago. I mean, I guess I knew you wouldn't mind, I just…" She shrugged again.

"Hey, no prob." Lea frowned. "I'd give you a hug, but that seems like it would be sending the wrong signal."

Kirsten gave a sad smirk and shook her head. "Yeah. How 'bout I get some clothes on?"

"If you think it would help." A laugh fought its way up Lea's throat. "Thought you said it was too late?"

"Yeah, well, your damn city is cold, and anyway, I'm feeling kinda stupid standing here butt-naked." She walked around the table and picked up her dress.

"So. Gianna? Seems… nice."

For the first time that Lea could remember, Kirsten turned away as she got dressed. "She is, a real sweetie."

"Hope I didn't scare her off."

"Me too. Actually, that's another thing I probably shoulda talked to you about before now." Kirsten turned around, fully dressed but uncharacteristically timid.

Lea walked over and gave her a hug — fuck sending the wrong message. "Talked to me about what?"

"Well, see…" After a moment's hesitation, Kirsten hugged her back. "See, we've gotten kinda serious, the last few weeks, and, see, she's got this nice little place on Leavenworth, just a few blocks from the store, and, um…"

Lea backed up and looked at her friend, whose expression had gone from humiliated to thoroughly miserable. "What? You… You want to move in with her?"

"Um. Yeah?" Kirsten's brows bowed down. "But see, I didn't want to leave you having to pay for this place on your own, so — "

Lea laughed and hugged her friend, so that some of the wine poured down Lea's back. "And here I was worried about having to tell *you!*"

"Tell…?" Then Kirsten gasped. "Oh! Sweetie! You got the job?"

"Yup!"

"That's so great! Hey! Congratulations!" Now Kirsten gave Lea a real hug. "Wow! Can't wait to tell Sean!"

"Um. He already knows."

Kirsten pulled back from her friend and peered into her face. "Oh?" Kirsten began to grin.

Now it was Lea's turn to blush.

Kirsten gave a whoop and hugged Lea again. "Are you telling me you and Big Bro finally got off y'all's asses and got *lucky?*"

"Oh, boy, yeah." Lea knew that she was turning bright red, but she too was laughing; it was hard not to laugh with Kirsten — or with her brother, for that matter.

"Thank *gawd!*" Kirsten gave Lea another squeeze and went to refill her wine, most of which she'd now spilled. "If I had to listen to the two of y'all *lust* after each other any more — " Kirsten turned back and shot Lea a supremely wicked grin. "So? Was it good? Did y'all fuck each other's brains out? I mean, I don't want details, this is my brother and all, but *still.* Dish, girl!"

"Um. Yeah. God. Kirsten!" That morning, in the back of Andy's Yukon, Sean licking Lea's pussy while Andy suckled on her nipples… They had made her feel exactly as if she had just had not one but two amazing men pleasure her in every way imaginable for three whole days and nights. Which in fact she had. Lea could barely bend her own brain about what had happened. She couldn't even begin to think how to tell her best friend, who happened to be one of her lovers' sister. She figured that nothing that she could say would come anywhere near to the truth.

"Wow," laughed Kirsten. "I always thought Big Bro was the mushy, romantic type. Didn't figure he'd fuck you speechless!"

"Had help," Lea muttered.

She hadn't meant to say it out loud, and so she was shocked when her friend blinked at her. "Say *what?*"

"Uh." Lea hid behind her glass of wine.

"No, no, no, Miss Lea, you don't get to drop a little bomb like that and then play *peek-a-boo!*" Kirsten squinted through Lea's Pinot Gris. "Now, did you say what I *thought* you said?"

Lea sighed. She'd figured that — if the arrangement continued, as it showed every sign of doing — she was going to have to tell Kirsten eventually. She just hadn't planned on blurting it out quite so soon. "What did you think I said?"

Kirsten made a face that was even more contorted viewed through the glass. "Sounded like maybe you and Sean had some *company.*"

Lea just nodded.

"Well, damn! What did...?" Kirsten gasped, reached out, and moved Lea's glass to the side. "Please tell me it was Andrew."

Again, all that Lea could do was nod.

"Holy fuck." Beyond that statement, Kirsten was speechless — a rare occurrence. After a moment she recovered. "I mean, those big country boys don't usually do a *thang* for me, but he is a beautiful piece of man-flesh, sure enough."

"Tell me about it," sighed Lea.

"No, honey, *you* tell *me!*" Kirsten laughed, then shook her head and held up her hand. "I mean, naw, bleh, don't. Don't wanna hear about it if Sean was... I mean, are we talking, you know, *both* of them?"

"Uh-huh."

"At the same time?"

"Well," Lea said, fidgeting, "first night it was one, then the other." She shivered, remembering the two mind-scrambling fucks, remembering the thunder. "But after I got the job..."

"Holy fuck," Kirsten said again, looking properly stunned. She bit her lip. "Um. Did Sean and Andrew...?" She pointed her index fingers at each other, sloshing some more wine.

"I think I'm going to let *Sean* tell you about that." Lea took a deep breath and a sip of wine. "And you can tell him about Gianna."

"Wow. Uh. Yeah." Kirsten drank from her glass, and shook her head again. "There's a conversation our mama won't ever want to hear about. And here I always thought Sean was the good one in the family."

"Oh," laughed Lea, "I think you're both wonderful."

As it turned out Lea *hadn't* scared Gianna off. Though the petite brunette seemed very calm when she picked Kirsten up to go to dinner, however, Gianna still couldn't look Lea in the face.

"You sure you don't want to join us, Lea?" Kirsten asked for the third time.

"No, I think I've interrupted you two enough for today," answered Lea, and after a moment all three women laughed. Even Gianna.

After they had left, Lea sighed and shuffled her way over to the fridge. Three heads of lettuce — the red leaf badly wilted, but the romaine and the butter lettuce still looking good — her choice of eight kinds of hummus, and a few leftover falafel. No pita, but some whole-grain tortilla — instant dinner.

As she pulled her plate together and moved over to the table — aware only after she already eaten most of her meal that she'd sat at the spot where Gianna had been dining on Kirsten earlier that day — she sighed, knowing she was going to miss California's food. *But Atlanta's a big city,* she reasoned, *I'm sure I can get good food.* Then she giggled as she thought, *And I sure know I can find some great meat there!*

After eating Lea retired to the bedroom she had shared with Kirsten since breaking up with John the Control Freak a bit over a year before. She started to watch *30 Rock*, but found that she kept glancing over at her roomie's bed. Would it be any different sharing a room with Kirsten now that Lea knew that her friend liked girls — had had a crush on Lea herself? Well, that had been years before. Kirsten was obviously fine with it. And they'd made (and so far kept) an agreement when they'd roomed together in college: no bringing anyone else into the bedroom without giving the other a chance to clear out.

Lea had just started to wonder whether she should look for another place to spend the night so Kirsten and Gianna could have some privacy, when Lea's phone chirped. A text from Kirsten read, *Spending the night at G's. OK?*

Smiling, Lea texted back, *Great. Have a nice sleepover. ;-)*

LOL! ILU! came back the response almost instantly.

As she was putting her phone back down, ready to dive back into the ever-entertaining travails of Liz Lemon, Lea's phone chirped again.

It was from Sean this time: *Hey, miss you. Both of us do.*

Lea's chest filled with warmth. She answered, *I miss you both too.*

Wanna see us?

?

Video chat. On the computer. Andy wants to be able to see too, for some reason.

Lea laughed, imagining the two burly boys fighting over the little phone. She flipped open her laptop. *Okay. Tell me when.*

Now? And he gave a link.

Lea entered it into her browser. The feed loaded... "Holy shit."

Two broad-chested, naked male bodies greeted her, visible from the neck down, so she wasn't immediately sure which was which. They were sitting on the edge of the pullout, knees spread, each stroking the other's cock.

Yes. The one on the right had a cock that curved away from his body: Andy.

"Holy fuck," she repeated.

"Nice to see you too," one of them murmured – over the tiny laptop speakers, she thought it was Sean, but wasn't certain.

"Guess you guys couldn't wait."

"Told you we missed you," said the other one, accent a bit heavier, so that had to be Andy.

"Uh-huh." Lea could feel warmth spread through her middle, could feel her still-sore pussy moistening and her nipples reaching out through her blouse toward the screen. "So... Tell me, boys, what part of me did you miss?" And before they could answer, she began to unbutton her top.

Stripping had always seemed like a silly exercise to Lea. She was a practical girl: the whole taking-clothes-off thing just got in the way on the way from foreplay to *play*. But men, she knew, were visual souls — and her boys, clearly, were men. As Lea slowly opened the front of her sensible blouse, their stroking slowed, and they visibly leaned forward.

Besides, this was the best they could give each other until next month.

Once the last button was undone, she slid a finger all of the way back up her torso. "Did you miss my neck?"

"Yes, ma'am," said one. "Uh-huh," said the other.

Taking the collar, Lea pulled the blouse away from one side. "My shoulders?"

This time, they both just grunted their assent.

Lea pouted down at her own flesh. "Someone clearly misses it — they left teeth marks there."

There was a hiss from the speakers.

Lea slid the other shoulder free. "No marks there though. Guess you don't miss this one as much."

"Nuh-uh," groaned one of the boys.

"Miss that one too," said the other. "Lots."

"Mmm." Lea slid the bra strap on that side down. "You sure?"

"Yes," they groaned together. Their hands had begun moving minutely more quickly.

"You sure you miss my left as much as you miss my right?" Down slipped the other bra strap.

"Oh, fuck yes," said one.

"Huh" was all the other could manage.

Lea let the blouse slide off of her, down to the bed. "What else have you missed?"

"Uh..."

She held the bra up with one hand and trailed the other downward. "My belly? I see some marks there too — you must miss that."

"Damn."

"Yeah."

Grinning, she turned away from the screen. "Tell me, did you leave any marks on my back?" And before they could even grunt, she added, "Oh! But you can't see the whole back. Here." She popped her bra open and let it join the top on her comforter. "Miss my back?"

"You know we did."

"Love… bites."

Lea wriggled, pretending to try to look over her shoulder. "Ooo, really? I wonder whose?"

"Pro'lly both," one of them grunted.

"I sure hope so," she said. "But have you checked my *whole* back?"

"Uh…."

She got up on her knees. "How about… down here?" She pushed her jeans down an inch.

"Um."

"Don't… see nothing."

"Oh, what a shame." She popped the button on the jeans and slid them another inch down. "How about… here?"

"Um, maybe."

"Can't quite, um, see."

"Well, we wouldn't want to have that." She bent forward, wriggling the jeans and panties down so that her whole ass was pointing at the screen.

"Sweet Jesus."

"Fuck."

Lea couldn't help it. She laughed. "Guess you do miss this part. Don't think either of you took full… possession, though."

Groans answered her, and the sound of each pounding the other's cock.

Stepping out of the jeans, she bent all of the way forward. "This part, though?" She reached between her legs and gently stroked herself. "This part? Oh, guys, you sure as hell took possession of this part of me."

Whimpering.

"This part of me? It misses you both too. Sooooo much…" Gingerly, she slid a finger in, and was amazed that it felt so good. "You guys fucked my lights out, but my poor little pussy is still weeping for more." Another finger. Lea hissed; it stung a bit, but honestly, it was true. She wanted it. God help her: she wanted *them*. She peered back between her legs and saw them stroking each other on her little laptop screen — another wet dream come to life.

Andy was rocking his hips, thrusting into Sean's hand. Lea could tell that he was close.

Apparently, so could Sean. Disengaging Andy's hand from his own erection, Sean knelt to the floor, staring first at Lea — Lea's bottom, spread for both of them to see, Lea's fingers thrusting slowly in and out — and then staring up at Andy. Sean kissed Andy's slick cockhead. "You can think about think about fucking that sweet poon there," he rumbled, "an' come in my mouth. If you'll let me come in yours." He gave Andy's cock a lick, from balls to head.

Andy gasped. Though he'd seemed to be okay touching Sean's rod, he'd been much less comfortable letting any part of his body other than his hand touch Sean anywhere — certainly not his mouth, and certainly not Sean's cock.

Lea wanted to be patient and kind, wanted not to force Andy to do something he clearly wasn't totally comfortable doing. But the sight of Sean on his knees between their lover's legs, licking his way up their lover's cock — it left Lea with no patience. No kindness. "Oh, Andy," she moaned, sliding her fingers in and out, arching her ass, "want you in me *so bad...*"

Sean's mouth reached the top of that long prick, and stayed there.

"*GAWD*," cried Andy, all restraint breaking, as he began to thrust into his friend's mouth. "Gawd, fuck, *fine, SHIT*, you can stick that *thang* in my mouth, *FUCK*, just, just let..."

Sean showed that he had been paying close attention when he'd been helping her suck Andy off. Smoothly, Sean took an astonishing amount of that long *thang* of Andy's down his throat.

"God," moaned Lea, "so fucking beautiful." Her thumb was trembling as it stroked her clit. "Fuck me, Andy."

And fuck her he did — fucking Sean's face as he grimaced at her, her cunt, at the fingers stretching it....

"Oh, fuck, fuck, fuck me, Andy, fuck me...!"

Andy screamed and arched, thrusting hard. Once. Twice. Then he collapsed back onto the bed. "Aw, fuck. Fuck."

Sean came coughing up, wiping his face. "Well, damn, boy, you just about broke my spine from the inside!"

"Aw, fuck..." Andy was still lying back, his cock leaning drunkenly down over his thigh.

Sean slid up next to Andy, and for a terrible, scintillating moment Lea was sure that Sean, the mushy romantic as Kirsten had said, was about to kiss his roommate. But after a second, Sean just reached down and gave Andy's softening cock a squeeze. "Andy-boy, you don't have to — "

Andy's hand shot out and grabbed Sean's, which was still hard.

Sean gulped, and Lea gasped in sympathy.

"Y'all both sucked me off how many times, last few days?" rasped Andy, stroking his friend's prick. "I mean, mean, if you can take *me* in y'all's mouths, shouldn't ought to be no big deal to take *this* little ol' thang in mine, right?"

"*Little?*" Sean scowled, and (upside down as she was) Lea couldn't tell if he were kidding or not.

But Andy didn't volley back. Instead he rolled on his stomach and held Sean's cock steady before him. He stared at it as if it were a stick of dynamite, liable to go off at any second. He leaned forward, face stony, and gave the head a kiss.

Sean pushed up on his elbows; his eyes darted between Andy, who had backed up and was now licking his lips, and over Andy's back at Lea, who was trying to assuage the fire in her loins as gingerly as she could.

Andy opened his mouth wide, as if he were about to begin a hot-dog eating competition — which, in a way, he was — but Lea had enough brain left to whimper, "Teeth."

Andy blinked up at Lea, and then back down. "Oh. Right." He carefully covered his teeth with his lips, closed his eyes, and took the tip of Sean's cock in his mouth.

It wasn't an expert blowjob, but Lea could remember her own first attempt, and gave Andy an A for diving right in.

Sean looked stunned. He still couldn't seem to figure out where to look: at Lea's open cunt on the computer screen, or at his friend's open mouth, bobbing up and down on his cock.

Lea decided that he deserved a bit of torture as well. "Feel good, Sean?"

His eyes flashed up to the webcam and locked on hers.

Lea flexed her ass, grinding on her own hand. "Looks so fucking hot, Andy sucking you off. Don't you think so, Sean?"

Sean growled. Scowled. But his eyes flashed down.

Lea grinned, astonished to feel an orgasm beginning to build up in her tired pussy. "Wish I was there… *Mmm...* Wish I was there to help Andy… Or… Or I could… *Mmmm...* Could suck on him while he…. *Hnh...!* While he, um, sucked on you, and…. Is he, uh, *god,* is Andy getting hard again, Sean?"

Eyes smoldering, Sean slipped his hand under Andy, grabbing something that made Andy lift his pelvis up, revealing that, yes, he was hard again, and yes, what Sean had grabbed hold of and was once more stroking was that gorgeous cock of Andy's.

"Oh, *fuck,* Sean, god… And you could use that amazing mouth of yours on *this...*" She arched her pelvis again, opening herself to him, thrilled and terrified to find herself sliding another finger in; she could feel the muscles protest, could feel them exult. "God, Sean, Andy, want you so much, *want...!*" She began to buck against one hand as she sucked the other into her mouth, seeking *fullness,* seeking completion such as only those two had ever given her…

Sean screamed. Her name, maybe. Or maybe the Supreme Being's. Or hell, maybe Andy's.

Lea couldn't tell, because to her own great and wonderful shock, she came, hard, squeezing tight the three fingers in her snatch, screaming into the fingers in her mouth.

Once she had returned to her body, Lea curled her knees to her belly and rolled onto her side, staring at the screen.

Her two boys were there, slick with sweat. Andy had come still dribbling down his chin, but he was hard in Sean's hand. Each was slack-jawed. Each was staring back at her.

Lea felt tears overflow — something she'd promised herself she wouldn't let happen. "Miss you both so much."

"Love you," they both murmured to her together, and Lea surrendered herself to the tears.

That night, they could barely say anything else to each other than to agree to talk again the next night. "Can't do it like this," mumbled Andy.

Sean added, "We're at the firehouse the next three nights."

"Oh," sighed Lea — sorry, even as her body was relieved.

The next night, they chatted briefly, both men looking very businesslike in their Atlanta FD t-shirts. The laptop was on Andy's knees, and so it felt as if Lea were looking up at them. It made her feel oddly small. It made her feel… oddly safe.

"Anyone else there with you guys?" Lea asked.

Andy's eyes flashed up, over the top of the computer, while Sean simply nodded.

"Oh, shoot," Lea pouted.

They both grinned sadly at her.

"Hey," said Sean, "Sis and I had… a really interesting conversation earlier tonight."

Kirsten was once again over at Gianna's. Lea grinned, relieved that the siblings had in fact not made her bring it up. "Did she tell you who *she's* moving in with?"

Sean scratched his head. "Uh. Yeah."

Andy looked at him quizzically.

Lea laughed. "Put it to you this way, Andy, their mama is going to have lot easier time swallowing her boy sharing a girl with you than her *girl* being with a — "

" — with a, yeah," Sean broke in, and whispered into Andy's ear.

Andy's eyes got very wide.

Lea laughed. "Yup! Kirsten told me that conversation was one your mother would probably be better off never hearing about."

"Well, she had that just about right."

"Hey." Lea felt her mischievous side rising. "I know there's other guys there, but they can't see the screen, can they?"

Both boys shook their heads.

"Good," said Lea, and lifted her shirt over her head.

Their twin stunned expressions was all the payment she wished for… that night.

Two nights before it was time for Lea to fly back to them, Lea got on their now-nightly chat full of excitement. She'd shipped boxes of belongings to their place — her place soon — had put in her last day at the tiny theater she'd managed to keep from folding, and had helped Kirsten finish moving into Gianna's. She had the bare apartment to herself, had nothing to do tomorrow but pack and see a few friends, and tonight her boys were home — the next night they were on duty.

She looked forward to a long, leisurely video threeway, their last, thank god, for a long time, because, really, she was ready to have them both take her again. And again.

She anticipated them being naked, as they had been every other night when they were at their apartment. Had anticipated watching them sucking each other off. Maybe, a secret, very adolescent part of her hoped, she could encourage one of them to let the other fuck him if she offered her own ass as a reward. The thought of taking one of those very sizable cocks up her backside was more than a little terrifying, but….

When she got online at the appointed time, however, both boys were sitting, still fully clothed in their fire department duds. Both very serious. Each holding a piece of paper.

"Guys?" Lea asked, nervous at their unaccounted solemnity. "Everything okay?"

They nodded, still grim-faced. Andy held up his piece of paper. "Got the results of our physicals back."

"Oh?" What the hell?

"Look in your inbox," said Sean, and that serious face suddenly had a spark of something smoldering beneath it.

Nervous, Lea opened her email. There was a message from Sean with two PDFs attached. She double-clicked on them.

At the bottom of each was the blood screening. Sean was O+. Andy was A+. Both had good cholesterol; Andy's HDL was marginally higher. Neither tested positive for any of several cancer markers.

Each had tested negative for HIV, HPV, genital herpes, syphilis, gonorrhea, and any one of a number of other communicable diseases.

They were clean.

Not certain why they were sharing this with her, she looked up at them. "Guys?"

They were both staring back at her. Andy's gaze too was full of banked flame now. "Wanted you to know," he said, "that you didn't need to worry."

"We'll still wear rubbers and all when we're, you know," Sean's face darkened, "fucking. But…"

"You don't need to worry," repeated Andy.

A thick gobbet of emotion stopped Lea's throat for a moment. "What about… you guys… worrying about *me*?"

"We trust you," said Andy.

"Also," added Sean, that wicked smile of his creeping in, "I know from Sis that you hadn't had, uh, intimate contact before us with anyone over the last two years except for John the Controlling Asshole. And he always wore rubbers 'cause — "

" — because he didn't want any Little Johns running around without his permission," finished Lea, trying but failing to match his smile. "Uh, guys?"

"Darlin'?"

"Baby?"

"I renewed my prescription for, um, The Pill."

Sean's eyebrows raised. "So…"

Andy licked his lips. "So…"

Love and desire swept through Lea. "So. Gentlemen. Next time I see you in the flesh, I am *soo* going to be able to feel both of you go off inside me. At the same time."

"Well…" Sean murmured.

"Golly," gulped Andy.

And each began to pull his t-shirt over his head as Lea unzipped the hoodie that was all that she was wearing tonight.

I'm going home! she sighed to herself, and then groaned as her two gorgeous, sweet men each pulled the other's pants off and began to stroke the other hard.

The Visitor Comes Again

Lea had just lowered her skirt and stood up when the captain came on the intercom and said, "Ladies and gentlemen, they've cleared the runway, and so we are now descending into Hartsfield-Jackson Atlanta International Airport. Please take your seats."

Out in the cabin, there was cheering — there had been threats of diverting to Miami.

In the bathroom, Lea was having a panic attack.

Fuckity-fuck-fuck. What was she *doing?*

Well, she thought, as she made her way back to her seat, she was moving to Atlanta for her new job, which started in just a week's time. The job she'd been dreaming of, at a theater she was overjoyed to be working at. She was going to have a *staff,* for fuck's sake! She wasn't going to *be* the whole staff — and the janitor, and the concessions-stand dishwasher, and…

And she was moving into her new apartment. Moving in with Sean. And Andy. Sean and Andy.

Thinking of Sean and Andy — her two boys, her two *men* — who, damn it, wouldn't be able to see her until tomorrow because they were, damn it, *working* — got her middle moving again, but this time it wasn't anxiety. She was thinking of the feeling of two cocks in her hands. Of one of them in her cunt while the other filled her mouth. Of Sean helping her suck Andy dry. Of the two of them whispering, "Love you," over the video chats that had been her life-line to them over the past few weeks.

Of the fact that she was *moving in* with two men whom she'd only really gotten to know over three days of bacchanalian orgy — well, and two weeks of passionate (if wistful) video-fucking.

She'd lived with men before. Roommates. Boyfriends.

But two of them *at once?* One she'd known for years, but how well? He was her best friend's brother, but really? What did she know about Sean?

And *Andy?* What did she know about him at all?

Well. That he came from Smoky Mountains. That he liked boiled peanuts.

That his cock bent away from his body, and he could make her come *so* hard....

That he made really good fried chicken.

It wasn't a whole hell of a lot.

She had her key in her purse. They'd made up the big sofa-sleeper for her use — and theirs, once they were off duty.

They were good guys. Good boys.

But she was going to have to make her way through — of all things — a snow-bound Atlanta, and then she was going to spend her first night in the apartment alone. Which shouldn't feel shitty — Lea liked being alone — but it did. Feel shitty.

The downside of living with two firefighters was definitely going to be that they had twenty-four hour shifts.

The upside, she knew, was that they only had two of them a week. Which left them the rest of the week to make Lea feel like a very, very natural woman indeed, thank you, Carole King.

Still, *thought Lea with an internal pout*, couldn't they have managed to have today off?

"Your boyfriend meeting you in Atlanta?" asked the grey-haired black woman in the floral print dress sitting in the window seat.

Not feeling like it was worth the trouble of explaining the complicated mess she was walking into, Lea just nodded.

"Thought so," tittered the woman. "I've seen *that* look before!" She graced Lea with a a self-satisfied smile. And before Lea could say anything, she turned back to her copy of *Fifty Shades*.

Fuckity-fuck-fuck.

As they descended into Atlanta, Lea found that *fifty shades of grey* was about right: the city, which had been verdant the last time she'd flown in just a few weeks before, was now monochromatic. Flat.

The lady next to Lea seemed to be just as disconcerted. "Why, will you look at that? If it's global *warming* what the hell is Atlanta doing looking like *that?"*

Lea decided not to get into a debate about climate change — it didn't seem like anything good would come from that. "Do you have someone picking you up?" she asked.

"Oh, yes, bless you, my oldest boy will be there. He's got a big ol' four-by-four pickup." She patted Lea on the knee with a mahogany hand. "He's a fireman."

Lea fought back a wave of irrational panic. She *knew* this lady wasn't one of the ladies she'd one day have to explain just how she'd contributed to her beautiful, upstanding son's downfall. She'd met Sean's mother, who was as fair and freckled as her children, and Andy was if anything paler. It seemed unlikely that he would have an African American mom. Still… "I… I'm seeing a fireman." *I am,* thought Lea with a guilty, swallowed giggle, *TWO of them!* "Midtown."

"Oh, how nice! My boy's down in East Point." The woman's hand flapped against Lea's knee again. "I'm sure they know each other!"

Lea tried to keep the nascent panic out of her smile. "I'm sure they do." *Oh, God,* Lea thought once more, *what am I* **doing?**

The plane touched down smoothly, though Lea's stomach still lurched — more from the fact that she was already close to throwing up than anything. The other passengers cheered.

Lea sat back and closed her eyes.

"Well, honey," burbled Lea's seatmate, "here we are!"

"Here we are," Lea agreed, voice thin even to her own ears.

As they shuffled up the big metal tube to the terminal, Lea could see her breath. *Weird,* she thought, and *How the fuck I'm I going to get to the apartment?* She had a rental car waiting for her, but there was sure to be ice, the car was almost certainly not going to have chains, and Lea wasn't exactly used to driving in winter conditions. For the four hundred and thirty-second time, Lea found herself wishing that even one of her boys had been able to pick her up. They both drove four-wheel drive cars, but beside that, Lea just wanted to *see* them. She felt pathetic.

"Well, now," said Lea's former neighbor, "you'll have someone to warm you right up soon enough." The woman laughed. "You give that fireman of yours a big squeeze for me, you hear?"

Lea nodded, trying to smile. She found herself trembling, and the cold had almost nothing to do with it.

As they entered the terminal, the woman patted Lea on the shoulder and strode off through the sea of disgruntled passengers, her copy of *50 Shades of Grey* held proudly to her chest.

Lea stepped out of the flow of traffic and closed her eyes, leaning against one of the glass walls that looked out at the plane she had just left. *It will be all right. I'll get to the apartment okay. I'll survive one more night with no one to keep me warm. And then tomorrow…*

"Excuse me, miss," said a low, gruff voice. A heavy hand touched Lea's forearm, which was clutching her purse to her chest. "Would you mind coming with us?"

Lea's eyes flew open. The hand on her arm was gloved — heavy, industrial gloves — and attached to an arm clad in a heavy, buff-colored coat marked *Atlanta Fire & Rescue.* Blinking, she followed the arm…

It was attached to Andy. Andy, in his full turnout gear — coat, overalls, helmet.

And behind him, Sean.

Both of them somber-faced, but each with a joyously evil glint in his eye.

Lea started to squeal, to leap at them both, to see if she could rap her arms and legs around both of them at once — to hell with people watching — but Andy's hand held her fast. "I... I thought you were working!"

"We are," answered Sean. His posture said *On duty*, but his eyes promised pleasure, a promise that Lea's body immediately began urging her to collect on. "Obviously."

"We managed to *volunteer* for an extra shift out here at the airport," Andy added quietly, and then said more loudly. "We just need you to identify something for us, miss, if you'd just follow us."

"Identify?"

"Yes, miss." Andy winked, and gestured down the terminal — not in the direction of baggage claim, but toward one of the thousands of non-descript doors that you never notice as you wander through an airport.

Andy led and Lea followed; she could hear Sean taking up the rear — an image that set *all* sorts of nasty thoughts going in Lea's nasty, nasty mind. Andy used a key to open the door and waved the other two through into a small stairwell.

As soon as the door *clicked* shut, Lea turned and leapt, grabbing both men's collars, wrapped her legs around both of them — as best she could, since even without these heavy coats on they were not exactly small guys — and proceeded to kiss them both soundly. Two big hands reached under her butt, each holding up one cheek, each pulling her tight.

After a few minutes — not long enough, *never* long enough — Andy backed away from her neck and Sean backed away from her ear. "Guess you did miss us," chuckled Sean.

She glared at him and then grinned. "What do *you* think?"

"I think," Sean murmured, "that we missed the fuck out of you too, begging your pardon."

Her grin grew. She pushed her hand down between the two men, feeling their erections pressing together through the heavy overalls. "So, gentlemen. You had something you wanted me to *identify*."

Sean hissed.

Andy grunted through gritted teeth, "Not here. Security cameras all over."

"Oh?" Lea pushed her hand down again and wriggled against them. "You don't think the TSA would want to watch me take both of you in my mouth at the same — ?"

Sean stopped that mouth with a hair-curling kiss. He turned and pressed her up against the cold concrete wall, and Lea was just as happy that it was cold, because she wasn't sure that that Sean's heat wouldn't have vaporized her.

She heard a loud *thwack!* Sean broke the kiss and snarled at Andy, "Hey! Keep your hands to yourself!"

Andy smirked at them both, panting steam into the stairwell. "Come on, you two. Let's take this somewhere a bit more private."

Somewhere a bit more private turned out to be a ready room for the AFRD's airport battalion. "There's one in each terminal," Sean said as they made their way through an endless maze of corridors. "This one happens to be assigned just for us for today."

"How... convenient." Lea was walking between the two men, her arms hooked through their arms. She'd never been more conscious of just how much bigger than she they were. "A nice coincidence that you happened to be housed in the terminal where my flight landed."

"Isn't it?" Andy chuckled. "We may owe a few favors."

"Oh." Lea looked from one to the other. "Well, I hope that it was worth the trouble. I mean, doing all of that *just* so that you could see me when I got in..." She was teasing them, but in all honesty she truly was deeply touched.

"It was our pleasure," said Sean.

"We couldn't wait to see you," said Andy.

Two maintenance workers sauntered past in the opposite direction, paying them no notice.

"Well, then," Lea sighed, "I suppose I'll just have to do my best to make sure that it was all worth your while."

"Er," said Andy.

"Huh," said Sean.

Lea just smiled and pulled their arms closer.

After what seemed like hours of meandering aimlessly through a labyrinth of anonymous corridors, they stopped at a door that looked exactly like several hundred other doors that they'd passed, except that this one bore a placard reading *AFRD BATT 7.*

As Andy pulled out the key, Lea asked, "BATT 7?"

"Battalion 7. That's the airport battalion," Sean answered.

"Wow. A whole other battalion. You guys *do* owe some favors." Lea grinned at him in a way that she hoped promised *just* how much she was going to make it worth their while.

Such good boys!

Sean grinned back, and it was his most wicked, pulse-quickening grin. "You have no idea."

A not-very-nice thought occurred to Lea. "You didn't promise anyone... *me*, did you?"

Sean's face fell, and Andy, who had just opened the door, turned around looking if anything even more abashed. "Lea! We wouldn't!"

She shivered, suddenly feeling the cold of the concrete floor flood up through her.

Sean led her through the open door; Andy closed the door.

Lea found suddenly that she couldn't look them in the face. She was staring at the battered, red industrial carpet.

Sean knelt so that he was looking up into her eyes. "Lea. It isn't like that. Honest."

"You think we'd *share* you?" Andy knelt beside Sean. "Like we'd share a truck or a hound?"

"You're pretty comfortable sharing me with each other," Lea joked — though it was a pathetic attempt even to her own ears.

"It ain't like that at all," said Andy, looking deadly serious. "It's not *sharing*, it's... I mean..." He reached a hand to her hip.

Sean took her other hip and, in fact, it felt as if they had rooted her back to the ground. "This is how we *get* to be with you, Lea-honey. And all," he added quietly, blinking at Andy, who blinked back.

"Lucky me." She was smiling, but she could feel that she was on the edge of tears. *Why?* "Sorry." She reached out and ran fingers through two heads of fine, blond hair. She was glad that they'd hung up their helmets — she could see them hanging on hooks by the door. Her boys in their gear, looking incredibly sexy... It was wonderful, but she was glad to be able to see their faces.

"What've you got to be sorry about?" Andy's hand drifted up to her ribs, sending predictable but unpredicted sparks to her nipples.

Sean leaned forward and kissed the point of Lea's hipbone, and that sent sparks further south.

Astonished to find the cold vacuum that had threatened to consume her filling with heat, Lea gasped, blinking at them both.

Their matching serious expressions of earnestness melted to smiles. Andy let his hand slide up along the bottom of her breast to where the nipple was now threatening to burst through the fabric, while Sean went back to kissing her hip, his eyes still raised to hers, his hand drifting up the inside of her knee....

"Lock... door?" Lea managed to splutter.

"Already locked," Andy said as his fingers began lightly to tease her nipple through the damned bra and the damned sweater and...

"And nobody else's coming in here until midnight," mumbled Sean into her skirt as *his* fingers slid up beneath the hem, blazing a path of glory up the inside of her thigh.

"Oh," sighed Lea, feeling as if it were a miracle that she was still standing, "Great..."

At that moment, Sean's fingers brushed along the length of her pussy through her panties, Andy pinched her nipple between his thumb and forefinger, and — not coincidentally — brought Lea herself to her knees.

Sean gave her a lazy smirk. "Nice of you to join us, Miss Lea."

She couldn't think of any response in that moment other than to stroke their coat-clad chests.

"I think we might be a mite overdressed for this next bit," Andy chuckled.

"Let me undress you both. I've always wanted..." Running her hands down to their crotches, she felt suddenly shy. Overwhelmed.

"Wanted to jump a fireman in his gear?" asked Andy, a smirk still coloring his voice. His fingers continued to tantalize her breasts.

Lea nodded, pushing their coats off their near shoulders.

"Sorry we can't do this with you on a truck," said Sean.

"Fuck the truck," panted Lea, pulling the heavy coats down so that they slid off of the men's arms and onto the floor behind them. She pulled the near suspenders off, then pushed the far ones. Her fingers trailed down their chests — both vibrating at her her touch — and came to rest on waistbands of their thick trousers. She couldn't see any fly or buttons. "Huh. Am I supposed to *tear* these off?"

"Uh," gasped Andy.

"Velcro," grunted Sean.

"Oohhh." Letting her fingers slide across the fronts of the pants — which were growing visibly tighter — Lea found the closed-away flaps. "Don't want to let go of either of you," Lea sighed. "So how am I going to open these pants? *Stop.*"

Each of the boys had begun to reach for his own fly, but Lea wanted no help. Grinning at them both, she leaned forward and gave the lump at the front of Sean's pants a gentle bite.

Sean sounded as if he might be choking.

But Andy was the less patient of her two men, Lea knew that, and so she turned toward his crotch, grabbed the waistband, and ripped the Velcro flap loose with her teeth. Gazing up into his eyes, she found his zipper with her teeth and pulled it slowly down over her lover's burgeoning erection.

All the while, she kept a firm grasp on the tented front of Sean's trousers.

"Fuck. Lea." Andy's molasses-dark eyes were half-lidded, smoldering.

Her gaze still locked on Andy's, Lea bit his boxers — being careful not to bite *him* (not too hard, at least) — and pulled them and the pants down to his knees on the floor. She kissed her way back up, grabbed his cock, and gave the head a long lick and a kiss.

Andy groaned gratifyingly.

Sean whimpered, and so Lea gave Andy's cock another quick lick, and then turned to her other lover and repeated the entire procedure, her hand stroking Andy's cock to keep it from feeling jealous.

"You want me to suck you?" Lea felt incredibly hot, incredibly powerful — two beautiful hard-ons in her hands, two beautiful mean nodding eagerly at her. "But who first?" she said with a pout — and then a thought came back to her — an incredibly nasty thought from earlier — and she went with it, not wanting to give them or her the room to get nervous: she pulled the two of them so that their balls were pressed together, their cocks a single spear of flesh in her hands. "Mmm," she said, and opened wide, taking both of them into her mouth at once.

Both men began to swear, and that heat, that power, flared even brighter inside of Lea.

She was amazed at how well their cocks fit together — Andy's reverse curve matching Sean's more typical one perfectly. The feeling of those two thick cock pressing over her tongue and into her throat was intoxicating — but almost too much. She backed off of them, just to make sure could still breathe.

Each of her men had grasped the other. Their heads were on each other's shoulder, their eyes closed. It was, Lea thought, the most sublime thing she had ever seen.

As Lea readied herself to take them back into her mouth, Sean began to rock his hips, pressing his cock through her grasp and along Andy's erection.

Andy gasped, "Damn!" He began to rock in opposition to Sean's thrusts.

If Lea had thought that her excitement couldn't grow any further, she'd been wrong. "That... feel good, guys?"

"Fuck, yes," murmured Sean. Pre-cum was spilling from the tip of his cock onto Andy's and onto Lea's hands.

"It's called —" She licked to the two erections into her mouth again. "— frotting."

"Huh," grunted Sean.

"Say what?" muttered Andy, one hand in Lea's hair, the other pulling Sean closer.

"*Frotting.*" A term she'd learned from fanfiction. All those years of reading Gundam Wing and Harry Potter slash had paid off after all! "Two girls rubbing their pussies together, it's called *tribbing.*"

Sean just repeated, "Huh."

Andy, however, opened his eyes again. "T-tribbing?"

"Uh-huh."

"Damn."

Lea took them both into her mouth again, evoking a pair of deep moans before she pulled off again and looked up. "You guys happy? 'Cause I'm pretty fucking happy."

Sean sighed, "Happy, yeah, but…"

"But… we'd kinda like to both wanna be…" Andy hissed as Lea sucked them both in again.

Sean continued, "Inside. You. *Please.*"

"Well," she laughed, "since you ask so politely, how can I refuse!" Letting go of Andy, she moved Sean back a bit, bent down and took him into her mouth.

Andy did as she knew he would: he moved behind her, flipped her skirt up, and gave her pussy a searing kiss.

Lea groaned around Sean's cock, and both men laughed. "Yeah," Andy said, kissing his way up her bottom, "she's got a lot to say when it's her at the receiving end!"

Lea was about to pull off Sean, turn around, and give Andy a piece of what was left her mind when Andy thrust into her, and she didn't have any pieces to spare.

Perfect. There was something about being with Sean and Andy that was just *perfect.* Didn't matter who was filling her mouth and who her pussy, or how well she knew them, or if both were in her hands or between her breasts or…

Sean reached down and cupped Lea's still-covered breasts, which were swaying wildly to Andy's thrusts. His fingers closed around her nipples and…

Mr. Sanderson, her senior-year Composition teacher had spent an entire class period once talking about how some adjectives can't be modified. *A bit pregnant. Really unique.*

More perfect — Mr. Sanderson had pointed up at the poster with the preamble of the US Constitution when he said that.

But Lea now felt she had reason to disagree. Before had been *perfect.* Now was *more perfect.* And then Andy's hands slipped around her hip and closed and her clit and…

Most perfect.

Sean and Andy were lying on the floor, each with his head at the other's knees. Lea was draped across them, her top and bra up under her armpits, her skirt around her waist. *Take that, 50 Shades Lady! Bet you didn't see* this *coming!*

Lea giggled moistly and then blinked. "Oh. Fuck. My luggage."

Both men laughed, literally rocking Lea's world. Andy snorted, "Knew we forgot something!"

Before Lea could jump up, Sean slid his hand — which had been resting on her thigh — up to her snatch, stilling her quite effectively. "Told you, Lea. We needed you to identify something."

Blinking, Lea looked at Sean and then at Andy, who laughed again and pointed over by the door. Her well-traveled back-pack and duffel bag were right there. "Oh. Thanks." She grabbed two semi-hard cocks and squeezed them, getting two rumbling groans for her trouble. "And thanks for meeting me."

"We couldn't stay away," said Andy.

Sean added, "And we didn't want you to have to drive with the roads like this." He stroked her hair. "If you don't mind, we get off shift at midnight."

"Mind? Hell, no!"

"Lea," said Sean, his fingertip running along her earlobe, the line of her chin, "You seemed a mite antsy. Is this really okay?"

She was going to answer *Are you fucking kidding?* But she recognized that it was a real question and deserved a real answer. "Yeah. Yeah. It's just..." She kissed Sean's hand and then turned and pulled Andy's to her lips. "I think this all scares me a bit. I mean, I barely know you guys, but this just feels so... *right.* You know?"

"Yeah," Andy said, as both men let their fingers explore her collarbones, her ribs. "Yeah, I reckon we sure as hell know."

"Indeed we do," said Sean. His fingers grazed the bottom of Lea's right breast so that she could *just* feel it. "And we know that worrying about it won't get us nowhere. Now what do y'all both say," he continued in his low, rolling drawl, "about seeing just how *right* we can keep this feeling before Andy and me have to get back out there in the cold?"

Andy and Lea both concurred that Sean's was a mighty good plan.

Perfect, even.

The Visitor Goes to Work

Lea's phone went off, crooning U2 at her.

First day of work.

Meeting with her boss, Sassy.

Meeting with Bob, the theater's artistic director.

Meeting with the box office staff and training on the ticket software with Zach, the theater's resident computer guy.

Tour with Gus, the tech director.

Lea needed to pee.

Heart racing, adrenaline singing through her veins, Lea leapt out of bed to go to the bathroom.

Well. She tried to leap.

Something heavy was holding her down.

Two somethings, in fact: Sean and Andy, whose legs and massive arms wrapped Lea in a cocoon that would have been incredibly sweet if she didn't need to get up and get ready for her first day on the job.

Also, she still needed to pee. "Guys?"

As Bono continued his ode to the glory of the day, Lea's boys snored on.

"Sean? Andy?" Wriggling, Lea realized that her hands were at each of their crotches. What a surprise. She squeezed two well-worn, well-earned morning hard-ons evoking two somnolent groans. "Boys. Get off of me or I'll fry these up for breakfast."

Andy's head shot up. "Uh. 'Morning."

Sean's face rolled off of Lea's right tit. "Hey."

Anxious as she was, Lea couldn't help but smile down at the shit-ton of male gorgeousness that she had somehow managed to snag for herself. "Hey, yourself. I need to get up."

Now Sean sat up. "Right. First day at the theater." He pronounced it as a three-syllable word: *the-AY-tuh.*

"Uh-huh. And as much as I'd love to stay and play — "

"No," both men said, and like the firemen they were sprang out of the bed, treating her to the sight of her shit-ton of pulchritude standing naked and cum-stained on either side of her bed, and making Lea briefly wonder if she *really* needed to be on time for her first day of work....

"We'll start some breakfast," Sean said, pulling on the pajama pants they somehow always put on but somehow never kept on.

Andy reached out to Lea. "You take a shower." When he pulled her up out of bed, momentum carried her body against his, and the feeling tempted Lea to stay.... He gently propelled her toward the bathroom. "You go. I'd say make yourself prettier, but t'ain't possible."

She beamed at him. "Flatterer."

From the kitchen, Sean called, "No, ma'am. Just the facts, ma'am."

"Uh-huh," said Lea with a very non-Southern smirk. "I've got my eye on you two. Don't think I don't."

"No, ma'am," answered Sean, his smile very Southern, and very wicked.

Standing under the spray, Lea contemplated the fact that tonight would be her first night alone in the apartment. Both of her boys would be back to the firehouse tonight, and that knowledge filled her with anticipated ache, even as it filled her with a bit of relief. Since Andy and Sean had met her at the airport three nights before, it felt as if most of her waking time had been spent in a fog of sexual satiation. One, the other, or both of the boys always seemed to be ready and raring to go, and that was hardly something Lea was going to complain about. Even so, Lea had lost count of the orgasms they'd brought her too, and she hadn't even tried to count the number of times they'd come on or inside of her. Her pussy. Her mouth. Between her tits...

The previous night, when she'd needed to catch her breath, on each other: frotting — grinding their cocks together, each grabbing the other's ass, pulling the other close, Sean on top, Andy with his head pressed against Sean's sweaty shoulder, his eyes locked on Lea's as he bucked against his friend and spurted up against Sean's flat stomach, setting Sean off....

It was just about the sexiest thing that Lea had ever seen, and was the closest she'd ever come to understanding her friend Kirsten's fascination with gay porn.

As the shower poured down on her, Lea felt her nipples hardening, felt the hot water streaming between her labia. *Oh, god....*

Sliding into the corner of the shower stall, trying not to think about time, Lea rubbed her hands over her wet body. She let her fingers trail down between her legs, and hissed as they encountered her pussy — satiated, yes; tired, perhaps; but still ready for more....

"You need a hand there, Miss Lea?"

Through the steam-fogged glass door, Lea could see that Andy and Sean were standing at the door of the bathroom. "Huh," grunted Lea. Bulges in their low-slung pajama pants made it obvious that they were having as hard a time as Lea was *not* thinking about about the last few days. "Uh-huh," she groaned. *"Please."*

They dropped trou — *why did they ever bother putting them on?* — and stepped into the shower. The brief flash of cool air that they'd let in was immediately replaced by the heat of their bodies pressing against hers. "Rolls in the oven," mumbled Andy, huge hands flowing over Lea's belly and hips. He leaned down and sucked Lea's right nipple into his mouth, eliciting a spark of pleasure and a small scream.

Sean stopped her mouth — gently, always gently — and began to slowly kiss his way across her cheek to her chin. Up her chin tortuously to her ear. He pulled on her earlobe with his lips, let it slide by the smallest possible degrees out of his mouth, and then whispered, "What you thinking about, Lea? What got you all hot and — " He let his fingers join Andy's sliding along the slick out lips of her pussy. " — ready for us?"

Whimpering, Lea tried to spread her legs, to open to them, but their massive thighs pressed against hers, and so she settled for letting each run his hand in the crease between either thigh and her pussy. It made Lea wonder why she hadn't ever tried masturbating two-handed.

Would she ever need to masturbate ever again? "Thinking... of you," she groaned as Sean began to apply his amazingly talented, *slow* mouth to her free breast. She reached down, taking two wet hardons into fingers that she could barely control. "Rubbing... 'gainst each other. *Fuck!"*

Sean had finally sucked her left nipple between his teeth.

Into right breast, Andy murmured, "Wouldn't you rather have us rubbin' 'gainst you?"

"Um..." Honestly, Lea had no ability to say what she'd *rather* have, but yes: that sounded very nice indeed. "Uh-huh...."

Grinning, Sean slid up Lea's body and turned her toward him. Andy pressed up against her back and reached around her, pulling Sean's ass, so that Sean's cock slid up along Lea's belly.

Sean pulled Andy close as well, and his cock slid against the length of her spine, his balls spreading her butt cheeks. Both men began to kiss and nibble at her neck, her cheeks, and to grind aganist her.

Fuckity-fuck-fuck.

They were fucking *through* Lea. Lea *was* the fuck. Her entire body felt like one enormous erogenous zone.

Each began to grunt ferally into one of Lea's ears.

FUCK....

But...

But as exciting as it was — and it was — Lea was aware of her own pussy weeping with need, the greedy thing, adding more moisture to the wet shower. "Um…" She found one leg sliding up onto Sean's hip.

Without any further prompting, Sean's hands slid to Lea's ass and lifted her, so that his cock was grinding against her clit and Andy's was sliding up the crack of her ass. "Damn," he grunted.

"Uh-huh," Lea sighed as the two erections sparked all sorts of fascinating sensations in her lower body.

"Damn," echoed Andy.

The two of them continued their steady rhythm. Lea hardly had do a thing other than enjoy herself and try not to pass out.

After a few minutes she felt the rhythm shift, speeding up. "Uh, Lea, honey?" moaned Sean. "Can I… inside you?"

"Please!"

In rhythm, he lifted her, then lowered her onto his cock.

Lea and Sean both swore in some Stone Age language that bore no particular resemblance to English. The feeling of Sean's sweet erection stroking her g-spot as Andy pushed against her pelvis, made her clit grind into Sean's pubic bone…

"Um, Lea? Baby?" Andy whined.

Lea threw back her head and kissed him. "Huh?"

Andy slowed, his expression pained. "Could I maybe…?"

"Oh. Sure. After Sean. I'd… *HNGH*… love… that." Sean had latched onto one of Lea's nipples again.

"Um, yeah, me too, um…" Andy panted, grinding against Lea's ass as Sean thrust up into her cunt. "Uh, maybe…?" He slipped one hand free and steadied his cock, lining it up with Lea's backside.

"Woah!" gasped Lea, her buttocks clenching around his head, her body stiffening, her cunt contracting so that Sean screamed his orgasm into her chest, and they all nearly toppled over.

"Sorry!" moaned Andy as Sean slid slowly to the shower floor, Lea on top of him. "I didn't — !"

"No, no, no, it's okay, I mean," panted Lea as she felt Sean pulsing inside of her as she lay on his chest, "I mean maybe we can do that, can talk about that, but, um, not right now, okay?"

"Okay." Andy sounded about five years old.

Sean slid his cock out of Lea, making her gasp again. "Don't worry, Andy. I think sweet Miss Lea here still needs some help gettin' off, and seems to me she's got a very sweet, very hot hole to file."

Lea tilted her pelvis so that Andy could see her pussy, washed by the shower spray, dripping Sean's spray, open to him.

"O-okay." Andy knelt behind Lea, between Sean's thighs, and buried his reverse-curved cock in her, and it was his turn to join her in screaming that Paleolithic war cry.

As Andy began to pound her from behind (and from his whimpers, he was clearly close, which was probably why he'd been so eager to stick his *thang* up her ass, the poor dear, and *oooo*, she was *sooo* close too), Sean's fingers slipped down Lea's belly and through her bush, finding her clit, and...

And...

As the mist cleared, Lea was first aware of *wet.* Wet Sean against her belly. Wet Andy gushing wet inside of her. Wet her. Wet air. Wet tile.

Tears. Water.

Wet.

"Think those rolls are done, Andy-boy?" asked Sean, reaching beneath Lea's overflowing pussy and squeezing his friend's balls, releasing more *wet* inside of Lea.

"Aw, *fuck yeah*," groaned Andy.

"Then let's go get this girl fed and off to her new job."

"Fuck yeah," panted Lea with a slack grin. "I'm definitely ready now."

Lea's first day was a whirlwind. Sassy, Lea's sardonic, Canada-born boss, was overjoyed to have a fulltime assistant for the first time in years, and showed Lea off around the office like a new baby. The theater was in the middle of producing one season and mounting its subscription drive for the next one, and so between the main office, the shop, and the box office, there were well over a hundred new faces and new names for Lea to learn. After her last job, where she and the artistic director had comprised the entire fulltime staff, the flood of new people and energy overwhelmed Lea, even as it thrilled her.

Everyone seemed incredibly friendly. She got five different offers of places to stay, and was asked out on three dates — two very different men and one woman — the office manager, Jaimie, who reminded Lea strongly of Sean's sister, Kirsten. It was quite nice to be able to say that she was all taken care of in both regards.

Nicer to be able to say it while she could still feel the remnants of Andy and Sean's passion inside of her.

After watching a few rounds of this, Sassy got an incredibly knowing, wicked look on her face. As they ate lunch in Lea's tiny new office (barbecued ribs, of course, which Sassy claimed was her main reason for staying in Atlanta), Sassy waited until Lea's mouth was full and shot her a sly grin. "So. Boyfriend? Girlfriend?"

"Um," said Lea, trying to swallow, trying to think how to answer. "It's... complicated."

Sassy's eyebrows shot up. "Is it, really? Well, well, well. It's always the quiet ones."

Lea knew she was turning the color of the barbecue sauce, so she didn't even try to answer, letting Sassy chuckle to her heart's content.

As they finished up their lunch, Sassy said, "Complicated is what we do best, of course, but if it becomes *too* complicated, don't feel shy about letting me know, eh?"

"Thanks," said Lea, trying to match Sassy's no-nonsense tone. "I think for now it's just complicated enough."

"Lucky you." Sassy's grin widened. "So, after your last meeting, I'd love to take you out to dinner with Bob." The artistic director of the theater. "Won't be stepping on any plans?"

"No," said Lea. "I'm on my own this evening anyway."

"Oh?" Sassy raised her eyebrow again, but apparently decided to move on. "Well, you've got a training session in the box office with Zach. He's sweet, but watch his hands."

"Okay," said Lea, thinking, *I'd rather watch Sean and Andy's hands, stroking each other...* Smiling, she shook her head, and then remembered her last meeting of the day. "No problem. Do I need to worry about Gus?"

"Oh, no." Sassy gave what was for her a soft, warm smile. "Gus is a sweetheart. You won't have any trouble with him."

"Great." Lea gathered up the napkins and sauce-soaked bags. "Well, let me strap on my armor and go get trained by Zach."

Zach turned out to be no problem. Lea short-circuited any potential ass-grabbing when she breezed into the box office and asked if he knew where Sean and Andy's firehouse was. "My boyfriend works there," she sighed, "and I'd love to drop in by surprise when I get off work tonight."

Politely Southern as most of the staff, Zach pulled up a map and showed Lea that the firehouse was only a half mile from the theater — which Lea already knew. After Lea had gone on about how wonderful her boyfriend was — and he was, whichever of them she happened to mean — she thanked Zach fulsomely.

He smiled back, a nervous, thin-lipped smile, and proceeded to teach Lea the intricacies of the box-office software.

Zach never touched her.

As Lea walked through the door that led backstage to the domain of Gus, the theater's tech director and senior designer, Lea texted the boys: *Miss me?*

Like crazy, came back Andy's immediate answer.

Think we're both addicted, added Sean.

Lea shivered and smiled. *Me too. Hey, I'm having dinner with my bosses tonight. Any chance I can swing by and visit after?*

After a minute or so, Sean's answer came back: *Afraid that's probably not a good idea. We kind of pushed our luck swapping shifts to meet you out at the airport. Another time?*

With a sigh, Lea sent them a frownie face, and then texted, *I'll be so lonely in that big pullout without both of you.*

She got two frownie faces in return. *See you tomorrow,* they both answered.

"Ah, Lea, how nice to meet you." Gus was grey-haired and small — pixyish, even — and though he was easily the oldest person working at the theater, his eyes and smile were bright and he was bouncing on the balls of his feet as he approached. "Sally's said such wonderful things about you."

"Glad to hear it!" Lea laughed. "You're the first person I've met here who doesn't call her Sassy."

"Oh, well..." He blinked at Lea. "My wife was named Sally, you know. My late wife."

"Oh." Lea felt all of the heat that had flooded into her middle as she texted Sean and Andy turn cold. "I'm so sorry."

"Oh, no need," Gus said with a bright, sad smile. "It's been four years, though there are days when it feels as if it was only yesterday. But we had a wonderful life together. Here. I'll show you." He led her into the bowels of the shop area behind the main stage; a group of artists were painting an elaborate starscape on what looked like an old barn door. "Look's gorgeous," said Gus, and the crew looked up. "Everyone, this is our new assistant business manager, Lea."

Lea waved. "The box office staff have already dubbed me *Mini-Sassy*," she laughed

The painters waved and introduced themselves; Lea despaired of remembering any more names, and then Gus tugged on her sleeve. "Come on," he said, "let me bring you up to my aerie." He led Lea up a steep staircase — almost more of a ladder — up to a room that was easily sixty feet above the shop floor.

"Whew!" Lea said when they reached the top. "No wonder you have so much energy! You climb that all of the time?"

"Oh, yes," Gus said, blinking, as if it had never occurred to him that it might be a difficult climb. "I suppose that's why I don't get too many visitors." He flashed his bright smile and ushered Lea in.

The office was easily three times the size of Lea's, but it didn't feel it. It was crammed with set models, blue prints, a wide-format printer, three work tables overflowing with sketches, swatches, paint chips and random pieces of hardware. And the walls were invisible, covered by dozens of brightly colored paintings. A number were of dogs and sailboats, but a number were amazing, impressionistic portraits of actors and...

"Here's my Sally," said Gus, that sad smile resurfacing. Behind what seemed to be his desk — it was difficult to tell, given the glaciers of beautiful bric-a-brac piled on top — hung eight different paintings that featured a beautiful redheaded woman. Well, it was difficult to tell what she *looked* like, but the paintings made it very clear how the painter had *felt* about her. "We were married over forty years," Gus sighed, "and she was as beautiful when I lost her — " He pointed to the portrait furthest to the right, which showed her red hair shot with white. " — as she was when I met her." He pointed at the painting at the opposite end, where her hair seemed to be almost a fire.

"Wow," said Lea, breath truly taken away. She gazed at the other paintings, each stunning, and noticed in three or four another figure: a tall, dark-haired man. "That's not *you*, is it? Do you have a son?"

"Hmm?" Gus followed Lea's gaze. "Oh. No. We didn't have children. That's Frank." Gus's eyebrows bunched, which looked almost unnatural on his face. "He was our friend. Good friend. Well, he was our boarder."

"Boarder?"

"Yes. He lived with us for nearly a quarter century, if you can believe that." Gus sighed. "We lost him nearly a decade ago."

"Oh, Gus, I'm so sorry." Lea felt as if she were walking through a minefield and tripping every last one.

"No, no, don't be, my dear." Gus's eyes were sparkling again, and his mouth was back in its usual bright smile. "One of the things about reaching my age — I'm seventy-eight — is that one loses people. Careless, I know, but it can't be helped! And in the mean time, I've known more than my share of love and laughter, and I've still got work that I enjoy, and a building full of young, creative people keeping me alive. I haven't any complaints!"

When Lea met up with Bob and Sassy, she was still laughing. "You told me Gus was a sweetheart, Sassy, but *wow!*"

"He's something, eh?" said Sassy with a wink. "I'm convinced he'll be here, running up and down to his office and giggling like a little gnome long after I'm dead and gone."

"Yeah," laughed Bob. "His crew believes he lives on paint fumes. They call him the Painter of Dorian Grey."

They all laughed at that, and the artistic director continued, "Mind, he's a brilliant designer. As much the reason this theater is still standing as anyone. I don't know how the heck we'd ever get by without him. Which, I hope and trust, we won't have to any time soon!"

"Here, here," Sassy agreed. "Now, Lea, let's get out of this building so we can show you that there is in fact food in Atlanta aside from fried chicken and barbecue. I know we're a little further away from the ocean than you're used to, but there's a seafood place just a few blocks away that makes some of the best sushi you'll find in the South. And while we ply you with seafood and sake, you can give us your impressions of the theater."

The meal was long. The conversation was fascinating. The sake flowed freely.

And the sushi was definitely fabulous.

I know Sean would love this place; wonder if I could get Andy here? Lea imagined their hulking forms in the beautiful, quiet restaurant. She imagined them nibbling at the sushi.

She imagined them under the table, nibbling at *her*, and she blushed.

When she arrived back at the apartment, it was almost eleven, and she was dead on her feet. Happy, but exhausted. She was almost glad that she would be able to fall into bed alone and simply go to sleep.

Almost.

There was a package in front of the door. Addressed to her.

Intrigued, Lea picked it up and let herself in.

The apartment was neat as a proverbial pin. There were roses on the table. A note that read *We can't keep you warm with our bodies tonight, but we hope our love can help at least a little.* They'd both signed it.

It made Lea's middle go soft and her eyes overflow, and she felt like such a *girl*, but what the fuck: she *was* a girl, proud to be one, and she had more than her share of masculinity at her beck and call (if not tonight) — and they'd been incredibly sweet.

Suddenly, she missed them terribly, even though she knew their purpose in leaving the flowers and the note had been quite the opposite.

She threw herself down into one of the chairs — usually Andy's chair — only then remembering the package.

It was from a store that sounded vaguely familiar, one in San Francisco, but not one that Kirsten had ever worked at, Lea was pretty sure. She couldn't think why it seemed familiar.

Using her keys to cut the packing tape (and trying to ignore the voice of her father telling her not to use her keys that way), Lea opened the box and pulled out the invoice, which included a note from Kirsten: *A housewarming present for my best friend, K.*

Intrigued, she pulled out the newsprint that had been used as packing material — reminding herself to ask the boys where to find a recycling center. In the box were three smaller boxes and a tangle of nylon, plastic, and fabric that, as Lea pulled it out, looked like some bizarre combination of sports gear and lingerie. *What the fuck, Kirsten?*

She lay aside the whatever-it-was, and pulled out the smallest of the three boxes. It contained what looked like nothing more than a plastic plumb bob, about three inches long, with a strawberry-shaped head. It was colored bright purple.

Alarmed now, Lea grabbed the largest box, having some sense of what it would contain — and it did.

A penis. Not quite as long as Sean's or Andy's, but a very nice size, to Lea's eye. Made out of silicone.

It too was bright purple. And had what looked like a handle at the back end.

Lea had her phone out and had hit her friend's number before she could even think to breathe.

"Hey, Leelee!" Kirsten's voice was warm, and bright, and welcome. "You get my package, sweetie?"

"Holy fuck, Kirsten!" Lea gasped. "What the fuck am I supposed to *do* with this?"

"Well, now, Lea, sugar," laughed Kirsten, "I am quite sure that you could figure out something to do with it all on your lonesome. But I kinda figured that with all of that boyflesh around you, there might be some fun uses you could put it too!"

"Kirsten!" Lea felt about thirteen, felt about as humiliated as she had when she figured out why the boys sometimes walked with their notebooks in front of their crotches. "I mean, thanks a lot, but I've got to tell you, I may be alone tonight, so I'm sure it will be great, thanks, but I've got two very nice penises already — your *brother's* being one! — so I don't see how having yet another phallus to stick inside of me is going to do me a whole lot of good!"

Kirsten cackled. "Oh, I know it'll do you a *whole* lotta good!" She laughed again and then said, "But Lea sweetie, that isn't just for you, you know!"

"Isn't just...?" Lea puzzled at the floppy plastic thing. "It's a dildo, for fuck's sake. I know what a dildo is."

Again Kirsten laughed maniacly. "And what do you think that doodad at the bottom is for?"

Lea grabbed it. "I don't know, a handle?" When Kirsten snorted, Lea growled, *"Kirsten!"*

"Heh! Okay. Okay. Well, did you try on the harness?"

"What, the nylon thing? I'm supposed to *wear* it?"

"Definitely," Kirsten said with a giggle, and before Lea could bark at her again, Kirsten asked, "You in pants or a dress, or what?"

Lea blinked, disconcerted. "Dress. It was my first day."

"Perfect. So slip that nylon thingee on like it was undies. You can slip off what you got or not, whatever."

Perplexed, Lea did as she was told; letting her panties fall to the floor, she stepped into what she could now clearly see were loops for her legs. "Okay."

"Really? Damn, I didn't think it would be that easy."

"Kirsten."

"Sorry. Yeah. So it's not all the way up, is it?"

"Nope." Lea had pulled it to just above her knees.

"Perfect. Now, see at the front, there's a kind of plastic ring, goes right over where your bush would be? Take the dong and slide it through there."

Lea did — and comprehension began to dawn. But still... "But... where will the handle go?"

Kirsten snorted again, but swallowed it. "Sorry! But that's not a handle."

"Not a...?" Lea pulled the harness up the rest of the way, trying to see how the whole thing would work.

As soon as she had pulled it the whole way up, the purple hard-on sprang proudly in front of her, and the protuberance that she'd taken for a handle pushed up against her entrance. *"Oh!"* As soon as Lea's body began to react to the pressure, it slid in. *"OH!"*

"It's called a double dildo, sweetie. A strap-on." Kirsten sounded very pleased with herself. "You ever wonder what it would feel like to fuck your guy, to have a cock? Well, now you have one!"

As the smaller end of the dildo pushed up into Lea's pussy, a nub at the front began pressing against her clit. Grasping the purple phallus with her free hand, she rocked her hips and felt the nub moving against her, the smaller phallus moving within her. "Oh..." she sighed.

"Uh-huh," said Kirsten. "Told you. Feel good?"

"Um. Yeah." Lea and Kirsten had talked about sex a lot, had even discussed vibrators a few times, but they'd never actually talked while *doing it* and Lea was feeling more than a bit uncomfortable — all the more so since she knew that Kirsten was even more bisexual than her brother Sean and had had a crush on Lea. "But, um, what am... How...?"

"Well, me," Kirsten said, all but purring now, "I like to do Gianna with it, right?"

"Sure, but — "

"But , see, there's *ways* to use it with a guy too. You see the butt plug?"

"Huh?"

"Thang looks like a big ol' strawberry? And there should be a bottle of lube in there, and a DVD."

Lea stared at the plumb bob. *Butt plug?* Still more than a little distracted by the feeling of the dildo inside of her, she searched the box; indeed, there was a small bottle of lube and a DVD. *"Guide to... Pegging?"*

"Yup. Peggin'. Trust me on this. Guys like gettin' it almost as much as they like givin' it." Now Kirsten was definitely purring. "God, what I wouldn't give to see you take big ol' Andy up the ass."

"Huh."

"But Lea, sweetie?"

"Huh?"

"I don't want to know what you and my brother get up to, okay?"

"Uh... 'Kay."

"Now, tell me, sweetie! How was your first day?"

Lea gave Kirsten the full rundown — though her mind was definitely occupied.

After her best-friend-forever hung up ("Gotta go use *my* srap-on on my girlfriend!"), Leah watched the video.

She was with Kirsten on this one. *Lea* wanted to see herself fuck Andy's sweet ass. And Sean's.

After the video was over, she brought all of her new toys into the bathroom, still wearing her harness and dildo, which she couldn't bring herself to take off.

She opened the lube and spread some over the butt plug, and then put a dollop on her finger and distributed it gently to the inside of her anus. Her *asshole.*

And then she slid the butt plug gently in.

She had tried anal sex with a couple of her boyfriends — well, they had tried it with *her*. It sure hadn't been her idea.

It hadn't been a whole lot of fun. But then neither of them had known what the fuck they were doing. John the Controlling Asshole had considered lube to be a sign of decadence. There wasn't any burning feeling now. Just a feeling of fullness, of *nastiness,* like saying forbidden words when she was a kid or touching her first boyfriend Sam's cock.

And feeling both of her lower openings spread, even as her clit was beginning to vibrate against the little nub... *Lordy-lord-lord.*

Lea stared at the purple penis in the mirror, holding up the front of her dress. What was it that was so fucking sexy about it?

But it was.

Having poured a little more lube onto her hand, she grabbed the dildo and began to rock her hips, thrusting the faux cock through her fingers — just *practicing,* to see what it would feel like.

It felt... weird. Good. Weird. The little dildo inside of her created a really nice sense of friction and of pressure. She was aware of her butt being spread every time she thust forward through her fist and clenched her ass cheeks — still, it didn't hurt at all, it felt good, but... weird.

The closest thing Lea could think of was the time that John had taken her out to dinner with a mini-egg vibe inside of her, and the control on his keychain.

Only this time, she was in control.

Did it feel like this for the boys when they jerked off? Well, she thought, it almost certainly felt even better. That being the case, she couldn't believe that they could manage to keep their hands off of themselves at all.

Her boys...

Watching through the mirror as her purple cock thrust through her slick fingers, Lea could feel her nerves beginning to catch fire — the little mini-dildo inside of her was rubbing her g-spot, the nub was rubbing her clit, and the butt plug in her ass and the dildo in her hand had her feeling *so* fucking sexy....

Her boys. Standing almost right here. Watching her in the shower. Getting hard. Rubbing themselves. Fucking *through* her. *Oh. Oh. Ooooohhh....*

The orgasm wasn't titanic, but it shook her — nipples buzzing, vaginal muscles, ass muscles, legs quivering spastically.

She collapsed, panting, against the counter.

Without even thinking, Lea took out her phone. She snapped one picture of the dildo in the mirror, her legs spread, the silicone glistening. Then she turned around and lifted the the back of her dress and took a picture of the little purple hexagon spreading the cheeks of her ass.

She texted the pictures to Sean and Andy and waited.

A minute later, Andy texted back, *WTF?*

Sean texted, *Video chat?*

You someplace private? Lea asked, knowing they were on duty.

Privateish.

Okay. I'll go get my laptop. Text when you're ready.

Okay.

Lea considered taking the strap-on off and removing the butt plug, but no — visual aids were always good for educational presentations. And they'd clearly gotten the boys' attention. And so she walked out into the living room, the silicone dick wobbling in front of her, her ass muscles squeezing around the plug, feeling incredibly silly and incredibly sexy, both a the same time.

She set up her laptop on her bed and knelt, waiting for Sean and Andy to get online.

She didn't have to wait long.

"Hey, Lea." They were crowded together in a small, dark space.

"Hello, boys. Where the hell are you?"

"Um. Cab of the ladder truck," said Andy sheepishly.

Sean gave an embarrassed smirk. "Biggest closed space we could find away from the bunks."

Before Lea could answer, Andy said, "But hey, how was your first day?"

"Oh! Great!" And Lea told them about her day from beginning to end, only vaguely aware that she was stroking the dildo in her hand or rocking against the one in her pussy.

She didn't tell them about Gus's paintings. It seemed... personal.

They *ooo*'d and *aaah*'d in all of the right places, promised to beat up Zach if she wanted, and then, when she was done, fell silent.

After a moment, Andy said, "So. Lea."

"Hmm?"

His expression was serious. "What the ever-loving *fuck* were those pictures you sent?"

"Didn't you like them?"

Sean answered, "Well, Lea, sweetheart, *like* isn't quite the word. *Nearly had to perform CPR on each other* is closer to it."

"Mmm," purred Lea. "Would have liked to see that."

"Uh-huh," Sean answered. "So...?"

"Well," Lea answered, aware that her voice was a bit higher than usual, "I got some toys for us to play with and I just wanted to show you." She thought that mentioning that she'd gotten them from *Kirsten* probably wouldn't make her brother very comfortable.

"Toys?" gulped Andy.

"Uh-huh." She got up on her knees so that they could see the dildo and the harness. "This lovely strap-on, and — " She turned around and lifted her dress. " — this lovely butt plug. And a video that taught me *all sorts* of interesting things that we could do with them. And I've been playing with them all by myself tonight, which is nice, but I thought, perhaps, we could play with them together."

Sean licked his lips. "Uh-huh."

Andy seemed to be sweating. "To... Together?" Andy jumped and caught his breath, and Lea was pretty sure that Sean had grabbed Andy's crotch.

Lea sighed. "Yeah. Together. See, the thing is, Andy, you asked if I would take you up my ass this morning, and, you know, I want to, because the idea of both of you inside of me at the same time is fucking amazing, but it's also kind of scary, you know? But I do want to give you that, because I love you both so much."

Both men gulped but nodded. "Love you too."

Lea felt heat spread through her whole body, and knew that it wasn't a blush of embarrassment or shame. "So, here's my bargain: if you want me to take it up the ass, I would love to, but you have to agree to take it up the ass as well."

"Jesus, baby," said Sean.

"Let *you* take us up the, um, ass," asked Andy, eyes wide, "or take, you know...?"

Sean glanced at his friend. His lover. "Andy?"

Andy's fair skin darkened and he looked down. "Or take, you know... each other?"

"Oh," said Sean.

"Oh, Andy, baby," gasped Lea. "That's... That's up to the two of you." Pulling her dress over her head, Lea smiled. "Now, if you'd like, I can show you some of the things we can do with these toys. Would you like that?"

"Oh, yeah," said Andy, face still dark.

"Please," added Sean, grinning.

And Lea did.

And they did like it.

And so did she. She took pleasure in the knowledge of a job well done.

The Visitor Entertains

Lea had never really been one to watch the news. She'd always read the newspapers for work — mostly the entertainment section for the reviews, and occasionally the sports. But by her second month in Atlanta, she had learned to tune into the five o'clock local broadcast — at least on the days when Andy and Sean were on duty.

She had also programmed an alert that would pop up on her phone whenever the words *Atlanta, Downtown*, and either *fire* or *fatality* appeared in a bulletin. Because when they did, the odds were good that her boys would be coming home sore of body and heart, and full of need.

The need expressed itself differently in each of them. Sean needed to touch and be touched. Andy needed to be inside of her. *NOW.*

And so on the evenings when Lea was able to be at the apartment when they came home, she would wear a bathrobe with nothing on beneath. Sean would come and kiss Lea and caress her and hiss at her caresses, while Andy would unzip, flip up the back of her robe and, after rubbing his cock head against her labia a few times to make sure that her juices were flowing, thrust in, *hard.*

Sometimes they would fuck just like that — standing in the middle of the room. Sometimes they would end up in a pile on the floor: a Lea sandwich.

And once Andy had come, which, if it didn't set her off, usually got Lea herself pretty fucking close, he would slide out and Sean would slide in, and all of their fear and sorrow and love would pour into her, and she would give them light. Respite. Surcease. Reassurance that they were alive and she was alive, and life was not all flame and tangled metal, but also joy and love and heavy doses of physical pleasure and all of the wonderful things that went with them.

She wouldn't have admitted it, but Lea was relieved that Sean and Andy were gone at least two nights a week. In the first place, it gave her poor, lucky body a chance to recover — each of the boys had at least as much stamina and desire as even the most energetic of her former lovers, and between them, they made sure that her body was ravaged. Every night.

A body wasn't really meant to take so much of that kind of pleasure. Not that Lea was ever going to complain.

The other reason that she didn't mind their being gone (even as she missed them) was that it made their homecomings so *amazing*....

That particular Saturday, she actually saw them on the big flat-screen while she was finishing preparations for dinner. It was between a story about the dearth of striped bass in northern Georgia's rivers and another on the debate about the fares for the new downtown streetcar (on which Lea's boss Sassy had already bought an ad reading *Desire,* with a picture from the theater's current production of the Williams classic).

The story, which lasted all of fifteen seconds, was about a six-car pile-up earlier that afternoon at the tangled cloverleaf that connected I-85 to Highway 10. The anchor reported blithely that the accident had been caused by a texting driver, and that Atlanta Fire and Rescue had transported four people to the hospital, where two were listed in critical condition, but that three people had died at the scene, including a two-year-old girl.

The video showed firefighters using the jaws of life to peel the roof off of one of the cars; it was crumpled like a beer can. As one of the firefighters reached through the hole, the one who had been handling the pneumatic cutter turned toward the camera. She'd have recognized that dimpled chin anywhere: Andy. The other firefight turned and shouted something. Square jaw. Eyes that were blue even through the face mask. Sean.

They looked grim.

They'd be headed home now — showered off, but still smelling of the ghosts of smoke and gasoline and adrenaline.

Pursing her lips, Lea picked up her phone and texted them: *Just saw you on TV. The accident. Okay?*

She'd expected a reply from Andy, because Sean usually drove them home. Instead, it was Sean who answered: *No. Not really OK. Bad day at the office.*

No kidding, thought Lea. It was always hard for the boys whenever they couldn't save someone. But a little girl? She texted back: *So sorry. ETA?*

Traffic sucks, came the answer. *Half hour?*

I'll be waiting, Lea answered. *Can I take your minds off your troubles? PLEASE.*

Then, a few seconds later, *Andy says fuck yes.*

Well then, I will give you the heroes' welcome you deserve.

A pause and then: *Not heroes. Not today.*

Yes you were. Yes you are. You are my heroes every day.

Sean didn't respond to that.

Damnity-damn-damn, she thought.

Lea found herself looking around. Considering.

Lasagna in the oven. A salad for Lea and Sean ready in the fridge; green beans boiled to hell the way that Andy liked them warming on the stove. Three glasses of good rye whiskey on the counter.

But their hunger wouldn't turn to their stomachs for a while.

She texted one last time: I promise, I will help make you feel much better. I have a surprise for you.

With a nod, Lea downed her shot — to give her courage — dropped her robe to the floor, and went to prepare.

When she saw the big SUV pull up in the parking lot, Lea — aided by a second healthy shot of rye — fought down rising panic and walked over to the table. "Please don't break tonight," she pleaded.

The sturdy if beaten-up oak table didn't look concerned.

And so she took two of the sets of handcuffs that she'd had since her days with her power-game asshole ex John, but that she hadn't yet used with Sean and Andy. Before she could have second — or eighteenth — thoughts, she spread her legs and locked her ankles to the legs of the table that were closest to the door. When she heard their muted voices coming down the walkway outside their apartment, she leaned across the table and bound each of her wrists with one of the other cuffs to the top of one of the far legs.

And she waited. Her naked ass pointed straight at the door, the bright purple butt plug that she'd inserted probably making her look like some very weird cyclops.

Too late to back down now, *she thought. And then,* Oh, fuck. I hope none of the neighbors is walking by when they open the door.

Their voices grew louder, though they still sounded less energetic than usual. They were talking about the Hawks. That was a good sign, at least.

The sound of the key turning in the door sent Lea's heart up toward her tonsils. *Oh, god. This is such a bad idea. What if they don't want to? What if they DO?*

But as she had already told herself, she was in no position to turn back now. Well. To turn *front.*

The door opened. Andy's voice rolled out in a flat drawl, "Hey, Lea, we're…"

Silence.

Lea heard two loud thunks. She hoped it was their duffles hitting the floor, that they hadn't both passed out and left her chained to the table where she couldn't do any of them any good. She was reassured when Sean gasped, "Holy *fuck."*

Silence.

"Um, guys, I'm glad this rendered you speechless, but would you mind coming in and closing the door? You are both welcome to look as much as you want — and touch, and anything else that you'd like to do. But I'd rather not have my naked bottom on display for all of Cobb County to see."

That broke the spell. The door slammed shut and suddenly her boys — her men — were around and against her. Sean, as she'd guessed, was leaning over the top of the table, kissing her, stroking her back, her arms, her neck.

Andy, to her surprise but to her great pleasure, knelt behind Lea and began to kiss the taut backs of her thighs, her butt cheeks, and finally, emphatically, her pussy, which was already moist with anticipation.

Lea groaned into Sean's mouth, her body pulling against her restraints, even though the last thing she wanted was to disengage Andy's wonderful lips, his lightning tongue, from her pussy.

And Sean's fingers began to glide slowly down her sides, counting her exposed ribs before brushing feather-light along the sides of first one breast and then the other....

Her image of this whole encounter had been about getting *them* off — about clearing the angst and sorrow from their hearts and simply giving them pleasure. Instead, Lea found herself submerged — as she so often did — in her lovers' very different rhythms, their very different approaches to pleasuring *her.*

And as Andy lapped at her, Sean's hands found Lea's nipples, revealed as she'd arched back under their ministrations. *Everyone needs to feel this way,* thought the small part of her brain that was at all clear. And then the typhoon of sensation blew out even that little bit of clarity, and all that Lea knew was that it felt *good.* And everyone else could find this feeling on their own.

Submerged as she was in the feeling, Lea forgot about the handcuffs. Forgot about the table. Forgot about the butt plug — except when Andy's nose occasionally brushed it and it sent a *different* tremor of sensation rippling through her. As far as her body was concerned, she might have been on a bed of rose petals or...

Andy kissed his way up her butt cheeks, alternating left and right, and then licked up the length of her spine, and suddenly Lea was very aware of her restraints. She heard him unzip his jeans and had just enough time for the thought of him replacing the plastic plumb bob in her ass with that long erection of his — just enough time for the whole of her body to break into goose pimples — when he pushed into her pussy instead, and the typhoon swept her away again.

Lea was spread-eagle over the edge of the table, and as Andy began to fuck her, her pubic bone was pressed firmly against the wood, and so his downward-facing dick stroked along the front of her vagina even more firmly than usual. She screamed.

Sean's lips pressed against Lea's ear, and he murmured, "Too hard, baby?"

"No," groaned Lea, "no, god, no." And she screamed again.

"Huh," chuckled Sean, finally releasing her nipples, which now bounced against the table top. "Then I think, if you don't mind, I'm going to go down the other end and lend the two of y'all a hand."

Andy continued to fuck her with everything he had — he was now holding onto the sides of the table so his thrusts didn't push it and Lea away. It wasn't surprising, then, that Lea forgot entirely about what Sean had said, until she felt two big hand push in from between Andy's thighs. She could feel him let Andy's balls slide over one even as the other found the hood of her clit and began to stroke it and squeeze it against Andy's thrusting cock.

"Aw, *shit!*" Andy shouted, and Lea felt him push even deeper into her.

Neither of her boys had anything like a quick trigger; unlike some of her former boyfriends, Andy and Sean were both quite capable of fucking her until she turned to jelly. Not even jelly.

If either of them was more likely to be thrown by a *surprise*, however, it was Andy, as he was currently demonstrating. Evidently, having Sean grab his balls while Andy was plowing Lea was just enough to make Andy pop his cork, which he proceeded to do, pushing into her hard enough that, even though he was holding the table down, he moved them both a foot or two toward the sink. He bellowed, and a flood of his come spilled into and — quickly — out of her, around his shaft. "Aw… *shit*," he repeated, panting into the back of Lea's neck.

Once they'd lain there for a moment, both sweating and gasping for air, both dripping onto the table and floor, Sean gave a laconic chuckle. "Sorry, Andy-boy." He patted something — probably Andy's ass, because Lea felt the cock planted deep inside of her twitch, felt more liquid spill from her cunt lips.

"Sorry," grunted Andy. "Like hell."

"Hey," Sean said, laughing, "you didn't exactly seem to mind! Not my fault that Lea's sweet pussy feels so good all it took to set you off was a little *squeeze.*"

Sean must have squeezed Andy's balls again, because Andy groaned, arched back, and poured more of himself into her. His cock, rapidly diminishing, began to slide out of Lea, and her attempts to *keep it*, to squeeze it hard so that it would stay inside of her, only pushed him the rest of the way out, to both of their loud disappointment.

"Damn you, Sean." Andy stumbled around the table and sat in a chair at the edge of Lea's sight. He may have been grumbling, but as he let his head fall back, she could see a small grin on his face.

Sean chuckled again. "Uh-huh. Damn me." Suddenly his hands, cool and rough, brushed against the heated flesh of Lea's ass. "Hey, baby."

"Hey," panted Lea, "baby." Now that Andy had departed, she could feel all of that spunk flowing down her left thigh, cooling as it dribbled.

She heard Sean drop his jeans to the floor — he must have kicked his boots off at some point — and felt him come up behind her, not *quite* touching. Lea tried to push back, to capture that beautiful erection that she knew was just behind her. But of course, she couldn't. She gave a quick moan of frustration.

Sean, standing right behind her, hissed.

"Well, Sean," said Andy — he was the one chuckling now. "You gonna leave our beautiful Miss Lea hanging like that?"

"No, sir," said Sean, and with a smooth, steady stroke, filled the space that Andy had just vacated.

Lea moaned again, but there was no frustration in the sound this time: only satisfaction and sensual delight.

As Sean began to fuck her — slowly, sensuously, making Lea's nerves sing — Andy got up and went over to where the whiskey glasses sat on the counter. He downed one tumbler, and then walked the other over to Sean.

Without stopping his gentle, overwhelming thrusting, Lea heard him toss back the shot. She felt it hit bottom, felt as his whole body shuddered — making her shudder as well. Sean leaned down and kissed her ear, the smell of the liquor wafting from his mouth to Lea's nostrils, intoxicating. His belly pressed against the butt plug, pushing it further into her. "Baby," he whispered, "if you're ready to seal that bargain you made with us, I am. You can fuck my ass any old way you want, if you'll just let me fuck yours."

"Please!" Lea screamed. She'd meant to whisper it, to match him, but somehow...

"Huh," answered Sean.

There was a *thunk* on the table as, right next to Lea's head, Andy dropped the bottle of lube, the condoms, and the strap-on that she had laid out beside the whiskey on the counter.

"Thanks, Andy," said Lea and Sean together.

"Y'all... 're welcome." There was a catch in Andy's voice.

"Turn you on, boy?" asked Sean, continuing to fuck Lea even as he picked up the lube. "Which part? Me fucking her sweet ass — " He reached between them and turned the butt plug just the *tiniest bit*, but enough that it sent lightning through Lea. " — or is it her doin' *me?*"

Andy's answer was monosyllabic and indecipherable. He went back over to the chair and sat. His cock raised its head drunkenly from his lap.

Sean leaned forward, pressing himself deep into Lea and biting her earlobe. "You ready? 'Cause if I keep thinking about this, I'm going to go off where I don't do either of us any good."

"Ready," whispered Lea, as goose pimples marched up and down her flesh. She arched her neck back; Sean took the hint and kissed her, letting his tongue snake between her lips and touch hers, even as his cock squeezed up into her, touching her cervix and setting her aflame.

Nonsensically, the voice of her high school physics teacher, Ms. Lighty, droned into Lea's head, talking about electrical current and how when you closed a circuit...

Sean's tongue and cock both retreated, and the circuit was broken, though the flame was by no means doused. He backed up until the tip of him just barely spread Lea's labia open. With one set of long fingers, Sean circled both of their sexes, pressing her lips gently against his head. With the other hand, he turned the plastic in Lea's rear end and pulled gently.

Lea had not herself been at all gentle in inserting the plug; she'd been aware that she needed to get it in as long before her men arrived as possible. She'd practiced with it often enough — they all had, on her, on each of the boys — that she knew to use plenty of lubricant, that she knew how to relax into the pressure. But mostly, she'd just shoved the thing in.

Removing it, however, Sean was his slow, irresistible self, and the sensation as the thick part of the butt plug stretched her, and then her anus squeezed out the long, tapered head, could only be described as *exquisite*. Finally he withdrew it, and Lea lay, panting, quivering on the table, asshole open and slick, pussy open and flowing, and she had never wanted anything more in her whole life.

Well. Almost anything.

No. *Anything.*

That was a surprise.

So was the sensation sparked by the feeling of Sean pressing against the overheated flesh of her sphincter.

A few of Lea's boyfriends had been into anal sex — Asshole John, of course, but also Kirby, her first experiment with anal, who argued that they might as well take advantage of his small endowment. She hadn't exactly enjoyed any of the experiences — John had made it actively unpleasant by insisting that they use no lubricant other than her natural juices — and so, knowing that her boys would enjoy it, Lea had hoped, at best, that she wouldn't hate it, given Andy and Sean's heft.

She didn't hate it.

She *really* didn't hate it.

Lea could hear as Sean smoothed a rubber down over his hard-on and then drizzled a hefty dollop of lube over his already-slick erection. "Okay?" His voice sounded strained.

Lea nodded and tried, against her body's loudly screaming instincts, to relax. *Like yoga. Just like yoga.*

Only not.

Sean leaned forward, trying to press in without pushing too hard, but his cock head slipped up the crack of her ass. "Oops." He put one knee up on the table to give himself a better angle, lined himself up again, and gently but insistently pushed.

"AH!" shouted Lea, aflame once more as she felt that cock head, which could do such amazing things to the inside of her vagina, slid smoothly a few inches into her ass.

Sean immediately stopped. "*Okay?*" he asked through gritted teeth.

"Great," sighed Lea, and she was surprised to find that, yes: she was. It was. Great. Fabulous.

Much of the discomfort that had accompanied her earlier experiences with anal sex, Lea realized — to the extent that she was thinking at all — had been the result of the fact that she had not, in fact, been *ready*. Even though she'd known what was coming (more or less), and even though Kirby, at least, had squirted KY on his lovely little prick, every time a man had pressed himself into Lea's rear entrance before, he had simply lined himself up and *pushed*, and Lea had found herself feeling....

Well. *Violated*, if she were to be honest.

For John, that had probably been the point, but Kirby and the couple of others she'd done this with would almost certainly have been devastated to hear that she had felt that way.

This was no violation. This was *sex*. Whether it was the fact that she and the boys had been talking about this for a month and a half, or the fact that Kirsten's house-warming gift had both planted the idea and educated Lea and her lovers in how to do this, or the fact that she had let butt plug help her relax and get ready — whatever the reason, the feeling of Sean lowering himself, inch by inch, into her, spreading the cheeks of her ass, sliding through that ring of muscle, felt...

Well, yeah. *Sexy*. Nasty. Exciting.

"Oh. God. Lea. Baby," Sean gasped as he leaned over her, his head resting now against her shoulder, his right knee up against her waist, his other leg pressing against the back of her chained one.

Lea could feel the tickle as his balls came to rest against her open, buzzing cunt. A sense of fullness, of heat, of just how deeply he was buried in her overwhelmed Lea. A sound ejected itself from her throat. Pleasure? Something. Ecstasy.

Answering her in kind, Sean began to withdraw, and then to slide back in. The amount of lube he'd added to what was already on the condom, in addition to the generous amount that she'd slathered onto the butt plug before inserting it, made the action smooth and frictionless, and so it felt amazing. Not the same feeling as having him fill her cunt definitely — *darker*, in a way that had nothing to do with *where* he was fucking her.

Where he was fucking her. He was fucking her ass. Sean was fucking her ass, Lea's ass, Lea cuffed to the table, and *god...!*

As Sean continued his steady, deliberate strokes and the heat poured from Lea's ass down into her pussy, she locked eyes with Andy, still sitting in the chair.

His eyes were half closed, his face dark, and his cock, no longer even the slightest bit soft, seemed to strain against the hand that fisted it. "Feel good?"

Lea just nodded, her tongue beyond her control. Through a clenched jaw, Sean grunted, *"Fuck yeah!"*

Andy shot them a tight grin and stood, still stroking his hard-on. "Think I'll give the two of y'all a hand. Or something."

Lea and Sean both grunted as he walked behind them — god alone knew *what* he had in mind, but Lea had too little brain-space to spare for any speculation, and it sounded as if Sean was just as lost in the feeling of their fuck as she was.

And so it came as an absolute surprise — though it probably shouldn't have — when Lea felt Andy's long tongue lap once again against her open, overflowing slit, running from her clitoris and along her spread labia, up toward the place where Sean's cock was now spreading her open, and the contrast in the two feelings was so… *so*, that every muscle in Lea's body contracted involuntarily — her legs and arms pulling *hard* against their bonds, her ass clamping down on Sean's cock, forcing him to stop and evoking a strangled gasp.

Chuckling against her pussy, Andy said, "Hey, Sean-boy, not my fault that Sweet Miss Lea's tight ass feels so fucking good that you nearly get set off by a little *squeeze!*" He licked again, starting once more at Lea's clit, but this time continuing onto Sean's cock, his balls.

Sean swore, saying words that would no doubt have gotten his mouth washed out with soap by his kindergarten teacher mother, but after leaning against her back for a moment, he growled and continued his strokes, maybe a bit less steadily, but no more quickly.

Andy laughed, and began to apply himself to torturing his lovers with his tongue. It was the sweetest torture imaginable and in all honesty Lea never wanted it to stop. Why would she?

And so as she felt Sean slowly begin to pick up steam, his thrusts coming jerkier, Lea found herself emitting a keening whine as she chased the feeling of Andy's tongue against her clit even as Sean's now-pounding cock pushed her in another direction entirely. *"Wait,"* she muttered into the table as her lips slipped over the wood, *"wait, wait, oh, god, wait…"*

Sean let out a low growl, and as he thrust deep and hard into her, Andy's mouth closed around Lea's clit, and sucked it in, and just like that, the deep, *dark* flame that flared out from where Sean was planted in her merged with the lightning sparked by Andy's mouth, and Ms. Lighty's voice whispered once again in Lea's mind: *A circuit closes, the current flows, and the filament…*

Ignites.

The first thing that Lea became aware of, once the impossible light receded, was Sean's breath, wet, hot, and gasping, against the back of neck — of her own hair, damp with her sweat and his, spilling over her face and onto the table.

Oh, and the swell of Sean's cock, still pulsing inside of her ass.

Andy's lips kissed Lea's labia, drawing a gasp from Lea, sending another ripple of orgasm through her, and her sphincter squeezed tight around Sean, and he screamed, pressing deep into her again, evoking an open-throated bellow from Lea herself.

Gasping again, Lea was shocked to see Andy leaning down to her, now kissing her mouth. "Hey, baby," he murmured.

"*Huh!*" was the only answer she could give.

Andy glanced up — at Sean, evidently, because Sean suddenly leaned forward and for a moment, Lea was certain they were going to kiss, but Andy suddenly flinched to the side, and Sean's lips met Andy's cheek.

After a moment, during which both Sean and Lea caught their breaths, Sean withdrew gingerly from her bottom. "Got the key so we can unlock you?" he laughed breathlessly, or are we going to eat dinner off your back?"

Smiling almost sleepily, Lea raised the key — which she'd been clutching desperately in her palm. She was almost sorry to be released from her voluntary bondage.

Ah, well, she thought, *I can always go back there again.* As she stood up on shaky legs, her muscles screamed. *Maybe not tonight, though.*

As they ate dinner at the very table that they'd just thoroughly debauched — and which had held up just fine, thank you very much — Lea smiled, even as she shifted gingerly in her seat.

The shadow of the day had passed from her men. She had given them heroes' welcomes indeed, and they sat, smiling, grinning at her as they ate.

They wouldn't allow her to help serve, clear, or clean. "You were already the main course," Sean joked. "You shouldn't have to do *anything*."

And so she sat, enjoying watching them move, enjoying even the feeling of her protesting muscles, because *man*, if you couldn't enjoy *that*, you didn't deserve a body at all.

After the meal had been cleared away and all of the dishes cleaned and stacked, Andy splashed another two or three fingers worth of whiskey into each of the three tumblers and carried them back to the table.

Once they had drunk a silent toast to each other, Lea grinned at her lovers. The heat from the sex and the heat from the liquor had her feeling *good*, *languid*, and she could almost see herself being able to play some more. Soon.

"What you smiling at, Lea-honey?" asked Andy with a smirk.

"You two," she sighed. "What else?"

"Lucky us," laughed Sean.

"Lucky me!" giggled Lea, and raised her glass.

They all drank to *that*.

"So," Lea sighed, "you guys up for the trip to the *the-ay-tuh* tomorrow?" She pronounced it as they would: a three-syllable word.

"The *what?*" Andy blinked.

Sean shook his head as if to clear it, and then nodded. "Oh, yeah. 'Course. Taking my mama to that *Streetcar* play."

"Yup! I'm looking forward to showing you where I work!"

They glanced at each other, laughed, and then grinned at Lea.

"What?"

Andy laughed again, "Well, was gonna be a secret, but…"

With a snort, Sean cut in, "But we want to make sure you're actually there."

"There?"

"Well, see," Andy jumped in, "we volunteered. To do the fire marshal inspection on Monday."

"So we wondered," said Sean, "if maybe you'd be the person to give us the tour."

"Oh." Monday. When the theater was dark, and most of the staff took what was essentially their weekend. "Uh. Yeah. I'm sure I can arrange that."

"Good," they both said with matching smirks. Sean's foot brushed against hers. "So we'll get to see the the-ay-tuh with my mama tomorrow." He exaggerated the Southern pronunciation. "But we kinda hoped you could give us the *real* behind-the-scenes tour on Monday.

Holy fuck, *Lea thought*. What in god's name do you two have in mind? *"Hope you don't get me fired!"*

"Oh, Lea, no," Andy said, more serious than serious, "we wouldn't that."

"Naw," agreed Sean. "We want you to be be able to give us the tour every month. Gotta make sure the theater's up to code, after all."

"Oh." Lea gave a mock-somber nod. "Yes. We've gotta make sure of that."

Afterward, they lay together on the pullout bed that somehow never got folded away and watched a basketball game. The Hawks were losing, and so somewhere around the third quarter, Lea simply reached into their boxers — they'd never put their pants back on — and began stroking them. Even though their focus remained on the game, she knew she had their attention. "Guys? You up to play some more?"

"Always," answered Sean, his eyes heavy-lidded in a manner that might have made her think he was falling asleep if she didn't know from experience just how much flame that look hid.

Andy simply turned away from the TV and looked at her.

"What you got in mind, Lea-baby?" Sean sighed, his cock gaining length under her fingers. "You want to try that strap-on tonight?"

Andy took a breath. Looking at Sean as she was, she couldn't tell if it was a gasp of surprise at Sean's question, or at the movement of her hand up and down his burgeoning flesh.

"Up to you, Sean," Lea answered, no more willing to push than he had been.

His washed-denim eyes met hers, and he nodded. It warmed Lea's stomach to see that, in fact, he was nervous. The sweet boy.

"Here," said Andy, dropping the strap-on, lube, and condoms again, this time in Lea's lap.

She stared down at them. Clearly Andy had been prepared, firefighter that he was.

"Guess you do wanna see this bit," Sean chuckled nervously, his eyes on the purple phallus that lay on Lea's thigh.

"Wouldn't you?" Andy said. "Wanna see what it looks like. Wanna see how it feels."

Sean chuckled again, his voice even higher.

"And you, Sean?" Lea squeezed his cock. "Do you want to see how it feels?"

Sean's eyes rounded, his focus entirely on Lea. He didn't answer her in words; he simply leaned forward and kissed her.

For a moment, Lea just lost herself in the heat of his kiss. Andy was a wonderful kisser, there was no doubt about it, but Sean... Sean kissed her as if there was nothing else going on in the whole universe but the kiss.

Tonight, however, something else was going to happen. Something that they'd been talking about and playing with the idea of for weeks, but that had never happened before.

Once the kiss found a breathing point, Lea backed up, her eyes still on Sean's, and ran her hand down his chest. She pulled up the bottom of his t-shirt. "Let's take this off, and why don't you lie down. On your belly."

"Yes, ma'am." Sean's voice was husky with desire. With fear?

Lea began to pull the shirt up, and found Andy's fingers helping. Andy winked at her.

Once the shirt was off, Sean took a deep breath, released it, and lay on his belly on the big pull-out bed.

"Want to help me give Sean a back rub, Andy, to help him relax?"

Andy nodded, and together they massaged Sean's muscular back — not a massage to get deep into the muscles and work out the knots, but a light one, to help Sean relax. Let go.

They'd done this much before, and so when Andy and Lea began to tug his boxers down, Sean didn't object, but simply raised his hips.

They kept rubbing, stroking, down Sean's legs — the soles of his feet. Sean purred contentedly, his head resting on his crossed arms. "Mmm. It's okay," he murmured. "You can… go ahead."

Trying to keep herself relaxed, Lea reached over with one hand and picked up the bottle of lube, careful to keep her other hand on Sean's calf. She lifted the bottle, offering it to Andy, but Andy shook his head. He'd never been comfortable enough to play with Sean's ass; with Lea a bit, sure, but not with Sean. Smiling, she leaned over and gave him a kiss.

And then she opened the lube and squirted a healthy dollop onto her finger.

Though the rest of him seemed to remain relaxed, Sean's tight butt bunched.

"Shh," Lea said. "Andy, could you keep working on his feet?"

Nodding, Andy did, and Sean once again let his muscles go.

Lea slid up Sean's side, letting her un-gooped hand float along the planes of his back, finding his neck. When he seemed all but melting into the bed, Lea whispered, "I'm going to touch that beautiful ass of yours. Okay?"

He nodded, eyes closed.

Lea ran her un-lubed hand down Sean's back and over the butt that she so loved to squeeze. Well. One of the *two* butts that she so loved to squeeze, and got to squeeze on a regular basis, lucky girl that she was.

She massaged one cheek and then the other, and Sean's breath quickened slightly, he didn't tense up. Reaching down with the hand with the lubricated finger, she parted the cheeks gently, revealing the puckered hole that lay between them.

Andy moved Sean's legs a bit further apart, giving Lea more access, allowing Sean a bit more comfort, and no doubt allowing himself a better view.

She lowered her slick index finger, letting the fingertip come to rest on Sean's anus. Sean's breath hitched, and Lea was surprised to find her own ass pulse in sympathy; it knew *just* what was coming. She ran the pad of her finger in a tiny circle around the opening, and Sean released a pleasure-filled sigh.

Lea had never been so glad that she was a nail-biter; the video that they'd watched together had talked about ways of dealing with long nails, but that was never a problem for Lea. After stroking his asshole for a minute or two, Lea asked, "What do you think, Sean? May I?"

Now it was *his* turn to groan, "*Please.*"

Grinning, Lea pressed her finger in — just to the first knuckle, just enough to feel the ring of muscle squeezing her finger. The couple of times they'd done this much before, she'd found the pressure a bit scary — she didn't want to hurt him. But now, for some reason, she found it incredibly exciting; the feeling of his ass squeezing her finger sent sparks to all sorts of interesting places.

She pushed down a bit more, wiggling her finger a bit as she did, and Sean let loose a full, deep groan that she could feeling buzzing around her finger.

"Looks like that feels a lot better than when the doctor does it," said Andy. Lea would have thought it was a joke, since Andy knew exactly how it felt, but he didn't seem to be smiling.

"Does," Sean answered. He *did* seem to be smiling.

"Glad," said Lea, grinning herself, and pushing just a bit deeper. With her free hand, she cupped Sean's balls and squeezed them lightly, evoking another groan.

When she'd released his testicles, Sean sighed, "In. Just... *Ahh.*"

Lea smiled as she felt what she now knew was Sean's prostate swell as she gave it a minute *come hither* stroke with her finger, which was now buried past the second knuckle.

Both boys liked this bit. A lot. And Lea liked it too — that with the smallest of movements in the most unlikely of places, she could bring them such pleasure. It was also more than nice that the movement she used on them was the same as the movement that she used on herself to stimulate her G-spot. Once she'd pointed *that* out to them, Andy and Sean's already impressive repertoire of ways to make Lea come had become truly and literally breathtaking.

Andy watched, apparently transfixed, stroking himself almost absentmindedly.

As Lea carefully tickled Sean's P-spot, as the boys had taken to calling it, Sean continued to give small sounds of contentment. A few minutes in, the sounds were becoming louder, and Sean began to push against the pressure, lifting his hips slightly.

Lea began to reach beneath his hip to stroke Sean's cock, but she found Andy's hand already there. "Jinx," she giggled, and began to help Andy stroke their lover's semi-hard penis — Lea from the side, Andy straddling one of Sean's legs and reaching up past Sean's balls. Though neither of the guys seemed to be able to achieve a full erection when she had her finger inside of them, both insisted that the feeling of being stroked was every bit as intense.

Though his upper body remained just as relaxed, Sean pulled his knees up underneath him, lifting his ass and making it easier for Lea and Andy to play with his cock, which was streaming pre-cum onto their hands. Sean's pale skin was turning redder as his excitement grew, and Lea contented herself simply to —

Sean reached between his legs to still her hand and Andy's. Before Lea could ask if there was anything wrong, he said, his voice low with lust, "Think I'm ready." His blue eyes stared over his shoulder, looking somehow darker than usual.

"You sure?"

He nodded, and then groaned as Lea withdrew her finger from his ass.

"Don't want the butt plug?" Andy asked, running his hands absentmindedly over Sean's balls, his thighs.

"Nope. Ready. Now."

"Okay," Lea found herself saying — mouthing, since her heart was now in her throat. She grabbed the dildo and harness and pulled them up her legs, marveling at the buzz of anticipation in her fingertips.

Shifting up onto her knees, she handed the bottle of lube to Andy. "Help get me ready."

Andy's eyes flashed as he took the lube with one hand and reached out to Lea's pussy with the other. "And here I thought you were *always* ready."

Staring at them over his shoulder through half-closed eyes, Sean chuckled.

"When you two are around, definitely," Lea answered, and then gasped as Andy's fingers squeezed her labia. "Doesn't... huh... Doesn't mean I don't like a helping *hand*..." She gasped again as one of those fingers slid between those lips and into her.

With his other hand, Andy slathered lubricant over the thick portion of the strap-on that was going inside of her, then leaned over and kissed her.

She found herself giving in to the kiss, to the feeling of Andy's hand — but then Sean cleared his throat and murmured, "I think she's ready, Andy."

Lea and Andy enjoyed one last breath, and then parted. Still staring into his deep, brown eyes, she pulled the thick back end of the dildo into her pussy, feeling the rippled surface sliding up into her, and she gasped again.

Andy tightened the harness straps and stroked the purple phallus that now protruded from Lea's *mons.* "Damn," he muttered, stretching the word out for what seemed like days. He lifted the condom packet to Lea's lips; she bit on the corner and he tore the packet open, pulled out the rubber, and then rolled it over Lea's *faux* cock. His hands trembled.

After kissing him again quickly — grinding her erection against his — Lea ran her hand up Sean's leg back to his ass and stroked it. "So. Sean. How do you want me to, um, fuck you? On your belly like this?"

"No. I want to see you." Even with his eyes half closed, his gaze burned.

"Okay." Lea felt a lump rise in her throat again, and wasn't sure why. Well, she could think of dozens of reasons why, but she really didn't feel like sorting through them in the moment. "Um. In the video, remember — ?"

Sean rolled and slid until his legs were off the bed. He remembered. As Lea shuffled off the bed, her dildo wobbling disconcertingly, he handed her a pillow.

To kneel on, Lea realized. "Thanks." Her eyes never leaving Sean's, her hand trailing down his body to his hip, Lea positioned herself between his thighs. She'd been *here* before — just never for *this*. Leaning down, she kissed the head of his cock — an activity that had grown quite familiar in the past few months, if no less exciting.

As Sean closed his eyes in pleasure, Lea slid her still-slick index finger back between the cheeks of his ass and stroked his asshole.

He groaned and lifted his legs to her shoulders, which Lea took as an invitation: she pressed her fingertip back into him, and he groaned again — louder this time. His ass opened to her more easily this time, and quickly Lea's finger was buried inside of his ass and she was playing with his prostate. He started to reach for his erection, but Andy beat him to it, giving Sean a long stroke that made Sean's ass contract. Sean gasped, "No fair. Teaming up."

"Aw, poor boy," Andy said; a joke again, but Andy looked grimly serious.

Taking in the pleasure that she and Andy were giving Sean now, Lea asked, "Sean, are you sure — ?"

Sean's eyes opened, full of blue fire. "Fuck my ass, Lea, baby. Fuck my ass."

"O-okay." Lea slowly slid her finger out of Sean, eliciting a hiss, and used the slippery hand to line up with his asshole, which was still open. She placed the purple head of the dildo against the opening and took a deep breath. "You want it, Sean?"

He nodded, gulping.

"Ask for it. Ask me again."

"Fuck me, Lea. Please, fuck my — *ah!*"

She pushed into him — just an inch or so, just enough that the bulbous head was fully planted inside of Sean. She watched his eyes cross before they closed, and Lea found every nerve ending in her body thrumming.

Andy stroked Sean's cock again, causing their lover's ass to tighten around the invasion, but then Sean fell back onto the bed, releasing his hamstrings and glutes, and whispered, *"More."*

And so Lea leaned over him a little, kissing Andy as she did, and then pushed her pelvis just a *bit*, sliding the dildo another finger's width or so into Sean, causing him to pant, *"Fuck!"*

That's the idea, thought Lea with a smile, excitement replacing nerves. She could feel the movement of the silicone inside of her, and she knew that this was going to be *fun.* Letting his legs fall around her hips, she leaned further over Sean, pushing the dildo deeper, and felt her belly press against the head of Sean's cock, which Andy was still holding, felt liquid spilling against her skin. She rocked her hips back minutely and then thrust forward again; Sean rewarded her with a high-pitched moan and more pre-cum on her stomach. She'd hit his prostate. *Will it feel good if I press past there?*

Only one way to find out: she leaned close to Sean, the tingling tips of her breasts brushing his panting chest, and pressed deeper into him.

The gasp this time was lower, and Sean's eyes flew back open. "Jesus. God. Lea." He lifted up on his elbows and kissed her.

It felt *so fucking good* to be there, planted in him as he had so often been planted in her, and she tried to rock her hips back and then forward again. She managed it, fucking him for a few strokes, each pushing a gasp from Sean.

It felt fabulous, her nipples bouncing against his chest, the pressure of his ass causing the part of the dildo inside of Lea to press against her G-spot. But it wasn't exactly *easy*. Well, it wasn't easy at all. *How the fuck do they do this for so long?* she mused. Leaning back, she lifted his legs back to her shoulders until it was his calves her breasts were pressed against. She found it easier to thrust this way, using her thighs and butt muscles to push into Sean.

Andy began stroking Sean's cock again, which was only semi-erect, but was streaming clear pre-cum as Lea stimulated the gland that produced it. "Feel good, boy?" His voice was low and husky, his eyes on Sean's face.

Sean, however, remained completely focussed on Lea. "You... *huh!* You have no... idea." Now his gaze shifted to his friend's. "God. Andy. Feels so fucking good, feels..." He gasped as Andy's strokes and Lea's found a rhythm, Lea's thrusts pressing Sean's cock up through Andy's fingers.

Holy fuck, Lea thought, aware that her own juices were now flowing freely over the dildo inside of her. *I'm fucking Sean. I AM FUCKING Sean!*

She'd had so many fantasies over the years about what it would be like to have sex with this gorgeous man, her best friend's brother. *All* kinds of fantasies she'd had back in the days before they'd ever actually fucked — fucking on his fire truck, fucking center-stage at the theater with a packed house watching, him tied up like one of the old paintings of St. Sebastian, only instead of him being pierced with arrows, he was piercing *her...*

Never this.

Thank you, Kirsten. Not that you're ever going to want to hear about me fucking your brother up the ass with the strap-on you gave me. Or that he's ever going to want me to tell you.

But thank you anyway.

Reaching out, Lea caressed Andy's butt for good measure. *What the hell! My ass is theirs, theirs are* mine!

Andy gave a gurgle and squeezed Sean's glistening cock, making their lover scream out once more to a higher power. To several. Of whom Lea was very pleased to find herself one.

"You feeling good, Sean?" She kissed his ankle and licked it.

Letting his head loll to one side — but keeping his eyes locked on hers — Sean laughed breathlessly. "What... the fuck... d'you *think?*"He started blinking, staring at his own cock in disbelief. "Aw, Andy, Lea, fuck, *fuck! FUCK ME, BABY, FUCK!*" he threw back his head and screamed, his face reddening as it so often did when he came — but instead of a geyser of pearly cum erupting from his cock head, more clear pre-cum spilled onto Andy's hand. "Aw, god, damn, what the — ?"

"You want me to stop, Sean?" Lea asked, but he shook his head vehemently.

Adding his own hand to Andy's, Sean began smoothing the slick liquid over his shaft. As Lea began to fuck him again, he laughed, groaned, and laughed again. "I just... Andy, when you were a kid, you ever beat off?"

Squeezing the semi-hard cock of his friend and lover, Andy chuckled. "Like, every chance I could."

"Yeah, yeah, I... *hnh!* I meant, like before you were all... Before you could really... I just... Coming just now, that felt so... I remember fuckin' my hand in bed, didn't even have hair down there or nothin'... *Hnh!* And... coming like that, just clear, no... And doing it again and... *Hnnh...*"

"Damn," sighed Andy. "Yeah. I kinda remember that. Remember doin' it till I felt like I had a bruise inside my..." He flashed a smile at both his lovers. "Damn. That was my P-spot, wasn't it?"

"Yup," said Lea, fondling his bum some more. "I reckon so."

"Think I can get you to come some more, Sean-boy?"

"Please."

Grinning, Andy leaned down and sucked down Sean's cock.

Sean closed his eyes, sighing as Lea's thrusts pushed his cock up into Andy's mouth, and then sidled underneath Andy, returning the favor.

And that was the image that etched itself into Lea's brain: her shit-ton of male pulchritude locked in a sixty-nine while she lovingly buggered Sean's ass. A 697? A 169? Whatever.

It was beautiful.

And even as her thighs and hips began to tell her that they were going to have words with her later, Lea's pussy told them to shut up; it was beginning to feel very, very nice.

And then Sean managed to lower his feet so that his toes squeezed and pulled at Lea's nipples (*holy fuck — the man must be part gorilla*) and she began to feel even nicer. Oozing pleasure, she began to let her hands run over her lovers' bodies, feeling their muscles bunching as they pleasured each other, as they pleasured her.

And her still-lubed finger found Andy's ass and slid in.

Ms. Lighty began to drone about circuits and filaments, and Lea didn't give a damn: she had better things to think about. The six-ninety-seven or whatever the fuck it was began to buck and groan like the single creature it had become, and Lea, Sean, and Andy where all lost.

Simultaneous orgasm is a remarkably imprecise term, especially when one is trying to describe an event or events sparked in the midst of such a timeless, out-of-body experience. Lea couldn't have said what led to what, who came first, who came last — the distinctions had no meaning.

But they all came. Even Lea, who didn't expect it at all, sensitive as her G-spot was. Even Sean, who had her strap-on filling him, and whose toes squeezed *hard* on Lea's nipples. And definitely Andy, whose ass clamped down on Lea's finger as he poured himself down Sean's throat.

They came. They came together.

Come together, right now…. under me.

As they lay in bed that night, glorying in the afterglow, Lea considered the possibility — not for the first time — that she was the luckiest woman on the face of the earth.

"Hawks lost," she murmured as they turned off the television and got under the covers.

"Fuck 'em," said Andy.

To which Sean added, "We won." And he turned off the light and spooned up behind her, wrapping his arms over her and Andy, his now-sleepy cock nuzzling between the cheeks that it had so thoroughly fucked earlier that evening — and Lea knew that *lucky* only began to describe it.

As they approached the theater the next day, Lea had her arms hooked through each of her boys' elbow, and the feeling of well-being still oozed from her every pore. Who cared about the aches in her muscles? Who gave a shit about the funny look their downstairs neighbor Lorelle had shot them as they walked by the laundry room on the way to leaving.

Life was as close to perfect as this imperfect life could provide.

Sean and Kirsten's mother stood waving at them from the theater entrance, her white hair gleaming in the afternoon light.

"Hey, Mrs. O'Connell!" Lea called, releasing Sean so that he could give his mom a kiss on the cheek, and then releasing Andy so that she could receive an embrace of her own from the older woman.

"Violet, please, Lea, I've told you." Violet gave Lea a squeeze and then turned to Andy. "Andrew, you're looking lovely as ever."

"You just say that because he looks like your son," Lea laughed, and laughed again as both men blushed.

"Perhaps," chuckled Sean's mom, "but I can see in your eye that *you* know that it's true."

Now it was Lea's turn to blush. "You caught me."

"Oh, Lea, honey, I'd have to be *blind* not to see it." Violet patted her son with a carefully manicured hand. "Just as I'd have to be blind not to see how this big old softie of mine appreciates how lovely *you* are." She peered at Andy. "And this big old country boy as well." She cast a cagey look at Lea that Lea had no idea how to interpret.

"Hey, Mama," Sean said, clearly trying to change the subject, "Kirsten call this morning?"

"Oh, yes." Violet went along with the course shift with a wink at Lea. "I think she misses her best friend here, though. It sounds as if your sister is having a hard time with her new roommate."

"Really?" Lea felt her face fall. "Oh, that's too bad."

Violet shrugged. "Or maybe it's boy trouble. She was pretty vague. My Kirsten can be closed-mouthed when she wants to be."

Nodding, Lea shot a glance to Sean, who was frowning. Not like she's going to tell her mother that her roomie Gianna *is* her boyfriend. Well. Girlfriend. Damn. I like Gianna. Hope things are okay.

"In any case, she sent her love to all of you, and says she wishes she could watch the show with us."

"Oh, yes," Lea said, smiling as brightly as she could, "she'd love this show — I know you guys will too. Come on, let's go in."

At the box office, and then in the lobby, Lea found herself introducing the O'Connells and Andy to the theater staff, and was surprised at how uncomfortable she was feeling. Some of the guys looked at her lovers as if trying to figure out which one to punch. A number of the women — and a couple of the men — looked at the two men hungrily and then stared appraisingly at Lea.

As the house manager, Jack (who had practically salivated at the sight of Lea's boyfriends) rang the gong that encouraged the audience to take their seats, Lea's boss Sassy came up with the theater's technical director, Gus. They made a funny pair: Sassy all squares, iron-haired, with a dead-pan expression, and Gus with his fly-away grey hair, bright eyes and pixy-ish build. Lea introduced them to her companions.

For once, there was no competitive heat aimed either at Lea or at her boys. "Nice to meet you," Sassy said. Turning to Andy and Sean she gave a grin so minute that Lea knew that only she would recognize it. "Lea has spoken very highly of you both."

"As well she should!" burbled Gus, bouncing on his toes.

"Agreed," laughed Violet, patting each of the boys on the arm.

"I think I recognize you, Mrs. O'Connell," Gus chirped. "Are you a subscriber?"

"Well, no, though Miss Lea has rectified that situation for next year. I believe... Is your wife's name Sally?"

Gus smiled his brilliant, heart-breaking smile. "Late wife, yes."

"I'm so sorry to hear that," said Violet, looking truly devastated.

"Yes," Gus agreed, his smile scarcely dimming. "It was terribly sad. But I like to remember the pleasure we had together." As Violet nodded sadly, Gus's eyes sparkled and he said, "Ah! Yes, now I remember. We knew you from the Fitzpatricks'."

Again Violet nodded, smile a bit brighter now with nostalgia. She seemed about to ask something when Jack rang the gong again. "Well, we should be getting in. Wouldn't want to miss the *Streetcar* now would we?" She shook Gus's hand and Sassy's.

"Pleasure to meet you, Mrs. O'Connell," said Sassy — and again, Lea knew that only she picked up on the emphasis that the laconic Canadian put on the first word. *What the hell, Sassy?*

"Lovely to see you again, Violet." Gus leaned down and kissed Violet's hand. "Enjoy the show." With Sassy, he wandered off to watch from the stage manager's booth at the back of the theater.

As they walked to their seats, Sean was staring at his mother with a look of amused bewilderment. "Was that old guy *flirting* with you?"

Violet shot her son a look of dignified authority that had no doubt commanded her kindergarten classes for decades. "That *old guy* is a very lovely man. We used to meet for bridge, but honestly, no one cared about the cards, thank goodness. The Fitzpatricks had a knack for inviting the nicest, most *interesting* people. Gus was simply being friendly and courteous."

"Uh-huh," said Sean, clearly unconvinced.

From Lea's other side, Andy waggled his eyebrows at Sean and mouthed *Flirting*. And Lea couldn't help but agree with him. *What the hell, Gus?*

As they walked Sean and Andy from the theater to their firehouse, the two men argued over whether Tennessee Williams wanted the audience to hate Stanley or Blanche more. Violet and Lea settled for occasionally interjecting, but mostly observed in amused silence.

"Stanley is a…. a *wife-beater* for goodness sake, Andy," said Sean, noticeably swallowing his expletives for his mother's sake. "And he *rapes* his wife's sister!"

Andy waved the broad-palmed hand with which he'd stroked the man he was arguing with the night before. "Which is just awful, definitely, but Blanche is, like, this huge black hole that comes and sits in his house and treats him and his wife like dirt."

"She's *crazy*, Andy. I mean, yeah, she's nasty to him sometimes, but I feel sorry for her."

"You would," Violet laughed. "My knight-in-shining-armor son."

Sean ducked his head.

Walking arm in arm with Sean's mom, Lea chuckled too. "And what about Stella?"

Both men turned back from where they were striding ahead of the women, their broad foreheads creased. "What *about* Stella?" Andy asked.

"Yeah, I mean, she's stuck with these other two. She's got a baby coming and all. What's she supposed to do?" said Sean.

Lea shrugged. "Well, yeah, fine, but she chooses Stanley over Blanche. She turns her back on her sister. She has to have at least guessed what happened the night the baby was born. Stanley and Blanche are who they are, and they're poison to each other, but Stella? She *chooses* how she wants things to be."

Both men pondered this, scowling.

Violet mused, "Well, it's not like either choice is exactly an attractive one. And a new mother in those days wouldn't have had an easy time walking away from her husband. You could argue that the choice was made for her."

Sean grunted, his eyes flicking to his mother's face. Sean and Kirsten almost never talked about their father, who'd disappeared when Kirsten was very young. He'd sent money regularly, and the couple had never divorced, but as far as Lea knew Violet hadn't seen her husband in a quarter-century. Kirsten and Sean definitely hadn't.

"Well," Lea said, trying to break the sudden cooling of the mood, "I think that's the point of the play. Each of the three main characters is sympathetic. Each of them is awful. It's one of the reasons I love this production so much — so often the play is about the Stanley and the Blanche, and you almost forget about Stella. This is like watching a threeway... um, car crash." That wasn't the simile that had actually popped into Lea's head, but she was going to be damned if she was going to reveal the depths of her depravity to Violet just yet. Well, hopefully, she'd never have to.

They walked up to the fire station. As every time Lea had come here, a group of the other firefighters was working on one of the trucks. This time they all stopped to razz Andy and Sean. "Hey! Look! The Twins brought dates!"

"Yeah," said the one woman in the group, "Andy's date is a knockout. The young one's pretty cute too."

Lea laughed and stuck her tongue out at the woman, while Violet blushed.

"Seeya tomorrow," Andy said, staring at Lea with a glum expression.

Sean was more cheerful. "Bye, Mama. Don't have too much fun without us, Lea." He squeezed her hand.

Then both men walked into the station, and Lea was aware that the eyes of all of the people on the truck including the woman — what was her name again? — were locked on Lea. Measuring her. Challenging her. "Hope you guys have a quiet night," she said, and waved.

They all waved back, and Lea and Violet walked another three blocks in silence to the restaurant where Sean's mother had insisted on taking Lea, "to repay you for the lovely tickets."

"You don't have to repay me, Violet," Lea said as the server seated them. "The tickets were comps, and it was my pleasure."

"Now, Lea, honey, the pleasure was ours. Let me buy you dinner; that pleasure will be mine, all right?" Violet's eyes, the same pale blue as her children's, sparkled.

"All right," laughed Lea, unable to refuse the eyes, just as she was unable to refuse Sean or Kirsten's.

They chatted about work as they looked over the menu. Violet had been trying to retire since Lea and Kirsten's graduation, but the district kept begging her to stay on — she was much beloved. She told Kirsten how odd it was to be teaching her students' children. Lea laughed, and told her how weird it was to go from being one of two full-time employees at a theater where most of the performers were younger than she was to one of nearly a hundred members of the artistic and business staff, of whom she found herself to be one of the youngest.

When their chicken Caesars were delivered to the table, the conversation slowed. At one point, Lea looked up to find Violet peering at her with a small smile on her lips. Lea couldn't help herself; she ducked her head and looked back down at her salad.

That didn't deter the older woman: "You've told me about your work, Lea, and I've seen for myself what a lovely place it is, but tell me, how is the living situation?"

Lea found herself turning bright red and choking on a croûton.

Laughing, Violet handed her a glass of water. "Oh, don't worry, dear. I knew what was going to happen the minute Kirsten told me you were moving in."

"You... you did?" Suddenly, Lea's stomach felt very full, and not in a good way.

Again, Violet laughed. "Well, of course! Kirsten and I have been expecting you and Sean to come together for years."

Not trusting herself to say anything that wouldn't make things worse, Lea simply nodded.

Reach across the table and taking Lea's hand, Violet took on a more somber tone. "My boy is such a romantic — I knew he wasn't ever going to push things, and so I was glad that circumstances... encouraged you together." Violet gave Lea's hand a squeeze. "But you have to tell me one thing, Lea, honey."

"W-what?"

"I saw the way that Andrew was looking at you. Please tell me that you and Sean are being sensitive to him. I know he looks like a big old country boy, but I suspect he's every bit as much a softie as my son."

Oh, Lea thought, *you have no idea how hard — or how soft — he can be.* When she was able, she said, "No, no, we're all really... careful. The boys both know how I feel about them." Well, that much was true.

"And how do you feel about my son, Miss Lea?" When Lea's face fell, Violet chuckled and added, "I know the answer, sweetheart, I just want to hear it."

"I love him."

Violet patted Lea's hand. "And I hope that he has told you how he feels about you."

"Oh. Yes." Also how he feels about Andy. And Andy's told me, and... *"Yes."*

"I'm so glad." The older woman's gaze became misty, focussed somewhere other than the restaurant, and Lea knew that she was thinking about the past. "Love is such a complicated business, isn't it?"

Lea couldn't help but concur wholeheartedly with that statement.

By the time that Lea finished walking from the bus stop to the apartment building, her heart had finally descended from her throat. The rest of the dinner had been nice enough, but all that had been going through Lea's mind had been been the image of thrusting her dildo into Sean's ass and her finger into Andy's while they sucked each other off.

Not something you want to be thinking about while having dinner with one of your lovers' mothers.

As Lea came to the bottom of the stairs, looking forward to nothing but some wine, some stupid television, and maybe a chat with Kirsten, a lumpy silhouette greeted her from the open laundry room door. "Hey, there."

Startled, Lea turned and watched the shadow resolve itself into Lorelle, the downstairs neighbor. She was carry her sleeping four-month-old on her shoulder. "Hey, Lorelle," Lea whispered back.

"Oh, you don't need to whisper or nothing," Lorelle said. "Once Peanut is out, it's hard as hell to wake her."

"Oh."

"Mind, last night, *someone* woke her up real good." Lorelle said this last with a smirk.

"Oh." *Fuckity-fuck-fuck.* Shame lit Lea's face like a beacon. "Oh, Lorelle, oh, god, I am so —"

"Naw, honey, don't, please, I mean, good *gawd!*" Lorelle, whose skin was usually the color of weak tea, darkened to something closer to coffee. "I mean, last night... You know Freddy's been on night shift last month or so, right?"

Lea shrugged. She and Lorelle had had perhaps four conversations, all while folding laundry.

"Well, and he hasn't... Um. Since Peanut was born, he's kinda scared to look at me, okay? Which was just fine with me for a while, but honest, um...."

Lea blinked at Lorelle, who was probably a couple of years younger than Lea herself, but like all new mothers, hadn't slept in months, and so looked a decade older; it seemed weird that she was acting so —

"See, even before, when Freddy and I moved in, okay? Those two men of yours, I mean, *gawdamn!* A woman'd have to be, like, a statue or something not to..."

Lea blinked some more.

Lorelle closed her eyes and took a deep breath. The baby shifted on her shoulder. "See... Even... When Nola here was, you know, *conceived,* I may have been in bed with my husband, who I love and all, but I was thinking about what it would be like to be in bed with those two boys of yours. Okay?" Lorelle's eyes flew open. "And this was before you moved in or anything, okay? This was last year and all, so..."

Lea found herself giggling. "No. Lorelle. It's okay. If I didn't get to climb into bed with them myself, I'd be thinking the same thing."

"Oh. Yeah." Lorelle shot her an embarrassed smile. "I guess. I wanted to say... Lea, honey, you're my hero, okay? I mean, I'm a happily married woman and all, but when I hear y'all get up to stuff, just, you know, I want you to know..." Lorelle's skin was now so dark that it was almost indistinguishable from her hair. "Well. I'm, um, cheering you on. Okay?"

Lea laughed, not knowing what else to do. "Okay. Thanks? I'm still sorry we woke Nola."

Lorelle laughed along. "Oh, don't be. That... I mean, I wasn't *exactly* sure what y'all were getting up to last night, but *gawdamn,* that was the sexiest sounding shit I *ever* heard. Helped *me* sleep real good, let me tell you."

They laughed together, and Nola wriggled on her mother's shoulder.

"And, listen, um, I don't know if you and your boys have anything planned for Wednesday night?"

"Not that I know of. We're all home."

"Oh. Good. Well, I was kinda thinking... It's Freddy's night off, and maybe y'all might... inspire him a bit?"

"You mean...?"

"Uh-huh."

"Oh. Okay." Lea dissolved into giggles again, because it seemed called for. This was, without a doubt, the weirdest conversation she'd ever had. Which was saying something when Kirsten was your best friend.

Again they laughed, and Lorelle hugged Lea, and wished her a good, *quiet* night.

But as Lea made her way into her peaceful, empty apartment, all she could think was, *Great. Now I get to think about our* audience *every time we fuck.*

Lea called Kirsten and shared the story, figuring her friend would at least see the absurdity of the situation, but Kirsten only chuckled politely. "Hey, K?" Lea asked. "What's wrong?"

And so Kirsten launched into a long, sniffly discussion of the state of her relationship with Gianna — how they hadn't really spent much time together recently, how they hadn't had sex in weeks, and, finally, about how Gianna's old boyfriend had been coming around and making noises about wanting to get married.

"Oh, fuck," said Lea.

"Yeah. And she isn't telling him to fuck off, which sort of leaves me hanging, you know?"

"Yeah."

"And when I tried to talk to her about it last night, her big answer was maybe we could try a threesome. Like y'all."

"Oh." Lea tried to think about that. "Well —"

"And yeah, honey, it seems to be working so well for y'all, and I'm so happy for you and Sean, but I kinda don't think it would be that way here — I think it would be about the two of them getting off, and me along for the ride, which would suck. Also, he's really short, and he has bad breath."

"Oh, Kirsten. I'm so sorry."

"Yeah, well, like I said, it sucks. And I think she's at his place now, which sucks more."

"Oh, K." And the two of them wept over the phone as they'd done together dozens of times over the years, until Kirsten was finally ran out of steam and laugh, "So Lea, honey, tell me about this young mother-of-the-year whose down jilling off to the sound of my best friend, my brother and their lover making the beast with three backs?"

That made Lea laugh too. "Oh, well, it's not poor Lorelle's fault. I guess we got kind of... carried away last night."

"Uh-huh." Kirsten's voice made it very clear that she'd be asking for details if one of the participants weren't related to her.

"And it's your fault."

"Mine?"

"Uh-huh. We finally put your housewarming gift to, uh, full use last night."

"Oh." It sounded as if Kirsten were the one blushing for once. "Um. And?"

"And we all had a very nice and, apparently, a very *loud* time."

"Damn."

"So thank you, Kirsten, for the lovely strap-on. I promise that it will be well used."

At that Kirsten cackled, sounding much more like herself, and Lea smiled as they went on to have a much more normal conversation. Normal for *them*, anyway.

The next day, the theater was very quiet. The box office was closed, it was the Equity day off, so there weren't any rehearsals, and the shop was closed, since *Streetcar* was the last show of the year — though Lea was sure that Gus was up in his aerie of an office, doing whatever it was that he did up there. The bookkeeper Chris was toiling away in his cubby. The telemarketing manager, Dave, had his feet up on his desk and — as always — a phone attached to his ear. The development director, Alice, seemed to have fallen asleep (she, like

Lorelle, was a new mom). And the office manager, Jaimie, was restocking the supply cabinet and flirting with everything that moved, including Lea. But only in a half-hearted, Monday-afternoon kind of way.

Sassy actually asked Lea to be the liaison with the fire marshal before Lea had thought to bring it up. (*Marshals*, Lea thought.) She said it with her usual flat voice, but there was something about the look in her eye that made Lea uneasy.

In any case, by 4:00, most of the staff had shuffled off early to beat the traffic. And so when Andy and Sean strode into the office, Sassy and Jaimie were the only ones left.

"Good afternoon, gentlemen," Sassy said, striding forward to shake their hands. "Nice to see you again. Since you already know my assistant Lea, I think I'm going to let her show you about, if that's okay."

"That'll be just fine, ma'am," said Andy with a nod.

I bet it'll just fine, Lea thought, looking at her two boys in their blue uniform shirts. *Just fine.*

Behind Sassy, Jaimie was all but drooling.

"Come on, Jaimie," Sassy said, grabbing Jaimie by the elbow and all but dragging her to the door. "Let's let the gentlemen do their inspection unmolested. I'll buy you a beer. Do you know why American beer is like making love in a canoe…?"

Once the door had closed behind them, Lea turned back to her boys, ready to pounce; they were still all business, however.

"We do have to do the inspection," Andy said apologetically. He was turned slightly away from her.

Lea lifted her hand to his chin and turned him toward her. He was sporting a black eye. "Andy? Was there… an accident?"

He looked to Sean, who shrugged. Sean said, "He was in a fight."

"A fight?" she asked Sean. "What about?"

It was Andy who answered. "It was Miller. He was…"

As Andy fizzled out, Sean picked up. "The guys were giving us shit 'cause of you. Which of us you were dating, and like that. Just shit. And Miller starts in saying, 'Well, why would they be dating her, they're dating each other,' and that gets a big old laugh, ha-ha, very funny, 'cause they have no idea, right? But he won't let it alone. All last night, keeps on calling us 'the Faggot Twins.' And…" Sean looked to Andy.

Andy grimaced. "We were coming back from a call this morning — false alarm — and he starts in on which of us likes taking it up the ass. And no one's laughing any more, but he isn't stopping, so I told him to shut the fuck up." Sean put his arm around Andy's shoulder, but Andy shrugged it off. "So we're back at the station now, and Miller sort of smirks at me and says it must be Sean, and I'm getting protective of my *girlfriend*. So I punched the fucker."

"Miller's an asshole." Sean embraced Andy again, and this time Andy let him. Sean continued, "It was a stupid-ass fight, like most stupid-ass fights. the two of them punching and wrassling, and Andy's got Miller in a head-lock when Joanie dumped a pitcher of ice water over them, which broke that up."

Joanie. Right. That's the woman firefighter's name.

Andy sighed and rested his head on Sean's shoulder. "Then the captain came in a gave both of us a tongue-lashing that still has my ears ringing, told us both that if he heard so much as a squeak out of either of us for the rest of the day we'd be home without pay for the rest of the month. And that was that."

Lea hugged Andy from the side not taken up by Sean. "I'm so sorry."

"Naw. The thing is," Andy muttered, "it wasn't that he was calling us *queer*, 'cause guess what? Whatever we are, it ain't whatever *straight* is. Not that it's any of their gawdamn business. It was just he was so *nasty*. And when he started on Sean… It was like, I don't know, like if he'd started in on your being Jewish or something; who the fuck is he to throw that sort of shit around?"

Sean patted Andy's back. "Yeah, well, the rest of the guys knew he was just being an asshole. I mean, he's been on Joanie all year, saying she's a dyke, which I'm pretty sure she's not, but it doesn't matter, 'cause what fucking difference does it make? He's fucking married."

Andy gave a short, bitter laugh. "Yeah, well, Joanie's tougher than me, that's for damn sure. She just keeps telling him to shove it."

Lea kissed the back of his thick neck. "But she doesn't have a girlfriend working right there with her." She laughed, and both boys looked at her. "Did you hear what your mother called you yesterday, Sean?" He shook his head. "Her 'knight-in-shining-armor son.' You're another one, Andy. You were protecting Seans's honor. Such a good boy!" She gave his butt a squeeze, which caused him to jump, and made Sean snicker. "You okay?"

Andy shot her a smirk, but nodded. "More embarrassed that I lost my cool than anything. Haven't been in an actual fist fight since I was, like, fifteen."

"Well, it's about time then," Sean joked, and he too patted Andy's butt, which made Andy's eyes go wide. "Come on, let's get the inspection started. I'm looking forward to getting it done with."

And so Lea led them around the theater: first the offices, obviously, since that's where they were, and then the lobby and the rehearsal studios, and then the back stage area. Sean and Andy kept checking the smoke detectors and the fire extinguishers, looked at the entrances and exits — including the few windows — to make sure that nothing was blocking them. In one of the studios they pointed out that a stack of set flats were blocking one of the exits; it was to a costume storage closet, but there was a fire escape from that room, so the doorways needed to remain unblocked. They pointed out a couple of doors that had been "ragged open," strips of fabric wrapped around the handles to make the doors open and close silently. This might make for better shows, but it would allow a fire to spread more quickly, since the doors were never fully shut.

Lea took notes on her tablet, creating a shared to-do list that would get the appropriate members of the staff to take care of each of the problems.

When they walked back into the shop, the men's eyes widened. "Damn," Andy said. "This is, like, my daddy's idea of heaven."

Lea laughed, looking around at the huge collection of power tools, neatly stored lumber and hardware, racks of painted flats, and even the shell of an old Chevy that had been used for a production of *Grease* a few years earlier.

"What's up there?" Sean asked, pointing at Gus's office, some sixty feet or so above the shop floor.

"Oh, that's the tech director's lair. You guys met him yesterday — Gus, he knew your mom, Sean."

"Oh. Right. We should probably check up there."

The drapes in the window glowed. "I think he's up there. Come on. I'll introduce you guys. He's a sweetheart. If he weren't 78, you guys would have competition, I'm telling you."

They climbed up the steep stairs to the office. "He's 78 and he's up and down these all day?" Sean asked.

Laughing, Lea nodded. "Yup. He's something." She knocked on the office door, and Gus's voice bubbled back. "Come in!"

Lea opened the door and followed her two firefighters through.

Gus was at one of the three drafting tables, working on sketches for God knew what. "Good morning, gentlemen!"

Lea smiled. "It's four, Gus. Everyone else is long gone. You should go home."

Gus blinked up at the hand-painted clock that was barely visible on his wall, surrounded as it was by set designs and paintings. "Four? Oh. My. So it is. Well, it's always lovely to see you, Lea. And it's nice to see your two friends as well. I've been thinking about your mother, Mr. O'Connell."

"My...?" Sean frowned.

"Oh, yes, you see, she and my Sally were very close for a while." He smiled his bright, sad smile and pointed at the purple-inked sketches on his drafting table. "I'm thinking of making another painting of Sally, you see."

Lea looked back over Gus's desk, where there was a line of paintings of Gus's late wife, her hair fading from flame red to snow white, and then peered at the abstract sketches on the drawing board.

"There's Sally, you see," Gus said, pointing to what Lea now recognized as the central human figure in the image before pointing at two other shapes, "and here's Violet O'Connell, and our friend Frank. This was at one of the Fitzpatricks's parties, about fifteen, twenty years ago." He ran his hand over the drawing, his smile saddening. "It doesn't feel so very long ago. These two are gone —" He pointed at the central figure and the one to her right. "—but seeing your mother again yesterday, Mr. O'Connell, it brought back some really lovely memories."

"I'm glad," said Sean.

"Well!" Gus said. "Given your uniforms, I assume you're not here to listen to me reminisce. Any problems with the shop?"

"No, sir," Andy said. "Do you have a second exit from this office?"

Gus showed them the exit to the fire escape — which in spite of having a lit EXIT sign was almost invisible because of all of the paintings and bric-a-brac around it, and let them check his smoke alarm. "Is this your last stop of the day?"

"No, sir," Sean said. "We still have to look through the theater auditorium."

"Well, much as I've enjoyed having you here, please, don't let me keep you." He waved to them from his drawing board, already immersed back in his new painting.

Lea, Andy, and Sean walked down to the shop, the boys shaking their heads. "Well, he's definitely what Mama'd call a *character*," Sean chuckled. "Nice guy. A little funny that he's putting my mama in a painting, though."

"Oh, I think it's because when they met yesterday, it reminded him of happy times with his wife. He was gaga about her, obviously."

"Not as gaga as we are about you," Sean answered, running his fingers through her hair.

"Oh, gawd, you're gonna get all mushy, aren't you?" grumbled Andy.

Lea turned to him. "It's all right, Andy. We're gaga about you too."

He blushed and muttered some more, but smiled even so.

They inspected the stage, Sean and Andy admiring the height of the fly system overhead, where scenery was lifted during shows. It wasn't Lea's favorite part of the theater, not by a long shot. She wasn't fond of heights. She wasn't *afraid* of them, exactly; she just had a healthy respect for them and avoided them whenever possible.

"So were you ever an actress, Miss Lea?"

"Yeah, in school a bit." Holding their hands, she walked them through the auditorium, its green EXIT lights all proudly on display. "Found out I liked being behind the scenes more, so I started directing, stage managing, that sort of thing."

"Stage managing?" Andy asked.

"Yeah. Stage manager is in charge of every aspect of the performance; makes sure the actors are in place, calls all of the cues, makes sure that any problems are dealt with invisibly."

"Kind of like a dispatcher," Sean said.

"Yeah, but roll the captain in with that and you've got a better idea of how central the job is. The old joke is that directors speak only to God, but that the stage manager *is* God. I'll prove it to you. Come on — I've been saving my favorite room for last."

She led them up a narrow staircase that ran from the stage-right wings up behind the wall of the auditorium. The lighting was dim — though the safety lighting limned every stair — and the carpet was thick. No sound- or light-bleed coming from here.

Lea opened the door to the booth, and as always felt as if she were entering a magical realm. The theater's tech booth was beautiful — a thick-paneled floor-to-ceiling glass wall at the front that gave a full view of the stage and the house, state-of-the-art sound and light boards, and between them, the stage manager's throne. But honestly, she'd loved every literal hole-in-the-wall booth she'd ever been in. There was something special about them — apart from the actors, above the audience, *private.*

And she'd always wanted to have sex in a booth, but there'd never been the right time.

Only now she'd found the right time.

"So, you said you'd prove the stage manager was God?" Sean said, shaking Lea out her reverie. She blinked at him and saw that he and Andy both had their serious, sexy faces on.

"God. Right." She turned away from them and walked toward the stage manager's station, pulling off her jacket and letting it fall to the carpeted floor. She began to undo her blouse, flashing one boob at them but stopping before continuing the strip tease because they were both standing there, completely naked. *How the fuck…?* By the time her chin had picked itself back up off of the floor, she had realized, *Right. I've fallen in love with a pair of firemen. Dress quick, undress quick.*

"God?" Sean reached out and started stroking Andy's cock; Andy returned the favor.

"Um. God." *God!* Lea moved backward and ended up falling back into the SM's chair, not able to look away from the spectacle before her — no matter that it was one she got to see all of the time. Reaching out to steady herself, she grabbed the first thing that came to hand: the mic. *Right.* "See this?" When both men nodded solemnly, she asked, "Do you know what it's called?"

They shook their heads.

Smiling, she pushed the big captain's chair back far enough that she could see the console and them at the same time. She turned on the PA system, grabbed the mic, clicked the trigger so that the red light showed, and spoke into it: "Ladies and gentlemen, your attention, please." Her voice rumbled from speakers all over the building — not just in the auditorium but backstage, in the lobby, and even up in the offices. Echoes rumbled through the building. "There's a fire in the booth. Could all members of Atlanta Fire & Rescue please report immediately to put it out?" Sean grinned, Andy scowled, and Lea laughed. "God mic! Ergo, the person who sits here is…"

"God," they said together.

Before putting the mic back, Lea said, "This has been a drill. No additional assistance is necessary. Thank you, and — "

Then they were on her, and all thoughts of the mic — or God, or anything — went right out of her head.

Sean was kissing her chin, her neck, her ear, in that unbelievably distracting way that he had, all while undoing the rest of the buttons to her blouse.

Andy undid the zipper of her skirt and had it, her panties and her stockings down in a heartbeat, her shoes off, and there she was, naked before them as they were naked before her, and as much as she had fantasized about fucking in a stage manager's booth thousands of times before, it had never been anything compared to this.

Lea fell into the sensation of her two lovers loving her, and was amazed that they could have her so excited so quickly. Or maybe not — she'd been waiting for this all day. Since the previous, lonely night. Since the end of their epic fuck the night before. If she were really honest with herself, she'd never really stopped wanting to feel them touching her, *adoring* her, as they were doing at that very moment.

From experience she knew that each of them was more than capable of bringing her incredible pleasure on his own. But from the first time that they'd all made love together, there had been something, something magical, about the way that they could make her feel together. It wasn't just the sexual part — though, *holy fuck*, that was beyond unbelievable — but also because she could feel them loving her, and trusting her, could feel their love and trust for each other, and it felt a bit like standing in the middle of the sun.

Then Sean's tongue found Lea's ear as Andy's found her clit, and honestly, the sexual part really would have been enough. Really.

She'd asked them a week or two before whether having two lovers pleasuring them short-circuited their nervous systems the way it did hers.

Andy, whom she and Sean had just finished sucking off, had simply laughed and said, "Hell, yeah!"

Sean had wiped Andy's jism off of his chin thoughtfully and had answered, "I think sex with even one of you guys starts me at short-circuited. By the time you're both involved, *all* the damned wiring is blown out."

Yeah, *Lea mused as her pelvis bucked against Andy's mouth and her chest against Sean's, that sounds about right. I don't need an electrician, I need the fire brigade, and what the hell! They're right here!*

Lea found that she was saying things, saying them pretty loudly, but had no clear concept of what she was saying. Their names, maybe. The seventy-two names of God. The capitals of all fifty states.

Love. That word featured in there a lot. Which made sense. To the extent that Lea had any sense left at all.

She was coming. Stupid word, *coming. Arriving* seemed more like it. Or *exploding.* Was there a word that meant both?

If there were, it would have described what she was doing. Again, very loudly.

It was only as their mouths began to disengage and the experience began to recede that she became aware of how *good* she felt.

Sean kissed his way back up to her mouth. "Hi," he murmured into her lips.

"Hi," she gasped.

Andy removed his finger from her, triggering another round of ecstasy. "God, you're beautiful."

Stroking Sean's cock, Lea laughed, "Which one of us?"

Lea could feel Andy bury his face in her belly, which was still trembling, so that she felt rather than heard him say, "Both."

The only answer she could think to give was, "I love you." And then into Sean's lips. "I love you." And before Sean could say anything mushy, she stood on shaky legs, pushed him into the chair, and then knelt between his thighs, and began to pleasure him with her lips, her tongue, her teeth.

If he could torture her, then she'd show *him* how it felt.

Somehow, Lea didn't think Sean would mind.

She felt Andy moving up behind her, unusually tentative. His hands found her pussy again, which welcomed them, and Lea wasn't surprised when one thumb meandered up the crack of her ass and circled her asshole. She murmured into Sean's shaft, "Either, Andy. It's up to you." She lavished Sean's rod with a long lick from balls to head, bringing a loud groan, and then looked back at her other lover, who was staring down at her backside like a kid at a candy shop window. "Really, Andy. I'm all yours." She gave Sean's cock head a lollipop lick. "And all yours too, Sean."

Andy's voice came dangerously close to a whimper. "We don't have the, um, strap-on."

"No," Lea answered between sucks. "But I trust you. I know you're good for it." He gulped. "The lube and condoms are in my jacket."

He shot her a nervous smile. "Brought some too."

"What a boy scout you are!" Lea took one of Sean's balls into her mouth ("Oh, Lea, *Baaaaby!*"). Releasing it, she wiggled her butt against Andy's fingers. "I'll give you anything you ask for."

"Anything?" When Lea nodded before swallowing as much of Sean's erection as she could, he whispered, "Can I fuck your ass, Lea?"

"Mm-mmm" she agreed, mouth full and focussed on pleasuring Sean as *slowly* as she could.

Behind her she heard the tearing of foil, the ripple of latex being smoothed over flesh, and the *slurp* of lube against her own backside.

She pulled off, eliciting a gasp from Sean. "Try to go as slow as you can, okay? I haven't been able to use the butt plug or anything today."

Andy nodded, and concentrated on helping Lea relax the muscles of her ass. He applied himself to the job with a real attention to detail. And he used his cock to keep her pussy from getting too envious.

Before this month, Lea had never experienced having a guy playing with her butt as *sexy*. Some of her boyfriends had really gotten off on it, and so that had been fun. But having Andy tease her asshole, gently relaxing it, pushing ever-so-slowly into it, all while she continued to lick languorously at Sean's cock — sexy was sure as hell the word for *that*. Having *Andy's* cock moving just as slowly inside of her definitely added to the general sense of sexy, sexy sex.

Eventually — if she'd had to guess, Lea would have said it had taken twenty or thirty minutes, all while Sean moaned to Lea's mouthly ministrations — Andy had patiently worked two fingers into her. Combined with the feeling of his cock filling her cunt, it didn't just feel sexy — if felt gloriously, wonderously, nastily *fabulous*.

Lea found that she was simply moaning incoherently into Sean's thigh. He ran his fingers through her hair. "You ready for him, Lea-honey?"

She nodded and then hissed as Andy withdrew his cock from her cunt and then slipped his fingers slowly from her ass. She knelt, gasping, Sean stroking her head like a frightened dog's.

She could hear Andy once again lubing his cock, could feel him sliding up behind her. He leaned over and kissed each of her butt cheeks reverently, and then blew gently on the still-open hole between them.

She shuddered — maybe a small orgasm? hard to tell, but whatever was going on, she moaned into Sean's hip as sensation sloshed through her.

Then she felt the tapered tip of Andy's cock sliding against her asshole, and suddenly everything was very still.

He pushed in as gently as he could, and the thick head pressed open her anus.

Andy was just a bit thicker than Sean — not enough that it had ever made any difference before, but she could definitely feel it now, and it took her breath away. That wasn't at all a bad thing, but as he began to push in, she realized that between that and the reversed curve of Andy's cock, this position wasn't going to be anywhere nearly as fun. "Andy, sweety," she gasped.

He grunted back, stopping his insistent thrust.

"Can I... pull a Sean, here?" She licked Sean's balls, which were right in front of her. "I'd... kind of like to see you."

She could almost hear Andy's teeth grinding as he tried to stop doing what his body clearly so wanted him to do. "Sure... baby." He pulled out — he was only a couple of inches in, but as soon as he had, Lea knew she'd made the right choice. Andy's voice came in pants: "How. You want. To do. This?"

Sean stroked Lea's hair. "Maybe you on top, Lea? So Andy here can just relax and enjoy?"

Also, Lea realized, so she could stay in control. "Um. Yeah. Let's try that, if it's okay with you, Andy?"

"Lea," Andy said, running his hand down her back and over her butt, "I am happy to do whatever you want, however you want."

Turning around on her knees, she kissed him. "Then lie back. Let me do the work."

"Okay," he sighed, and lay back on the thick plush carpet. "We don't have to —"

She straddled his waist on her knees. "I'm going to take that beautiful cock of yours up my ass, Andy, and there isn't a thing you can do about it." When his eyes grew huge, she laughed, then leaned forward and kissed him, letting her body flow against his. As they melted into each other, Lea felt Sean's hand gently stroke her back, felt Sean insinuate the length of Andy's rod between the cheeks of Lea's ass — not thrusting in, just up between the cheeks, but it still felt fabulously intimate and fabulously nasty, especially because it was their partner doing it, not Lea or Andy.

Andy groaned into Lea's mouth and then gasped when she flexed her butt cheeks, squeezing the length of him, pushing him against Sean's hand.

"Feel good, baby?" she asked, her lips still pressed to Andy's. She didn't mind that the answer he gave was incoherent. She could feel Andy trying to hold back from thrusting. "Want to try?" He nodded against her mouth, and so she kissed him again and sat up. "Sean, baby, I'm going to lift up; could you do the honors?"

"My pleasure," said their lover.

And so Lea lifted herself up — just high enough that she could feel the tip of Andy's erection piercing her cheeks. "You ready, guys?"

Andy nodded, eyes enormous, and Sean simply answered, "Ready."

And so, trusting Sean to hold Andy steady, willing herself to relax, she backed down onto Andy's cock. "Just stay still, Andy, let me move, okay?"

He nodded again.

Closing her eyes, she worked to relax her muscles — the muscles in her butt, the ones in her legs — and let gravity lower her onto Andy's waiting penis. Held firmly by Sean, Andy's erection once again spread the ring of muscles in her anus. Once again it slid through — but this time, it went smoothly, as if filling a space where it was meant to fit. Inch by inch she let her own weight bring him up into her.

After a time, she felt Andy's pubic hair against her open cunt, and she opened her eyes. "Hi."

"Hi," Andy said. She could see that he was working hard at not moving. His expression was transported, full of wonder. "I... I've always wanted —"

Lea lifted back up, Sean's fist continuing to hold Andy's prick steady, and she grinned as Andy's eyes closed and he lost the power of speech. "Wanted to fuck my ass?"

He gave a quick pant of a laugh. "Yeah. Yours. Gorgeous. *Tight.* But... *Any...!*" He groaned as she began to lower herself again.

"Anyone's?" Sean asked.

Continuing to groan, Andy nodded. "Never... Never wanted t'ask... 'cause... *Shoot!*"

Lea was lifting back up again. "Because you're sweet and considerate, but baby, what is mine is yours."

"And mine too, Andy-boy," Sean rumbled, his free hand finding Lea's breast, stroking her ice-hard nipple.

Andy looked close to crying. "Know. Love... *God...!*" His hands came up and joined Sean's on Lea's breasts. "Want... Sean? Play with my...?"

"With your balls?"

Andy shook his head, biting his lip.

Continuing to move, Lea put her hands over Andy's and Sean's. "Your butt, Andy? You want Sean to play with *your* ass?"

Still biting his lip as if he couldn't say the words, Andy managed a short, emphatic nod.

With a low, rumbling chuckle, Sean withdrew his hand from Lea's breast, from under his lovers' hands. "With pleasure."

As Lea continued to ride Andy exquisitely slowly, just a fraction of an inch or so with each stroke, she heard the *slurp* of lube — *Have to get more of that stuff!* — and then felt Andy tense, pushing up into her despite himself, and she gasped.

"Easy, Andy-boy," Sean said, speaking as if to a frightened animal. "Easy. This is going to feel good, I promise, but you gotta relax."

Andy nodded, lowering his pelvis again, and then groaned — Sean must have found his asshole, must have been circling it as he had with Lea.

They fell back into a rhythm, a slow, small fuck, very different from some of their more athletic endeavors, but no less mind-scrambling for it. "So," Lea said after a little while, "you've never actually had anal sex, Andy?"

He shook his head, face darkening. His brown eyes were open now, and locked on hers. "Always... wanted to."

"But you were saving yourself for Miss Lea, here," said Sean, his mouth suddenly right by Lea's ear, and now it was her turn to tense, and she and Andy both swore.

When Lea's ass had relaxed its grip on his cock again, Andy said — all but sobbed, really — "An'... for you, Sean."

Lea and Sean both stopped. Though Andy's attraction to and affection for Sean was very clear, he never spoke about it. Sean whispered, "You can fuck my ass if you want, Andy. Just like Miss Lea here said, what's mine is yours."

"And mine's... yours." Now Andy was crying, face red and voice thick not just with lust, but with some other emotion.

Still poised mid-stroke, Lea reached out and caressed Andy's cheek beneath the bruised eye. "You want Sean to fuck you, Andy?"

He turned away, scowling his Andy scowl. But after a moment he nodded. "I... Always. Yeah." Then he loosed a groan and his cock head swelled inside of Lea, making her moan as well.

"Sorry," Sean said, chin still on Lea's shoulder. "I should have given you both warning before sliding my finger in like that." Reaching his free hand under Lea's arm, Sean stroked Andy's nipple with his thumb; Lea reached down and began to caress the other. "When Lea here's done taking one kind of ass-fuck virginity from you, Andy-boy, I'd love to take the other."

Their lover turned back to face them, and his expression was full of an unguarded passion that Lea had never seen there before. "Maybe," he groaned, arching up against his lovers' hands on his chest, so that his cock moved minutely inside of Lea, "maybe you could, you know, do me while I'm, *huh*, doing Lea?"

There was an image that had never occurred to Lea, but that would probably be stamped into her erotic imagination forever. She tried to visualize how such a thing would work, but between her arousal and the fact that she could see dozens of possible ways to put that puzzle together, she found herself just blinking down at Andy.

Sean wasn't feeling quite so overwhelmed. "Man. Holy fuck. I can do that if you... Lea? You up to try this?"

Very aware of Andy's cock inside of her, of his hands on her tits, Lea nodded. "But... how?"

"Know the stretches Cap has had all of us doing, Andy?" Andy nodded, and Sean removed his hand from Andy's chest as well as — apparently — removing his finger from Andy's ass, since Lea could feel the cock inside *her* backside flare again at the same moment that Andy arched again and gasped. "Hamstrings," Sean said, lifting Andy's legs until they were pressing against Lea's back. Next came the familiar sounds of a condom and lube being deployed. Sean grunted, leaning forward until his forehead was on her shoulder.

"Maybe," gasped Andy, "if you get your legs up under my, um?"

"Sure," muttered Sean. "Lea, baby, think you can lift just a bit so I can get Andy's, uh, yeah, off the floor?" Once she'd done so — Sean lifting Andy's legs so that Andy's cock remained in Lea's backside — Sean said, "Okay. I don't know how much I'm gonna be able to control how hard I thrust in, with y'all both pressing down."

"Don't care," Andy panted. *"Please!"*

"Damn," Sean said, and Lea was right there with him. "Okay. Let me just…" He shifted, his hips pressing up against the backs of Andy's thighs, and then suddenly both men tensed… and then relaxed. *"Holy fuck."*

Andy screamed, arching and pushing his own cock deeper into Lea, who echoed his shout.

"Sorry!" grunted Sean. "Sorry. Didn't mean —"

"No." Andy moaned, "God, Sean, no, feels *so fucking good,* oh, *GOD!"*

They lay there for a moment, stunned, catching their breath.

Andy reached up and caressed both Lea's face and Sean's. "Please. Sean." Then he gasped, and Sean's thrust pushed him deeper into Lea once more, and all three of them screamed, *"FUCK!"*

They fell into a rhythm fairly quickly. Lea had the odd, out-of-body feeling that Sean's cock was actually pressing up inside of Andy's, that they were both fucking her ass at the same time. She knew the image was nonsensical, but…

But as the three bodies pressed together, small, rocking motions moving them within and against each other, it really didn't matter much. The sex, the *fuck* — it floated through them as if it were the sentient creature and they merely the conduits through which it flowed.

In slightly less astral moments, Lea was aware that Andy's hands had found her breasts again, that Sean's, which had been gripping her hips, had slid forward, so that one thumb was playing with her clit while the index finger of the other hand had slid inside her. *Come hither,* it beckoned, and she did. Or it did — the feeling, the pleasure, the *orgasm,* surfing the wave between Sean's fingers and the *dark* feeling of Andy's cock moving through her asshole, pushed by Sean.…

Andy was weeping, hands groping, moving. Sean was panting, swearing almost inaudibly into Lea's ear. And that *feeling…!*

Lea felt another finger slide into her pussy — blinked down and saw that Andy's hand had joined Sean's, and that she had one of *each* of them inside of her, and for whatever reason it was that thought as much as the feeling — the feelings, of pussy stretching and clit buzzing and nipples aching and ass *squeezing,* and skin sliding against her and around her and within her, front and back, inside and out…

Come hither, their fingers called to her.

And she *came.*

And they came. All of them, howling a wordless war-cry to the God Love, screaming their claim as his most devoted, most rewarded worshipers.

Lea was not a particularly religious woman. She had grown up in a family that looked at its Jewish heritage as an interesting academic aspect of its own identity. She'd gone through her *bat mitzvah,* had learned enough Hebrew to read the prayer book, had sporadically attended synagogue services, but had never felt any connection to God there.

At that moment, in the temple of her lovers' tangled limbs, Lea felt the presence of the Divine close by, immanent and imminent — everywhere and everywhen — and it was a sublime feeling, one that made her feel infinitely powerful and infinitely small, both at the same time.

A good fuck can make even an agnostic see God — a fact that explained Lea's parents' fascination with Tantra, something about which Lea thought as little as possible.

But this hadn't been a *good* fuck. This had been something else. Something had happened.

Lea just wasn't certain exactly what that something was.

She felt Sean disengaging himself, sliding his hand from her pussy and his chest from her back as a *slurp* announced his departure from Andy's ass. Andy's legs lowered, and his spent cock slid from Lea's backside, sending another tremor through them both.

Andy was still crying. Not crying — *weeping.* Convulsing with tears. Beneath Lea, he rolled onto his side and curled into a ball around her left thigh.

"Andy?" She stroked his back, his heaving shoulder. "Okay?"

He curled tighter around her leg, shaking his head. The answer wasn't necessary. Clearly he *wasn't* okay.

Lea pressed herself against him, kissing his hair, his ear, his black eye. "Love you," she whispered.

"Why?" he groaned through gritted teeth. "I'm a faggot! A queer! *A fucking fudgepacker!* Everything Miller said —!"

Sean was kissing Andy's forehead, his nose and Lea's brushing each other. "Miller's a son of a bitch. You're not any of those things. You're Andy. You're the boy Lea and I love."

Fast as thought, Andy turned beneath them, grabbed Sean's face, and kissed him. Nothing sweet or delicate about this kiss: it was desperate and angry, a kiss that couldn't help itself. Then Andy's big hand pulled Lea into the kiss, and their lips met: six lips, sliding around and against each other, impossible and fantastical, but very real.

They kissed for a while, until Andy's sobs had stilled and Lea's lips were raw, but she wouldn't have pulled back from the kiss if they'd been bloody.

"Love you, Lea," Andy whispered. "And dammit, dammit, *dammit,* I love you, Sean. Loved you since we went through training. Every day, wanting to kiss you, and hold you, and suck you, and *fuck you*…!" Another sob wracked Andy's muscular frame. "And that's not how guys are *supposed to feel,* and I didn't want to, but lying in the bunk above you, thinking what would happen if I just climbed down? And then Lea comes, and holy *fuck,* she's so *beautiful,* so *fucking sexy,* and all of the things I feel for you, Sean, I'm finding myself feeling for you, Lea-baby, and watching y'all fuck, and fucking both of y'all and Sean, you sucking on me, and me sucking…. I could sort of pretend, you know, that it was something we were doing for Lea, that I was really just a straight boy sharing my girlfriend with my best friend, but *fuck...!"* Andy was sobbing again, and Lea and Sean just held him.

After another while, they found themselves lying there on the tech booth carpet. Lea was wrapped around Andy's back, while Sean held their lover from the front. Sean murmured, "Andy, I've always felt the same way about you. Don't know that I'd have known what to do about it if we all hadn't ended up in bed together, but you know what? I've loved Lea forever. Longer. And the feelings I have for you don't change the feelings I have for her — they're the same feelings, Andy-baby." He kissed Andy on the lips, that sweet, slow, only-thing-in-the-universe kiss of his.

Andy whimpered into Sean's mouth.

Lea didn't blame him. She knew just how wonderful and terrifying that kiss could be. Kissing the back of Andy's ear, she whispered, "Andrew. I love you. I love *Andy.* I love that he loves me, and that he loves *Sean.* I love that love works that way, that it is infinite: the more I give you both, the more I have to give. The names aren't what's important. The love *is.* And I'll be damned if anyone is going to be able to tell me or either of the men I love that we shouldn't love each other the way that we do. Point Miller out to me the next time I'm at the fire house, and I'll kick him in the balls."

That brought a surprised laugh from Andy and a chuckle from Sean, who added, "I think you'd have to stand in line, Lea-honey."

"But he was *right,"* sniffled Andy. "Sean is my, you know...."

"Who cares?" asked Lea. "The words he used didn't have anything to do with what you feel for Sean, or for me, or what we feel for you. And the *feelings* he was talking about sure as hell don't. He can go fuck himself, since no one else is likely to take the job."

Now Andy laughed — truly laughed — and Lea hugged him from the back as Sean hugged him from the front, and Lea knew that it was going to be okay.

As they slowly got dressed, her overflowing sense of well-being didn't even diminish when she saw the red light that was still shining at the base of the God mic. Well, it didn't diminish *much. At least everyone's gone.*

The boys walked her back down to the lobby — all of them walking a bit more gingerly than they had before. They had to go file their report and sign off duty. "We'll meet you back here, and then let's celebrate," Andy said, looking taller and lighter than Lea could remember seeing him. "I'll take you two out to that sushi restaurant you've been telling us so much about, Lea."

Lea was going to ask him if he were sure, but his expression told her not to bother; Andy was happy. He was sure.

She let them out, relocked the front doors, and made her way up to her office. There, on her desk, was a note written with a precise draftsman's hand on heavy sketch paper in purple ink.

Lea,

I need to apologize for listening to you and your lovers today. As soon as I heard that you'd forgotten to shut off the God mic, I turned off the feed everywhere in the theater — except in my office. I found that I couldn't stop listening, and for that invasion of your privacy and your lovers', I am terribly sorry, but it brought back so many memories that I truly couldn't help myself.

I've told you about my beloved wife Sally, and about our boarder Frank. I have never told another soul this, but I think perhaps that you are one of the few who can understand: Frank was not merely our friend and house mate. He was our lover for over twenty years.

In those days, sexuality was a much more black and white thing: you were <u>straight</u> or you were queer. Now, this was after Masters and Johnson and all of that — the Sexual Revolution should have made distinctions like those irrelevant — but as your lover Andy has found, labels can be terribly hard to avoid.

In any case, I had always been attracted to men. I loved Sally with all of my heart, soul, and body, but had dreamed of making love to another man for as long as I could remember having sexual feelings at all. Sally knew this; for many years, she indulged my fantasies by using a dildo in a harness and pretending to be a man. I believe it excited her nearly as much as it excited me.

When we met Frank at a party, neither Sally nor I had any thought of bringing a third into our marriage, and yet from the moment that he became a member of the household, I think that we all knew that our <u>folie à deux</u> was destined to become a <u>ménage à trois</u>.

Frank was a giant of a man — you noticed that he was much larger than I when you pointed him out in the paintings — and he very much identified as gay. Not that he subscribed to any of the stereotypically flamboyant fashions of gay behavior or dress in those early days of Gay Pride; he was a very masculine, very conservative man. Women loved him. Sally certainly did; and so, to my own shock, did I.

For the first few months after Frank moved in, it was, in fact, very tense among us. Frank, you see, found me extremely attractive — I was small, pretty (in his eyes, I'm happy to say), and, so far as he knew, straight. For him this was a fatal combination. I found him irresistible as well — for the first time the imagined man whom Sally became while we played gained a name: Frank.

Sally was the one who moved things forward. After trying and failing to convince me that here was my chance, at last, to live my fantasy, she told me that if I wasn't going to be a man and seduce our lodger, then she'd have to do it. She got the three of us quite drunk on bourbon — for a tiny woman, Sally truly could hold her liquor —and proceeded to do her own Dance of the Seven Veils. The moment is burned into my mind's eye; it's the third painting on my back wall, the one where Sally is dancing while Frank stares up at her.

And of course, when she was done, she was completely naked except, to my and Frank's mutual astonishment, for the strap-on that she was wearing. She told Frank how much I desired him. She told us both that she was happy to share, facilitate, fuck, be fucked, or just to watch, but that she really, really wanted to see what would happen when her husband got what he wanted.

I'll be honest with you: that first night is very much a blur for me. But it became clear from the first time that Frank kissed me — and then kissed Sally — that we were building something very special.

We had our difficulties. Frank was uncomfortable to discover how attracted he was to Sally, just as I had been uncomfortable with how attracted I was to him. It is funny to think how much the label of being gay constrained him as much as the label of being straight constrained me. And Sally more than once became jealous, because there were times when the intensity of the sexual connection that Frank and I shared threatened her. We each dallied outside the threesome — usually with each others' permission, though not always. We each slept with other men and women — Sally even moved in with a lady for a time — but always we found that our home was in our <u>ménage</u>.

We were lovers for nearly a quarter of a century. I shared a bed with each of them right up to the end. They are with me now in everything that I do, and I miss them both terribly.

I suppose that, aside from apologizing for listening in on the very beautiful love-making that you, Sean, and Andy were engaged in today, what this rather odd, rather dirty old man wants to tell you is this: do not take what you have with these two boys for granted. Even in these times, what you have — what Frank and Sally and I had — is rare. I have already heard how much you all enjoy it, and so I can only urge you to <u>treasure</u> it. Even a lifetime is not enough for a wonder such as the three of you are creating.

I will never mention any of this again to you — and certainly never to anyone else. But if you ever need advice, or simply want to talk, I will always be at your service.

I'll make sure that the God mic is off.

Yours,

GUS

The Visitor Takes a Trip

"Mmm," purred Lea, lowering herself onto Sean's straining erection as he sat on one of the kitchen chairs. She gloried in the flare of the head spreading her open. "Feel good, Sean?"

"Damn, Lea-honey," Sean growled into her breast, "you know it does." His big hands pressed gently but insistently down on her hips, pushing her further onto him. His cock pressed past the place where her pussy and her ass was pushed tight by the butt plug that was planted deep inside of her, and now it was Lea's turn to growl.

Then she gasped as his teeth clamped onto her nipple. Her whole body tingled, and she slid the rest of the way onto him — the rest of the way home.

Gazing up into her eyes, Sean sighed, "Love you. Love you so fucking much."

Suddenly the pressure of imminent tears narrowed Lea's vision. "Love you too, Sean."

Behind her came a deep, muffled moan.

Sean's eyes flashed over Lea's shoulder, but she rocked her hips, giving him (and herself) a taste of the delicious fuck that was yet to come.

"Ignore him, Sean."

Blue eyes, lust heavy, floated back up to hers, and Lea smiled. She didn't need to turn around to see Andy, their lover, gagged and handcuffed to another chair, just close enough to hear and smell *everything*. Lea kissed Sean. "Andy's got no one to blame but himself. Isn't that right, Andy?"

Another moan came from behind, but beneath Lea, Sean smiled ferally. "Uh-huh." Sean's cock was pulsing inside of Lea, his fingers twitching where they dug into her hips.

Her lips still against Sean's, Lea murmured — just loudly enough to be sure that Andy could hear — "Fuck me, baby. Show me you love me. Fuck me *hard*."

It really was Andy's fault. Really.

In the weeks after Andy had finally admitted what had been obvious to Lea for a while — that he was as in love with Sean as he was with Lea — Andy had grown more and more withdrawn.

It wasn't that he didn't seem to love fucking Lea and Sean, or that he didn't love having each of them fuck him. It wasn't that they hadn't tried and enjoyed every sexual permutation that they could think of combining all of their various body parts since that first mind-blowing threeway fuck in the stage manager's booth at the theater where Lea worked.

It wasn't that he didn't seem to love them any less.

It was more that Andy seemed less and less able to talk to them about anything.

Anything.

He became monosyllabic. Sullen. And then his schedule and Sean's at the firehouse, which they'd kept in sync since before Lea had even met Andy, mysteriously changed. Instead of being on duty the same two days a week and off the other five, Andy and Sean had only one day a week at work together.

In some ways, Lea was delighted. It was a treat after all these months to be able to spend some time alone with each of her boys. But while her nights with just Sean were wonderful — a fulfillment of the daydreams (and the more nocturnal ones) that she'd had about being with him since she was in college — Andy seemed closed off to her. Except of course when they were fucking.

And so, one steamy, early summer evening, Lea pressed the issue while Andy's calves were over her shoulders, and she was more literally pressing her strap-on cock deep into his ass. Leaning into him, Lea squeezed his weeping erection, making him gasp. "So. Andy. What's gotten into you?"

For once his answer had two syllables: "*Wedding. . .*"

"*WHAT?*" For a moment Lea thought he might be trying to propose, which she thought would be sweet, but kind of weird timing.

Well, the two times she'd been proposed to before had been even weirder — but only because she'd been trying to break up with the men at the time, not because she was fucking them with a bright purple silicone phallus. "You want to *marry...?*"

He shook his head and whimpered, "Naw, naw... But... Don't stop, please, I'll... Promise. I'll... Just... *don't stop,* please, fuck, Lea, fuck me, baby, *FUCK!*"

Lea began long, hard thrusts with her hips, driving her dildo into his ass and driving his cock through her fingers in a way that she knew drove Andy wild.

Fine. He'd promised. He'd keep his promises. He was a Boy Scout, even if he was a mute Boy Scout.

She fucked him hard, both of them screaming, sweating, until her muscles were beginning to burn (*How the hell do they keep going...?*) before Andy closed his eyes and arched, his butt clamping around the dildo, and a pearlescent geyser streaming onto his belly and chest.

By that point Lea herself was so excited, the blood pooling around her clit, her nipples buzzing, that she knew she was close. Deciding the answer to her question could wait just a little longer, thanks, she shifted to the smaller, rolling thrusts that pressed the strap-on's nub against her own, and rocked the other, bulbous end of the dildo against her g-spot, bringing her quickly to a small but very satisfying and very well-earned orgasm.

They lay, panting and sweating on Andy's much-neglected bed. "Damn," Andy grunted.

"Uh-huh." agreed Lea. Honestly, that was all she could manage in that moment.

When Andy began to lap at her breast as he unbuckled the strap-on, however, she found the energy to stop him by gently grabbing his ears. Slack-faced, he looked up at her, his brown eyes managing convey both satisfaction and hunger.

"Wedding?"

"Huh?" He blinked at her before shaking his head — not telling her *no*, just trying to remember what they'd been talking about. "Oh. Yeah." He began to look down again, either to kiss her boob or maybe to talk to it, but Lea had gotten tired of him *not talking*. She held onto his ears until his eyes met hers again. "Right," he sighed. "Wedding."

Lea ran a finger down the length of his nose. Really, what she wanted was to be on her belly, him plowing her into the mattress. But he needed to finish this. She needed him to.

"So." He was frowning down at her boobs. A part of her wanted to cover them, to close them away, but she couldn't afford to distract him. He repeated, "So. Wedding. See… My best friend. Prior."

"That's his name? Prior?" Lea just managed to hold back asking if his parents were big Tony Kushner fans.

Andy nodded, brown eyes focussed far away. "Did just about everything together growing up."

This time Lea couldn't hold back the tease: "Everything?"

As she'd known he would, Andy blushed and scowled at her. "Football. Baseball. Fishing. Getting drunk. Getting high and looking for Indian arrowheads in the woods. Everything. Damn, woman. I wasn't *always* a cocksucker."

"Uh-huh."

His scowl twisted, so that Lea wasn't sure if he were fighting off laughter or tears. "Don't give *me* no *uh-huh.*" Then he shook his head. "See. We always promised each other… We'd be each other's best man. You know? I mean,

I just had Jessie and Danielle — " His older sisters. " — and Prior, he had nothing but brothers."

"Uh-huh."

"So." He leaned down and kissed her breast. "Wedding. He's getting married. To Cherry." He kissed the other breast. "My old girlfriend. First girl I ever did any of — " He sucked the nipple into his mouth as his fingers traced the spreading lips of her pussy. " — *this* with."

"Uh. Sounds complicated."

"Yup." That was all that Lea got out of him for the next forty-five minutes. Well. That's all that she got out of him about the wedding. She got lots from his hands, and his lips, and she definitely got a goodly amount of his thick, hard cock pounding her into the mattress. On her belly.

It's difficult to complain while you're being fucked magnificently. So she didn't.

Instead, she waited until they'd both stopped gasping for air — he was still blanketing her, his cock slowly weeping its way out of her — before asking once more, "Wedding?"

"Huh," he sighed. "Yeah."

"Best friend marrying old flame?"

"Uh-huh."

"And you're supposed to be the best man?"

"Yeah."

"So, when are we going?"

A huff of wet breath against her neck. "Two weeks."

"Fine. Settled."

"But…"

Ah, Lea thought, *here it is.* "But?" She squeezed *her* butt for emphasis.

He groaned, and then whimpered as his cock finally slid out of Lea. "But, um… See, my ma and pa and all want to meet you. And Prior'nd Cherry do too. See…"

When he didn't finish, she turned beneath him. "What, Andy?"

"See… See, when Prior texted me, he kind was giving me shit, saying Jessie — " The younger of his sisters. " — could be my date, since he knew no woman would ever want to grace my sorry ass with her presence."

"Uh-huh." Jesus, *Lea sighed to herself.* Men. Constantly playing Whose Pecker's Longest.

"So, I told him about you, and see…" He ducked his head against her neck, and for a moment Lea thought Andy was going to say that he'd told his friend about *Sean*. But no. "I kinda told him… we were engaged."

"You WHAT?"

"I… See, I kinda said, you know, *Ha-ha, very funny, it's good you texted, 'cause I was going to ask you to be my best man*, and so then he asked all about you, and I told him — I mean, not about the whole threesome thing or anything, 'cause fuck! But yeah — and he told Cherry, and she told Jessie, and *she* told my folks, and…"

Lea grabbed him by the ears and pulled his face up so that she could see it. She *wanted* to yell at him — what the fuck had he been thinking? — but she was so stunned and he looked so miserable that all that she managed to say was, "Jesus, Andy."

"I know, right?" His brow worked for a moment before he said about the only thing that he could. "I'm so sorry, Lea."

"Uh-huh." Sure. Of course he was sorry. But still… It wasn't as if she had told her family the truth about what she, Andy, and Sean were doing. The only person who knew about *that* was Kirsten, who'd figured out almost immediately what was going on between her best friend, her brother, and her brother's roommate. Well. And Gus, from the theater. Who'd listened to the three of them fucking up in the booth. "Andy. I'm angry with you. I mean, you've set it up so we have to lie to your family the first time I meet them."

"I know. I'm sorry." He looked up at her with the whole puppy-dog eyes routine — it didn't seem to be at all put on, but the sincerity just made Lea want to giggle, which really wasn't what she *wanted* to do right then.

"Yeah. Fine," she huffed, trying to keep a straight face. Not able to manage, she snorted and flopped back onto her belly and lifted her pelvis. "So, Andy, you're going to have to show me *just* how sorry you are."

Like the good boy he was, he dove right in, tongue first. He'd eaten her this way the very first night they'd made love — when Lea hadn't even been sure who the visitor to her pull-out bed was — and it had been the most mind-blowing sexual experience she'd ever had. Until Sean woke her from the ecstatic haze in which Andy had left her and lifted her to another plane entirely.

Lying there once more, ass in the air, face in the pillow, Andy igniting in Lea pleasure that truly made everything else seem unimportant, Lea released thoughts of the wedding for later and focused purely on enjoying the neverending, evanescent moment.

It wasn't, then, until much later — after Andy had licked her to one screaming orgasm and fucked her yet again to some number more — when Lea's mind cleared enough for the one truly awful thought to come clear: "Oh. Fuck. What's *Sean* going to think about this!"

When Sean arrived back at the apartment the next evening, his reaction was absolutely not what Lea (or Andy) had expected. He threw his head back and howled with laughter.

As he stared down at the two of them and wiped tears from his eyes, Lea silently questioned the wisdom of choosing to live with not just one man, but two.

They were both *impossible*.

When at last Sean had stopped snorting and giggling, Lea asked, as calmly as she could, "So, Sean. What are your thoughts on this mess?"

He tittered, then pulled a semblance of a serious face, and said, "Guess I'm wondering, do I get to be the best man, or the bridesmaid?"

Lea gaped up at him, but Andy joined in the sniggering. "Damn, boy. You'd look cute as fuck in a lavender dress."

Which inspired Lea to grab the Braves cap from Sean's head and smack them each with it.

Sean was much more somber, however, when he appeared on the sidewalk as Lea left the theater at the end of the next day.

Part of his sobriety probably had to do with the presence of his mother, who somehow could manage to make just about anyone feel like one of her five-year-old students.

"Hi, Violet," said Lea as she kissed Sean's mom on the cheek. "What a pleasant surprise."

"Oh, honey, I was surprised too, when this boy of mine showed up at as my little geniuses were trouping off this afternoon."

"Hey, Lea-honey," murmured Sean as he leaned in to give Lea a kiss — on the lips.

"So how did I happen to be honored with the presence of not one but *two* O'Connells?" Lea took Sean's hand.

"Well," Violet laughed, "I gather that my son has another surprise in store for you. I, however, took advantage of the opportunity to come and say hello to Gus."

"Oh!" Lea glanced up at Sean's face, which remained stony. "Well, would you like us to walk you back to the shop?"

Violet squeezed Lea's free hand. "Oh, no, honey, he said he'd meet — oh, there he is."

Gus bounced out of the same nondescript side door through which Lea had just exited the bluff-colored concrete-and-glass theater building. "Hello, Violet! Lovely to see you out of uniform, Sean."

At first Lea panicked, thinking that Gus was referring to Sean's naked tryst with her and Andy — but no, she hadn't told the boys that Gus had overheard everything. That he'd apologized and told her that he too had been part of a *ménage à trois* for many years. Which was something she still hadn't quite reconciled her mind to.

"Yeah, nice to be here off-duty." Sean took Gus's tiny hand in his enormous paw and shook it. Whatever the excitable old man had meant, Sean had understood him to mean nothing but the fire marshal inspections that he and Andy had done over the past few months.

"Well, Violet," Gus turned to Sean's mom, bouncing on his toes, "I was so excited when you called. I'd love to show you the new painting — it's almost finished, as much as any painting is ever finished. But I thought perhaps you might join me for dinner?"

When Violet hooked her arm through Gus's elbow, Sean cleared his throat. "Now, Gus, don't you keep this young lady out too late, you hear?"

Violet shot her son a scandalized glare, but Gus laughed. "I promise I'll have her home before curfew, Mr. O'Connell."

"Hmm. She's got school tomorrow, you know. Bye, Mama. Bye, Gus." As the older couple walked off, waving, Sean's smile dissipated.

Lea squeezed his hand. "So, you've got another surprise for me?"

He nodded. "When we get home. Come on. I'm parked just 'round the corner."

He wouldn't talk about whatever it was that he'd cooked up all through the ride home, preferring to sit there, uncharacteristically silent, and so, after she'd run out of things to tell him about the theater, which was just ramping up for the new season, she started talking about her feelings about the mess that Andy had landed them all in. "I mean, it's hard enough to look your mom in the face — but at least she doesn't think you and I are getting *married*, for god's sake!"

"Don't you want to get married?" His eyes didn't stray from the road.

"But…" Lea gaped at him. "Sean, how the hell am I supposed to answer that question? What the hell does marriage… And how could I marry either one of you? I mean, hell, you guys could probably marry *each other* here soon."

"Then *you* could wear the lavender dress."

"*Sean.*"

But that was all that he had to say on the subject for the rest of the ride.

They parked and walked up to their apartment, waving to Lorelle, the downstairs neighbor. (*Oh, god, ANOTHER person who knows what the three of us get up to!*) They entered their home to the familiar smell of fried chicken cooking and the familiar sight of Andy's tapered back at the stove. "Hey, Lea. Hey, Sean-boy."

"Andy," said Sean, slouching over to the kitchen table and sitting. He began to dig in his pants pocket.

If he's going to sit there and fucking play with himself…! Lea fought down two days' worth of frustration and grunted. "Guys, what the hell —?"

Andy, who had turned around with a serious expression on his face held up one hand, begging time. He was staring at Sean, who pulled something from his pocket: a small, lumpy envelope. Sean held it out to Andy, who shook his head.

Sean looked down at the envelope and then up at Lea, who was now not just angry but a bit bewildered — not a good combination. Before she could think of anything to growl at them both, Sean tugged a white gold diamond ring from the envelope, slid down on one knee at her feet, and took her hand. "Will you marry Andy, Lea?"

Lea's jaw dropped.

"Or marry Sean, baby," said Andy. He was suddenly standing behind Sean, his hands on their lover's massive shoulders.

"We don't much care which," Sean said, those blue eyes of his absolutely sucking her in. "Because honestly it doesn't much matter. But will you wear this for... one of us? Or hell, like you said, wear it as a sign of a promise between this country dumb-fuck and me?"

Andy swatted Sean's head. "See, we know that right now what we've got is how it's going to work. And we're both happy with that if you are."

Annoyance giving way to complete bewilderment, Lea shrugged.

Sean squeezed her hand. "But we also know that none of our families are going to be okay with that. At least for right now. And yeah, I know Kirsten, but come on: *Kirsten.*"

Again, Lea shrugged. His point was well taken.

"So what we're, um, proposing is that you take this as a sign of a promise that the three of us are making to each other. And you can decide which of us you want actually to go through the whole ceremony with. Or hell, we can fly off to California and get Andy and me hitched. Whatever. But wear it. And it will... calm down everyone's family a bit."

Still unable to form words, Lea nodded and held out her hand. Sean slid the ring onto her finger.

They all stared at it for a moment.

"It was my mom's. It's been sitting in her jewelry box for as long as I can remember. I didn't tell her what I meant to do with it, but she was happy to let me have it."

"Oh," rasped Lea. "That explains the twinkly look she was giving me. Do you think she'd understand if I were to tell her it was for Andy to give me?"

Sean shrugged. "Dunno. But in any case, the point is, now y'all can head up to Andy's little backwater of a home and everyone will see this ring, and you won't be lying."

Andy grunted and ran his fingers through Sean's hair. "Won't be telling the whole truth, neither. But no: we won't be lying."

Lea gazed at the sparkles from the diamond. It wasn't big but it was *bright....* "And you aren't coming with us, Sean?"

He blinked up at her, and then at Andy. "Guess. I mean, would it be okay if I came? Would it even be a good idea?"

She leaned down and kissed him. "Wouldn't want to go without my fiancé. Would we, my other fiancé?" She looked up and kissed Andy.

"Nope," said Andy, sounding deeply relieved.

"Good," Sean said, standing between them. "Now, let's eat that delicious-smelling chicken, drink some good bourbon, and keep our down-stairs neighbors thoroughly entertained for a few hours, shall we?"

Lea and Andy both concurred that this was an excellent plan.

> **Lea:** Take a look at this. Sean gave it to me last night. [Picture]

Kirsten: HOLY FUCK!

Kirsten: Wait. I know that ring!

> **Lea:** Yeah.

Kirsten: So Sean popped the question?????

> **Lea:** Well. A question, anyway.
>
> **Lea:** He asked me if I would marry Andy.
>
> **Lea:** It's complicated.

Kirsten: Uh-huh. Sounds like. So did you say yes?

> **Lea:** Maybe? I'm not exactly sure.

Kirsten: How much alcohol was involved?

> **Lea:** None.

Kirsten: Yeah, right. Then how much lube?

> **Lea:** Well. None until AFTER. We used a lot last night actually. Want to hear about it?

Kirsten: NO.

> **Lea:** But I love bending your brother over the back of the couch!

Kirsten: NO. STOP.

Kirsten: I can take that strap-on back, you know!

> **Lea:** Just you try.

Kirsten: Then don't make me. God. Yuck. Over the COUCH? Remind me not to sit there. :-p

Driving up to the mountains, Lea didn't really know what to expect. First of all, she kept waiting for the *mountains.* Well, there were *peaks.* Peeks of peaks. But everything seemed very gentle and small, not like the mountains she was used to. It felt, she realized, a bit like going to Disneyland as a kid — the Matterhorn rising out of the smog, and looking like a real, snow-capped mountain, but… tiny.

"How high are these mountains?" Lea asked, peering out of the window from her seat behind Andy, who was driving.

Andy said over his shoulder, "I guess some of the mountains up here are four thousand, forty-five hundred feet." It was the first thing he'd said since they'd got in the car.

"Oh," Lea said. "Wow."

Sean turned around. "Don't be disrespecting our mountains now, Lea."

"I'm not!" She felt her eyebrows purse and tried to release them. "It's just..."

"I know," Sean laughed and turned to Andy. "Where she comes from, mountains like these shoot straight out of the ocean."

"Really?" Andy's shoulders looked they were up around his ears.

"Really," said Lea. "They're just... really different." She reached up to rub his shoulders. They were beyond tense. It felt as if the muscles were trying to tear themselves loose from Andy's bones. "Andy...?"

"Listen," he said, looking straight forward, "when we meet my folks... Y'all aren't in Kansas any more, okay?"

"Kansas," said Sean with a smirk, but Andy shot him a look that wiped his face clean.

"Yeah. Up here... My folks are about as conservative as it gets, okay? And I don't just mean politics, though, yeah, we probably don't want to talk about that. Or religion."

This was making Lea distinctly uncomfortable. "I wouldn't do that anyway with anyone I was just meeting, of course not." Then a thought occurred to her. "Andy. Do they know I'm Jewish?" Of all of the things about Lea's life with Andy and Sean, it seemed like the least important, most innocuous detail, but suddenly the fact that she was about to meet people who might *never have met a Jewish person* scared the crap out of her.

"Um," said Andy. "Not really. No. But they've seen your picture."

"I'm not sure I understand," Lea said, trying to stay calm.

Sean intervened. "Um, if I follow what our country boy is saying, most of the folks up hereabouts have about as much pigment as Andy and me do. Are there even many black folks up here?"

"Not many," mumbled Andy. "But... Um... Cherry. And Prior."

Lea waited for more. None came. "They're black? Your ex-girlfriend and your best friend are black?"

Andy nodded.

"Well..." Lea looked to Sean, who shrugged. "Yay?"

Andy grunted. "Sure. Yay. But... I don't want y'all to think my folks are, like, KKK or nothing. But there were only like six black kids in my high school. And Prior, his brothers and Cherry were five of 'em."

Sean's hand came to rest on Andy's shoulder beside Lea's. "How'd that go with the folks?"

"Well… They never said nothin'. But then, my pa never says nothin' anyway. And Ma always said they was welcome in our home, so… But you could kinda see, the idea of me bein' with Cherry, or with… hangin' out with Prior, you could see they wasn't exactly, you know, *comfortable* with it." Andy's accent was thickening with each mile.

"So are you saying they'll see Lea here as an improvement?" Sean said. His tone was light, but his eyes were deadly serious. "'Cause her skin is a few shades paler?"

"*Jesus,* Sean, I have no fuckin' idea, okay?" Andy grabbed both of their hands in one of his. "I have no fuckin' idea how my fuckin' family is gonna react. But I *hope* —" Andy's knuckles whitened as he squeezed their fingers. "— that they're gonna see, like I do, what an amazing *person* you are, Lea, baby."

In spite of her anxiety (or perhaps because of it), Lea tittered, causing Sean to quirk an eyebrow at her. "*Mensch,*" she said, trying to regain her composure. "That's the Yiddish word. *Mensch.*"

"*Mensch,*" the two men said, and then all three of them laughed, though Lea was sure they had no more idea than she did why they were laughing.

When Andy pulled his Yukon into the gravel driveway, a collection of what could only have been Andy's family gathered on the porch.

Andy's father looked like an older, scruffier, slightly weather-worn version of his son — he was even wearing one of Andy's Atlanta Fire & Rescue t-shirts, and his arms were, if anything, even more heavily muscled than Andy's. The older sister Danielle, tall and broad-shouldered like her brother, dwarfed her husband and held a baby; her hair was the same dirty blond as Andy's — the same as their father's had probably been once upon a time. Jessie too was tall, though her hair was brown; her face was rounder than Andy's, but she sported a softer version of his dimpled chin, and they had the same bottomless brown eyes.

The only person there who didn't seem cut out of the same Harris cloth (aside from Danielle's husband Robby, who was skinny and had dark hair) was Andy's mom, who was short, round, and pink-faced, with a massive head of bottle-blonde hair, big green eyes, and a smile that was every bit as bright and as large. "Welcome, welcome!" she called as they got out of the truck. "It's so good to see you, Andrew!" She ran up and gave her son a hug, and then turned to Sean, who was standing at his friend's shoulder. "And you must be Sean. It's a pleasure finally to meet you."

Then everyone's eyes focussed on Lea, and their weight stopped her in her tracks as she walked up to Andy's other side.

Andy reached out and grabbed her hand — the left one, with the engagement ring sparkling in the late-afternoon sun. "Mama, this is —"

"You must be Lea," blurted Andy's mother, grabbing Lea's free hand in both of hers. She pronounced it as one syllable: *Lee.*

Andy cleared his throat. "Um. Le-a, Mama. *Le-a.*"

The woman's smile didn't dim a watt. "Oh, like in the bible, how sweet. Well, it's so nice to meet you, to welcome you into the family. I'm Nadine."

Her husband appeared at her shoulder. His eyes were darker than his son's — they were almost black, and piercing, and made Lea feel very much as if she were being hunted.

Nadine tittered and said, "And Le-*a*, this is my husband Davy Harris. He's been wantin' to meet you."

Jessie appeared over her mother's other shoulder. "We *all* have, mama, c'mon! Hi, Lea. I'm Jessie. The pretty one."

"Hey!" called Danielle with a smirk that told Lea that this was an old family routine, "everyone knows that's *Andy*. Ain't that right, Lea?"

Blushing, trying not to think about all of the things that this family *didn't* know about her relationship with Andy, Lea nodded, and added, "Of course, you're *all* lovely. But yes, I think Andy is gorgeous."

Andy blushed and looked at his feet, squeezing her hand. On his far side, Sean shot Lea a smirk, as if to say, *Nicely done!*

"Mind," said Jessie, "I think Sean here gives lil'Andy a run for his money. Don't you think, Lea?"

Now Sean's smirk said, *And how are you going to get out of this one, Miss Lea?*

"Oh," she said, breathily, "I think Sean is lovely too, yes."

They all laughed at that, and Nadine invited all of them around back for dinner — *supper* — which was (naturally) fried chicken, served with grits, collards, watermelon, lots of lemonade and beer, and Andy's favorite boiled peanuts. Sean proclaimed it "the pinnacle of Georgia cuisine," and Lea hoped that no one heard from his tone how much Georgia cuisine bored him.

No one seemed to notice, except Andy, who took the opportunity of kissing Lea on the cheek to reach across her lap and squeeze their lover's balls. Sean was well-behaved after that.

The meal was lovely. The back yard afforded them a view of the valley that was already lovely, but that became absolutely spectacular as the sun set and the sky turned from blue to scarlet to silver to black. When they were finally done and clearing the plates and platters back to the kitchen, lightning bugs lit their path.

It was magical.

And so Lea was a bit thrown when, after Danielle and her family had said goodnight, Nadine turned to Lea by the sink and asked, "And where does a name like Krakowicz come from?"

"Poland," coughed Lea, and then looked at Andy, who shrugged from behind his father's massive shoulder. "Krakow is a big city there..." She took a deep breath. "It used to be one of the major Jewish centers in Eastern Europe."

Her smile undiminished but noticeably tighter, Nadine just said, "Oh."

Lea nodded. "Yeah. My mom's family were mostly from what's now the Ukraine, though. Not far from where all the fighting's been happening." *Kiev — another Jewish capital*, she refrained from saying.

Lea was very aware of Mr. Harris's predatory gaze, even as Nadine Harris re-established her hostly smile. "Well, that's nice. Poland. Well, you young'uns need to let us old folk go get our rest. Papa's got a big order to finish, and company always leaves me tired. Now, Lea, honey, I hope you don't mind — you'll be sharing Jessie's room. And Sean, I'm sure you'll be fine bunking with Andrew, I know y'all do at the station, so that's all right. Well, good night, all."

"'Night, Mama," said Jessie and Andy in unison.

"Good night, Mrs. Harris," said Lea and Sean.

"Nadine! I told you both to call me Nadine," Nadine laughed as her husband escorted her up the stairs, squinting over his shoulder at Lea.

The four *young'uns* stood quietly until the bedroom door upstairs closed.

"Sorry about that," Andy groaned.

Sean patted him on the shoulder. "Don't worry 'bout it, Andy-boy. I'm sure the lovely Miss Lea can spare you to me for one night."

Andy glared at Sean, which just made Sean and Jessie laugh.

"Hey," Jessie said, "what you say we walk down to Prior'n'Cherry's? I told Cherry you was going to be here tonight, and she said they'd love to see y'all, to meet Lea here. And the lovely Sean as well."

Lea nodded at the idea — less because she wanted more company than that she needed to clear her head — and so the four walked down winding roads past what passed as a town center. Jessie took Sean's elbow and seemed inclined to laugh at everything that he said.

"So what's with your sister's boy-crazy sixteen-year-old act?" muttered Lea.

"Well, she's only been divorced a year or so. I guess the last time she really was on the market, she *was* a boy-crazy sixteen-year-old." Andy turned to her. "Listen, Lea, I'm so sorry about Mama."

She huffed and stared up at him. It was hard to be angry with that face — but she could feel herself working at it. "Andy, what the hell *was* that? I mean, what's she worried about, that I'm going to *infect* you or something?"

"Naw," Andy sighed. "Not that. It's... I'm guessing it's that she's worried that you'll raise the grandkids so's they won't be able to go to church or nothing. That they won't really be part of our family."

"Oh." That actually made sense, but still — "*Children*, Andy? What the fuck?" She said this last in a tone that she hoped Jessie couldn't possibly hear, but Sean turned around. Lea smiled thinly and waved him on. "Andy, sweetheart, you've got to make this right. I don't know how you're going to do that, but please — I can't have you're mom thinking I'm going to snatch her grandkids and your dad staring at me like he's going to grind me up and sprinkle me on his grits. Okay?"

"Aw," Andy sighed, "Papa's not so bad. He —"

"Not so bad? He never said a word, Andy, and he kept *glaring* at me!"

"Naw, Lea-baby, that's just Papa. He don't talk much, but when he does, he sure as hell means it. I know it can make folk uncomfortable sometimes. He ain't *glaring* at you."

"*Ain't* he?" she snapped, and then shook her head. "Sorry, Andy. But yeah — you've got to fix this, or the wedding is *off*, you hear?"

Andy chuckled sadly. "*Which* wedding?"

"Well," said Lea, watching Jessie flounce on Sean's elbow remarkably nimbly for a woman who was nearly six feet tall, "if your sister has anything to say about it, I think we've lost our chance with Mr. O'Connell there for good."

Andy laughed, and Sean shot a nervous glance back at his lovers, which made Andy laugh again.

Prior and Cherry's house sat in its own little valley — *hollow* — and looked as if it were half-way between being rebuilt and falling down out of exhaustion.

"He works in construction. So it's kinda like the shoemaker's kids not having shoes," Jessie said when she saw Lea's expression. "Bought it couple of years back as a fixer-upper, ain't quite fixed it up. But it won't fall down. At least, probably not. Not tonight, anyways."

When they approached the house, the couple were sitting in a glider in the front yard, and something about their body language told Lea that they'd just finished fucking — or were just getting ready to.

Well. Maybe that was just in Lea's own perverted brain.

In any case, when Jessie opened the gate, the woman who must have been Cherry jumped up to greet her and them, while her fiancé stood slowly, rearranging himself before sauntering over. So it probably wasn't just Lea's brain.

"So nice to meet you," said Cherry, whose skin was indeed a few shades less pale than Lea's own — a shade somewhere between *café au lait* and mahogany, if the moonlight could be trusted. She shook Sean's hand and gave Lea a surprisingly warm hug. "I always wondered what kind of woman would finally snag Andy. I should have known."

Lea was about to ask what it was that Cherry thought she should have known when Prior stepped up. "You must be Lea," he said in a surprisingly high, smooth voice. "Pleasure to meet you." If Cherry's skin was *café au lait* there was no other word for Prior's skin tone but *black*. Lea had seen folks so dark their skin almost shown, but not many born in the US.

Prior turned to Sean and shook his hand, greeted Jessie warmly, and then turned to Andy. "So, you pasty-ass pansy. What makes you think you're good enough for a real woman like *this?*" He pointed a thumb at Lea.

Andy narrowed his eyes at Prior. "*Good* enough? I know I'm good enough 'cause she *chose* me — I didn't have to chase her all over the county for two years like your sorry excuse for an ass did, pining after *this* fine example of womanhood." Andy gestured at Cherry.

"Sorry excuse —!" Prior gave a scowl of what Lea assumed was mock indignation. "This *sorry excuse* for an ass can still beat yours into the ground any day of the week, and twice on Sunday, you —!"

But Lea never found out what Andy was, because Andy decided to jump on top of his best friend, knocking him to the ground, where they wailed on each other. It couldn't really be called anything so civilized as *wrestling*; it looked more like they were trying to rip each other's limbs off.

It was… surprisingly sexy. Lea couldn't for the life of her figure out why that might be. "They do this often?" she asked Cherry and Jessie.

"Every time they see each other," Cherry said, and Jessie added, "No idea why."

All three women turned to Sean who held up his hands. "Hey! Don't look at me! I have no idea what this kinda bullshit is about!"

Suddenly Andy and Prior were laughing, still tangled on the ground. "*Pasty ass?*" Andy snorted. "*Twice on Sunday?*"

"Hey!" Prior chortled. "*Pining after this fine example of womanhood?*" He gave Andy's shoulder a wallop just for good measure, and then pulled his friend back up to standing.

"What are you two, ten?" Cherry asked.

"Naw," sighed Jessie, "if they was ten, they'd be more mature about it. Y'all are useless, you know that?"

"Aw, Jessie," said Prior, "you know you love us just the way we are!"

"Him I have to love, 'cause he's kin." She pointed at her brother. "You, Prior, I only tolerate 'cause you're his friend and 'cause I'm getting to wear a fucking bridesmaid's dress at your wedding on Saturday. So don't push it. I can find another excuse to wear that dress. Hey, Sean, you getting married any time soon?"

Sean's brow twisted, seeing the trap, but not knowing how to get out of it. "Uh… Not that I'm aware of."

"Good." Jessie grinned at him, then turn to Prior. "Anyway, the point is, you're not worth the dress. So act like a grown man, already."

"Oh," Cherry said, "my baby may be an idiot, but he's definitely a grown man. Ain't that right, baby?" She twined her arms around him.

"Damn straight," he said, and kissed her.

"There," said Jessie, "*that's* how a grown man is supposed to act."

"That so, sis?" asked Andy, and pulled Lea to him and kissed her more soundly than he had ever done in front of anyone else but Sean.

When they broke apart again, Lea was breathless, her crotch was singing, and she was very glad that it was dark.

"You have to watch that all of the time?" Jessie asked Sean, her arm through his again.

Sean's expression was uncharacteristically blank as he answered, "It has its charms."

Andy chuckled. "Thought that was how a grown man was supposed to act, Jess."

They went inside to the upstairs sitting room and drank until all of them were beginning to get woozy. Cherry turned to Lea at one point and whispered, "I think our men like each other more than they like us."

Lea looked at Prior and Andy, who were laughing, their arms up on the back of the couch over each other's shoulders. Sean was leaning in toward them, smiling, but it didn't reach his eyes — though that might have been because Jessie was draped over his back. "You know," Lea mused, "maybe they should marry each other rather than us." When Cherry started, Lea asked, "What?"

"Um. I'll have to know you a hell of a lot better or get a whole lot drunker before I tell you what I was just thinking. But yeah. I've always felt like a third wheel with these two, even if I'm the one they both slept with."

"Lucky you," Lea said, admiring both — all three — of the men. "They don't exactly build them small down here, do they?"

"Well," laughed Cherry, "we have our scrawny boys too, but no, this set is quite the bonus-size package, ain't they?"

"Definitely," Lea agreed, and the two women laughed until they started crying, which made the men — and Jessie — stare at them. "Sorry," Lea snorted, "we were just talking about how Georgia boys don't seem to come in the single-serving size."

"Are you saying we need to lose weight, Miss Lea?" said Sean with a smirk, and it was only then that Lea caught the double meaning in her own words.

"Uh." *Fuckity-fuck-fuck.* The men, Cherry, and Jessie all laughed at Lea's embarrassment, but she let them laugh, happy that they couldn't see what her perverted, perverted, *sick* mind had served up to her: a vision of herself with Sean and Andy sandwiched around her, making love as they had come to do so well together, with Prior fitting himself in... wherever. And hell, Cherry watching. Why not? "Uh. Lose weight? No."

"Never," snorted Cherry, "We love y'all *just* the way y'all are!"

And the way her skin darkened made Lea wonder just what image the bride-to-be's mind had served up to *her*.

Eventually, the visitors stumbled off with promises to continue the conversation at the bachelor and bachelorette parties the next night. As they stumbled their way out of the ramshackle house — which had indeed managed not to fall — Andy said, "Hey, guys, you think you can find your way back to the house? Sis and I got some catching up to do."

Lea was about to say that, no, she had *no* idea where they were or how to get back to the Harrises' house, but Sean said, "Sure thing, Andy-boy. Cherokee Ridge Road, yeah?"

Andy nodded and led his bemused sister off in the opposite direction.

Lea watched them go and turned to Sean. "What was that about?" she whispered.

"I'm hoping he's trying to warn her to back off of me a bit."

Lea grinned up at Sean. "Aw, poor boy."

"Hey," he muttered, "she's *scary*." Sean led her uphill at slow pace, and Lea could feel the heat pouring out of her into the warm, sticky Georgia night. Moths and lightning bugs played a game of shadow-and-light tag. "Also," he said when they'd gotten a couple of minutes up the road to a place where the winding road passed through a dark copse of pine trees, "I'd like to think that he's trying to make it up to us for all of the entertainment we've provided his family by givin' us a bit of *alone time.*" And before Lea could say a word, he lifted her up onto the split-rail fence, stepped between her surprise-widened legs, and kissed her in that whole-body, nothing-else-in-the-universe way that Sean could kiss.

Within seconds, Lea's libido, which was already at a simmer, went to a full boil. "Oh. God. Sean. Want you. Want you so much...."

"Then by god, honey, you're gonna have me," Sean murmured as he slid his cock out of his jeans and, tugging her panties to one side, slid all of the way home in a single, smooth, pussy-filling, satisfying stroke.

Lea screamed, but it was into Sean's huge palm, which lightly covered her mouth, and her whole body reacted, both to the feeling of him fucking her, and to the realization that they were fucking on the side of a public road. That added a touch of panic to the wild gumbo of sensations and feelings that were chasing around inside of her, but... No one was likely to come along. And even if they did, in that moment Lea couldn't have cared less.

And now the heat was flowing *into* Lea — warm as she already was, the heat of Sean's fabulous cock and of the night were sending her past the boiling point. She felt as if she were turning to steam — to flame — and only the very, very solid point of contact between her body and Sean's kept her rooted in the world.

"Honey," panted Sean. "Baby, wanted... wanted to do this to you all through supper, all through sitting there with Jessie treating me like a damned teddy bear... God, watching your nipples go all... when Andy'n'Prior were down wrassling... Turn you on, Lea-honey? You want to watch me'n'Andy all tangled up at your feet?"

"Uh-huh," she panted, the image now clear in her head — Sean and Andy, sweaty, naked, wrestling, their cocks straining — "Oh, god, god, fuck, *yesss!*"

Somehow, Lea's shirt and bra were up over her tits, and Sean's mouth found one of her nipples and...

Usually, Sean had a devastatingly slow approach to pleasuring Lea — slow, meandering, and insistent, where Andy was usually the more stereotypically passionate of her lovers. But that night Sean's urgency was intoxicating, and now that both of his hands were digging into the flesh of her ass, pulling her close to him, she had to stifle her scream on her own, and so she shoved a hand into her mouth, howling into her own knuckles as Sean suckled, pounding away, groaning into her breast, "Come, gonna, gonna, *aw! —*"

And then he thrust into her so hard that she lifted up off of the fence. He arched back and she arched back, and honestly, it would have been so easy for them to fall, but they didn't — they each released themselves into release in perfect, ecstatic balance.

And then they slowly came down, and uncoupled and rearranged themselves, pulling their clothes back into place and attempting to look like anything but the thoroughly debauched couple that they were. And they stumbled their way back up Cherokee Ridge Road to the Harrises' house. They walked in to find Jessie and Andy waiting for them. Lea had to work hard to pretend that she couldn't feel the residual of the fuck dribbling down her thighs. She could only be thankful that Jessie was, if anything, more drunk than Lea was herself and so didn't seem to notice.

Brother and sister led their guests up to their childhood bedrooms. Andy's room actually had a bunk bed — with a wrought-iron fireman's pole down from the upper bunk. Sean and Jessie waited while Andy kissed Lea good night, whispering into her lips, "Hope he fucked you good enough for both of us, sweetheart."

She nodded, blushing, and then whispered back, "But I bet he's got enough left for you, Fireman Andy."

Which made him sputter and blush right back. Sean winked at her and pulled their lover into their bedroom while Jessie led the way quietly back to her room, which was stuffed with a combination of childhood furniture and what were clearly the leftovers from the home she'd created and left — stuffed animals on top of a glass and chrome liquor cabinet, a leather recliner next to a doll house. A trundle bed with both mattresses made up with satin sheets. "You want to sleep on the inside or the outside?" Jessie asked.

"Whichever," Lea said, "I don't want to take your bed."

Jessie shrugged and took the bed that was against the wall. She didn't bother turning away as she stripped off her skirt, top and underwear, which left Lea to do the same, hoping that the insides of her thighs weren't glistening to much. Lea grabbed a sleeping shirt and waited while Jessie climbed naked into bed, and then slipped under the covers. "Man," Lea said, yawning only partially for effect, "I'm dog-tired."

"Never did understand what that meant," Jessie sighed. "Hey. Um. Can I ask something?"

Uh-oh, thought Lea. "Of course."

"See, Andy, he was trying to tell me..." Jessie flicked off the light, and suddenly Lea could make out glow-in-the-dark stars on the ceiling. "He was saying that Sean's love life is kinda... complicated. Do you know what he was talking about?"

Shitty-shit-shit. "Uh. Yeah. I do. And yeah, it kinda is." Lea lay there, staring up at Orion on Jessie's ceiling. "See, I shouldn't... I think it's not my place to talk about it."

"Yeah. That's what Andy said."

"Yeah." And then Lea had an inspiration. "I don't think Sean wants to talk about it either to be honest."

"Oh." Jessie was quiet long enough that Lea began to fall asleep, but then Jessie sighed. "Yeah. I guess that makes sense, why you'd end up with my twerp of a brother instead of *him.*"

Lea couldn't help but give a nervous laugh. "Well. Um. I've kind of known Sean since I was a kid." Nineteen. That's still a kid, right? "His sister's my best friend. So..." So your brother and I are both in love with him, have been for years, and we all fell into bed together when I moved here, and now we share pleasure in ways that would so not be appropriate for me to tell you. *"So. Yeah."*

"Uh-huh." Jessie sighed again. "'Night."

"Good night," said Lea, and was asleep almost instantly.

The next morning, Lea thought the pounding in her head must be a hangover — though she didn't think she'd drunk *that* much. When she lifted her head, though, she realized that, no, the metallic banging was coming not only from outside her head, but from outside the house.

"Papa's hard at it," sighed Jessie. "Been working on whatever it is for days, won't tell anyone what he's working on. Then again, Papa never tells nobody nothing."

"Quite an alarm clock."

"Yeah. Least he waited until after dawn. That's always my favorite." Jessie slid over, her naked, Harris-scale body suddenly very intimidating to Lea. "Sorry. Gotta pee. Anyway —" Jessie threw on a nylon robe. "—I don't miss much about living with Booger. But not having to wake up to the hammer and anvil, that was nice."

"Must be hard living back with your folks."

"You have *no* idea." Jessie ran a brush through her hair and grabbed mascara from the liquor cabinet, applying it while staring at her reflection in the chrome. "Makes me feel like a damned twelve-year-old again."

"Yeah." Lea was fascinated to watch Jessie continue to apply her makeup — in preparation for going to the bathroom. "Was your ex's name really *Booger?*"

"Yeah," Jessie snorted as she blotted a fresh layer of lipstick, "Robert actually, but everyone called him Booger, he even called himself that. *Booger's home, baby-doll!"* Jessie shuddered, and Lea couldn't blame her.

Battle-face on, Jessie smiled at Lea and opened the door, running into Sean. "Why, good morning, Sean!" she said brightly, and Lea suddenly knew *exactly* why Jessie had been so careful before stepping out of her room. Aware of her own disheveled state — feeling the sticky remains of her fuck with Sean — Lea waited until Jessie had stepped into the bathroom, looked carefully down the hall, and kissed both of her boys quickly. She lingered a bit longer with Andy. "So, fiancé, did you and your other fiancé make any boyhood dreams come true last night?"

Sean grinned wolfishly in a manner that made Lea think that indeed, they had debauched the boyhood bunk bed.

"Gawd." Andy chuckled nervously and whispered back, *"No!* That room shares a wall with my folks!" He shook his head. "Can you imagine *what* the heck they'd've thought if we started bangin' the wall last night? Mama has *no* idea what she was doing to torture me when she had the two of us share a room."

"Her loss," said Lea, and licked Andy's ear. "Poor boy." He spluttered, which caused Sean to smile some more.

"C'mon," grumbled Andy, "Mama's making blueberry pancakes."

"Well, damn, boy!" laughed Sean. "Why didn't you say so in the first place!" And so, once Lea had thrown on a robe of her own, the threesome trooped downstairs for breakfast.

The blueberry pancakes were wonderful, but Andy and Jessie's mother wouldn't even look at Lea, let alone talk to her. At least Mr. Harris wasn't there to stare at her.

The day was a long and schizophrenic one.

On the one hand, it was wonderful getting to see where Andy had grown up. He showed them the high school two towns over where he, Prior, Cherry, and the rest had met. He showed them the firehouse where he'd started volunteering at fourteen. ("You do know most boys *stop* wanting to be a fireman at some point, right?" Sean asked, to which Andy responded with a smile, "Uh-huh. So what's *your* excuse.") They saw the honest-to-goodness drive-in where, apparently, all three Harris siblings had lost their virginity — not at the same time, Lea was fairly sure. They even visited Andy's favorite skinny-dipping hole.

Of course, what made everything a bit uncomfortable was that Jessie stuck with them the whole day. Not that Lea could blame her — what else was she supposed to do, since she had the day off work? Lea didn't blame her for wanting to get out of her parents' house. And she wasn't throwing herself at Sean quite the same way, though she was clearly still stalking him.

But when they got to the swimming hole, all that Lea could think was what it would be like to fuck both of her boys in the cool, green water. And then, of course, Jessie suggested they all strip off and jump in, an idea that Sean nixed immediately, and so all four of them walked away a bit grumpy.

They attended the wedding rehearsal at a Baptist church a few towns over in a plain building that actually reminded Lea more than a bit of the synagogue her family had very occasionally attended — except of course for the huge cross over the altar. Cherry looked nervous. Her mother, a generously wide woman with eyes an even more astonishing green than her daughter's, seemed to be spending a lot of time whispering in Cherry's ear while her father stood stoically on the far side. Based on Cherry's grey expression, it was tough to tell whether she was telling Cherry that everything was going to be great, or that it was all going to be crap.

Prior was bouncing on his toes amidst three other big, plum-black men — his brothers, clearly. He grabbed Andy when they walked up and the two men looked as if they were having to restrain themselves from wrestling right there in front of the altar.

Then the minister showed up, and the walk-through took all of fifteen minutes.

Andy and his sister were the only white members of the wedding party.

After what Lea (the former stage manager) could barely consent to calling a rehearsal, everyone trooped over to Prior's family's for a barbecue, which was lovely. Andy and Prior finally got their opportunity to *wrassle,* much to his family's amusement and Cherry's family's dismay. Prior's brothers were hooting the whole time, telling their brother he was a wuss. Well. That wasn't the word they used. But *wuss* basically covers it.

Sean happily helped at the barbecue, working with Cherry's dad and an uncle, flipping enormous racks of ribs and half-chickens and generally ignoring Jessie's chatter.

Lea almost felt bad for the woman. Almost.

Cherry sidled up to Lea as the men all sprinted to form a line when the uncle banged on a battered old gong. The bride-to-be laughed. "No surprise that my man and yours are at the front of the line."

"No," Lea agreed. She looked at Cherry, who seemed to have regained her equilibrium. "You doing okay? You looked a bit overwhelmed at the rehearsal."

"Oh." Cherry shot Lea a furtive glance. "I just got… jitters, you know? Y'all walked in, and I saw Andy and Prior there, and… I don't know. It all seemed… real. You know?"

"Yeah," Lea said. "I mean, I've never been where you are, not yet, but yeah, that makes sense. Hey, can I ask something?"

"Sure."

"Is it... weird for you, having Andy here? I mean, I'm trying to imagine having one of my exes in my wedding party."

Cherry laughed. "Naw. I mean, yeah, a bit. But... Me and Andy, that was a long time ago. We was high school sweethearts, you know? Regular Romeo and Juliet. No one wanted us together — not the other kids, not our parents. Made everyone uncomfortable. Andy just said, fuck them, you know? Oh. Sorry."

Lea shook her head. "Don't worry. I live with Andy *and* Sean. I've heard a hell of a lot worse."

"I bet you have." Cherry's eyebrows lifted. "Is *that* weird? I mean, living with your fiancé and his best buddy — other than my Prior, of course."

"Yeah, it's..." Lea struggled to find a word that expressed the situation without saying to much; she settled on the word that Andy had used with his sister the night before: "It's complicated."

Cherry's look now was appraising. "Uh-huh. I bet. Now, come on, let's go get some food before our boys decide to go back for seconds and there's nothing left."

After the barbecue, the *young'uns* separated out — Prior's brothers dragged Andy and Sean over to one side of the yard with many sideways looks and sniggers that told Lea something really Neanderthal was in the offing for the bachelor bash. Lea walked up to her boys and said, "Listen, guys, I really don't give a shit what goes on as long as no one catches anything and any, uh, performers are treated respectfully. Okay?"

They both promised solemnly that they'd make sure that both of those stipulations were met.

Lea had figured that she'd head on back to the Harrises' and see if she could get Mr. Harris actually to say three words to her, but Jessie and Cherry insisted that she join them and a trio of Cherry's cousins for the bachelorette party. "Nothing very wild, I'm afraid," Cherry said.

"Naw," said one of the cousins, "you got all the *wild* saved up for tomorrow night." That evoked a lot of cackling and speculations about just what Cherry and Prior were going to get up to on their wedding night.

Cherry rounded on them, lips pursed primly. "Tomorrow night, my husband and I are going to *fuck*. It's what newlyweds do. Y'all can snigger about it, but all *I* know is none of *y'all* are going to be getting what *I* do tomorrow night. Now, tonight," she said imperiously, "aren't y'all going to get me drunk and play stupid games or something?"

"Yes, ma'am!" said Jessie. "Your carriage awaits!"

They trooped off on what turned out to be a tour of just about every road house and dive bar in the district — they definitely crossed into Tennessee for a while, and Lea wasn't sure that they didn't spend a little while in North Carolina. Cherry turned out to hold her liquor quite well — much better than her cousins, in fact — but it turned out that she was a *flirty* drunk. She started sidling up to men in each bar, and Lea and Jessie had to fend off some of the more aggressive men from taking advantage of her. "She's gettin' married tomorrow," Jessie told one would-be suitor who barely came to Jessie's shoulder, "and it ain't to you."

Some time after midnight, Lea convinced them all it was time to head back to Cherry and Prior's and play whatever silly games they could think up.

Lea — who was the most sober of them — drove the whole way back, hoping that Sean and Andy were okay. And that they weren't doing anything too stupid.

When they got back to the house, bottles of booze magically appeared, and Lea finally felt like she could partake now that she wasn't driving, and the cousins, who were already pretty well gone, started getting sloppy. When they were trying to come up with something suitably embarrassing to do, one of them turned Cherry and said, "Naw. Nah g'na play Truth or Dare'th you. Y'always asking us to kiss each other or get all nekkid or something. Naw." That brought an indignant look from Cherry, but everyone agreed: no Truth or Dare.

"How about Never Have I Ever?" asked Lea as she sipped a very smooth rye whiskey.

"W'zat?" asked the drunkest of the cousins.

"Well, haven't any of you guys played this?"

They all shook their heads.

"Oh. Simple. So, we take turns. And whoever is It says something they've never done. Like, if it were me, I could say, 'Never have I ever walked on the moon.' So after I say that, if any of you *have* walked on the moon, which I'm guessing you haven't, you have to drink. Okay? And, um, if only one of us *does* have to drink, she has to tell all."

All of the eyes in the room were now focused on Lea. She licked her lips. "So, shall I start?" When everyone nodded, Lea said, "Okay. So… Never have I ever kissed another girl."

"*Really*," gasped Jessie. "I thought you was from San Francisco!"

"I am," Lea said. "Even so. Never."

Cherry turned to two of the cousins and raised an eyebrow.

The cousins were indignant. "No fair! 'S'only 'cause *you* dared us!"

But the others all started chanting, "Drink!"

And so they did.

Jessie went next. "Um. Never have I ever... I dunno. Never have I ever given a blow job to a guy while he was driving."

Everyone looked around the room; no one drank, which sparked a round of relieved laughter. "It's a good thing!" Cherry said. "That's a good way to get yourself killed! And maybe *he's* gonna die happy, but..."

Another round of laughter.

Cherry said, "Anyway, my turn. Let's see. Um. Never have I ever let a guy tie me up."

Fifty Shades strikes again, thought Lea, and lifted the rye to her lips. It was only when she lowered the glass that she realized that the whole circle was staring at her open-mouthed. *"Really?"* said Jessie. "I mean, *please* tell me that wasn't my brother!"

"NO!" said Lea. "God, no! I mean, Andy may have, you know, *things* that he likes —" *Like having me take him up the ass, or licking at me and Sean while we're fucking, and I* did *handcuff myself to the table once, but he didn't tie me...* "God no." The circle waited. "Oh. God. Yeah. So this was my ex-boyfriend John, who was kind of a dick, actually. He liked to tie me up and keep me just on the edge of... you know, for as long as he could before he'd let me, um, you know." Eyes glistened. "Come. Before he'd let me come. And it felt really good, but honestly, he was a controlling bastard."

"Wow," said Jessie.

"Tell me about it," Lea agreed.

The game went on as the game always did — raucous laughter, embarrassment, surprises. Lea got to know more about this group of strangers than she did about some of her close friends.

Well. Not Kirsten. Kirsten told Lea *everything*. Almost everything. It had taken Kirsten seven years to tell Lea she was bi. But yeah.

Eventually, the cousins, who lived the next county over, decided they needed to head home if they were going to make the wedding. One of them had actually stopped drinking a couple of hours before, so she offered to drive. When they were gone, Jessie, Cherry, and Lea looked at each other. "So," Lea asked, "you guys want to turn in?"

"Nah," sighed Cherry. "To be honest, I'm worried about the boys. I'd love the company, if y'all don't mind."

Lea agreed, and Jessie did too. She picked up her glass and gave Cherry an evil grin. "Never have I ever slept with a black man."

Cherry was about to say something — probably that it was unfair — but she stopped when she saw that Lea had taken a drink and downed one herself. "So?" she asked Lea.

Lea shrugged. "Yeah. Dated a black guy for a little while. Also a couple of Asian guys. Never a Hispanic guy." She shrugged again. "Okay, my turn.

Let's see. Never have I ever… been on a honeymoon." She smiled at Jessie, who glared back.

"Fine," Jessie said, and drank. "I mean, what is there to tell you? I spent a week in Orlando with Booger. We both got sick and if we fucked, I can't remember it, because, I mean, sex with Booger was so quick anyway it was more like a sneeze than a passionate love-making session or anything. So fine. I was on a honeymoon."

"Ouch. Sorry." Lea turned to Cherry. "Hope you and Prior have something nice planned."

"We're heading down to New Orleans. It's supposed to be beautiful."

"That's what I hear," Lea agreed. "I've never been. The food's supposed to be amazing."

"Uh-huh," Cherry said, but she had that mischievous, flirty look she'd gotten at the bars, and Lea felt suddenly nervous. Cherry smiled and said, "Never have I ever slept with two men at once."

Jessie laughed and said, "I wish," but Lea's stomach went cold. Cherry was looking at Lea like she *knew*; but Lea couldn't just *admit* that she slept with Sean and Andy — not in front of Andy's *sister!*

At that moment, the front door opened and Sean's blessedly welcome voice called out, "Y'all here? The house hasn't fallen on anyone?"

Cherry rolled her eyes. "Naw, we're upstairs in the sitting room. Is my man with you?"

"Yeah, he'll be here in a bit. He and Andy are both trying to hold the other up. It's not working very well." Sean's head appeared at the stairwell. "Hey, now. You guys look cozy."

Lea had to stifle an urge to kiss him. Instead she reached out and took his hand. "So. Anyone going to be too sorry tomorrow?"

Sean shrugged. "Well, not Prior, not me, not Andy."

"So I'm hoping," Cherry said, "that Prior's brothers didn't drag him down to some so-called *massage parlor* down in Chattanooga."

"Naw," Sean said, running his fingers through his hair. "They'd just arranged for a dancer-lady. Who was Well, she moved real nice, I guess I can say that. And Prior's brothers kinda tried to get her to take things beyond the, um, entertainment level, but your man's a gentleman — very respectful of the young lady. So. You guys. Nice bachelorette soirée?"

"Great," Cherry said, "We hit about every bar in about four counties in three states. And we've been playing Never Have I Ever."

"That so?" Sean winked at Lea.

Jessie, who suddenly seemed much drunker than she had a few minutes before, stood and leaned her whole body against Sean's. "You ever play, Sean?"

"Uh, no, Jessie, I can't say as I have."

"Well," Jessie sighed, throwing her arms around Sean's neck, "never have I ever kissed —"

Sean tried to back up, but she held him tight. "Hey, now!"

"Jessie," said Lea, "remember — complicated."

"Fuck that!" Jessie growled. "What does that even mean?"

"It means," said Sean, grasping Jessie's face, "that I like guys. I like men."

Jessie froze. "What?"

"I have a... boyfriend, Jessie." Sean relaxed his grip, cupping her face in his hands.

Jessie flinched from him as if his fingers were on fire, stepping back and staring.

"I'm sorry." Sean shot her a sympathetic smile.

Jessie gave a groan so low that it seemed to come from her knees. Her face a mask of abject humiliation, she ran down the stairs.

Sean started to move after her but Lea grabbed his hand. "No."

Cherry nodded as the door slammed below. "I think she's just embarrassed. Haven't seen her throw herself at a guy like that since high school." She moved to the window where they could see her fleeing across the porch and into the front yard. "She'll be okay. So. Sean. You like guys."

Sean shrugged.

Cherry looked from him to Lea. "'Cause it sure looked like you liked Lea here well enough last night in the pines."

Suddenly, Sean's face went ghostly pale.

Cherry smiled, however, and raised the tumbler of rye in her hand. "Never have I ever slept with two men at once. Lucky bitch."

"Uh." Lea didn't know how to feel — embarrassed to have been seen fucking on the fence, terrified that Cherry would tell Andy's family, amused that the whole farce of pretending to be engaged to Andy had been pointless. She looked out the window to see that Jessie was stock-still in the middle of the front yard, staring at the glider. "What the hell?"

Sean grunted. "Looks like Prior'n'Andy passed out in the swing-seat."

Cherry gasped and said, "I don't think they're passed out."

Sure enough, the two friends were moving, tangled in each other. But instead of *wrassling*, they were... "They're *kissing*."

Jessie shot a look up at the house — Lea couldn't tell if she saw the three of them at the window or not, but in any case, she ran out the gate and into the night.

Oh, thought Lea, *damn.*

But then Cherry and Sean both hissed and Lea looked at the two friends making out on the glider. Andy, who was on top, had started grinding his crotch against Prior's. "Frotting," sighed Lea.

Sean grunted. "Uh-huh."

Lea grabbed his bicep, which was rippling with tension. "You okay, Sean?"

He grimaced. "I dunno if I should be angry... or really turned on."

"I know what you mean," sighed Cherry. Then she held her hand in front of her mouth. "I mean..."

"We know what you mean," Lea said. The other woman's nipples looked as if they were getting ready to take off. It was mesmerizing, in a disconcerting way.

Cherry nodded and they all turned back to watch the two men dry-hump on the glider. "What you call that there? Sean?"

"*Frotting*," said Sean. He flashed a look at Lea and managed a small grin. "Andy-boy's mighty fond of frotting. Two girls, it's called *tribbing*, ain't that right, Lea?"

"Yup."

"Oh." Cherry shuddered. "I guess... Every time the two of them idiots started wailing on each other, rolling around on each other... Every time they do that, all I can think about is what it would look like if they was naked. You know."

Lea and Sean both nodded. Lea *did* know, had had exactly the same fantasy watching her boy and Cherry's wrestle. Maybe Sean had too.

Out in the moonlight, Andy reached between them and Sean swore quietly. "I think we're about to see it for real." As Andy yanked open his fly and Prior's, Sean groaned and swore again. "Should I stop them?"

Lea couldn't think how to answer other than to ask, "Do you want to?"

Sean came up behind Lea and embraced her. "Dunno. I really don't know."

"No," said Cherry, reaching back and grabbing Lea's hand. "I mean, I kind of want to kill them both, but I kinda think they've both wanted to do this for a while."

"Uh-huh," agreed Lea and Sean. His erection was pressing against her back.

Cherry groaned. "I guess... Better they get this out of their systems now, right?" Her hand clutched Lea's.

"Sure, yeah," Sean said.

Lea stared down at her boyfriend — her lover, her fiancé — fucking his best friend. "I guess."

As Andy ground away, his jeans slid down his tight ass, revealing a flash of pale skin.

"Damn, I've missed that. That boy of y'all's has a truly beautiful backside, don't he?" said Cherry.

"Uh-huh," they agreed again.

Cherry moaned again and unselfconsciously pulled Lea's hand against her chest; the feeling of those bullet-like nipples rising and falling against Lea's knuckles was *really* disconcerting. Especially in contrast with Sean's fingers, which were clenching and unclenching at the waist of Lea's skirt — as if he were having to work very consciously not to let them stray higher. Or lower. Lea let her free hand rest on one of his. Just to reassure him. Or, maybe, to encourage him. To encourage him *down...*

Sean gurgled into the back of Lea's head when *his* knuckles found forbidden territory through her light summer skirt: Lea's crotch, which was humming with need.

"Don't know about y'all," Cherry said, "but the sight of the two of them grinding together like that is getting me all tingly. You know?" Then she glanced down at where Sean's thumb had begun to insinuate itself between Lea's legs. "I guess y'all do know."

"Fuck yeah," Lea found herself gasping.

"Definitely," Sean groaned, sliding his crotch against the small of Lea's back.

"Well, then," Cherry said, lancing the pair with an intent stare before turning back to look at the two men outside, "I say we enjoy the show and kill them both later. Okay?"

"Okay," Lea and Sean agreed.

Down on the glider, Andy slid down between Prior's thighs. In the dark, Lea couldn't see Prior's cock, but she watched as Andy lowered his head down into the space where it must have been.

"Oh," said Cherry. "Oh, my." She pulled Lea's hand harder against her chest. And Lea never knew why she did it, but she turned her hand and cupped the other women's breast. *"Oh,"* Cherry sighed and shuddered. "That's... Oh. My."

Lea's fingers trembled. She watched the pale flash of Andy's face bobbing up and down like a flame at the end of a black candle.

"Yeah," agreed Sean into the top of Lea's head. "My, my, my." And as he began to stroke her with one hand, with the other he pulled up the back of Lea's skirt and opened up his jeans.

It was an indication of how wild the whole situation had gotten and how quickly that only a small part of Lea's brain panicked at the thought of Sean taking her from behind right next to a woman whom Lea had only met the day before. Most of her brain, however, was sending out a very clear *PLEASE!* signal, and that was the part that leaned her forward, put her free hand on the window sill, and tilted her pelvis so that, once Sean had shoved her panties down, he was able to slide into her in one smooth, long stroke.

Lea groaned, naturally, which caused Cherry to look down at them and gasp.

"Sorry," Sean grunted. "We can —"

"Naw," Cherry sighed. "G'wan." And then she slid her hand across Lea's back and began stroking ribs and the side of her tit.

Lea obviously wasn't new to the sensations sparked by having two people pleasure her at the same time — had had two people pleasure her quite thoroughly, lucky bitch that she indeed was. But she was very aware of the edges of Cherry's long, manicured nails through the fabric of her top and bra. Her breath caught, and her hand slid from Cherry's breast and grabbed the sill, less to keep her balance that to hold onto something solid.

Down in the yard, Prior arched and twisted as Andy sucked him.

"Damn," said Cherry. "Looks like Andy has got real good at that."

"Oh, yeah," Sean panted. "Hell, yes."

One long finger nail traced the outline of Lea's nipple, and she could feel her eyes cross. "So, you like boys, Sean?" Cherry asked.

"I love Andy," said Sean.

"Huh." A rustle made Lea turn her head, and she saw Cherry pull up the hem of her dress and slip the fingers of the hand that wasn't tantalizing Lea's boob down the front of her panties, bright red to match Cherry's name.

About six inches from Lea's face.

"And," Cherry continued, voice even breathier, "I guess you like girls."

"Oh, yeah." Sean hissed, slowing his thrusts. "Would you like...? If it's okay with you, Lea, would you like me to... Can I help you, Miss Cherry?"

"Oh. Sweet Jesus. Please."

Sean swore, but Lea recognized this profanity: it told her just how turned on he was. But Sean was Sean — he always wanted to do the thing *right.* Instead of simply grabbing at Cherry's pussy or her tits, he reached up and unzipped the slinky purple dress.

Cherry let it slide off, along with her panties, and leaned next to Lea against the windowsill. She let out a gasp; Lea assumed that Sean had begun to tantalize her with his hand — he would never go straight to the finish line, not Sean. At least not usually.

Lea turned her head and saw in fact that, while he was fucking Lea very, very nicely, he was letting his hand float over Cherry's ass, *just* touching it. Lea smiled, knowing how amazing that feeling could be.

"This boy of yours's got nice hands," Cherry sighed, confirming Lea's assumption. An army of goose pimples appeared on Cherry's ass, her back — down the arm that led to the hand with which she was playing with herself.

"Yes," Lea said, "yes, indeed he does."

"I aim to please," said Sean, sounding, in fact, very pleased with himself. "And you, Miss Cherry, you..." He slid his cock out of Lea so that just the tip of the head split her labia, then slid all of the way back in. "You have a very nice ass."

Lea reached between her legs and squeezed his balls, making Sean gasp, which made Lea and Cherry both laugh. Lea became very aware of the green of Cherry's eyes, which was startling amidst the dark skin of her face.

"Bet he's got a nice cock too," Cherry said with a smile.

"Oh, yes," Lea answered, smiling back. "Yes, indeed he does." Weird as this was, it was kind of nice, being fucked fabulously, all while chatting with a girlfriend. Surreal. Nice.

"Does it do that bendy thing Andy's does?" Her eyes crinkled.

"You mean...?"

Cherry pulled the hand from her panties and demonstrated the downward bend of Andy's erection. "Prior's always wondered why I love getting it, you know, like you are."

Her eyebrows flying up, Lea blinked at the other woman. Truly, this was without a doubt the *weirdest...* Again, Lea giggled and Cherry followed, and it all felt so wild and so weird and so *good* that Lea didn't notice that Sean had stopped his steady thrusts.

"I think Andy-boy's about to give Prior an introduction," he murmured, "to that, uh, bendy thing."

Lea and Cherry both looked out the window, and saw what Sean meant. Apparently, Andy had finished Prior off, since Andy was now the one sitting on the glider — lying on it, staring up at his friend, who was straddling Andy's waist, reaching back and holding...

"Sweet Jesus, what is Prior *doing*?" Cherry gasped.

Once again, Lea felt anxious. "Um, are you guys sure we shouldn't stop them?"

Sean leaned down and kissed Lea's back, doing something with his hand that made Cherry gasp again — higher this time. "I think... I mean, sex is sex, right?" he murmured.

Below, Prior was lowering himself onto Andy's cock; he let out an audible cry. Andy's hands flowed over Prior's body, soothing, calming.

"Sweet Jesus," said Cherry.

"It's another thing Andy does really, really well, Miss Cherry." Sean began to fuck Lea again; his voice sounded calm, easy, in spite of the fact that his lover was introducing Cherry's fiancé to anal sex down on the swing. Sean gave a grunt as he slid home again — making Lea kind of forget about Prior and Andy, forget about *everything*. "Y'all had to get blood tests and all, right, for the wedding?"

Cherry, who was biting her lip, nodded. "Tests for everything known to man, I swear. Stupid. We only slept with each other, last three years. What we gonna catch? But— *Oh!*" Cherry's eyes crossed as Sean once again did *something* with his hand that clearly made her feel very good indeed.

"See, me and Andy, we get screened every three months; don't want us picking up something — home or work — and passing it along to someone else when we're trying to rescue'em and all. So we're clean. And Miss Lea —"

"I had myself tested too as soon as I got here," she gasped. She didn't want to be talking about STDs. She wanted to be *fucking.*

Sean's hand had worked under Lea's skirt and his thumb began tracing the insides of her thighs.

Prior called out again — Lea couldn't quite make out what he said, but she could see the white length of Andy's erection disappearing inch by inch into Prior's backside.

"Damn," Cherry said, staring down at the men. Lea assumed that the other woman was as turned on as Lea herself by what they were seeing, an assumption that was confirmed when she arched back into Sean's hand, her own hand grasping at Lea's shoulder.

"You can say that again," Lea sighed. Sean had picked up the pace slightly, and it felt *soooo good...* "Oh, God, Sean."

Sean just let out a long, steadying breath, as if he were preparing to jump out of an airplane, and then began plunging deep and hard, pressing the breath out of Lea.

"Damn," repeated Cherry staring back to where his hips had slapped against Lea's ass. As Sean withdrew painstakingly slowly, her green eyes widened. "Oh, my."

"Uh-huh," Lea panted. "Nice, right?"

Cherry licked her lips. "Um. Can I...? I mean," she said, her eyes flashing back to the window and her man and Lea's fucking, "I mean, I don't wanna do, um, but, Lea, can I *touch* that?"

Lea found laughter bubbling up again. "Don't you think you aught to ask Sean? *Huh!*"

Sean slammed home again. "If it's okay with Lea here, how could I say no?" He slid back out until, once more, only the tip of his cock remained inside of Lea, and her toes and fingers curled.

Cherry reached back over Lea's ass, her breasts sliding along Lea's back — again, short-circuiting Lea's brain — and her hand sliding over Lea's ass, fingers closing around Sean's cock.

Sean gurgled and thrust through Cherry's fingers, pressing back into Lea and... "*Oooo...*" she sighed.

"Ooo," echoed Cherry. "My, my, my..." Fingers were pushed against Lea's pussy by Sean's thrusts — Lea was not even having to work hard not to think about whose fingers those were, because it felt *sooo* good.

"Jesus, God," groaned Sean, and his hand in Lea's crotch pulled her hard back against him, trapping Cherry's fingers, and now Lea and Cherry both groaned with him.

Gripping the battered window sill with both hands, Lea looked over her shoulder. Cherry's cherry-colored panties where just inches away. Sean's hand curled around beneath them from the back, while Lea could see Cherry's hand working at the front.

Prior and Andy were groaning loudly enough to be heard from this distance; the glider outside groaned beneath them.

"Oh, say, now," Cherry sighed, "could I, maybe…? I have kind of a fantasy. And if my boyfriend's gettin' *his*," — And getting it *hard*, by the sound of it, Lea thought. — "maybe, you know, I could kinda get mine?"

"Sure," Lea said, lost on the feeling of the fuck.

Sean just panted.

"'Kay." Cherry's voice was suddenly rising in pitch. She stood, and for a second Lea thought she was going to kiss Sean, which Lea wasn't sure she was okay with. Instead, when Sean was once again barely inside of Lea, Cherry swung her leg over his cock, facing Lea. Her legs were longer, and so although Lea knew logically the other women was standing astride Sean's erection, it suddenly felt weirdly as if the cock that split Lea's labia were Cherry's.

"Um," Lea began, but then Sean thrust in, his thumb pressing against Lea's clit, and honestly? The bounce of Cherry's boobs against Lea's back, the whir of Cherry's knuckles, covered in silk, pushing against Lea's butt — Lea couldn't have cared less. "Oh. God."

"Jesus," Cherry and Sean answered together.

As Sean once again fell into a steady rhythm, Lea lifted her head. Down in the yard, she could just see the pale blur that was Andy; his rhythm seemed to be matching Sean's. "So Sean," Lea sighed, "you like fucking two women at the same time?"

"Fuck, yeah," he grunted. His left hand, sticky, grasped Lea's breast firmly. "You… like fucking two guys at the same time?"

Lea laughed, setting all three of them shivering. "Fuck… yeah."

"Y'all talk too much," said Cherry, and they all laughed and shivered again. Cherry lay her forehead on Lea's shoulder. "Always… wanted… to have a cock…"

And from in between Cherry's legs thrusts *Sean's*, not as deeply as usual, perhaps, but deep enough, and Sean's thumb against her clit, and his fingers on her breast, and Cherry moaning and Sean growling and Lea —

Coming.

Lea would have thought that she was an old pro at having an orgasm brought on in close proximity to not one but two other people. She would have thought that coming while one person was pounding away at her pussy and another moaned ecstatically into her shoulder was a familiar, almost everyday occurrence.

Of course, *everyday* didn't include the person doing the moaning being a woman, and a woman whom Lea liked, but had certainly never thought about sharing a lover with. It wasn't that the orgasm was any less wonderful — it was just that, where Lea so often felt as if she had left her body when she came, now she was very aware of her body: of the feeling of her pussy pulsing around Sean's cock, of the sweat on her nose, of the trembling whir of Cherry's fingers against Lea's ass.

Cherry came next, a high sigh and a shudder.

Sean, astonishingly, kept going.

"Damn," gasped Cherry, shuddering again.

Lea would have reached back and fondled his balls, knowing that would most likely set him off, but she wasn't sure that she would be able to stay upright if she let go of the windowsill, and so she looked over her shoulder. "Hey... Cherry... *You* ever... kissed another... woman?"

Startling green eyes blinked. "Never... have I ever." Then she took the hint, leaning forward and capturing Lea's lips between her own.

It wasn't weird or unpleasant. It wasn't a turn-on either.

When Lea had been in college, while she was still acting, one of her teachers had challenged the class to choose scenes that forced them to do something that they would never do in their own lives. Lea and Helen Kim had decided to work on a scene from play called *Stop Kiss* in which two women who think of themselves as straight find themselves extremely attracted to each other and after a long back-and-forth share a kiss (and are subsequently assaulted — but that happens off stage). The scene had been Helen's idea, but she had been incredibly uncomfortable with the idea of actually kissing. She kept stopping the scene before they got there. Finally, the night before they were supposed to present the scene, Lea had come to Helen's dorm room with a bottle of wine and refused to start rehearsing or leave until they'd finished the bottle off. They'd talked about their boyfriends, they'd talked about their politics (Helen was from a very conservative family), and they'd talked about how they felt about the idea of kissing each other. Where Lea was moderately uncomfortable with it, Helen was frankly terrified. Lea had tried a dozen ways to see if they could just touch their lips together — no emotional content, no nothing — but Helen finally simply freaked out and asked Lea to leave. It had left Lea feeling frustrated as hell, though not in a sexual way.

The last time Lea had seen her, Helen had been waving a rainbow flag while marching down Market Street in the Gay Freedom Day parade.

Kissing Cherry was fine — just lips touching lips, no big deal, no turn-on. At least not for Lea. Cherry really seemed to be getting into it. And Sean...

As Lea had suspected, the sight of his girlfriend making out with another woman — while he fucked his girlfriend between the other woman's legs — sent Sean over the edge. "Aw, damn, fuck, *shit, holy* —!" He pulled hard with both hands (at Lea's breast and crotch) and thrust as deep as Cherry's presence would allow.

And then, as Lea felt aftershocks of orgasm ripple through the three of them, she heard a shout and loud crash from below.

"Oh, damn," Cherry sighed into Lea's lips. "I think they just broke the swing."

Once they'd disentangled themselves and looked out the window, Lea could see that, yes, indeed, the glider had collapsed. Prior and Andy were fighting their way out of the tangled mass of wood and stumbling toward the house.

Sean and Lea followed Cherry downstairs — Lea distracted by the line of cum that Sean had splattered across the back of Cherry's panties and up her back when he'd pulled out of Lea.

When they reached the front door, Cherry opened it, revealing her boyfriend and Lea's standing unsteadily, kissing.

"Gentlemen," said Cherry, and the two men broke and blinked through the door. "You had fun tonight?"

"Um," muttered Andy.

"Yeah," sighed Prior, staring at his fiancée's half-mast red undies.

"Well, good. We had ourselves a nice time too." Cherry crossed her arms. "But Prior Isaac Lawrence, after tomorrow, if you *ever* touch another man — or woman — without *telling me first*, I am going to cut off your *thang* with a rusty pair of shears and use it for fish bait. *Do you hear me?*"

"Yes, Cherry," said Prior, staring now at his own feet.

Cherry leaned over and gave Lea a kiss — once again on the lips. "Lea. Sean. It has been lovely *entertaining* you while our boys *had fun* out here in the yard. We look forward to seeing you tomorrow at the wedding."

Andy wouldn't talk, the whole way home.

And when Lea finally slid into the trundle bed, trying not to wake Jessie, Andy's sister spat, "*Complicated.* Like fuck."

Shitty-shit-shit. *"Sorry."*

"Are you and Andy even engaged, or is that all just some bullshit smoke screen?"

Lea tried to think how to answer that. "We are. And Sean. Too."

"What?"

"All three of us, Jessie. It's —"

"That's…!" Jessie growled. *"Disgusting."*

Lea lay there, heart beating. *What the fuck do you say to that?* "Sorry, Jessie."

At breakfast the next morning, none of the Harrises — not even Andy — would look Lea in the eye, let alone talk to her.

Fuckity-fuck-fuck.

Mr. Harris got up from the awkward table first, tapping Andy on the shoulder and muttering something about *Delivering the present*, and they disappeared.

Sean tried to start a conversation about the wedding, and another about the weather — faced with the silent antipathy of Andy's mother and sister, however, he muttered something about going for a ride and dragged Lea out to Andy's truck.

They drove up to an abandoned fire tower that Andy had shown them. Where the silence at the table had been smothering, stifling, the quiet in the car was a relief. When they reached the lookout, Sean parked, sighing, "Well, it could be worse."

"How?"

"A hundred years ago, they'd have tarred and feathered me'n'Andy, stoned you'n'Cherry just because, and lynched Prior on principle."

"Oh."

They looked out at the valleys spread out beneath them.

"God, it's pretty," sighed Lea.

"Uh-huh."

"Wanna fuck?"

"Sure."

And so Lea and Sean made love there, overlooking three states' worth of the Blue Ridge Mountains in the front of their lover's SUV — their lover who was feeling less like their lover every day.

It was lovely, and it was a relief from the oppressive dread that was crashing down on Lea.

For a while, at least.

When they arrived back at the Harrises', Nadine, Jessie, Andy and Mr. Harris were sitting at the table. The men were silent and sweaty. The women were just silent.

"Hey, there," Sean said, flashing his sunniest smile.

As Sean later put it, "I might as well have been peeing in a thunderstorm for all the good it did."

Trying to keep from wringing her hands, Lea took a deep breath. "So. I guess it's time to get ready for the wedding?" She hadn't meant to ask it as a question, but the Harrises' stony expressions made it difficult to state as a fact.

Nadine smiled a brittle approximation of her usual grin. "I don't think we will be going to the... wedding, Miss Krakowicz." Jessie nodded in affirmation.

Lea's heart plummeted.

"Ma!" whined Andy.

Mr. Harris merely rumbled, his dark eyes boring into Lea.

Mrs. Harris cleared invisible dust from the linoleum table. "I do not think that I can, in good conscience, celebrate what is so clearly a sham of a sacred sacrament. A sham perpetrated by the couple themselves, my *son* —" Her voice and face both bespoke acid distaste, and her eyes too slashed toward Lea. "—by his *so-called* fiancée, and by their *boy-toy."*

"Ma!" Andy was crying. Lea had never seen him cry — except during sex.

She felt as if she might be closer to vomiting than to tears.

Jessie didn't look any happier, but she was nodding solemnly, her eyes too locked on Lea.

Nadine Harris stood, imperious. "You may do things very differently in California, Miss Krakowicz, and I am not surprised to find that perversion has found its way into a cesspool like Atlanta, but that is *not* how we behave here!" She began to turn to make a dramatic exit.

Before she could clear the table, however, her husband's enormous hand grasped Nadine's elbow. *"SIDDOWN."*

Eyebrows disappearing into her teased, bleached hair, Nadine sat down.

Davy Harris's eyes flicked back from his wife to Lea, and any urge she might have had to speak disappeared. After a moment, he said, "You love my boy, Lea?"

Now she felt like crying. She nodded.

"You love my boy, Sean?"

Eyes enormous, Sean nodded as well.

"You love these two, boy?"

Still blubbering in a manner that broke Lea's heart, Andy nodded as well.

"Well, then." Davy added his own gruff nod. "Least none of 'em likes to fuck animals like my uncle Billy." When Nadine started to speak, he turned his intent gaze on her. Her mouth slammed shut. "And least none of 'em likes to beat up little black girls and rape 'em like your grandpa, Nadine. We got plenty of perversion around here, and it's always been pretty darned *mean,* 'cause can't no one talk about it." He turned from his wife, who was bright red, to Andy. "That's why we's uncomfortable about you'n' Cherry, son. Not 'cause she's black, though, *dang,* my pa woulda been sure it was the 'Poccalpse if he'd seed his grandson with a... black girl. No. Her ma and your'n is sisters. You's cousins."

Oh, mouthed Andy.

Jessie's mouth was hanging open, and Lea thought hers was too.

Davy stood, towering over the table. "Preacher al's talks about *love.* How it heals all things. Well, I can see that the three of y'all love each other. And I can't think how the Lord would see that as a bad thing." He surveyed the five stunned people around him. "Now let's get dressed for the danged wedding."

Later, Lea could barely remember the wedding service itself. Shock, probably. Well. Certainly.

Cherry and Prior made a beautiful couple. There had been singing. That's about all she could remember.

At the reception, Lea did see Cherry's mother and Andy's talking very politely. *The same green eyes. Oh, my god.*

Jessie got good and drunk and disappeared with one of Prior's brothers. Lea wished her well.

Sean danced with just about every woman at the reception, and he kept grinning at Lea in a way that reminded her that the ring on her finger was *his*, whatever everyone else thought.

Andy was very quiet, but he held her close when they danced. Lea wasn't surprised to find that he danced quite well.

As the reception began to spin out of control, Cherry bounced over to Lea and Andy and whispered, "We're getting ready to leave. Come back with us, okay?"

Before Lea or Andy could answer, she'd shimmied her way back over to her husband.

And so about a half an hour later they strode down into the *holler* where Prior and Cherry's house still improbably stood. Sean was giving Andy grief, saying as the only person who'd slept with both the bride and the groom, *he* should have been the minister.

Prior was laughing. Andy was glowering, but there was a bit of a smile there.

Lea had her arm hooked through Cherry's. "So... you said last night you'd always wanted a cock?"

Cherry's face darkened, but she laughed.

"Well," Lea whispered, "I think I might have a wedding present for you." And she held her finger in front of her mouth — *secret!* — and both women dissolved into giggles.

The Georgia evening was thick and sweet. As they turned into the front yard, lightning bugs lit the path, revealing....

"Holy fuck!" Prior barked.

"It was my present for y'all," Andy said. "Pa made it and we delivered it this afternoon. Didn't realize how badly you'd need it."

An iron glider stood where Prior and Andy had destroyed the old one the night before. The black beams were bedecked in ribbons and flowers.

Cherry ran to Andy and threw her arms around him. "Oh, Andy, baby, that's so beautiful!"

Prior laughed, joining her, "And it ain't fallin' down like the rest of this damned house!"

They all laughed, even Andy.

Cherry's green eyes caught Lea's and then flicked up to her husbands. He nodded.

Cherry's voice which was usual self-assured, quavered slightly. "Would you three... like to join us tonight?"

Andy blinked, flushing, though Lea didn't think it was due to embarrassment. He looked back to Lea and Sean who both shrugged the decision back to him. He looked at his first lover and his most recent, licked his lips, and shook his head. "Naw. It's y'all's wedding night. This is a night for you two." He leaned forward and kissed the bride. And then the groom.

"Maybe a raincheck, then," Prior murmured into Andy's lips.

They were all happy with that idea.

The next morning, the whole Harris clan was gathered on the gravel drive again. Danielle and her family seemed to have missed the previous day's storm, but even Jessie showed up to say goodbye.

Davy Harris said not a word, of course — Lea was sure he'd used up a year's supply — but Nadine made a point of kissing Sean and Lea each on the cheek and telling them they were always welcome in her home.

Back in Atlanta, everything returned to something like normal. Andy's shift and Sean's mysteriously shifted back into sync. The three of them went back to sharing a bed and employing it fully.

As she'd promised, Lea sent a strap-on to Cherry (and Prior) as a present. It was the same model as Lea's, only in Cherry's namesake color instead of purple. Cherry informed Lea that she and her husband had *both* enjoyed it enormously.

The one thing that didn't change was Andy's distance.

Nothing that Lea or Sean could think of seemed to make their lover *himself* again. No laughter. He seemed to have been infected by his father's reticence. In bed, where Andy had always given as good as he got, he became passive and much less assertive.

And Sean, thrown off balance, became uncertain as well.

It was putting quite a damper on the life they shared — not just sexually, but in every aspect.

It got to the point where Lorelle from downstairs asked if something were wrong. And Lea didn't know what to tell her.

Finally, at her wits' end, worried that Andy's funk would destroy not just the threesome but her relationship with Sean, did the thing she's sworn she'd never do: she went to Gus, the septuagenarian tech director who was the only other person she knew who had created a successful *ménage à trois*.

Sitting in Gus's office high above the theater's shop, Lea found herself apologizing, but Gus would have none of it. "I told you that I'd be happy to help, Lea, dear!"

She sighed, staring at the newest of Gus's oil-and-canvas tributes to his wife. It showed Sally — recognizable because of her brilliant red hair — laughing with a slight blonde woman while the large, dark figure of Gus and Sally's lover Frank loomed behind them. "Is that... Violet O'Connell?" She pointed to the blonde.

"Oh, yes," Gus said, smiling as always. "Violet. Sally was very, very fond of her." He blinked and looked back toward Lea. "But it sounds to me as if your young man Andy is wracked with guilt."

"*Guilt?*" Lea snorted, shaking her head. It seemed like such a Jewish reaction from such a *non*-Jewish boy. "You really think so?"

Gus steepled his fingers in front of his mouth and nodded. "Hmm. Sally was a Catholic — not a very observant one, of course, but once a Catholic... In any case, I told you that she once left me and Frank... for a woman. For nearly a year. It destroyed the woman's home life, but Sally finally found that she belonged with us. But when she returned, she was so crippled with guilt — guilt at having made a mess of the young lady's marriage, at having abandoned me and Frank. It didn't matter that the woman was happy to be out of a loveless marriage. It didn't matter that Frank and I were ecstatic to see her back. She couldn't give herself to us fully until she had... atoned for her sins."

"That sounds more Jewish than Catholic."

"Hmm. Nonetheless." Gus looked back to the painting.

Staring at the piece of art too, Lea puzzled at what he was saying. "So... we need to find some way for Andy to find... absolution?"

Gus simply nodded and patted Lea's hand. Then they both stared at the painting for some time.

"Oh, god, Sean, baby, fuck me, fuck me *hard!*"

Sean was answering Lea as best he could, pounding up into her as she straddled him on the kitchen chair.

Behind her, Lea heard a long, high, keening moan. "Tell me, *huh!* Is... Andy crying?"

"Looks... like."

She turned her head, which bounced as Sean continued to pound away. Tears were indeed flowing down Andy's cheeks. And his cock, bending away from his body as always, seemed to be straining to reach Lea and Sean. "You... sorry... Andy?"

Blinking the tears out of his eyes, he nodded.

"You *sure?*" Lea found that she was quite enjoying the role of the dominatrix, but she wasn't sure she could hold out much longer.

Andy screamed into his gag, nodding harder so that some of his tears crossed the gap landing on Lea's bouncing ass.

"Sean," Lea said, "why don't you walk us over there. I'd like to hear Andy tell us what he's sorry for."

Sean stood, still planted deep inside of her; she had a momentary flash of feeling very small next to her two lovers. Still, she was the one in charge, for all that they out-weighed her together by much more than three times.

When they were next to Andy, Lea said, "Look at Sean's cock, how it's spreading me. Don't you wish you were inside of me like that? Or that he were inside of *you?*"

Andy howled into his gag.

Lea leaned back and undid the bandana.

Andy's breath was raspy and labored. "Gawd, Lea. *Gawd....*"

"What are you sorry for, Andy?"

He sobbed, "Sorry I embarrassed you with my family. Sorry my family treated you both so crappy. Sorry I fucked Prior without askin' either of y'all.... *I'm so, so sorry, Lea, Sean!*"

He was wailing in earnest now.

"Do you apologize?"

"YES!"

"Will you ever do it again?"

"NO!"

"And if you do, sweetheart, because we all break promises sometimes, will you simply tell us, instead of bottling it up and punishing yourself, which is much less fun than having us to it?"

"YES!"

Lea turned back to Sean, who had managed to keep his steady rhythm going. "What do you think, Sean?"

"Sounds... huh... like he means it."

"Hmm," Lea said. "*Do* you mean it, Andy? Are you heartily sorry?"

"*Yesss!*" he sniveled. "Please, Lea, Sean, I'm so, so, so, sorry!"

Nodding, Lea whispered to Sean, who bit back a chuckled. Lea looked back at their bound lover. "Okay, Andy, we believe you. Open your mouth."

Blinking, he did.

Sean backed Lea up so that the end of the butt plug protruding from Lea's ass was between Andy's teeth. "Take it out," Lea ordered. "Gently."

Andy's mouth clamped down on the plug. He tried to pull his head back enough to move it, but couldn't, bound as he was, as so Sean helped, pulling Lea in the opposite direction. Lea felt the plastic plumb-bob stretch her asshole and then slide through. She swore.

A *clunk* let her know that Andy had let the butt-plug slide out of his mouth to the ground. Lea could feel his breath against her open asshole, and it made her shiver, contracting around Sean, which made him groan. "Kiss it," she sighed, "and we will release you. Kiss my ass, Andy."

Andy leaned forward, and his lips found the quivering flesh of her anus. And his tongue.

That got Lea swearing again. Which got Sean swearing.

When they'd caught their breath, Lea gasped, "Well, Sean? Should Andy be released?"

"Fuck, yeah."

"And has he earned his reward?"

Andy whimpered. Sean just chuckled.

And so Lea pronounced, "Yes. He has earned his reward."

And Sean — ridiculously strong Sean — slid himself onto Andy's knees, so that the head of Andy's cock bounced against Lea's backside. Steady now between her lovers — where she belonged — Lea reached back, held Andy's erection steady, and let Sean lower her onto it, so that, for the very first time, Lea had one of them in her cunt at the same time that the other was in her ass, and she felt as if she were finally complete.

"You're... forgiven, Andy," she moaned. "Now fuck me. Fuck me, *both of you. Fuck me* **hard!**"

Continued in

The Visitor Has Company: A Friendly MMF Ménage Tale

COMING JULY, 2015!

Something's coming for our trio....
But it's not what they expect!
*Lea, Andy, and Sean are settling in for a nice quiet evening at home —
handcuffs, some lube...*
*But the doorbell rings, announcing an unexpected guest. The Visitor has a
visitor, and who knows what that will bring?*
(New adult MF erotic romance. Bondage, submission. Adult readers only.)

Juliet Takes Flight

In the first story in this series, Juliet Takes Stage, *as Allison celebrates her reunion with Ken — her lover, her former teacher, her Romeo — she remembers how she fell in love with him.*

In the second story, Juliet Takes Off, *Allison recounts the story of how she finally became Ken's lover — his Juliet.*

In the third story, Juliet Takes Her Leave, *Allison has left for college and finds herself missing those she left behind: her best friend Jordan, and her lover Ken. She finds, however, that sometimes love can transcend distance.*

In the fourth story, Juliet Takes a Chance, *Allison gets a visit from her BFF Jordan, and to both of their surprise the visit becomes a more than friendly one. As her exploration of her own sexuality continues, she is left to ask herself what love is. She loves Ken. She loves Jordan. Is it the same?*

Juliet Takes the Floor

Kissing my cunt gently, Ken shrugs my legs off of his shoulders and lets me pour down into his lap. We kiss.

Well, he kisses me. My lips, like the rest of me, are fluid, unresisting.

He grins into my mouth. "Still think I need that army?"

I manage to shake my head.

By the time I brought Jordan to the bus stop, three days after that first night together, we walked hand-in-hand without even thinking about it. My school's pretty liberal, but still: rural Ohio. The one other person waiting for the shuttle, a middle-aged man I vaguely recognized from the financial aid office, got up and walked out of the shelter, even though it was freezing. Not the *OMG-it's-chilly* freezing that Jordan and I had grown up with, but actual water-turning-to-ice freezing. Once he was outside, however, he turned back toward where we were standing.

"That guy's staring at us," Jordan muttered.

"Fuck it," I sighed, my breath turning my glasses opaque. "Let him stare." And I kissed her.

"Damn," Jordan groaned. "Don't want to leave."

"Stay," I murmured into her lips.

"Aren't you usually the one who tells me to be more responsible?" It was the kind of thing Jordan usually said as a tease when I'd been nudging her into studying more.

"Fuck responsibility."

A puff of her hot breath steamed my glasses even more. She backed up and put her mittened hands over my lips. "Stop. Please stop. I don't want to go..."

I nodded. "I guess you should get back to your so-called college out by the beach. And we really shouldn't fuck with poor Franny's mind any more than we already have." My poor roommate hadn't ever seen us doing anything, but seemed very jumpy every time Jordan and I entered the dorm room.

Jordan snorted. "Yeah. Have to save something. For next time."

I smiled.

By the time the shuttle bus to Columbus came we were both laughing, though why I doubt either of us could have told you. Jordan got on and sat by a window right above me—the guy from the FA office sitting as far from her as he could—and mouthed I love you through the glass.

"I love you," I sighed back, though the bus was already pulling away and I knew she couldn't hear me.

It was almost dinner time, and so I walked to the Old Dining Hall, the place that Jordan had dubbed Hogwarts because of its stone walls and long wooden tables. Franny, who often ate early, was sitting at our usual spot; I sat next to her with my bowl of soup and mug of cocoa. "Hey."

"Hi. Jordan get off okay?" Then Franny's incredibly fair sking caught fire. It was kind of cute. "I mean, did she catch the bus?"

"Yes, Franny, Jordan caught the bus." I figured that if Franny had something to say or ask about my relationship with my BFF, I'd let her say it.

She nodded, chewing on her lip.

Here it comes, I thought.

Cheeks still bright pink, but lips pale, she said into her dinner, "Jason and I slept together Saturday night." Her fingers tightened around her fork. "Had. You know. Sex."

"Oh." I tried to think of what to say. "Okay?"

"It hurt."

"Yeah. But it does feel better after a while."

She nodded, still not looking at me. "It did. When we tried it again last night. I mean, it still hurt some, but it also felt pretty nice." Now she looked up at me and I saw that her eyes were red. "I'm trying to figure out what this means. About my promises to Joe."

"Yeah. I bet. You want to talk about it?" She'd already told me way more about her relationship with her fiancé than I really wanted to know, but I figured she might need someone to talk to.

She shook her head, however. "Thanks. Maybe later."

"Oh. Okay."

Now she nodded, as if we'd come to some sort of decision. "So. You. And Jordan."

"Me and Jordan." As I said, I wasn't going to make it easier for her.

"Are...?" She took a deep breath and released it. "You...?"

Are we lesbian lovers? Sapphic sweethearts? Have we been making out, making love, fucking like demons every time you're out of the room? I had to work neither to blush nor to grin maniacally.

Another round of lip-chewing. "When I came back last night from... Jason. You were already asleep?"

Spooning naked in my twin bed. "Yeah. Tired." Once we'd gotten too sore actually to fuck. Which we both thought was hysterical. "We talked about stuff until we got sleepy."

This, as it happens, was true. *Stuff,* I didn't mention, included whether it would be fun to use a strap-on, and would it feel good for both of us, or just the one being fucked. Also, whether both of us waxing our bushes completely would give us more of a road rash or less from rubbing our crotches together— the rather gymnastic act that Jordan swore was called tribbing, though that sounded like a remarkably silly name to me, even for a sex act. Also about Ken, and the phenomenally detailed fantasy that Jordan had developed when we were still in his class involving the old wooden desk chair in the theater, whipped cream, and lots of rope. Also our mutual ex, Lucas-of-the-Quick-Trigger. And some funny stories about the guys Jordan had dated and/or fucked before she swore off sex. I didn't think Franny wanted to hear any of that, so I only added, "About boyfriends and stuff."

"Oh," Franny said, and then blushed, looking down. "I was thinking maybe... maybe she was... your boyfriend back home?"

Well. Shit. I looked over my shoulder at the mostly empty dining hall. "As a matter of fact, no. She's not my boyfriend back home. She's just... Jordan."

"But...?" Franny frowned.

"But my boyfriend knows about Jordan. Knows about everything."

Her frown deepened.

"Franny? This isn't... too weird for you, is it?"

"What, you mean...?" She shook her head, shrugged, and then nodded. "Well, yeah, a bit, but... It's not that. It's... Your boyfriend? He doesn't... mind?"

"Well," I said, trying to think how to explain, "we're not exclusive, you know? He said he actually expected me to see other people." He'd told me to, as a matter of fact, but I wasn't going to say that to Franny. "Also, I hate to say it, but, see, if it had been another guy, it might have bothered him more."

"Oh." She stood up straight then, picking up her tray. "Thank you, Alli."

        Allison: Hey, girl

        Allison: Jordan?

Jordan: Hey A

        Allison: Miss you

Jordan: Allison?

        Allison: ?

Jordan: That was a big deal for u right?

Jordan: When I visited?

Allison: Yes. It was a big deal.

Jordan: Good. Me too.

I spent the rest of February with my head and heart absolutely whirling. I tried to think about how what had happened between me and Jordan had changed me. Had changed my life, my choices.

I consciously looked at women for the first time in my life not just as friends, classmates, and teachers, but as potential partners. I noticed after a bit that some of them were looking back. Jeannie, the redhead who had played Titania in the *Midsummer Night's Dream* that I'd been in that fall, started smiling at me in a way that made me, in fact, quite uncomfortable.

Well, Allison, *said a voice in my head that sounded remarkably like Ken's,* do you want to kiss her? Fuck her? Or don't you? What do you want?

I was standing in the vestibule of the library one night, a couple of weeks after Jordan's departure. I'd been doing research for my Psych project: The Eternal Triangle: Freudian, Adlerian, and Jungian Interpretations of Threesome Fantasies. Sounds like it should have been fun. It wasn't.

The weather was bitterly cold and I found that I couldn't make myself leave the relative warmth of the library. I was about to chicken out entirely when an arm slipped through my thickly bundled one.

"Come on," said Jeannie, her voice low and throaty as always, "it doesn't get any easier if you wait. We'll keep each other warm."

"O...kay." It's funny: when people are swathed from head to foot in winter gear, what you notice is their faces. Jeannie had lots of freckles, and grey-green, mischievous eyes. "Um. Thanks."

"Least I could do for my favorite fairy."

Huddled together, arms around each other, we stumbled along the icy streets of the campus through the blustery winter night. We didn't talk. It was too cold.

Jeannie's dorm was closer. "Want to come warm up?"

"Um."

"I've got a single. You can spend the night here if you want." She said it purely factually, but I didn't have to work hard to hear a subtext.

"Um." I was looking at her eyes. Trying to decide whether I actually wanted to kiss her or not.

She took the choice away, pulling down the scarf that covered my mouth and pressing her chapped lips to mine.

It was okay. It wasn't Jordan. Or Ken. Maybe it's just the cold. Or the ten layers of clothing. Maybe if you went up to her room and warmed up...

I realize however that, in fact, I really wasn't interested. Not that she wasn't pretty. And nice, in a smirky kind of way. But kissing her really wasn't doing much to me. I broke the kiss.

"So?" she asked, a hunger on her face that I felt badly not satisfying.

But no; I really wasn't that interested. Not turned off the way I might have imagined kissing another girl would make me feel before Jordan. Just not turned on. I shook my head. "Thanks. But my life is already so complicated, I think that would probably be a really bad idea."

"Complicated can be fun," she said, moving to kiss me again.

I leaned back. "Maybe. And it's not as if it doesn't sound fun. But no thanks, Jeannie."

"Hmm." She stepped back and squinted at me from under the hood. "Let me know if you change your mind."

"Thanks." I tried to smile, even as the chill took hold of me again. It didn't leave me until long after I'd gotten back to my dorm.

Allison: Jordan?

Allison: Jordan?

Allison: Remember the redhead with the huge tits I introduced you to after my acting class? Jeannie the Junior? She kissed me just now and invited me up to her room and I told her no and I'm really kind of confused.

Allison: Jordan?

Allison: Ken?

Allison: I know you're probably in rehearsal. Something really weird just happened. Well, not weird, but I can't figure out how I feel about it. Call?

Neither of them got back to me that night.

Shit, I thought as I lay in my bed listening to Franny snore, *if you're both going to ignore me, maybe I should just have gone up to Jeannie's room after all.* I tried to work up some enthusiasm about all of the freckles dusted across Jeannie's skin, about the wide, pink nipples that she'd shamelessly showed off in the women's dressing room. About the feeling of her lips, chapped but warm, against mine.

But it was too cold to go back out. And the idea still didn't strike me as terribly exciting.

The next day I met with the Psych professor to talk about my project. Professor Green was short, shapeless, and ruthless in her pursuit of making the students in her classes feel as unsettled as possible. She like to flirt mercilessly with both the guys and the girls, and describe in full, breathless detail assorted fantasies and fetishes, and then cackle at the looks on our faces, saying, as she put it, "I love it! You can't think of me and sex at the same time!"

Well, I could, but only when thinking of sex in the driest, most academic, least exciting terms possible. "The limitations of the three schools' views of sexuality are making it really frustrating trying to come up with a thesis that's worth arguing," I grumbled.

"Oh? How do you mean?" she asked with a look of bland innocence so out of character that I knew that I must be on to something.

"Well..." I tried to think through the research I'd been trying to do the previous night when not stealing off to the library bathroom, my head filled with thoughts of my two very different lovers and just what I wanted them to do to me. What I wanted to do to them. "Well, none of them really accepted the idea of bisexuality as nearly as I can tell, and all of them viewed homosexuality as pathological, so their views on menage fantasies are incredibly phallocentric and heteronormative. Freud and his followers saw them as expressions of some sort of inverted, un-introjected Oedipus complex, wanting to have sex with Mommy and Daddy, I guess. Adler argued that it was all about the desire either to dominate or be dominated; I don't get the feeling he cared much about the genders of the other fantasy participants. And Jung's camp argued that it was some sort of defect in the Animus or Anima, the inability to develop a clear subconscious view of the Other."

"Sounds like quite a lot to talk about to me," the professor answered wryly.

"Well, yeah, I guess, but it's all stupid."

She raised her eyebrows. "Stupid?"

"Okay, fine, I know that Kinsey didn't come along until later. But because they started with the idea that wanting someone of your own gender was sick, something to be cured, that seems to have limited their whole take on threesome fantasies."

"That's a fair critique, from a twenty-first-century point of view. Don't you think that's worth discussing?"

I huffed. "Not really. It's like saying that Freud was obsessed with sex. Well, duh."

"All right. You want more of a challenge." Professor Green's expression remained neutral but her voice was getting bouncier. "What are your views on these sorts of fantasies, Allison?"

The truthful response came unbidden to my mind: That I'd like to lick both my lovers while they fucked until they screamed. "Um. Well. From a Kinseyan point of view. Um. Innate bisexuality..." I scowled, trying to fight down the blush that was threatening to light me up like a beacon.

"Ah-hah. Well, perhaps a foursome for you then." When I goggled at the professor, she smiled. "That is, showing how Kinsey and other later models have answered each of those three early-twentieth-century schools' views on ménage and harem fantasies."

I did my best to smile back. "It would ruin my title."

"You're a clever girl. I'm sure you'll come up with something fitting."

"Thank you, Professor." I gathered up my laptop and books.

"By the way, Allison," said Professor Green, face and voice bland again, "I find it interesting that you seem to be so focused on bisexual threesomes. As I'm sure you're aware, most people..."

Well, damn. "Most people visualize themselves with members of the opposite sex."

"Mmm." After shooting me a quick smile, she turned away to her desk. "Have a nice evening, Allison."

"Um. Thank you, Professor."

Ken: Allison?

Ken: Allison?

     Allison: Hi

Ken: Sorry I couldn't get back to you last night. I
   was in rehearsal.

     Allison: Figured

Ken: You okay?

     Allison: Yeah. Think I figured some stuff out.

Ken: Yes?

     Allison: Yeah. :-)

     Allison: Ken?

Ken: Yes?

     Allison: Do you know what my psych project is?

Ken: Nope

     Allison: Threesome fantasies

     Allison: You ever fantasize about a threesome, Ken?

Ken: Research?

> **Allison**: Absolutely. :-D

Ken: Ah. So. Yes.

> **Allison**: I see. And do you fantasize about being with a man and a woman or two men

Ken: No

> **Allison**: I see. So you think about being with two women at once

Ken: Yes

> **Allison**: Interesting. :-)

> **Allison**: Ken? Are you hard?

Ken: And humiliated. Thank you

> **Allison**: You're welcome, Ken. It's an extremely common fantasy, you know. There's no need to be embarrassed, young man.

Ken: I know.

Ken: I've been having threesome fantasies since before you were born, young lady.

> **Allison**: Oh.

> **Allison**: Had any recently? (she asked, strictly as a matter of research)

Ken: Good night, love of my life.

> Allison: Good night, Ken. Oh. By the way, Jordan had this very funny idea involving her, you, me, and a bunch of whipped cream.

Ken: Good night. Fire of my loins.

> **Allison**: Good night, Ken. :-)

I had barely signed off with Ken when my phone started crooning a K-pop version of "My Girl," the old Temptations song—Jordan had set it as my ring tone for her when we were in eighth grade.

God, how could I not have known?

"Hey, J!"

"Hey." It sounded as if she were talking through a really thick muffler.

"Were are you? It sounds as if you're in a closet."

A pause. "I am."

"Drunk?"

"Oh, yeah."

"Okay?"

"Love you."

"Love you too. You okay, Jordan?"

"Fucked Beech." She sounded suspiciously sniffly.

"You... Your roomie?" Jordan had sent me a couple of pics of her: classic beach blonde, long-legged. Tan. A nuclear engineering major, if that could be believed.

"Yeah."

"Oh. Nice?"

"No." Her voice thickened. "Actually, it sucked. I mean, it sucked ass. And she kinda freaked."

"Oh, fuck, Jordan."

"I mean, seemed like a good idea, you know?"

I wasn't sure I wanted to hear. She'd only been gone from my bed for a couple of weeks. But still, she's my bestie. "Yeah. I know."

"Thought of you 'n' that redheaded bimbo 'n' thought, Shit, Beech's cute, 'n' up for anything, 'n' Lizie's over at her boyfriend's, so..."

"Jordan," I said, trying to keep my voice low and even. I was very glad that Franny was over in Jason's room, though I knew that was going to mean another round of self-flagellation from my roommate. "Jordan, you know I didn't do anything with Jeannie, right?"

"Whatever," she mumbled miserably.

"Not whatever, Jordan, come on." But that wasn't the point. "So. Beech freaked?"

"Fuck. Yeah." She groaned. "Were tribbing—"

"You on top."

I could hear her grin even as I heard her sniffle. "Yeah. Me on top." We had found that having Jordan grind her clit against mine, straddling my left leg with my right up between those wonderful tits of hers, could bring us both off together, which was kind of amazing. "Though, you know. Clothes on. Some."

"Uh, yeah?"

"Dry humping, really. Shit. Haven't done that in years."

"Nice?"

"Yeah," said Jordan, sniffling again. "Nice. Anyway, tribbing, me on top, and, um, yeah, and she's lying there like a fucking blow-up doll while I'm grinding away, and yeah, nice, feeling good, getting close, and suddenly she's, like, coming and she's screaming and I'm still going, 'cause I'm almost there, and I figure she's feeling good, but she pushed me off and started shouting at me."

"Fuck."

"Yeah. Screaming I was a dyke and shit."

"Fuck."

She was sobbing now.

"Jordan. I'm sorry."

"For what? Sorry I fucked someone else? *FUCK.*" A loud clunk pushed my ear from the phone.

"Jordan? Okay?"

"Yeah."

"Is she there?"

"Passed out on her bed."

"And you're in the closet?"

"Not any more, I guess." She laughed moistly. "But yeah. Couldn't look at her any more."

"Oh, Jordan. I'm so sorry."

"You should be." I couldn't tell whether she was teasing or being legitimately nasty; Jordan was capable of both, though usually she was only nasty if provoked. "Should be. You fucking ruined me, Alli. I mean, shit."

Being the sober one in any conversation is no fun; being the sober one when your best friend and lover is imploding and you're not completely sure that you understand why is so beyond not fun that the word fun shouldn't even appear in the sentence. "Love you," I said, because I couldn't think of anything else to say.

"Yeah, well, love you too. I mean, really. So, then, why does it feel like my whole life is going through a fucking blender?" Now the sobs were coming back.

"Because, I don't know, Jordan, I mean I know what you mean, but..." I was beginning to tear up too. "Because we're not exactly who we thought we were and that's fucking scary?"

Jordan was silent. Silent for a while. Just at the moment where I was beginning to think she'd passed out on me, she whispered, "Yeah. Okay. That sounds about right." A sniff. "Though having Beech screaming at me while I'm there just trying to get off sucked fucking ass too."

"I bet." I was now gladder than ever that I hadn't let Jeannie the Junior lure me upstairs. Not because she would have freaked out on me, I knew she wouldn't have, but because sex was also clearly very fucking scary and very fucking complicated, which was as close to profound as I could get in that moment. "You never did get off, huh?"

"No." She sounded so thoroughly miserable that I couldn't help but chuckle. "Oh, fine, laugh away, you bitch."

"At least I'm not a stupid twat who could have your fabulous, sweet cunt rubbing against mine, those breast bouncing around my leg, and somehow leave you hanging!"

She groaned, and I knew that, miserable as she still was, I had a way to make her feel at least a little better. "No. You'd never do that."

"Unh-uh. If I came and I couldn't take any more of how fabulous you were making me feel, you know what I'd do?"

A sniff? Her breath catching? Another little sob? A hiccup? Couldn't tell. But I would have bet every piece of winter clothing I had that she was beginning to touch herself. That those long nipples were stretching and those ruffled labia were beginning to spread beneath her fingers.

"Do you want to know, Jordan?"

"Fuck yes." Her voice was breathy now—just like that—and it made me laugh again. "Fuck you. Tell me, Alli."

"Oh, I won't leave you hanging, baby." I could feel my own middle warming. "I'd push you down on the bed. And I'd cover your body with mine and feel our nipples bounce together."

A hiss.

"I'd kiss you. I miss kissing you."

A whimper.

"I'd nibble my way down your throat and lick along your collarbone." My free fingers slipped under my nightshirt and ran along my collarbone. "I'd pull at those fabulous nipples of yours. With my teeth."

A groan.

"Then I'd roll you over. On your knees. So your skinny ass was up in the air."

"Huh."

My eyes closed, I ran my fingernails over my own nipples. "I'd kiss that sweet ass. One cheek. Then the other. And then..."

"Then?"

"Then..." I could see it. Could see her bent over in front of me. Open to me. I pinched at my nipple and hissed; Jordan answered me. "Then, I'd lick. Starting at your clit—"

She whimpered.

"—and licking up along you pussy. Sooo sweet."

"Fuck, Alli..."

"Mmm." I slid my hand away from my breast and under the bottom of my nightshirt. "And then—"

"Hnh..." Her voice quivered as it did when she was getting excited. Feeling orgasm coming. It was a sound that I'd quickly learned to recognize—quickly learned to love.

"—I'd lick all of the up to your ass. I'd run my tongue up one cheek—"

"Damn!"

"—and then the other. Did you know there's a beauty mark on the inside of your left cheek?"

"Uh..." A gasp. "Uh-huh."

"It's so cute. I kept wanting to kiss it."

Another whimper. A long one.

"I felt funny, though, 'cause it was so close to your asshole."

A full-on moan, and I can't help answering it.

"Would you've liked that? Jordan? Me to kiss your asshole?"

"Aw, fuck, Alli!" I could actually hear the liquid movement of her fingers in and out and against her pussy. "Fuck yes!"

"Mmm," I groaned. "Kiss it. Lick it. While my... fingers..."

"God... Alli..."

"...push into your pussy. So tight. So sweet."

"Aw, *FUCK, ALLI...!*" Her breath was roaring through the phone—roaring through my blood. *"MAKE ME... I'M...!"*

"Come for me. Jordan. Come."

And she did. Loudly sobbing. Calling my name.

Which made me come too. Not quite as loudly. But it was sweet, making love to her again. Even if it is over the phone.

After I beamed back into myself, I could hear her breath rasping slow and steady into the phone. I thought perhaps she had fallen asleep. I whispered, "Jordan."

"Hey, Alli," came back her low, immediate answer. "Thanks."

I laughed. "Oh, hey, thank you. You got me off too, you know!"

"Glad." She sounded relaxed now. Sleepy maybe and still drunk, but not sobbing.

"You do, you know. Have a little beauty mark. Right near your asshole." I didn't know why I was saying that to her.

"Huh. Yeah. Corey was always talking about it." I could hear that she was actually smiling, which made me smile.

"Yeah. He would have had lots of chances to look at it." Jordan had had a notorious on-going thing up in the tech booth with Big Corey, who'd run sound for our school's shows. I could imagine Jordan, bent over the mixing board, both of them with their headsets on, him plowing into her from behind for hours. "Did you guys really do it while we were performing?"

"Oh, hell yeah. Never missed a cue, either, fucking-a right." Her tone was proud, smirky, and nostalgic. "Anyway, reason he kept talking about that mole was just because he wanted to fuck my ass."

"Did you?"

She snorted. "With that big ol' thing? Fuck no! I may be a slut, but I'm not stupid!"

"Not a slut."

"Yeah, I am, and proud of it." She was quiet for a moment. "Or was, I guess."

"Well, no one ever said you were stupid, anyway."

"Except me. I mean, come on. If I'd known you could get me off like that over the fucking phone, why'd I ever have spent all those nights just texting you?"

"Because we didn't know. And you were seeing lots of guys."

"True. I sure can't complain for lack of dick."

"No." I bit my lip, then shook my head. "Have you, you know, thought about hooking up with guys again?"

"Um. Yeah. Thought about it. But I didn't..." It was weird to hear Jordan sounding timid. Uncertain. Her flare came back. "Anyway, you just want to pull me into bed with your old-fart boyfriend."

"Jordan!" I was surprised by her suddenly shift. "I... I'd never..." But I wanted to. I'd been thinking about it since before Jordan had left, and my Psych project—my conversion with the professor—had only made the images clearer.

"Admit, come on, you just want to have both of us fucking you—" Now she was sounding angry again.

"Jordan, come on!"

"Come on yourself, girl." She gave a savage snort. "You telling me you wouldn't like to have Ken fucking you and me sucking on your fucking tits?"

"Well... Of course I would, Jesus, Jordan!" Now she'd supplied me with yet another image that I knew would haunt me. Why was she...? "Jordan? Do you want to have a threesome with me and Ken?"

"Just 'cause you're in a fucking Psych class doesn't make you a fucking shrink, okay?"

"Jordan—?"

"Good night, Alli."

"Night, Jordan." My head was spinning, as if I were the one sitting drunk in the closet. "I love you."

Her tone softened again. "Love you too. Night."

"FUCK!" I shout as I slide, shower-slick, onto Ken's cock.

"Shh." He holds me close against him, that cock pushed far, far up inside of me.

"FUCK!" The walls of my cunt haven't entirely stopped pulsing from the orgasm he set off in me just now with his tongue, up there against the shower walls, and they begin to pulse again almost as soon as his head presses up against my cervix.

As I release myself into the void again, it occurs to me, not for the first time, that sex is nothing more than the removal of the membranes between two liquid creatures, which allows them to mix.

Am I the cream or the coffee?

That night, Franny stumbled back in before midnight—early for her and Jason.

"Calling it an evening?" I asked.

"Calling it quits," she sniffled, which was for her an extreme emotional display. "Told Jason we couldn't do this any more."

"Oh." I felt torn. Franny and Jason really had seemed like an incredibly happy couple when they were together—holding hands, giggling. Talking about everything under the sun. Fucking like bunnies. But Franny still carried the little splinter of diamond on her left hand. I didn't know Joe at all, aside from reading a couple of his letters, and so it was difficult to feel too much loyalty to him, but they were engaged. And cheating on him had been tearing Franny apart. "I'm sorry. How did Jason take it?"

"Not well," Franny sighed, her face glummer even than usual.

In fact, Jason walked around for days looking like a kicked puppy. I tried to talk with him about it, but he just pouted at me and slumped away.

As spring break—and my birthday—loomed, I worked, I talked to my two lovers, I tried to keep my roomie from having a nervous breakdown. I fended off a few more gentle advances from Jeannie before I finally told her I already had a girlfriend. And a boyfriend. And that I wasn't sure I could handle more.

She smiled at me. "Poor little fairy. Lucky them. I don't suppose either of them likes to share?"

I laughed, because even though I knew she meant with her, there I was again: I couldn't get that image, of fucking Ken and Jordan both at once, out of my head. I told her no, they didn't, but all I could think was how amazing it would be if they would.

The Psych project didn't help. When I finally turned it in, I got an A-. The only thing that kept me from getting a straight A, Professor Green said, was that I needed to do more research. She said it with a particularly lascivious grin on her face that got me turning bright red before she looked back to the paper and pointed out assertions that I needed to flesh out further, or to substantiate. What I was thinking, however, was Research? I'll go do some fucking RESEARCH!

It was a relief that the class turned away from sexuality and toward apparently congenital mental illnesses like schizophrenia and bipolar disorder. And unlike sexual addiction, which I began to fear that I was suffering from.

Because even though the class moved on, it didn't stop me from thinking about having one hand wrapped around Ken while the other slid into Jordan.

They weren't playing along, however. Every time I tried to get one of them to bring it up, each of them would change the subject. It was kind of frustrating.

What do you want, Allison? I asked myself finally.

That was easy: a threesome. Bringing both of my lovers off. Pleasing them both simultaneously. And maybe not just once. Maybe a true ménage à trois. (I could remember Jonathon laughing as he told us that he'd learned in French that that literally meant Keeping house for three. Katie and I had laughed along. I didn't find it funny now.)

What's in the way?

Their reluctance—knowing or unknowing. My own reticence.

What are you going to do to get what you want?

Well, I couldn't think of a way to get their reluctance to change without confronting it, which brought me up against my own native shyness—my best, oldest friend, aside from Jordan. And Ken.

Come on, idiot, I yelled at myself. *They've both seen you naked. They've both seen you weeping after you've come, snot-nosed, dripping from both ends. They both love you. The worst that can happen is they both say no.*

Fuck you! I yelled back. But I knew that I was right.

> **Allison**: Jordan? Ken? You guys both getting this?

Ken: ?

Jordan: yo

> **Allison**: Yo?

Jordan: :-p

> **Allison**: I'd say "I wish" but that would be getting ahead of myself

Ken: Ladies?

> **Allison**: Sorry. You must be wondering why I called you here today.

Jordan: very funny are u reading a will?

> **Allison**: Sort of. I'm telling you something I want for my birthday

Jordan: birthday?

Ken: What do you want, Allison?

> **Allison**: You two.

Allison: I want to have sex with you both at the same time.

Allison: I want to have a threesome with the two people I love more than anyone.

Allison: I want to feel you coming inside me, Ken, while I feel you coming against my tongue, Jordan.

Allison: Guys?

Jordan: i think u broke ken

Allison: How about you, J? Did I break you?

Jordan: a bit yeah

Allison: Sorry. Ken?

Ken: Not broken. Just not sure what I can say, here.

Allison: You can say yes.

Allison: I know you two have both thought about it. And I know you find each other attractive, and the idea of the two of you fucking turns me so fucking on, but you don't have to touch each other if you don't want to. I'll do all the work.

Jordan: talking 2 much.

Allison: Sorry

Ken: Can we think about this? It's not a small thing.

Allison: Of course you can. I'm coming home next Friday but J isn't until the Friday after so we couldn't even try until that weekend because I have to leave that Sunday but we could get together that Saturday I think.

Allison: I can't believe I just asked you guys that.

Ken: Are you sorry?

Allison: Fuck no.

Allison: But yes, think about it. Just let me know, okay?

Allison: I want to fuck you both so bad.

Jordan: shit

Jordan: ur a bad influence Ken

Ken: ME???

        Allison: Nope. I'm corrupting you both. Bwahaha!

I didn't hear back from either of them for a couple of days. I spent the intervening time completely out of my mind.

It didn't help that Franny and Jason were each pestering me—her about whether I thought she'd done the right thing, which I didn't think I had any right to tell her one way or another; and him about whether I thought Franny really meant it.

I told him I didn't know, but that he would be better off waiting for her to make up her mind than pushing it. He didn't seem happy with that advice, but he at least seemed to hear it.

Three nights after I had made my indecent proposal to my two lovers, and just at the point where I was about to text them both and tell them it was early April Fool joke, winky-face, my phone buzzed with Jordan's Korean "My Girl" tone.

Franny blinked owlishly up from her copy of Wuthering Heights.

"I'll, um, just take this, um, outside," I said, grabbing my phone and sprinting toward the door to our room. "Oh. And Heathcliff is an asshole."

"Who's an asshole?" asked Jordan.

"Heathcliff. From Wuthering Heights."

"Sounds like my kind of guy." I could hear her Jordan smirk firmly in place; it was a relief that she wasn't sounding sorry for herself.

"No, Jordan," I said, as I had said to her a thousand times. "Assholes are assholes. Even if they're well hung."

"True," she answered. "Anyway, my type apparently is smart-ass girls with glasses, juicy butts, and really amazing tongues."

"Oh?" Blushing, I ducked into the hall bathroom, where I'd had to start doing my diddling again now that Franny wasn't over in Jason's room nearly every night. "Am I your type?"

"I guess so. Smart-ass girls with glasses, juicy asses, amazing tongues, and really twisted brains."

"Um. Yay?"

"Yeah," she said very slowly. "Yay. I think."

"So yay, then." I walked into the shower and closed off the stall.

"Where the fuck are you, the bathroom?"

"Yeah."

"Beats the closet, I guess."

"Yeah." I laughed weakly. "I guess I'm out of the closet too."

"Oh?"

"Well, Franny knows. She kind of figured it out."

"Hey! She's not as clueless as she looks." And we launched into a discussion of the ups and downs of my roomy and my hallmate's messy love lives. Finally, we wound down. Jordan cleared her throat. "But I don't really want to talk about the Well-Hung Munchkin and the Not-so-pure not-so-Virgin."

"No? Have you, um, thought about what I asked?"

"Jesus, Alli," sighed Jordan. "How could I think of anything else?"

I sat on the damp tile floor. "And?"

"Ken and I talked about it and—"

"You talked to Ken?"

"Jesus, Alli, you want us both to play Hide-the-Salami with you. I hope you're not going to get all bent that we decided to talk with each about it."

"No," I gasped. "Of course not. I'll do whatever you guys want."

She sighed. "Fuck. Alli. What we want..." Another sigh and a snort. "What I want is you here, sitting on my face, okay?"

I giggled, uncertain how else to respond.

"What Ken wants... Well, I think he wants basically the same thing—" and before I could break in she said "—sitting on his face, asshole, since I know you were going to make the fucking joke."

"Sorry."

"Sure you are." Jordan chuckled. "What we both want is to make you happy. God fucking knows why."

"Because I'm really lucky?" I whispered.

"Lucky," echoed Jordan. "Jesus. Alli?"

"Jordan?"

"Do you really want to do this?"

"With you and Ken?"

"Uh-huh."

"More than anything."

Jordan sighed.

"Jordan?" I asked tentatively. "Have you ever done this before?"

"Well," she started and then paused. "I mean... There was those football players. But that wasn't like this. I mean. It was just them getting off and me getting off. There wasn't any, you know..."

"Love. There wasn't any love."

"Well. Yeah. That." She was silent.

"Jordan? Isn't it better this way?"

"Alli. You know this might blow up, right?"

I started to say that I knew it wouldn't, that I was sure, but I knew that was a lie. "Yeah. I know. I mean. I'm sure it won't. I mean... "

"Yeah, I know. I know." Jordan took a deep breath. "See, what do I know? But Ken, he agreed with me. He said—"

"He said?" I was aware of my wet ass. Of my trembling hands. "Has he, you know, done anything like this before?"

"He hasn't told you?"

"No."

"Oh. Um. Then I won't..." She cleared her throat again. "Um. The thing is, I said to him, even if we try to pretend that it isn't, this is going to, you know, change things, right? And he agreed. He said..."

I waited. Then I prompted, "He said?"

"He said... Yeah." She took a deep breath. "He said the three times he'd tried, it brought stuff up. Stuff none of them expected."

"Well. Yeah. I guess."

"He said he'd write you about it."

"Oh? Um. Cool."

She laughed hollowly. "Yeah. Cool."

"Jordan? What's wrong?"

She snorted dismissively, as if she were about to say, Wrong? What could be wrong? I've got this so covered. Instead, a small, young-sounding voice said, "I'm scared, Alli."

"Scared? Of what?"

She blew out a breath, and the voice that answered me was more Jordan's. "I guess, you know, that you're going to actually realize that he's got a dick and I don't."

"Oh." I tried to think of a way to answer that, and realized that a joke was the only option. "You'd look kind of weird with a dick."

"Oh, fine." I could hear a bit of a smile. "And anyway, I told you: you would look fucking hot with a cock."

"Uh-huh. And anyway, he doesn't have your tits. Or your sweet pussy."

"I'll have to take your word for that."

"Not after my birthday."

"No. Not after your birthday."

"Jordan?"

"Yeah, you little shit?"

"Thank you."

"Don't thank me yet, Alli. If you still want to thank me after, give my ass a good lick and we'll call it even."

"Okay. I look forward to it." I grinned. And then we got each other off. It was very nice. Even if my ass was wet, and my neck was getting sore from holding onto the phone while my hands were busy.

I slept better that night.

The next day, a new package of stories arrived from Ken.

Juliet Takes Charge

Cream, I decide. I'm the cream. I'm too pale to be the coffee.

"Allison?"

Cream, I am. Poured around Ken, who is kneeling on the floor of the girls' dressing room showers. With me, limp and liquid, flowing over him. "Hmm?"

"Oh. Good. Thought I'd lost you for good."

I shake my head. "Unh-uh. Don't want to miss anything."

The spray from the shower gives Ken a kind of halo, though his expression is anything but angelic as he clenches the muscles of his thighs and ass pressing his cock up into my cunt and I feel liquid again—liquid fire now. "Love you," I murmur—or at least I try, since, yes, my lips too are liquid.

Having said the words just a handful of times, I haven't yet gotten used to the feel of them. They are still fresh and sharp and cut me as they leave my mouth.

"Love you," he rumbles, lying back and lowering me onto his chest. His words too are fresh, and balm, and I slide atop him—steamed milk now? Something frothy and insubstantial.

But, oh, that cock still, still deep within me—it is very, very solid.

Dear Allison,

Well, after our chat with Jordan the other day, I don't

think I can even pretend to be your teacher at this point. When the girl who could barely say the word fuck when I first made love to her is suddenly proposing a threeway, I think need to admit that you've learned what I have to teach. Congratulations. Pick up your diploma at the office.

Here's where I admit my own weakness and admit I'm not ready to wave goodbye to you yet, however—and I hope that you aren't ready to leave me in the dust quite yet either. Given what you're asking, however, I feel as if I need to share my own experiences with attempting to expand beyond a couple, none of which ended quite the way any of us intended. I want to offer these, not as a teacher, as I said, but as your friend and your lover.

I've got three stories to share, aside from the one that we're about to write. Two involve Cindy—they're about the only sexual stories I can think of about my time with her that are worth sharing—and one is a story I've already mentioned involving Veronica and our friend Jenny.

I'm still looking forward to giving you your birthday gift. I just wanted you to understand why it scares me.

Love,

Ken

I wasn't sure how to feel about this package of Ken's stories. First of all, Cindy had become this bugbear, the way he *didn't* talk about her. Reading about her struggles with her own bisexuality, I couldn't help but feel a bit sorry for her. Though I didn't blame Ken for being angry with her.

Also, I couldn't help but think, But this time is different. This time it's something we are all going into with our eyes open. This time it's something we all want.

Well, *I admitted to myself,* I want it. I don't know if they do, or if they're just going along with me. But still…

Midterms kept me busy; sometimes, even an impending threesome has to take back seat to schoolwork.

And if I'd had any room for thinking of what was coming, my roomie Franny filled it by approaching what was either a nervous breakdown or a nuclear meltdown trying to decide how she was going to tell her fiancé when she went back to Anchorage that she'd been boffing Jason from across the hall, and that, in fact, she'd really kind of liked it. A lot.

As I was walking out of my last class—clothes already in my backpack, ready to catch the shuttle to the airport—my phone buzzed. It was Jonathon.

Jonathon: Hey Alli!!!

    Allison: Hey JonJon. What's up?

Jonathon: Looking forward to your birthday!

    Allison: ?

Jonathon: The party! Katie said we were having a party at Kens saturday

    Allison: Oh cool

Jonathon: Oh shit I hope it wasn't supposed to be a surprise!

    Allison: I'm sure not. No sweat. How's school? How's that cutie Sam?

    Allison: Ken?

Ken: ?

    Allison: Did you know that I'm having a birthday party at your house on Saturday? I mean, before the one we talked about?

Ken: Yes. Katie emailed today. Just assumed it was happening.

    Allison: Oh. Fuck.

Ken: :-) I didn't feel like I could say no.

    Allison: Yeah. Katie's too nice to say no to.

Ken: Well, it'll be a fun evening.

Ken: What did you think of my stories?

    Allison: I liked them. And yeah, I get what you were saying. But don't you think this is different?

Ken: Perhaps.

    Allison: Does this make you nervous?

Ken: Of course. I don't want either of you getting hurt.

> **Allison**: What about you? Aren't you worried about your feelings?

Ken: I'm a big boy. I can deal with my feelings being hurt.

> **Allison**: Well, we're both big girls, Ken.

Ken: As you keep proving to me every day. Even so.

> **Allison**: Trust me. Trust us both. Okay?

Ken: Okay.

Ken: Jordan really cares for you, you know. It's very sweet. It's a side of her I've never really seen.

> **Allison**: Is that okay?

Ken: Wonderful.

> **Allison**: And believe me, you're going to see a whole side of her Saturday you've DEFINITELY never seen.

Ken: Yippee.

I wasn't able to get away from my family to see Ken until the third day I was home—Monday—and by then I'd barely been able to keep my panties on.

I told my family that I was going out with some of my friends, and not to wait up.

It wasn't even a lie: I shared a joint with Katie, parked in our old high school's parking lot. She gushed about her reunion with her longtime boyfriend Bram. (They'd been together since they were fifteen—both with bright red hair, they were so cute even I found it almost disgusting.)After some typical giggling, girl-talk, and gossip—just like old times—I said I'd see her later that week, dropped her at Bram's house, and took the familiar drive across town to Ken's.

And Ken was certainly a friend. A very, very close friend.

We didn't even make it out of the front hall before he was planted deep inside of me, me up on the table just inside his door. Once he'd gotten me to scream once, he groaned that he really didn't need his neighbors thinking he was a vivisectionist, and carried me—my cunt pulsing around his still-unspent cock—a bit further into the house. He sat in the big chair, the one where he usually sits when my friends and I invade his house to watch bad movies. My legs over the arms of the chair, I rode him until he sprayed up into me, sparking another flutter of an orgasm.

It made me feel a bit funny to admit that, yes: this was something that Jordan couldn't do for me, her many splendors notwithstanding.

Ken and I stayed there, breathing heavily. Without moving, barely talking, Ken still inside of me, we began to kiss, we began to caress, we began to rock, and we settled in for our second round, which was developing very slowly, very nicely.

"So," Ken murmured, his voice low and rumbling, "you still feel like this dirty old man has something to offer?"

"Not old," I pouted as I always did, and then leaned down and sucked at his nipple, earning me a groan and a pulse of his hardening-once-more cock inside of me.

"Old enough," he grunted, as *he* always did, and began rocking against me, so that I could feel him stiffening again.

I smiled and purred, knowing this was going to be a nice, long, slow ride.

Ken. My friend. My lover. My *first* lover. Whose hips I was astride, having just indulged in a frantic, apart-too-long, chair-top fuck.

I moved to the other nipple.

Ken groaned again and arched, that thick, thickening cock pushing back up into me, and now it was my turn to moan. Buried deep in me, he shuddered and then stilled my pelvis with his huge hands. "And you're avoiding the question."

"Question?" I sat up and peered down at him through my skewed glasses. I wasn't being coy—in that moment I couldn't have told you the day of the week or my name, let alone the answer to whatever question Ken had asked. All I could think about was that I'd just been fucked, and was about to get gloriously fucked again.

"Is this"—he kissed one of my nipples (left? right? no idea)—"still worth"— he licked the other one—"your time?"

"Oh. Uh. *Shit, Ken!*" I shivered with pleasure. How could his mouth on my tits make my pussy pulse and my toes curl? "Uh. Yeah. Uh. Wanted to talk to you… huh… about that."

Suddenly his stillness was not tense, but guarded. He backed away from my breasts, leaving them buzzing.

"Uh, Ken?"

"Sorry." He put both hands over my breasts, warming them. Covering them away. "So. You wanted to talk to me?"

"Ken?" I was too distracted by the fact that his cock had stopped moving inside of me to focus on what he was saying.

"So." He had his teacher face on, and while I find that incredibly sexy most of the time, right then I'd have rather be seeing his slack mid-fuck face, or his I'm-about-to-come-so-hard grimace. "Are you sure you want me there on Saturday?"

"*Want —*?" I whined.

"Yeah, you know." He smirked, and his thumb grazed my clit. *Evil, evil man!* "Want."

"Um, yeah, *want*, yeah."

"Allison?" He clearly wanted me to pay attention, but he was going about it in the most perverse way possible. "Why do you want to do this, with Jordan and me?"

"Uh…" I was trying to rock against him, trying to get back that feeling he'd ignited with his thumb. "Uh…" I was also trying to think how to answer his question.

"I mean," he said, having some pity and rocking minutely in the chair so that his pubic bone pressed against my clit, "I want to be there. I'm not completely stupid. But also—" He stopped rocking and press down on my pelvis, so that that *feeling* skittered just out of reach. "—I kind of need to know if this is something you're doing because you can't disappoint one of us. I mean, here I am, balls deep in your wonderful pussy, and I couldn't be happier, but I do worry that you're just doing it to avoid disappointing one of us."

"Disappoint… Worry?" I shook my head. *How could anyone feel this good and worry?* "Unh-uh."

"Good. So you —?"

At that I laughed, and started moving my pelvis in counterpoint to his. "Ken, trust me, I want you. And Jordan. And what you're doing right now feels so fucking good, Ken, and I want to tell you all about why I want to make you and Jordan come at the same time, give you all of the juicy details, but right now?"

"Uh-huh?" His eyes were wolfen, hungry.

"Don't want to think about anyone else, Ken." I leaned forward and kissed him. "Just want you to fuck me. Talk about it after. Okay?"

He latched on to one of my nipples—left? right? no idea—and growled into my breast: "*Okay!*"

As we fucked there on Ken's chair—as I began to feel the blood rushing to my pelvis more and more, and he thrust up into me—I couldn't resist gasping into his ear, "Wanna hear…*uh…* 'bout what… Jordan… *tastes like?*"

He didn't answer me in words. Instead, as I'd kind of hoped, he began pounding harder, so that any thoughts of Jordan, or Saturday, or anything else, quite left both of our minds.

As my cunt pulses around Ken's cock, as his cock sprays up into me, as each of us screams into the other's mouth, I think *NOW. Now is perfect.*

Lying on top of Ken in the girls' dressing-room showers.
Yes. Perfect.
Every time is different. Every time is…
Now. Now is perfect.
"C'mon," pants Ken. "School is out. Let's get home."

Jordan: i am so fucking ready to be fucking DONE

    Allison: Friday

Jordan: want it to be friday now. make it friday NOW

Jordan: thing that sux about being allisexual is theres only one and shes never around when u need her

    Allison: :-(

    Allison: ILU

    Allison: But you get me AND Ken on Saturday!

Jordan: okay fine

Jordan: friday ur (Y) is MINE though. ur all MINE

    Allison: LOL Yes, Jordan, on Friday, my pussy will be all yours.

Jordan: MINEMINEMINE!!!

By the time that Friday arrived and Jordan texted me that she was driving up I-5 at 90 miles per, Ken had more than managed to to satisfy me, but somehow knowing that my girlfriend was speeding up the interstate ("*with 2 fingers in my popo*") and that we would be alone together again that night left me just as fluttery.

When her dusty Toyota pulled up to our curb and I ran out, it was just like a bazillion sleep-overs that we'd had over the years. There were three differences: I wasn't bringing a sleeping bag, her nipples looked as if they were trying to push their way through her top, and as I slid into the passenger seat and went to hug her, Jordan pulled my hand up under her skirt and against her very naked, very slick *popo*. "Missed you," she murmured with an evil sigh.

"Me too." I was having to exercise what restraint I had left not to kiss the hell out of her.

"Think your folks would mind," she said, rocking her pussy against my trembling hand, "if I jumped on your face right here?"

"Uh." I gulped and gave her pussy lips a squeeze. "Yeah. I think that might kind of freak them out. I mean, maybe not the girl-girl part, but definitely the steaming-up-the-windows-and-rocking-the-car part."

She pouted. "Fuck. Want you so bad."

"Soon." I nodded, withdrawing my hand from her skirt.

"Yeah." She shot me a grin, grabbing my hand and drawing my sticky fingers into her mouth, and then laughed when I turned crimson. "Soon."

I love Jordan's family. Really. I do. And I've been over to their place often enough for dinner that I had my own special spot at the table: across from Jordan and next to her younger brother Alex.

But that night, as I sat across from my girlfriend while her parents asked us both about how we were surviving, Robbie (the eldest) kept trying to swap war stories about late nights and early mornings (he was currently in his sixth year at a state school with a reputation as a party capitol), and Alex, who was finishing his junior year in high school, kept calling his sister *Dog*(she called him *Poop*) and asking me about whether I was dating anyone, I just kind of wanted dinner to be over and to drag Jordan back to her room where I could think about stripping her clothes off and painting her body with my tongue and not have to worry about whether those thoughts were visible on my face, or on other parts of me.

When Alex started up on my love life again over the blackberry crumble (a specialty of Jordan's dad), Jordan came to my rescue. "She's seeing someone, Poop."

His face fell. "Oh. Someone from school?"

Careful not to look at Jordan, careful not to think of the naked pussy beneath her skirt, I said, "Yeah, Alex. From school." I didn't say from *which* school. And I very specifically didn't say *Two people, one of whom is sitting across the table from me and running her toe up the inside of my calf.*

"Why is Alex so obsessed with who I'm seeing?" I grumbled after we'd excused ourselves from the table and were on our way to the upstairs bathroom, which Jordan had informed her brothers would be off-limits for the next hour or two, since we would be doing *girl things.*

Jordan shot me a quizzical look. "Really? Come on, Alli, don't be stupid. He's got a crush on you. Has forever."

"Oh."

She pulled me close and whispered in my ear, "And I can't blame the little shit. But he can't have you."

"Nope," I giggled. "He can't." We closed the bathroom door and I finally, *finally* was able to pull her close and kiss her. "I'm all yours tonight." When Jordan's body tensed, I bit her ear, causing her to shiver, and whispered, "Tonight is tonight. Tomorrow is tomorrow. And I promise, I will make sure that you enjoy both, okay?"

"Okay," she sighed, and proceeded to reintroduce her body to mine. Just a *hello*, not a *full*reintroduction, but a long, friendly, very welcome one.

When we paused, I was sitting on the edge of the bathtub, with Jordan side-saddle on my lap. "One more reason to thank J.K. Rowling," I sighed.

"Huh?" Jordan's eyes and mouth were wide, her gaze unfocussed.

"For introducing us to the word *snog*."

"Oh." By that point, Jordan's grin was just as hungry, but not quite as manic. "Thank you, J.K."

"Thank you, J.K."

We kissed a bit more, each teasing the other's breasts lightly through our tops.

"Hey, J?" I asked as she began to tug my t-shirt up out of my jeans, "how're we going to, um... I mean..." Her fingers slid their way up my ribs and I swallowed a gasp. "Your... family?"

"You made *me* be quiet in your dorm." With one hand she undid my bra. "Besides, Mom and Dad'll be downstairs watching PBS news, Robbie'll be off at the Aces —" A local dive bar. "— and Alex will probably be in his bedroom with a bottle of baby oil, a box of tissues and a picture of *my girlfriend*." Her fingers found my nipples.

"Um. Okay." And, trying hard not to think about it any more, I let me hand slid up the inside of her leg to her pussy, which was in full flower, and flowing.

She gasped. "Can't... uh... complain. He's got good taste. As long as he doesn't try... *huh*... to touch you."

"N-no," I said into her lips, "just you."

The scary thing was just how easy it was to fall into that literal no-man's-land between *making out* and *making love* with Jordan. The experience was so *fluid*—not just in that we were both wet (though we were), but also in that there didn't seem to any firm lines between *touch* and*caress*, between *hug* and *embrace*. There wasn't the kind of pyrotechnic explosion that had consumed me that Monday night with Ken—but the flame was just as hot, the desire just as undeniable.

The kisses were definitely just as sweet, for all that the lips and cheeks against my own were smooth and soft.

After a long, leisurely re-introduction, Jordan and I ended up sitting at either end of her big tub, our legs tangled, our skirts around our waists, each enjoying watching the other play with herself.

Jordan frowned. "Aren't you right-handed?"

"Huh? Oh, yeah." To be honest, I was barely listening; I was lost in the sight of her dark outer lips glistening as her fingers moved up and down the length of them.

"You're masturbating with your left."

I looked down to where the first two fingers of my left hand were in fact moving across my clit. "Oh. Yeah. I guess I mostly do. Sometimes I use my right, though."

"Should have known you swung both ways." When I stuck my tongue out at her, she laughed. "You know, there are better uses for that tongue."

"Didn't we come in here to wax?"

"Oh, fine. Pain before pleasure."

"Um. I'm kind of close. Maybe a little pleasure first wouldn't be such a bad idea?"

"Okay. I can live with that."

Watching Jordan masturbate—masturbating in front of her—felt surprisingly intimate. Which was funny, when you think that we'd touched and tasted everything that we were watching each other tease and stroke.

But somehow having just that much distance made me feel even more naked.

More naked than naked. *There's a thought.*

Little things: where I rubbed myself from side to side, Jordan slid her fingers up and back over her clit. But each of us had a hand under her own shirt, stroking her own breast.

"I've seen you do this in here before," said Jordan, her lazy grin belying the whir of her fingers.

"Yeah, asshole," I answered, trying to sound just as casual, though I could feel the heat beneath *my* fingers building. "Hope your, *hnh*, brothers remember to knock."

"*I* remembered to lock the door," she sighed, "unlike you. Lucky me. Best day of my life." She threw her legs wide, over the edge of the tub, and gave a gasp of of exaggerated ecstasy: "*Oh, Ken!* Diddled myself to that sight for years —*ahh!*"

I had slid my foot between her thighs and squeezed her pussy lips with my toes. I think I'd meant it as tweak, a friendly punishment, but in fact I'd sent her over the edge. Her eyes closed, her back arched, and an army of goose pimples broke out all over those lovely legs and breasts. *Little skin hard-ons.*

When she came back down, Jordan's eyes and mouth were wide and hungry. "Um. Do we really need to wax?"

"Unh-uh. I like your bush. And I think tomorrow Ken would rather have a reminder that he's not with a couple of pre-teens."

A feral grin on her face, Jordan slithered over and kissed me. Vulpine. Foxy in every sense of the word. "Then I think," she murmured into my lips, "that I really, really want to bring you into my room and fuck your brains out. Okay?"

"Oh." Suddenly I felt very much as I had with Ken: aflame. "Okay."

Once Jordan had made sure the coast was clear, we tiptoed into her room— our skirts and tops still up, our breasts and asses still on display. She closed the door to her room behind us and leaned against it. "I have a present for you." She picked up a gift bag with a picture of a fairy godmother waving her wand, spelling the words *Happy Birthday* in glitter.

I took the bag from her, frowning. "I thought tomorrow —?"

"Yeah, well, that's your present from both of us." She licked her lips. Vulpine. Foxy. Oh, hell yes: foxy. "*This*—" She held the bag out "— is just from me. Open it."

Pulling out the tissue paper—I was careful not to tear it, since I knew that Jordan and her family always reused it—I saw in the bag a nylon harness and a long, life-like penis. I pulled it out. "A… strap-on?"

She nodded, eyes bright with excitement but also biting her lip. For the first time that night, she seemed nervous. "Remember, how I said you'd look so fucking hot with a, um… "

"With a cock?" Grinning now myself, I held the dildo against my bush.

"Huh." Jordan looked as if her mouth were literally watering. "Uh, yeah. Fuck. Alli. I mean—" Her eyes flashed up to mine. "I could, you know, I mean, I'd like to, um… "

I was dropping my clothes and stepping into the harness, adjusting it so that the silicone erection stuck straight out ahead of me. I walked over so that it slid between her thighs and our breasts were barely touching. "You want me to fuck you with my big… hard… cock?" I thrust gently with each word.

Her eyes now enormous and locked on mine, Jordan gasped, "Please?"

"Well, if you ask so *politely*…"

She knelt before me, and kissed the dildo. "Please." She sucked it into her mouth, keeping her eyes locked on mine—a sight that made my breath catch. "Please." She turned her back, keeping her face on me, and leaned over her bed, presenting her whole bottom to me—ass, cunt, both wide open. "Please."

That was a sight that made my heart stop.

Clearly seeing exactly how she was affecting me, Jordan grinned, reached back, and pulled me by the strap-on down and into her.

I guess most girls—most women—wonder what it would be like to have a cock. To be the one fucking and not the one fucked.

It was… It was wonderful, leaning over her, feeling her tremble as I pushed the dildo in with my hips. Wonderful to hear her groan as I began to slid out and back in, feeling my hip bones slap against her skinny, sweet ass. Watching her back arch and her face bounce against her pillow, mouth open, eyes closed.

It felt nice too—but only because the straps slid on either side of my clit and squeezed it just a bit each time I thrust in.

But then Jordan's fingers slid back between my thighs and began sliding over that excited little nub as I thrust, and then? Then it felt glorious. I wasn't fucking her any more; *we* were fucking.

Glorious.

And so without even thinking I returned her favor, reaching past her hip to find *her* clit, and letting my motion do the diddling for me.

I watched a flush of pleasure wash up her ass, up the length of that sinuous back. "Hey, J?"

She answered with a high moan as I continued to thrust into her.

"How come Alex calls you *Dog?*"

She began to mutter something—I'm pretty sure it started with *Poop*—but then speech left her and orgasm took its place.

I love watching Jordan come. Her eyebrows shoot up and her mouth falls open even as her eyes slam shut. And, usually, she lets out a high-pitched groan that is wonderfully gratifying—but incredibly inappropriate. Feeling her begin to lose control, hearing that sound boiling up, I clamped my hand lightly over her mouth.

She screamed into it, pushing back into me, onto me, and then collapsed onto her bed, panting.

I slid forward with her, still planted deep. I could feel her pussy pulsing against my fingers. I leaned down and kissed her. "You're not a *doggy*, Jordan. You, my sweet, are a *fox*."

At first I thought she was laughing, her belly convulsing against my wrist. But then I realized that—*fuck!*—I had made her cry again. "Jordan?"

She reached up and pulled me down to her, kissing me blindly. "Love you."

"Love you, too, Jordan."

She sobbed into my neck for a minute, and, to be honest, it felt incredibly intimate, but also more than a bit overwhelming.

Once she had calmed down a bit—but not before the tears had stopped completely—Jordan began fumbling with the harness, pulling the strap-on off of me. "Told you you'd look fucking hot with a dick."

I swung my legs around so that she could pull the contraption all of the way off. "Uh-huh."

"First dick I've had in me in months, and holy fuck…!" Then she pushed me onto my back. "And now I'm going to show you just how it fucking feels."

I watched her hunter's eyes narrow as she yanked the buckles tight around her own hips. "Um. Okay."

She leaned over me, that glistening cock held steady at the entrance to my pussy, growling, "I am going to fuck you *so hard*, Alli."

"Okay," I squeaked—or began to. But she pushed the dildo all of the way into me, and honestly, I don't think I made another intelligible sound for quite some time.

She fucked me for what felt like an hour, my legs wrapped around her soft hips or pressed up over her shoulders, those steel-hard nipples bouncing against my calves. I came, and came again, her hand clamped over *my* mouth this time.

We fucked until she finally collapsed and I lay limp beneath her, both of us out of breath. Both of us slick with sweat, each of us panting *Love you* into the other's ear.

It wasn't like Ken. It was different. And it was fucking amazing.

Driving me home after breakfast, Jordan was laughing. "Jesus! *That* was funny!"

"Alex?" He had stared at me the whole time we were at the table, and I'd spent the whole time looking anywhere but at him.

"Yeah, Poop. And his *dream girl*." She shot me a look and snorted. "Couldn't tell which of you was funnier—him trying to get your attention, or you trying to avoid his."

"Come on. I feel awful for him."

"Hey," she said, and snorted. "Don't go feeling *sorry* for the kid! He's been playing twist-the-undies with Izzy Fry. He's fine. He'll survive."

"Yeah, but all I could think was whether he'd heard us last night." It hadn't been something I'd wanted to admit to Jordan.

Jordan grinned at me. "I've got to teach the kids *somehow*, right?" When my face fell, she laughed. "Trust me, Poop didn't hear anything—even if he had... Well, I mean, he's actually walked in on me a few times—Lucas, Bill, a couple of times with Corey last year up in the tech booth—and all he's ever done is give me shit. Though I guess it's an even bet whether he'd be more turned on by you fucking a girl than turned off by the fact that it was me."

I smacked her shoulder.

She rolled her eyes, but her skin was darkening. "Think we aught to get Robbie into the act. Turn the whole family Allisexual."

I smiled and kissed her on the cheek. "Only one of you matters."

She giggled. "Aw. Sweet." But she was definitely pleased.

After we'd driven a few blocks more, I asked, "Hey, have you heard from Corey at all?"

She shook her head. "Nah. Funny: he's probably the guy I fucked the most, but I don't think it ever occurred to either of us that it was ever going to be anything more." She shook her head sadly. "What does that say?"

"That you hadn't found the right person yet?"

She stopped at a red light and turned to me. "Or that I had, and I never in a million years thought that I'd ever actually have a chance with her." She leaned over and kissed me, open-mouthed and deep. "Lucky me."

"Lucky me too," I gasped into her mouth. "Jordan?"

"Hmh?"

"Light's green."

Smiling broadly, she turned back to the wheel and started forward. "Yup. Lucky me." And then she started singing: "*Roxanne! You don't have to put out the red light...!*"

We were both still giggling as she pulled up to my house. Jordan tucked the strap-on demurely in my bag, said she couldn't wait to see it on me again, and drove off.

When I arrived at Ken's that evening, nearly everyone was already there—except Jordan. Katie and her boyfriend Bram, Jonathon with *his* boyfriend Sam (a first—not the boyfriend, but bringing him to meet us), Lucas, and a few others. Ken, naturally. Everyone was happy to see me. I was happy to see everyone. But Jordan wasn't there, and that made me nervous. Had she decided not to come? Not to join me and Ken?

Ken too worried me. I'd expected him to be as excited as I was, if nervous, perhaps, as he had been at my birthday party the year before, or at least smiling and chuckling at his former students as he had at so many of the get-togethers at his house. At worst, I thought he might be impatient for all of my friends to wish me well and go away—all of my friends except Jordan, of course.

Instead, he was contained. Quiet. Somber.

Not exactly what I was looking for. I stood there in my red party dress, smiling, but in anything but a party mood.

I was sitting between Jonathon and Sam, listening to them tell the story of how they'd first gotten together—a story that Jonathon had texted me at the time (as in, while their first date was underway, though thankfully before any clothes came off), but I didn't mind, since they were both so giddy and Lucas didn't seem comfortable insinuating himself onto the couch with us.

Sam and Jonathon were just getting to what I knew was the punchline of the story—Sam's roommate walking in on the two making out in Sam's dorm room and saying, "Dude! No wonder you thought I had a better chance with Anne than you did!"—when my phone buzzed.

Jordan: sorry

    Allison: Jordan???

Jordan: can't make it.

Jordan: u wore me out

    Allison: You okay? Everyone here's worried.

Jordan: everyone?

    Allison: Okay fine. I'M worried. And I'm sure Ken is too.

Jordan: headache. staying in bed

    Allison: Oh. Okay. Hope you feel better.

I was thinking that if she stayed in bed over at *Ken's*, we could probably help, but didn't want to push.

I was pouting at my phone when Ken sauntered up behind me. "Okay, Allison?"

I showed him the phone, which he frowned at, poor boy. For Sam's sake, I said, "My best friend Jordan isn't coming. She's sick."

"Classic college break," laughed Jonathon. "Come home to party, get sick instead." The whole room laughed; we had all barely seen each other over Christmas break because so many of us had come down with the flu after weeks of grinding pre-vacation exams.

"So, birthday girl," Ken said with a chuckle that sounded distinctly forced, "cake next, or movie—and no vote from you, Lucas, because I know you'll always vote for the food."

The room laughed again at that—even Lucas—and so my own smile was *unforced* when I answered, "Let them eat cake."

The cake was store-bought, decorated with a *Romeo and Juliet* theme. That of course launched a series of raunchy rehearsals of my performance in Acting class our sophomore year, doing that Juliet monologue.

You have no idea, I thought, and looked around the crowded, noisy room for Jordan, who *did* have some idea. Somehow, it didn't seem *real* that she had just blown the party off. It felt as if she were actually right there with me.

"So, guys," Ken said over the hubbub, "what's the movie choice for the night?" He favored me with a smile that was so minute that I almost might have imagined it.

The movie was, naturally, the truly awful Leonardo di Caprio *Romeo + Juliet*. I'd always liked Claire Danes in everything I'd seen her in.

Not in *that* piece of crap.

My friends laughed at the deaths and threw popcorn at the screen during the love scenes—in other words, they behaved exactly as we'd behaved for every dumb teen flick we'd ever watched at Ken's.

It was fun watching my friends have fun. My heart wasn't in it, though.

I was thinking about Jordan sleeping at home and Ken's aloofness, and all of the terror of what I'd asked them to do with me pressed down on me—and now it had all just fallen apart.

After the movie, everyone started to wander off—none of them *ever* stayed to clean up. Katie and Bram were first out the door, looking very much like they were off to find someplace to get horizontal, and Lucas skulked out not far behind. Jonathon hugged me while Sam held his hand; JonJon whispered in my ear, "I hope Jordan feels better." He let go of me, gave me a wink, gave his boyfriend a kiss, and then disappeared after the rest.

What...? My heart aching from being pulled in so many directions, I turned around, looking to help Ken pick up. *Well,* I thought, *I guess we're back to junior year—helping him clean up, then just going home and...*

Going home and diddling myself raw, thinking of him.

He wasn't in the kitchen. I frowned, calling into the bathroom, "Ken?"

"Upstairs," he answered.

Oh. The bedroom. THE bedroom...

The lights upstairs were all out, but a gentle glow came, not from the room that Ken had shared with his late wife, but from the office. I staggered my way to the door.

Jordan was kneeling on the guest bed in a red silk teddy that I'd helped her buy. She held her arms behind her. The single candle burned at the head of the bed, starkly lighting those amazing nipples of hers.

Ken was standing beside her, unbuttoning his shirt. His face was in shadow, as was his crotch, but I thought I could make out the growing shape of his wonderful, familiar erection.

"Happy birthday," they both murmured.

"Oh," I squeaked.

"That's what I love about Alli," purred Jordan. "She's so fucking articulate."

When I merely blushed, they both laughed. I detected some nervousness in their laughter, even so.

"Did you like the little show Jordan put on?" Ken said, letting his shirt slide to the floor.

"Show?" I walked closer.

"Uh-huh," said Jordan, her Jordan smirk firmly in place. "Didn't want Jonathon and the rest knowing Ken and me were just hanging around, waiting for the rest of them to leave so we could fuck your brains out. Also, wanted it to be at least a *bit* of a surprise for you."

"Oh." I don't think the sound even qualified as a squeak that time, but I didn't care. I was entirely focused on watching Jordan reach over to unbutton Ken's jeans. "Surprise."

He put his hand over hers. "Are you both sure you want to do this?"

With an exasperated snort, she pulled her hands away from his waist and pulled me into a searing, truly satisfying kiss, washing all of the anxiety from me.

Evidently it had the same effect on Ken. "Fuck," he groaned, "I am so going to the *special* teachers' hell."

"If you're going to hell in a bucket," I sighed, reaching out to him as Jordan began unzipping my dress, "at least you're enjoying the ride." And I pulled his beloved lips against mine, which were still moist from Jordan's fuller, softer ones.

Ken's mouth was warm and wide and welcoming. Wonderful.

Almost enough to keep my mind occupied while Jordan lowered my dress and peeled off my bra—but not quite enough that I didn't gasp into that mouth when Jordan latched on to one of my nipples. Ken and I both gazed down at her; she was grinning up at us quite evilly.

"Mind if I join you?" Ken asked and when she shook her head – not letting loose my breast—he knelt on the bed and suckled at the unoccupied tit.

I know I'm not the first person ever to have lovers sucking at both of his or her nipples, but I honestly felt in that moment as if I were exactly that: the pioneer, the woman experiencing a new, previously undiscovered sensation, walking into an ocean that had never been swum in before. *Stout Cortez,* and all of that.

Except, of course, I couldn't have told you that at the time. In spite of the fact that I had been looking forward to that moment—literally dreaming of it—for weeks, I was so caught off-guard, so surprised by the intensity of the sensations that their very different mouths were sparking in my flesh that, even though I had promised myself to *pay attention,* to *notice,* I was literally sucked into the oblivion of total pleasure almost immediately.

I think I may have come just from that sensation, because when I became aware of their fingers sliding together up the insides of my thighs, my tiny pink panties—the same ones I had picked so carefully for Ken to take off of me the year before, the night he had relieved me of my virginity—were soaked through.

I blinked down at my lovers. Jordan had her lascivious fox-grin on, and Ken the smoldering, sleepy I'm-going-to-fuck-you-so-hard look.

"She looks so hot like that, doesn't she?" said Jordan, pulling on my left nipple with her teeth.

"Yup." Ken ran his tongue around the right one and murmured, "Incredibly innocent and incredibly nasty, both at the same time."

I would have answered them, no doubt with a comeback that was both properly indignant and scathingly clever; however, at just the point where the words were forming themselves on my tongue, their fingers both reached the crotch of my undies, and there I was: back in that unswum ocean, without words, without thought, and losing control of my body altogether.

My lovers lifted me down to the bed—at least, I think that's what happened. I know that I found myself on my back, and I'm pretty sure they'd switched sides. Ken was now suckling at my left breast, while Jordan was nuzzling at the right, leaning over me from above.

Her nipple, insistent, silk-clad, dragged along my cheek, and I turned to it instinctively as an infant, sucking silk and flesh into my mouth. Jordan hissed.

Ken grunted, and began pulling down my panties.

Both of my lovers are incredibly attentive. Each is capable of filling my senses and bringing me to a level of pleasure that, as I've said, I can't find the words to describe—though obviously I'm happy to keep trying. Having *both* of them teasing and tantalizing…. Well, it was almost a relief when Ken's mouth let go of my nipple and he began to kiss his way down my chest.

Almost.

As it was, the feeling of Jordan's teeth and tongue torturing my nipple while Ken's lips brushed my ribs did a pretty good job of scrambling my thoughts, and when his tongue dipped into my navel, any thoughts or expectations that I might have had were swept away on a wave of sensation.

Thinking about it now, I almost want to laugh; it was obvious where Ken was headed. And yet by the time his mouth met my hot, open pussy, I was so lost in *feeling* that I squawked in surprise, letting go of Jordan's nipple and pulling my own out of her mouth. We both looked down at Ken, his face planted firmly between my thighs. I could feel his tongue and lips begin to explore my cunt, and it was glorious, but honestly? The thing that got me most was the look of wicked intent on what I could see of his face.

"Shit," murmured Jordan. "That looks like fun."

Ken gave the length of my pussy a long lick, making me arch my back. "It is."

"Eat… Jordan," I whimpered. "Wanna see —"

Jordan kissed me. "Nope. It's your turn, birthday girl." Her hands joined Ken's in sliding onto my now-vacant breasts, pinching and caressing. "What do you think, Ken?" she asked. "Is there room down there for one more?"

At that thought I whimpered again, while my legs made their opinion clear by spreading wider.

"Only one way to find out," he said, and turned back to teasing me with his tongue.

"Geronimo," laughed Jordan, gave me another kiss on the mouth, a nip on each nipple, and a long lick down my belly until her face and his were side by side—though upside-down to each other—between my spread thighs.

For the first time, I was sorry that Jordan and I hadn't waxed the night before; as her tongue joined Ken's in dancing around my clit, what I wanted more than anything was to see *everything*,without the screen of my bush.

Within the first second or two of their tongues tangling around my sensitive pearl, however, I couldn't have cared less. I was blind, deaf, without smell or taste. The feeling of the two of them pleasuring me took up all of the available bandwidth. The rest of my senses shut down.

Sightless as I was, some part of my brain remembered vision. "Kiss… Wanted to see you…"

But then fingers closed around my nipples and another slid into my pussy—Ken's? Jordan's? Hell, *mine*? No idea.—and even my sense of touch shorted out, and I was lost.

How long did they eat me together? No idea of that either. I know it was a period of time, that, as much as time ceased to exist for me in that eternal moment, I didn't come instantly, though how I didn't I'm not sure.

I know that they were patient, that they played with me, that they worked together to bring me closer and closer to a pinnacle that they weren't in any hurry to reach. I don't *remember* this, but I'm certain of it, because by the time I finally reached that crest and the infinite light of that orgasm exploded through me, I was covered in sweat, my hair (which I'd arranged in a carefully messy bun before I came to Ken's) was tangled and wet around my face. My fists were tangled in two very different heads of hair, pushing them into me, my pelvis pushing up into them. I could smell the heady aroma of my own excitement (and Jordan's, just inches from my nose), and could taste the iron tang of my own blood—I'd bitten my cheek. *"OH, GOD!"* I howled, and I've truly never taken the Lord's name less in vain. Agnostic though I have always been, I never believed in Her more strongly than at that moment.

I lay, gasping, weeping, gazing up at the ceiling. I was vaguely aware of lips against my belly—Ken's—until I felt him gasp and heard the sound of a zipper.

"Jesus, Ken," Jordan said, "here she's been sighing about how nice and hefty you were and I was all sure it was just because this was the only one she'd ever seen. Damn." And then Ken's gasp turned into a growl.

Infant-weak, I lifted my head. Jordan had taken that *hefty* cock into her lovely mouth, and that sight sparked the flame in me once more, even though my whole body was still quivering with the aftershocks of that monumental orgasm.

If I'd thought about it, I would have realized that all of my fantasies involving this threesome had involved me pleasuring the two of them. Which seems kind of strange. But it is the reason that the vision of Ken's cock pressing through Jordan's lips shook me so thoroughly. It was sexier, nastier, more beautiful than anything that I had imagined, and I couldn't begin to tell you why. Why it set my crotch and nipples buzzing, instead, for example, of making me jealous. Here, I'd broken up with my first boyfriend because he'd screamed Jordan's name while I was jerking him off, and now Ken, my Romeo, was planted in Jordan's mouth, and it only made me wet.

And it did. Make me wet.

She sucked him deep into her mouth—once, twice—and then she slid her mouth off of him, a string of pre-cum stretching between them, and pulled him between my thighs and into me, and we both screamed.

Jordan had fucked me with the strap-on the night before, and it had felt fabulous. Ken wasn't any bigger—if anything, the dildo was a bit longer—but there was something about the knowledge that this phallus was *alive,* that it could receive as well as give pleasure. Something too about knowing that my lover's cock was slick with my lover's spit. I felt hotter as he slid into me than I had even as they had both been eating me. "Oh, Ken, Jordan, *oh!*"

Jordan turned around and kissed my cheek, which was bouncing from Ken's gentle thrusts. "Hey, Alli."

I turned and kissed her mouth.

They say we can't really multi-task, that at best we switch our attention very quickly from one thing to another. I don't think I truly believed it until that evening. Intellectually, I knew that Ken was the one fucking me, but I was only truly conscious of Jordan's mouth on mine.

That is, until Ken's rough chin slid up my neck and he murmured, "Is there room up here for one more?"

My response consisted mostly of consonants. Jordan laughed against my lips and slid over to one side of my mouth. "Come on in, lover-boy."

He moved over, and there I was: kissing them both, being fucked, and past my poor single-track mind's ability to think, lost in the fuck.

At some point, I realized that once more there was only one set of lips on mine: thick, rough—Ken. It was a gloriously familiar feeling, his heavy erection thrusting into me, our chests bouncing together, my legs crossed under has clenching ass....

But then I felt a long tongue run up the back of one of my thighs, causing me to gasp into Ken's mouth and clamp my pussy down on his cock, which made him groan. That tongue—Jordan's tongue—slurped up the back of my other thigh and I arched, moaning into Ken's lips. Growling, he began to thrust again, jerking occasionally (when Jordan's mouth teased *him,*apparently). We fell back into rhythm, even as Jordan continued to tease us with her tongue.

As we fucked, as her mouth nibbled and tasted at us, I felt a pair of thin fingers sliding up the inside of my hip to the point at which Ken's body was slamming into mine. They found my clit—already engorged—and began to rub me. With what little awareness I had left, I realized that she was using my side-to-side motion, rather than her own up-and-down, and as the pleasure began to peak again, I started to cry, because it was so, so sweet, and it felt *so, so good,*and...

And...

And Ken, whose build to orgasm I had grown to know well, and who I could have sworn was still a ways away from coming, reared back, bellowed, and unleashed a torrent inside of me that quickly overflowed.

That (on top of that thrusting cock and those whirring fingers) set me off too, and we both screamed, gripped each other hard, and then collapsed.

When we'd caught our breath, Ken pushed up and we both looked at Jordan, who sat beside us, grinning.

"Holy fucking *shit*," gasped Ken. "Jordan, you could have given me a warning!"

She laughed. "What, Ken, never been tea-bagged?"

"Well," he grunted, "never had my balls sucked on while I was buried deep in a woman's pussy, no." He continued to move in mine. I could feel that he was still hard, and knew that we were nowhere near finished.

"Huh." She looked as if she were thinking about it. "Yeah, I suppose that wouldn't happen often."

"No." His eyes were slitted as he glanced at her, even as he continued his gentle post-fuck fuck. "No, it doesn't."

"Hey!" Jordan crowed. "I taught *you* something!"

He growled at her, which just made Jordan laugh—which made me laugh. Which made my cunt squeeze Ken hard, which made him gasp.

"Uh," Jordan said, staring down at his now-erect hard-on, slowly plowing me again, "didn't you just…?"

"Fuck, yes." God, the sound of him swearing was almost as much of a turn-on as the feeling of him fucking me. Almost. He looked down at me, and when I nodded, smiled evilly at Jordan. "So. You ready for me to teach *you* a lesson, Miss Jordan?"

Her eyes widened. "Um… Yeah?"

He was the one grinning, now. "Allison, do you know her brother Alex's nickname for Jordan?"

I did—but I didn't know that *he* knew. "Um. Dog?"

"Doggy." He leaned down and kissed me, and then withdrew, causing us both to hiss. "Do you know *why* he calls her that?"

I shook my head, but mostly I was astonished by the sight of Jordan blushing. *Jordan. Blushing.*

"Apparently young Alex has walked in on his older sister on several occasions—including several times with Corey up in the booth last year. And every time, she was being taken from behind."

Oh. As I had taken her the night before.

"Jesus!" spluttered Jordan, "I can't believe he told you that!"

"Oh, he was trying to talk his way into Izzy's pants when they were hanging lights. He didn't realize that I could hear him."

"Oh." Jordan had a sheepish expression on her face that was totally at odds with her erect nipples and revealing silk undies.

Ken reached over and took her hand. "Jordan. I already knew about you and Corey. It's okay."

"You… knew?"

He chuckled. "Well, I preferred to think that you were using all of those rubbers up in the booth for their proper purpose, because having a water balloon fight with all of that electronic equipment around…?"

That got a laugh out of Jordan, and I laughed along in relief as much as anything.

"And it never affected your work up in the booth, so…" Ken shrugged.

"Never missed a cue!" Jordan said.

"Nope," said Ken. They were staring at each other cautiously.

It was time for me to take charge. "I would love to watch the two of you fuck doggy-style."

They both blinked at me; I knew they hadn't forgotten me, but I could tell that my interjection had surprised them both.

"I would," I continued. "And before you go down the whole STD-and-pregnancy path, either of you —"

"We —" Ken began, but Jordan finished: "— already talked about it." Suddenly their expressions were both deadly serious.

I knelt up and kissed Ken, squeezing his cock, which was still dripping from me. Then I turned and kissed Jordan, with my other hand giving the frilly lips of her pussy a gentle squeezing, feeling them beginning to flow again. Not letting either of them go, I backed up. Each favored me with a hungry, simmering look. "So I've kissed you both. And fucked you both. It's time for you two to get to know each other."

To my surprise, I watched a flutter of panic pass over each of their faces. "Alli —" said Jordan, while Ken grunted, "Allison —"

I fondled the two of them, stopping their protests. "Shh. Just a kiss to start. Please. I want to see you kiss *so* much…"

They broke from my gaze and stared at each other.

"Please," I said, surprising myself as much as them this time, and stroked them both.

Jordan shook her head. "Come on, Ken. Your girlfriend's asking you to kiss another girl. What's wrong with you?"

"I'm not sure," he said, smiling now. "*Your* girlfriend is asking you to kiss an old dude. I can see not wanting to do that."

"Would it make it better," she said, "If I told you I've wanted to jump your bones since freshman year?"

Ken snorted. "I'm not sure that it doesn't make it worse." They both laughed nervously. "Come on. Let's make our *belle dâme sans merçi* happy." And they leaned into one another, and kissed. After a moment, their hands replaced mine on each other's genitals and I stepped back.

I was… It is impossibly hard to describe how watching them kiss made me feel. Excited, certainly. Terrified. Perhaps a bit jealous. But they *fit*. It was if I had taken two pieces of broken pottery and slid them together and found that they matched *perfectly*. Their coloring—both dark. Their heights—he leaned over her just *so*…. (Mind, I'm exactly the same height as Jordan. Nonetheless.)

After a while, during which neither his cock nor her nipples showed any sign of softening, they both turned toward me. "Satisfied?" asked Jordan.

"Oh, I don't know," I answered, reaching out and squeezing her nipples gently between my fingers. "Are *you* satisfied... Doggy?" And when she didn't answer, I let my fingers trail down to her pussy. "Believe me, I know Ken can satisfy you." Over her shoulder, I could see that Ken was biting his cheeks; I knew what would satisfy *him*. "And I'll help. I promise." I planted a kiss on her lips, which she returned with fervor. When I tried to break from the kiss, she wouldn't let me go; she began to kneel on the bed, pulling me down with her. When I began to reach for her breasts, she shivered, and then pushed me gently backward. "Lie back. Pussy."

I laughed. "Yes. Doggy." I spread my legs and lay back on my elbows.

Jordan smirked at me. "Woof." She leaned down and lapped at my cunt, which knew well enough to begin responding immediately.

I gazed back over Jordan's raised ass to see Ken stroking himself, but otherwise looking as if he were trying to remain very, very patient when that was the last thing he was feeling. I ran my foot down her back and over her ass. "I think, Ken, that this constitutes a clear invitation. Don't you?"

Just in case Ken wasn't getting the point, Jordan wiggled her silk-covered backside at him. He shot me a bemused grin. "Christ, Allison. You've come a hell of a long way in a year." He slid forward on his knees, reaching out with one large hand and putting it on Jordan's ass while the other continued to stroke his darkening erection.

"I have, haven't I," I sighed as Jordan lapped at me. "And I have you two to thank for that."

Ken lined himself up with her, unfastening the crotch of the teddy; as he began to press in, Jordan groaned into my pussy. All three of us swore. Once he was fully inside of Jordan, he opened his eyes. "Actually, Allison, I think we—*huh!*—are the ones who should be thanking *you.*"

Jordan grunted and nodded against my crotch, and I found myself feeling inexplicably shy. I gazed down at her, and then up at him—both faces slack with pleasure. I had seen those expressions on those faces before, but never from a distance, and it was weird seeing those faces so deeply transported—and knowing that even though my touch wasn't making their pleasure happen, that I was still its *cause.* That these two, whom I loved, were fucking, and enjoying each other as I had enjoyed each of them—and that they were doing it for *me.*

Well, obviously, they were doing it for themselves. But still, they'd never have been in that bed, with Ken taking Jordan hard from behind, if I hadn't asked.

Weird.

Wonderful.

Weird.

I found that I was crying—smiling, but crying—and that Ken's thrusts had made it all but impossible for Jordan to keep her mouth against my pussy. I leaned down, pulling her face up to mine, and kissed her. "Thank you."

She grunted what passed for "You're welcome."

I slithered along her body to Ken. His eyes had stayed open, locked on mine, but the feel of Jordan's cunt had his mind focused elsewhere—just where I had wanted it to be. "Thank you." I kissed him too, and he shuddered, his thick fingers gripping Jordan's hips hard.

"Can I show you something, Ken?" I whispered, and his eyes actually focused on me. He frowned, but nodded. "Look down."

My boyfriend blinked at me, but did, all while continuing to fuck my girlfriend. I had to admire his concentration.

I lifted the back flap of the red teddy. Together we watched Jordan's haunches rippling with Ken's strokes. I ran a finger down the crack of her ass to where there was a mole, just to the left of her asshole. "Isn't this beauty mark cute?" I touched it with my fingertip, brushing her asshole at the same time; Jordan gasped and tensed; Ken groaned. "The first time I saw it, I wanted to kiss it."

I ran my fingertip lightly around the beauty mark, brushing the puckered opening of her anus, causing another chain-reaction of groaning.

"Do you remember what you said on the phone, Jordan? About how I could thank you?"

"Uh-huh…" She voice was high and thin and very not-Jordan-like.

"Good," I said, trying hard not to think too much about what I was doing, and leaned down. I kissed the base of her spine. "Thank you, Jordan," I said, and licked my way down, letting Ken's thrusts do most of the moving for me, feeling my tongue-tip brush lightly across the wrinkled flesh of her asshole.

Jordan shrieked, arching like a cat, but Ken's cock, pushing deep into her, and his big hands, gripping her hips, held her steady as I pressed down, pushing my nose down between my lovers, and kissed Jordan's ass.

Kiss my ass. I've heard that so often as an insult, or a tease. I'd had the phrase thrown at me in anger, in hatred (thank you, Erica Travers), and even occasionally in playful affection. Hell, Jordan and I had each told the other to kiss her ass dozens, hundreds of times.

I'd never thought of it as an expression of love.

That's how it felt, though, pressing my lips against that most reviled of body parts: an expression of the deepest possible love and trust. *I love you. I love ALL of you.*

I withdrew my lips from her, and peered up at Ken. His face was lust-dark, as it should have been in the middle of fucking Jordan's amazing cunt. But his eyes, which I had expected to be half-mast with lust, were wide, and his jaw hung open.

I smiled up at him and kissed his belly, and then his rocking hip. Jordan continued to scream as Ken banged away at her.

I crawled around behind Ken, kissing one clenching butt cheek and then the other. I reached between his thighs, letting his balls slide over my palm and wrist, pressing Jordan's clit up against Ken's driving erection.

"Thank you, Ken," I sighed against the small of his back, and then kissed the dimple where his back and pelvis joined.

He bucked, his breath hitching, and while he was still, I pushed between his butt cheeks and found *his* asshole, and kissed it.

I love you. I love ALL of you.

His musky Ken scent, pooled beneath my nose at the base of his spine, was heady. I touched my tongue to Ken's sphincter while compressing Jordan's clit between my fingertips.

Their reactions were immediate, volcanic, and gratifyingly loud. My lovers howled together, pulling away from me as orgasm gripped them.

They collapsed on the bed, both gasping.

I slithered up the length of their bodies and hugged them both. "I love you both. So much." Now *I* was crying again.

And they began kissing me—sloppily, stilling gasping and trembling. Which only made me cry harder. Which eventually made Jordan begin to giggle. "So, Ken?"

He grunted into my shoulder.

"You know how Alli was saying she was corrupting us? I kinda think we need to take her at her word."

We played until we were all exhausted, trying just about every variation that we could imagine—other than using the strap-on on Ken (he asked for a rain check).

At around two in the morning, we were all collapsed in a heap, legs, arms, bodies sprawled every which way. I could feel my worn-out body calling me into sleep; I think I heard Jordan begin to snore.

With a great sigh of reluctance, Ken pulled us back from the edge of slumber. "Much as I hate the idea of you guys leaving this bed, I don't think your parents would be cool waking up to find *your* beds empty. And you, Allison, have a plane to catch in the morning." He goosed my boob and Jordan's ass, making both of us yelp and sit up blearily.

"Jeeze, Ken," Jordan grumbled in mock indignation. "What kind of host are you? Kicking two lonely little girls out in the middle of the night?"

"Trust me, I really don't want to—but I think I can honestly say that neither of you could be described as a *little girl*, thank God." He stroked our cheeks. "And after tonight, I hope that you're not feeling lonely."

I pouted. "Lonelier over there —" I pointed toward the door. "— than we are snuggling in*here.*" I managed to wrap my legs around both of them.

"Be that as it may," sighed Ken, detaching my calf from his butt, "it's time for you two Cinderellas to go home."

We protested some more, but both Jordan and I knew the night was drawing to a close. Within far too short a time, we were out of Ken's office, more or less dressed (I couldn't find my panties) and standing in the entry hall. "I don't want this to be over," I said, fighting to keep from weeping yet again.

"Hey," said Jordan, holding my hand, "the whole point of this was to make you happy!"

"And you so, *so* did," I sniffled pulling them both to me yet again. I gave each of my lovers a long kiss. "That's why I don't want it to be over."

Ken gave a sad chuckle. "Good night, good night. Parting is such sweet sorrow, that I shall say good night till it be morrow."

"Wow, Ken," Jordan laughed. "You really are her Romeo."

"Not just mine anymore," I replied.

They blinked at each other, and then at me.

"Would…" I felt suddenly cold, though Ken's house was warm and I was thousands of miles from the Ohio chill. "Would you guys want to try this again? Because I really, really do."

They both looked completely overwhelmed by the question. In fairness, I was completely overwhelmed by *everything* in that moment, but I did know that what they had given me was something so special that I wasn't sure how I was going to survive the three long months until the end of the school year.

Carefully *not* looking at each other, they both shrugged and then nodded.

Giddy, I kissed them both again. Pulling them close, I whispered, "While it's still sort of my birthday, and I can still make ridiculous demands of you, there's one other thing I want to ask."

"Jesus, Alli," Jordan groaned.

Ken sighed. "Tell us, Allison. What is it?"

"Since Jordan's just starting her break, what I want…" I took a breath. "I want… my Romeo and my… Ganymede? Cesario? Whatever. I want you two to try to get together without me this week."

They stepped back—from me and from each other—and frowned.

"This," Ken said, shaking his head and laughing, "is not usually what a girlfriend asks after a threesome."

"As you'd know," said Jordan, smirking.

"Hey, you are both now *way* more experienced with threesomes now than I was before tonight."

Still feeling cold, all the more so since they'd let go of me, I blurted, "I know it's a lot of me to ask, you don't have to, but if… Either way, could you tell me what happens?"

Again they peered at each and then nodded. Relief flooded through me—and then confusion. Why was I relieved that my boyfriend and girlfriend had agreed to consider, at least, hooking up without me? But relieved I was.

Ken reached out and took Jordan's hand. "Good night, *Doggy*." She growled at him, and he smiled and gave her a quick kiss before turning to me. "Good night, *Pussy*."

I purred and grinned.

After he had kissed me—a longer kiss—Jordan said, "Well, we'll have to think about what animal *you* are, Ken." Opening the door, she gave me a long, wet goodbye kiss. "Hope you aren't too sore to sit on the plane for hours," she murmured into my lips. Releasing me, she turned to Ken. "Give me a call, okay, Ken? Just, um, give me a few days. I don't think I'm going be walking straight for a while."

We all laughed. Ken wished us both good night once more. And then Jordan and I walked to our cars, waved and drove off to our separate, lonely beds.

"What do you think I should do for my next birthday?" I ask Ken as I slip back into my panties.

He squints at me. "Jesus. Already? I feel as if I've just recovered from the last one."

"Aw, poor Ken."

He turns to me, zipping his fly, his eyes filled with low flame for all that we've just fucked and fucked and... "If you're determined to kill me, at least I know I'll go be with a smile on my face." He pulls me to him and kisses me, and my body—still feeling his passion in every part—responds.

After a moment, he steps back, a grin on his face, and hands me my bra and dress. "Come on, my America, my new found land, get your clothes on. I have a surprise for you back at my house."

"*Oh.*" Nipples, pussy, lips, ass all buzzing, I gasp. "Okay."

Wedding Belles

Wedding Belles *is a collection of nuptial-related naughtiness with stories by K.D. West and Mary Cyn.*

In the other stories in the collection, part of the Kat McKinney, Wedding Slut *series, Mary Cyn explores her heroine's extremely non-traditional views on love, marriage... And sex. Lots and lots of sex.*

Folding Herself In

"Can't believe we're actually sitting here quietly like it's just another Friday night," Gil muttered, taking a pull from the bottle of oak-aged port that Sean had bought him as a joke. He'd already polished off an impressive amount of the vodka that Frank had provided.

"Well," Sean said, waving his eighth snifter of whiskey at the disaster that was their apartment, "we had a nice little stag bash, didn't we? Sent your brothers home properly drunk."

"*Home*, yeah, right," Gil snorted. "Will, maybe. James, sure. But I'd be willing to bet that the twins and Frank, Scotty and them are off giving our single days a proper send off, and here we are winding down for a good night's sleep. I mean…"

Smiling, Sean said, "I suppose I know what you mean. But I'm not planning on getting a whole hell of a lot of sleep *tomorrow* night. You?"

Gil blushed, as Sean had known that he would—whether at the idea of Sean enjoying *conjugal relations* with Gil's sister or at Gil's own soon-to-be-legitimate debauchery with Phoebe, Sean wasn't sure. "No," he grunted, taking another swig.

They sat there in silence, surveying the thoroughly be-messed sitting room for some minutes. Sean knew that they should clean up—this apartment would be Gil and Phoebe's after the honeymoon, and she wasn't likely to appreciate coming home for the first time to upturned furniture and four-letter words painted on the walls. Still they sat, however, more than mildly drunk and hugely content.

He was *marrying Diana*. Unbelievable. It was if his whole life—every horrible accident and wonderful, serendipitous happenstance had been pushing him to this place, this time. Into her thin, strong arms. Her thin, strong fingers…

After tomorrow, no more having to sneak or hide. He could take her hand, tell her and Gil's parents that they were going upstairs, and fuck her until she screamed, and nobody would mind. They'd probably be *pleased!*

"We're marrying them," Gil said blinking up at the letters sprayed on the wall opposite: *Bullshit!* it read in alternating purple and red.

"Yeah," Sean answered.

"Fuck," Gil said.

"Yeah."

"You… happy?"

"Oh, yes," Sean said.

Gil grinned. "Me too." He lifted the port, Sean lifted his whiskey, and for the fiftieth time that night, they toasted their luck.

Putting down the glass, Sean knocked over one of the bottles of lube that Frank had given them as a joke. After another silence, he asked, "What do you think the girls are up to?"

"Well, I know Connie and F'licia were going to throw them a bachelorette party, but come on," Gil said dismissively, "you know Phoebe's had them both home and in bed for hours."

Sean nodded and glanced at his watch: almost 1:00. "Speaking of which—"

A loud *thunk* sounded from the front door, and then two more.

"Fuck," Gil grumbled, "that's got to be the twins come back to paint on the walls some more."

Sean waited for Gil to get the door; his friend barely moved.

Three more *thunks* thudded against the door.

Resenting having to budge from his comfy chair, Sean groaned his way to his feet and shuffled over to the door. "Fine, fine," he grumbled, reaching out to the nob.

Opening the door, he expected to find Gary and Jerry, drunk out of their skulls. Or perhaps Scotty held up by Tom and Liam.

What he didn't expect to find was Ruth Thorson, one of his and Diana's brainiest and quietest friends, standing at an angle with her lipstick smeared (since when did Ruth wear lipstick?), her blouse unbuttoned to her navel and her black skirt down around her hips, revealing a red lace bra and sky blue panties.

At least she was wearing a bra and panties. "Hullo, Sean. I'm very invert… inebriate."

"Uh. Hello, Ruth." Sean was having a hard time not staring down his friend's unsuspectedly canyonous cleavage. "Uh. How was Phoebe and Diana's bachlorette party?"

"Still going," Ruth sighed. She threw her arms around Sean's neck and gave his cheek a wet kiss. "Mmmmm. Hullo, Gilbert," she said blearily, stumbling towards Gil, her breasts rubbing past Sean's chest in a really diverting way.

Gil blinked at Ruth as she floated across the room toward him. "Damn, Ruth. You're plastered."

She stopped and looked down. "No, Gilbert. I don't seem to have any stucco on me." Stepping toward him again, she tripped over an empty bottle and flopped across Gil's knees. "Wee!"

Gil stared down at Ruth's backside—the skirt had now flopped up onto her back, revealing her panties not only to be blue, but semi-transparent. His chin trembling uncertainly, his hands gripping the arms of the chair, Gil looked to Sean for aid.

Transfixed by a backside as surprisingly round as the topside had proved to be, Sean was at a loss to give any. "Uh… Ruth?"

"Wee!" their friend giggled again, wriggling face-down across Gil's lap. Gil remained motionless.

"Ruth," Sean repeated somewhat more steadily, "what brings you here?"

"Well," Ruth said, still folded across Gil's thighs, "Diana and Phoebe wouldn't let me share, so I decided I'd come here and be your Jonny."

Over the years, Sean had learned to count to ten to give himself time to think Ruth's statements through. Knowing himself to be somewhat plowed, he counted a full fifteen. "I'm sorry, Ruth," he said finally, "I don't understand."

Gil nodded enthusiastically, his eyes fixed on the ceiling—as far from Ruth's backside as he could get them.

"Oh," Ruth said in tone of the mildest possible surprise. She began to push herself upright, one hand on the floor, the other on… some part of Gil that caused his eyes to bulge. She wobbled to a standing position, teetered and plopped back into Gil's lap, sitting this time. "I fell," she said, her head lolling back against Gil's shoulder.

Gil squeaked. Sean hadn't heard him squeak in years.

"Ruth," Sean said, trying to keep his I-may-be-drunk-but-I'm-reasonable voice going, "I'm afraid we're still in the dark as to why you're here."

"Ah," Ruth said. "Well, I told you. I tried to climb up on the table with Phoebe and Diana and Jonny, but they wouldn't share."

"On the table?" Gil rumbled.

"Yes. I said. Phoebe and Diana and Jonny where there on the table. I would have folded myself in anywhere, you know."

"What were they doing on the table?" Gil asked.

Sean had a very vivid idea of where this was headed, but somehow couldn't manage to stop the train.

"Well, Gilbert, I would have thought that was obvious. I've heard you and Phoebe often enough that I know you've got a clairly fear idea…" Ruth shook her head, her hair flying in Gil's face, and she giggled. "Fair. Ly. Clear."

Sean's stomach seemed to be filling with something cold and heavy.

"Gilbert, I wish you wouldn't keep poking my butt, it's distracting," said Ruth, wriggling in a very distracting manner.

"So," Sean managed to say, praying against all odds that this would all end well, "Jonny… took his clothes off?" Jonny had been part of their group of friends after college — well, part of the *girls'* circle, anyway. Sean'd always found him incredibly self-involved. And *pretty.*

Ruth nodded and began to sway against Gil, causing him to begin to turn even a deeper shade of red. She began to sing breathily, "'I want to be, a…' Did you know he's been working as an escort? Really a good job for him, I think, suits his temperament and his skill set quite nicely. In any case, I always find having sex with him nice—his stamina is rather remarkable—and of course, I've always wanted to have sex with Diana, and Phoebe too, when it comes to that—"

"Sex," Gil said. Well, it was more a hiss than a statement, really. "Sex. Phoebe. Jonny. Sex."

"Oh, yes," Ruth said. "He'd already done quite a nice job with Diana, you see—and Diana really had done a nice job of entertaining Phoebe in the meantime, she really does have the most talented tongue, that girl."

Sean groaned.

"In any case, when he began to take care of Phoebe—" Gil echoed Sean's groan. "—Diana looked so all alone, and so nice, and I thought I'd go on up with them and help out, but—"

"They said no," Sean muttered.

"Yes," pouted Ruth, "they wouldn't share, and Felicia and Connie started pulling me down, and I never did like them, you know, though Susan and Tila were trying to talk them into at least letting me watch from up close, which I thought was rather nice. But Fellatia and Connili… Connie pulled me down, and Diana said she wanted them to herself—"

"Wanted…?" Sean began, knowing he didn't really want to finish the question, absolutely certain he didn't want an answer.

"Phoebe and Jonny, of course. And I thought…" She peered around the room. "Did you not have stripers? Connie and Felicia swore that you were having stripers—which they very clearly understood to mean *having* stripers, which I have to imagine means something thoroughly sexual—swore that Liam and Tom swore that Frank swore that you'd have them, and that was the only reason that they were able to talk Phoebe or Diana into it. What's good for the gander is really good for the goose, you know."

"Not *stripers*, Ruth. *Strippers.*" Trying not to watch Gil's face growing dangerously red, trying not to stare at the way the blonde hair was peeking around the crotch of Ruth's panties beneath the useless skirt, Sean said, "Ruth. Ruth. Our strippers were Gary and Jerry in drag. It was one of the most disgusting things I've ever seen."

"Sex. Phoebe," Gil moaned. His eyes snapped to Ruth's; she returned his stare with an equanimity that was all the greater for being utterly trashed. "*Sex.* Phoebe would *never…* No fucking way! With Jonny fucking Powers?"

With Diana, Sean thought, and in spite of himself, he felt his libido stir to life, jealousy and horniness its favorite meals.

Ruth blinked at Gil and then pointed at where *Bullshit!* was painted over the fish tank. "Your wall doesn't agree with you, Gilbert." She finished this pronouncement very seriously, but then giggled. "I do think she liked the bit with Diana best."

Both men stood, Gil toppling Ruth to the ground.

"Wee!" she giggled. "Was sex with the twins fun?"

"I'll *kill* him!" Gil bellowed.

Sean nodded, but a part of him wanted to watch for a bit, and *then* kill them.

"Can't get in, you know," Ruth said. "Private. Invitation only. And you know, Gilbert, Phoebe will only think that you didn't want her to have what you got. She won't like that. *Patriarchal, sexist attitude.*" This last was declaimed in so Phoebe-like a tone that it brought both Gil and Sean up short. "And you know what Diana's like when she's disappointed, Sean. She'll be *sooo* disappointed, I think, if you interrupt. Well, I suppose you didn't *both* have sex with your stripers, did—"

"*We didn't have sex with my... STRIPPERS, Ruth!*" Gil yelled, still glaring toward the door.

She winked. Ruth Thorson, of all people, *winked*. "Oh, of course. What a shame. Gary and Jerry. I've always rather wanted that experience, myself." Ruth smiled blissfully at Gil and then at Sean. "Well, how nice! I'm glad that I've come after all. I *can* be your Jonny."

Sean felt Gil turn with him to look at Ruth again. She was sprawled against the chair where Gil had dumped her, legs spread, hair wild.

She was unbuttoning what little was left to unbutton of her blouse. "Macho, macho man," she sang breathily, baring one shoulder and then the other.

"Ruth," Sean said, knowing that he had very little leeway here—if he didn't do something soon, either Jonny Powers was going to be the most thoroughly hexed wizard since the end of the war or Ruth was going to have more drunken revenge sex coming at her than she could possibly know—

"I rather like having sex with men whose adrenaline is running high," Ruth sighed, removing her blouse and tossing it in Gil's face. "It's so exciting. Sex with angry women isn't anywhere nearly as much fun."

The bra was semi-transparent too, it seemed, and Sean was fascinated to discover that Ruth's left nipple was pierced.

Dropping to his knees between Ruth's thighs, Gil worked at the blouse that he had balled in his hands. "Is he? Really? Fucking?"

"Oh, yes," Ruth said, wriggling the skirt past her feet, "and Phoebe was making that high-pitched sighing *OH-OH-OH* sound she always makes when Diana and I come to visit and you and she are off—*OH!*" *Off* went the blouse, *rip* went the brassiere and *slurp* went Gil's mouth as he pulled the ringed nipple into his mouth. Sean watched in a kind of fascinated dread as Gil's hands made Ruth's panties disappear as effectively as they'd eliminated the bra, and suddenly there was no pretense—Ruth Thorson was quite naked on the floor of their apartment, and Gil was moving his thumb up and down her vulva in a manner that caused Ruth's wide-set eyes to cross. "How nice," she said.

Sean stood there, frozen. Really, he had never been one to lock up. When decisive action was called for, Sean was always the first to commit—a tendency that Gil and Phoebe had been trying to rein in for a decade.

Not Diana. She'd never tried to make him be someone else.

But here he was, watching as one of his best friends diddle one of his fiancée's best friends, watching her attempting to undo the zipper to his trousers by main force, and he couldn't move, couldn't think, couldn't speak. Stop them? Join them? Go to bed? Go to Connie and Felicia's and bay at the windows like a lovesick hound smelling a bitch in heat? Two. *Two.*

Three.

"You know, Sean," Ruth said over Gil's shoulder—she had apparently opened his fly and was worming her hand in; Gil had switched to the unadorned breast—"Do you know—OH! Goodness, Gilbert, what nice hands you have!—I've wanted to fuck you both since we met at that birthday part of Diana's, and the thoughts were so clear and I—*MMMM*—kept laughing, the thought of you both wrapped around me like bread on a sandwich..." Ruth's hands were working manically at Gil's shirt, but her voice was as calm as always—with occasional outbursts of sexual transport. "And Diana does say that your mouth is so nice, Sean, I bet it's as good as *hers!"*

Gil plunged a finger into Ruth, causing her back to arch. His long thumb kept up its wild dance at the front of her vulva—which was reddening and slickening as Sean watched.

Sean's cock was as hard as he could ever remember it being. Diana had never made him this hard.

He had never forced himself to wait this long with Diana.

Jonny's dark flesh, stallion-long, plunging into pale and pink and copper... He shook his head.

"Oh!" Ruth said, voice still airy and distracted—and Sean could see a reason for the distraction for a change, as he watched Gil add a second finger. "Do. Come fuck. Sean. *Please.*" She pushed herself up into the chair, yanking Gil by his shirt so that he stood beside her, his crotch at her face level. Sean watched in awe as she drew Gil's enormous erection out of his trousers.

Damn! Not a stallion, but...

Ruth lowered her mouth to that amazing piece of befreckled manhood. Gil threw back his head and groaned, his hands flying to her hair.

Ruth began humming "Macho Man" as she slurped him into her mouth. One hand stroked Gil's cock in time with her lips while the other slipped between her round thighs and began to stroke at her pussy.

Sean had walked in on Gil and Phoebe once—they apparently hadn't had the restraint to make it all of the way back to Gil's room—but all that Sean had gotten was an eyeful of bountiful, bouncing breasts, since though her blouse had been quite gone they hadn't removed her skirt. He had only seen one cunt in his life, and it was thin-lipped and topped with a tuft of flame-colored hair.

Ruth's was amazing, but very, very different. Exotic and puffy, it seemed to be calling him from across the room while Ruth's pale eyes seemed to plead with him vaguely from the other end of her as her cheeks filled and hollowed.

Gil turned his head toward Sean; his jaw was slack and his eyes wide. "Damn, Sean. Come on."

"I… I don't know if I can," Sean groaned.

"Sean—*Nnnnnnn*—my fucking sister spread her legs—"

Ruth spoke around Gil's penis. "Actually, she was on all fours. *Phoebe* spread—"

Gil thrust into her mouth.

Sean's feet led him to the chair. His knees gave way, placing him level with Ruth. She smiled and sucked. Gil was beginning to pant.

Sean reached out and ran his thumb up the length of Ruth's lips as Gil had done; she shivered, causing the ring to bounce against her round left breast. Decisiveness flooded back into Sean sure and simple, and with the same certainty with which he had gone off to slay monsters and rescue fair maidens (and others), he bent forward and kissed the nearly hidden bud of Ruth's clit.

They say that smell is the most primal of the senses, connected to the most primitive part of the brain, and so tied closely to memories. Taste is a close second though, and the minute Sean's tongue began to lap at Ruth, her tang sent him back into his mind to another night just before a wedding, Will and Nancy's, when he'd been slightly less drunk but a lot more anxious. Diana had talked Gil into switching rooms without telling Sean. He had been about to pull his I'm-not-good-enough-for-you, I'm-going-to-be-gone-at-the-end-of-the-summer act again, terrified as he was that he wouldn't be able to let her go if she so much as touched him. She hadn't touched him, not at first. She had simply removed her clothing. Very slowly. Silently. Her eyes still on his, challenging, pleading, she had climbed into the bed next to him, and waited. She hadn't had to wait long.

They hadn't fucked that first night—neither of them felt ready, or at least *Sean* hadn't, and Diana had respected that. But they did explore in other ways, and after she had timidly kissed him to an explosive ejaculation—white droplets like pearls in her hair—he had returned the favor, kissing at her privates and then lapping at them, catlike.

The look of astonishment on Diana's face when she had come had filled Sean with more pride and joy than any other single accomplishment that he could remember.

Ruth's tasted similar, tangy and tart, but the texture against his tongue, around his fingers was quite different. And the sounds...

Ruth loosed a muffled shriek, her cunt pulsing against Sean's mouth, and Gil howled. Sean knew that howl well, though he'd never been in the same room before when it was bellowed. Sean's friend collapsed to the floor, his cock splattering come across Ruth's body and Sean's face. "Damn," Gil said, and blinked. "Sorry. Damn."

"'S all right," Sean muttered, wiping his cheek with his sleeve. "Well, that was nice..."

"Oh, no, Sean," Ruth burbled, her eyes bright as Sean had never seen them. "It wouldn't do for you to leave now. I really do want to make you come, you know."

"Uh..."

"Also," she continued, her tone returning to its normal airiness, "I still want someone inside of me."

"No problem," grunted Gil. He stood, and Sean was astonished to note that Gil was still hard. He lifted Ruth into the air—"Wee!"—sat in her place, and lowered her back onto his lap.

"Oh, how nice," purred Ruth, arranging her knees on either side of his hips and lowered herself onto his stiff, speckled cock. "*OH*, yes, *very* nice!"

Sean began to back away, but Ruth arched around toward him. "Well, Sean, what would you like? You can fuck my bottom, or Gilbert and I can take turns licking you."

Gil blinked.

"Uh, not that, Ruth, no," sputtered Sean.

"Oh, good," Ruth said. "I've always enjoyed anal sex, especially when I've got something occupying my vagina. I've never had penises in both at the same time, however."

Again Sean's body began moving before his mind had really absorbed the situation, let alone considered the proposition. He had dropped his pants and shuffled back to where Ruth's plump, moonlike bottom was rising and setting on Gil's horizon before he had time to think.

"Here," Ruth said, leaning over and grabbing the bottle of lube and opening it expertly with one hand. She smoothed the slick liquid over Sean's cock, leaving him breathless. "Oh, what a nice penis you have, Sean. It's just perfect. *Ahhh!*" Ruth gasped as Gil began nibbling on her nipples.

Touching his cock, Sean realized that it was as slick as ice in a warm drink. Lovely or not, its need was urgent. Sean's hunger howled as he reached trembling hands out and touched Ruth's soft, white haunch, stopping her in mid-bounce.

"Oh," she managed to murmur—Gil was continuing his assault on her breasts—as she squeezed what seemed like most of what remained of the lube onto two of her fingers and deftly worked it up her ass. Then her fingers slid out and it was there, waiting for him. Open. Glistening.

Grasping his erection by the base in numb fingers, Sean whimpered as his cock touched Ruth's puckered rear hole, pressed, and pushed through the tight ring of muscle.

"*FUCK!*" all three of them cried out.

Sean was only a few inches in—two thirds of his cock still waited outside of her ass—but as he began to thrust in as gently as he could manage, he could feel Gil's cock jumping inside of her cunt through the thin membrane separating the two passages. Sean felt Gil's huge hands clamp over his own; together they kept Ruth still as they began to move together inside of her.

"*FUCK!*" Ruth screamed as they began to find a rhythm together, thrusting up into her, front and back. "*FUCKING FUCK! DAMN!*" Her head was flung back against Sean's shoulder, her chest against Gil's face. She was flush from her nipples up, and a string of most un-Ruth-like obscenity spewed from her mouth. "*GOD! FUCK MY...! FUCK!*"

Her bottom was tight; even with the lube it took him two minutes of thrusting before he felt his balls brush against Gil's and he knew that he was all of the way in.

He and Diana had tried anal sex twice—once by accident when they'd been fucking for so long that Sean had flipped her, pushed in, and only realized that he'd pressed into the wrong entry when she squawked. In her shock she had squeezed him so hard that, even after three rounds earlier that day, he had came instantly. They'd tried it again on his most recent birthday, but while he had loved it, she had complained of discomfort afterward, and so Sean hadn't suggested it again. There were plenty of other ways to play, and he didn't want his playmate

Ruth seemed to be enjoying herself enormously.

Sean was going to have to ask Frank about that lubrication.

That was if he ever had a reason to sleep with Diana again.

The wedding.

Could they get married now?

Sean loved Gil. He loved Ruth, after a fashion—at the moment, his hips slapping against her bottom as Gil's thighs squeezed Sean's, he loved her a *lot*—but even buried in another woman's ass and with full certainty that Diana'd had Jonny Powers buried in *her*, Sean was certain as he could have been that

Diana was the person he wanted to wake up to for the rest of his life, that he wanted to have children with, that he could see himself growing old beside, that he could trust to stand beside him in sickness and in health.

Trust.

He and Diana were going to have a *very* interesting conversation tomorrow. Later today. Before the wedding if he could manage it. After if need be.

"*GuguEWR-AAAAAAAAAAAAA*!" Ruth screamed as Sean and Gil slammed into her from either side. She pulled Sean's hands from her hips up to her breasts, where Gil was still grazing. Gil's cock thrusting along the length of Sean's own. The tight loop of Ruth's ass squeezing him tight, *pulsing*.

A scream answered by two more as first Sean and then Gil poured into Ruth's body.

Breathless, slick, they collapsed.

"Fuck," Gil gasped.

Sean's softening cock twitched, triggering another spasm through Ruth, followed by a giggle. "Bread around a sandwich," she sighed followed by a last, diffuse, "Wee!"

Sean could feel Gil's breath hot on his neck as they both laughed limply.

"I hope I can walk for the wedding," Ruth said. "I wouldn't want to miss that."

Sean saw Gil's brow furl, guilt and uncertainty playing across his friend's broad, open face. Gil and Phoebe had never seemed to trust each other or themselves quite as much as Sean and Diana did. "'S all right, Gil," Sean said. He kissed the back of Ruth's neck.

"Hmmm," she murmured. "'I want to be... a macho man...'"

And with that, she passed out.

Sean backed away from Ruth, his softening cock disengaging from her ass with a loud *plop*. She shuddered and curled tighter around Gil.

Gil, who was panting. Staring wide-eyed at Sean. "Damn. Sean. We just... Phoebe'll *kill* me."

"You can take turns killing each other," Sean said, trying to calm the tumult in his own chest.

"I... How can we get...?"

"Talk to her, Gil. They're going to feel just as terrible as we do."

"But we aren't supposed to... Before the..."

"Talk to her."

Gil nodded, "Yeah. *Talk*." He looked up at Sean over Ruth's slumped head, his face contorted as if he were working on a particularly challenging chess problem. "I just... I couldn't stand it if... She doesn't handle booze well, Phoebe. I know she only did it 'cause she was drunk and 'cause she thought I..." Gil blinked and stroked Ruth's back, then gave a small grin and looked back up at Sean. "I... I've always wanted to..."

In spite of the nagging sobriety that was creeping over him, Sean smiled. Ruth's face was slack on Gil's shoulder; naked on his friend as she was, Sean found to his surprise that she was quite beautiful. "Yeah," he said. "That was pretty amazing. I've always wondered what it would be like with her."

"Oh. Yeah. That too," Gil said, and then, for some reason, blushed. "Think we should try to get her home?"

"Let's put her in my bed. I'll sleep out here." Sean murmured, his eyes still moving over Ruth's form. "If the girls come over... Well, I wake faster than you do."

"True," Gil said with a weak grin. He stood, still holding Ruth.

Her legs wrapped instinctively around his waist. "I want to live at the Y... M... mmm... C...'" She buried her face in Gil's neck and fell back to snoring.

"Need a hand?"

"No," Gil sighed, shifting his hands to her ass. "Sean... Do you...? Are we going to be okay?"

"Yeah, Gil," Sean sighed, righting the sofa and pulling a blanket from one of the ferns. "We'll be just fine."

Fantasy is More than Black and White

Most straight guys would have considered dating a hot bisexual girl a fantasy — even if it only lasted a week and she never did get around to inviting one of her girlfriends in for the porn-requisite threesome.

Unlike most straight guys, it hadn't ever occurred to Trey to fantasize about any of that. Besides, it had been years ago.

But when that hot bisexual ended up marrying Trey's sister Dianne… Well, that wasn't the stuff of fantasy *at all*.

Trey didn't mind that his sister was marrying a woman. He was happy to serve as her best man. Ecstatic.

No.

What was throwing Trey for a loop through the whole ceremony wasn't that Dianne, who'd come out to him when she was twelve, was marrying another woman. It was that she was marrying *Lara*. Lara Jefferson. Who had slept with everything that moved during college, and after. Including — for one very, very weird week — Trey.

There was something really disturbing about watching your sister say *I do* to the only woman that *you* had schtupped since graduation other than your own beloved wife. Something unsettling about watching your sister kiss her bride, and having that bride give you a really nasty wink.

It was like having a wet dream turn into a nightmare.

Trey liked Lara. She was smart. Funny. Had a really amazing repertoire in bed. An amazing mouth, which Trey had been working very hard not to think of as touching his sister in any way. He liked Lara. He just didn't trust her.

She enjoyed making mischief way too much.

No one knew about their brief fling. It had been during one of the occasional… breaks that he and Jeanne had taken from each other. The last one, actually, before Trey had proposed for the fourth time and Jeanne had finally accepted. Even at the time, he'd known his fling with Lara was a one-time thing. Fun and games. And Trey had been too conventional to find that anything but sad — *way* too conventional for Lara. She'd made that clear over and over. Kept laughing and asking, "How the hell did I end up in bed with *you?*" Usually right before she jumped on top of him again.

They'd both agreed at the end of it that it had been nice, but that they'd never tell anyone about it. And so far, they'd both stuck with that. At least, Trey had. So far as he knew, Lara hadn't told anyone. But with her, one never knew....

If Dianne had known, she'd have given him shit about it, he was sure of that. Dianne — with her gallery of tattoos, her vegan food business, and her Buddha-like acceptance of whatever the universe threw at her — was much more Lara's speed. And Lara really did seem to love Dianne. More to the point, Dianne loved Lara.

Still, as Trey watched the brides walk in matching white dresses back up the aisle while the guests cheered, he had to shake himself and tell himself that everything was great. Wonderful. Happy. Fantastic.

A familiar whiff of two parts Estée Lauder and one part book mold enwrapped him, making him truly happy as Jeanne's unique scent announced a more substantial embrace, and turning Trey's world better again.

"We've done it," he sighed.

Jeanne kissed his ear. "Done...?"

"They're married. We've discharged our duties."

"Well," she said with her small, deceptive librarian's smile, "we do have the pictures. And the speeches. But then, yes, I think you and I have earned a chance to get royally drunk. And then, you know what, Trey?" She bit his ear.

Shivering, he shook his head.

"Well, I think, after we've danced and had plenty of good food and drink, I think we should retire to our room and fuck like bonobos."

"Uh, okay."

Yes. Trey's world was rapidly improving.

The pictures went incredibly smoothly — thanks to Will, the photographer, who had been a friend of Dianne's and Trey's since they were kids together.

Dinner at the reception was an amazing spread (vegetarian, naturally) — though there was a mix-up about the wine that the caterer and Trey agreed to talk about *later.*

Trey got up and told a few obligatory embarrassing stories about Dianne, said that he knew that his sister was incredibly lucky to have found someone like Lara (though he didn't say that he knew just how lucky Dianne was), and he wished them the happiest of lives.

Once the polite applause died down, Jeanne stood up and told the assembled crowd that she had known both of the brides for over a decade and had never seen them happier than they were both that night, and that she knew that they would be only happier as the years went on. That she knew that, for Lara and Dianne, the reality of marriage would outstrip the dream of the wedding.

Then she quoted what her own father had said at their wedding: "Marriage is a journey that starts long before a day like this, and carries on, we dearly hope and trust, for many, many decades into the future. It is not a place at which one arrives or a point in time at which the couple can rest easy. It is a path that leads down the aisle and into the future. This wedding is more our celebration of your partnership than any bonding that any institution could fashion." Jeanne lifted her champagne. "Dianne, Lara — tread the path well."

After the room all toasted and gave another round of applause, Jeanne said, "And now, it's time for cake, and fun!"

That brought the largest cheer of all.

As the band — led by another old friend, Jeff — rocked away at a waltz, Trey found himself dancing with his sister, of course. He congratulated her for what felt like the four hundredth time, and she laughed and cried and kissed him on the cheek.

When Lara's father broke in to dance with his new daughter-in-law, Trey turned and found himself dancing… with Lara. Of course. Who had that supremely mischievous smirk on her face.

"Congratulations," he said. "Welcome to the family."

"Thanks." She threw her arms around his neck and kissed him on the same cheek that Dianne had just smooched. "Funny to think of you as a brother, when I know just what you've got in your boxers and just how well you use it."

Trey felt himself go red, but as he took her in his arms and began to one-two-three, he managed to spit out, "Uh… Thanks." After a deep breath, he added, "Of course, if the kind of thing that's in my boxers was that important to you, you wouldn't have married Dianne. And I'm working very hard to avoid thinking of what you know about what my sister has in her panties."

"Good point!" Lara laughed, as Trey had hoped she would. Then she pushed up on tiptoe and whispered wetly in his ear. "Of course, Dianne's not wearing any panties. Neither am I."

When she stepped back, Trey just stood there, staring at her, and Lara laughed again. "Sorry! Well, not really. But, Trey, bro, I want you to think about *that* when she takes off my garter." She raised her eyebrows in exaggerated suggestion. "And look! Here comes your wife. Why don't you dance with her, and I'll go see if I can smooch mine. Hi, Jeannie!" Lara gave Jeanne too a kiss on the cheek, leaving a bright red lipstick mark, and then she moved off into the crowd.

"You've got lipstick on your cheek," Trey said, pulling out his hankie to try to cover his discomfort. He wiped his wife's cheek clean.

Jeanne took the hankie from his hand. "So do you — two sets, actually. Well done!" She tidied him up as well, and they began to dance. After a moment, looking off at the newlyweds, Jeanne asked with a small frown, "So... what were you and Lara talking about?"

"Oh," said Trey, fighting down the queasy feeling of having to lie to his wife, even a bit, "she was just giving me shit, the way she always does."

"Yes," agreed Jeanne, and they danced.

The evening wound down, the guests wandered off to their rooms or to their homes and at last, it was time to get really drunk.

Trey grabbed a bottle of first-rate scotch from the bar (knowing it was already paid for) and Jeff, finally off of the stage, corralled the brides, who were still going strong, Will, and Jeanne, and they all sat at one of the tables and began to swap stories about the wedding — about other weddings. About school. After a half hour, one of the caterer's staff apologized, but asked if they'd mind heading somewhere else, since they needed to clean up, and Dianne invited everyone up to the bridal suite.

"You sure you want us up there?" asked Trey.

"Oh, brother-in-law of mine," said Lara, "I've been boffing your sister for four years, and I intend to keep doing it for a good long time. I think we can keep our hands off each other for a little while."

Dianne squealed the way that she'd always done as a kid when Trey had teased her about the girls that she'd had crushes on. It made Trey smile to hear that sound again.

Everyone seemed in agreement: up to the bridal suite it would be for the after-party. As they all headed out the door, the caterer ran up and buttonholed Trey. "About the shiraz...?"

Trey groaned and waved his wife and friends on. "I'll join you guys as soon as we've got this sorted out."

Jeff lifted the bottle of scotch in salute, and the five left the ballroom.

"So," sighed Trey, "it wasn't supposed to be shiraz, it was supposed to be..."

When at last, a good forty minutes later, Trey finally slouched his way up to the hotel's bridal suite, Will and Dianne were both weeping with laughter on the huge bed, while Jeff stood beside them, apparently examining the carpet really, really carefully. Lara was sitting at the small table, lips parted, eyes sparkling, an almost-empty drink held at a dangerous angle at her shoulder, her pale eyes boring through Trey.

Jeanne sat primly beside her, slightly flushed but barely holding in a small grin. *Damn.*

They'd polished off a considerable proportion of the scotch.

"Trey! You're back!" Dianne raised a glass that sloshed whisky. "The hero's hero! You really are the best man!"

Trey flashed her a salute.

Jeanne lifted her chin; a subtle invitation, but one that Trey knew to promise heaven — or possibly hell. He walked to her and started to lean down, when she threw her arms around his neck and pulled him into a knee-weakening, peat-tinged kiss.

The onlookers cheered, his fucking sister loudest of all.

Once he had accepted Jeanne's whisky-flavored smooch, he poured himself a full tumbler. He'd just wasted nearly an hour bickering with the damned caterer about the difference between shiraz and pinot noir, and he really, really wanted to get on with the fun. He kissed his wife again once he'd pounded down the whole shot, poured himself another, and asked, "So what's so funny? Sounded from outside like you guys were dying."

"God, death by laughter! What a way to go!" snorted Will.

"We were talking," said his wife, enunciating very carefully, "about fantasies."

"Fa...?" Trey blinked at Jeanne, and then at the rest.

"Yes, Trey," said Lara, her voice managing to sound simultaneously utterly innocent and absolutely lascivious. "I was just telling everyone that I don't have any."

Whatever Trey had been bracing himself for, that wasn't it. He tried very hard not to laugh, but failed spectacularly, inhaling half of his drink and snorting most of the rest painfully through his nose. "Don't...?"

"Apparently," laughed Dianne, "whenever lovely Lala gets an itch, she just sort of scratches it, so she never gets to the fantasy stage."

Trey stared at Lara, who smiled malevolently back at him and sighed, "Well, it doesn't seem like a good idea to hold those sorts of impulses in, does it? I've had sex with just about everyone I've wanted to have sex with, in just about every way I have wanted to. I quite enjoy it. Why should I wait?"

"Good question, Lara," chuckled Will, winking at Dianne. "So long as your bride's in the mix, it sounds like a great idea."

Lara smiled at Dianne. "Of course. I would never, *ever* want to disappoint her."

Dianne snorted and asked, "You mean there isn't *anyone* you've wanted to screw that you haven't?"

"Well," said Lara, staring at the ceiling in something like thought, "I suppose that technically there are a few people... For example, Jeff, I haven't slept with you or...." Lara suddenly trained all of that evil focus on Trey. "Jeannie, may I fuck your husband? You've always said how nice his cock is." She gave him an echo of the wink she'd shot over Dianne's shoulder at the end of the wedding.

Trey started to cough uncontrollably, while Jeff and Will dissolved into laughter again, and Dianne, naturally, squealed.

"I'm afraid," answered Jeanne, eyes bright, "that that is one impulse that we shall have to ask you to refrain from indulging. For the moment." Then she pinched his ass and he yelped, leading to another round of general merriment.

"Oh," sighed Lara, once the room had settled again. Lifting her glass, she winked. "How nice. I suppose that I can keep that as a fantasy then, after all. Thank you." She turned toward the trio on the bed. "Well, I would still like to fuck Jeff's brains out. Dianne, would that be all right with you?"

At first Trey thought Lara must be joking, but she got up and floated toward her wife and the guitarist.

Jeff got a predatory look that always gave Trey the heebie-jeebies — since it had so often been aimed at Trey's sister, who didn't like boys...

But Dianne inexplicably said, "Since you already know... Depends on if I get to join. Jeff?"

Face suddenly softening, Jeff squeezed her hand and reached the other out toward Lara, who took it and purred, "Works for me. Okay, Will?"

Trey's jaw was somewhere around his ankles. He knew he should say something, but couldn't even think where to start.

"Uh... Umm," Will stammered, eyes wide.

"We haven't talked about *your* fantasies yet, Willy-boy," Jeff said gruffly, an arm around each bride's waist, "but I bet they aren't too far from mine, right?"

"Actually," said Lara, "I happen to know that your fantasies and his aren't the same, but they fit together pretty fucking well."

Jeff blinked, and Will just nodded mutely, his dark skin darkening even further.

"Will likes to watch," said Dianne, reaching across Jeff's legs and running a finger up her wife's thigh.

"And take pictures," added Lara, drawing out that last word in a way that made it sound... incredibly nasty.

The four of them locked eyes, looking as if they might go at it right there and then, and Trey would have exploded, but fortunately Jeanne cleared her throat. "Well, now that that's settled," she said, as if addressing a city council meeting, "perhaps Trey and I should head off to our room. Good night, everyone."

Four sets of eyes owled at them. Before Trey could think of anything to say, Jeanne grabbed his hand and pulled him out of the bridal suite.

Trey's brain began to boil with images like some obscene stew: Lara, well, he'd always known, but *Dianne...?* She'd never even been with a guy, so far as he knew. And Jeff, well, a guy *would*, but *not with Trey's sister*, and... *Watching?*

At the stairwell, he turned to go back down the hall and stop whatever they were getting up to before it got too far, but Jeanne grabbed his shoulder, pushed him against the banister and very demurely stuck her tongue down his throat.

Any thought of Lara or Jeff or any of the rest of it went right out of his head. Part of him was boiling still, but it wasn't his brain, and his senses overflowed with curly brown hair and his wife's whisky-hot mouth and *ass*....

"Have I got your full attention, now, Trey?"

He grunted and reached to pull her back, but she wiggled away, flashing the *I'm-a-wicked-girl-but-only-for-you* smirk that always drove him wild.

Fuck Jeff and the rest. Fuck Lara. Trey chased Jeanne down the remaining two flights to their room, her giggling the whole way, but staying just out of his grasp. At their room, he finally grabbed hold of her, and she wriggled again, but he had her now, pressed between him and a thick oak door, his hands working under her dress, up her thigh, fingers along the edge of lacy undies, pulling, and...

She opened the door and the two of them tumbled through onto the floor of their room with an *oof!* from him and a high-pitched squawk from her.

Just as he was about to kick the door closed and ravish her right there on the floor, she rolled out from under him — and he ended up full-body-planting on the very nice but very hard floor.

Not only had he fallen on his nose, he'd fallen on his erection, thank you very much. "Fuck," moaned Trey as he closed the door, rubbing both sore spots, "gonna be hard getting *that* hard again."

"It is?" pouted Jeanne. Somehow, she had made her way to the bed, and was draped across it, her dress shed, lying there in nothing but the really naughty, really tiny sapphire blue silk things that Dianne'd helped him buy for Jeanne's last birthday.

"Uh," said Trey, finding himself stumbling towards the bed with no memory of having stood, "no."

He slid himself between her thighs and kissed her hard. She pressed the whole of her bountiful body against him, and helped him peel away his tux without breaking the kiss.

When they were almost to the point of no return — just enough brain cells and clothing left to keep them from plunging over the cliff, and knowing that if they plunged now, he wouldn't last as long as he'd like — he pushed back on both arms and gazed down at her.

There she was, the Jeanne that he loved most: hair tangled, cheeks red, lips wet and red. Eyes wide with lust. *Damn.* "So," he began, not knowing what he was going to say. "Fantasies?"

"Mmmm," said Jeanne, her legs wrapping around Trey's and causing her lacy, silky panties to tangle against his boxers in a really, really distracting way.

"Jeff's was, what? Being with two women?"

"Yes," she sighed, shivering as goose pimples sprang up across her chest. "Not surprising, but it was so funny, because he was so embarrassed."

"Well, yeah." He reached between her breasts to try to unbuckle the bra. "Who wouldn't be? And Jeff, he's embarrassed to talk about anything without a mic in his face."

"True!" she said, laughing; her breasts bounced on either side of his struggling hand in a manner that really didn't make the task any easier, but which he really couldn't say he minded. "And of course, *Lara* wasn't at all embarrassed. Nor was Dianne, for that matter. She — "

"Yeah, never mind what her fantasies were, thanks. Probably something I'd really rather not know."

She stroked his chin. The damned buckle still refused to operate, and now, with one of her arms up, that breast pressed up against his hand, and he really wanted — "Trey?"

"Hmmm?"

"What's yours? Your fantasy? Two women? Or watching, like Will? Or just... another woman?"

She was suddenly very still. She had her frightened-little-girl face on, the one that always killed him — not the put-on pout, but the one that she'd used to get when they were young, when all the nerdiness and bossiness melted away because he'd done something...

"Jeanne?"

"Trey... When we... Before we were married. I don't want to know. But... Did you ever...? Were you ever with anyone else? While we were not together?"

He'd never said anything about Lara — he'd rather swallow ground glass, because he knew it would kill Jeanne. But he couldn't lie, not to her. "I... Yeah."

The little-girl face got even sadder. Even smaller.

"Jeanne, it wasn't ever... It was — "

She lay a finger across his lips and he stopped. "I don't want to know."

He nodded. Tried not to scream *Thank God!* though that's what he felt like doing. They lay there, staring into each other's eyes, still as they were so infrequently still. "Uh. Jeanne?"

"Yes, Trey. I did too."

"Oh." A weird mix of feelings steeplechased around his guts: cold fear, hot anger, and — weirdest of all — liquid desire. "Oh."

"Do you want to know, Trey?" Her voice was so quiet, he'd almost believe it wasn't there, if he couldn't feel it humming against his hand, which was still sandwiched between her silk-encased breasts.

Did he? He wasn't sure. Well, to be honest, he *didn't* want to know, definitely not, but he had learned his own weaknesses well enough over the years to know that it would eat at him, that it would grow like one of the tumors that old

Aunt Agnes was continually complaining about the doctors cutting off of her. "Uh. I think I need to."

She nodded.

"Who?"

"Well," she said and bit her lip.

"Come on, Jeanne," Trey said, more cheerfully than he felt. "It was before we were married. I promise not to cut the guy's dick off. At least, not while anyone's watching."

She tried not very successfully to smile. "It wasn't… That's why I asked actually."

Trey frowned down at his wife, confused for once not by her ridiculous vocabulary and stratospheric logic but by her unaccountable timidity.

She took a deep breath. "When… Up in bridal suite, when Lara was talking about not having fantasies…"

"Yeah," he prompted. "When she said she'd slept with everyone she'd wanted to?"

Jeanne nodded. "You see, she was very clear. I was sure that you would work it out. I mean, she's been living with Dianne. And of course she and Will saw each other for a few months right after graduation…" She looked up into his face, and then back down. "And *then* Lara mentioned that she had always wanted to, to sleep with you and with Jeff. And that left…" She stopped and bit her lip again.

Trey waited for her to finish, but she just stared up at him, eyes wide and pleading, waiting for the dime to drop. Which it finally did. "*LARA?* You and *Lara?*"

She gave a small, timid nod.

"Wow." He couldn't think of anything else to say.

"It was just for a couple of weeks, that last winter that you and I were, were not seeing each other."

Around the same time *he* was shacked up with Lara.

Lara and Jeanne…

Wow

"And it was very lovely," Jeanne continued, her voice pitched as it always was when she was embarrassed or upset and trying to pretend not to be, "but I didn't think it was something I needed to explore any further, and you're all I ever really wanted, even when you leave your clothes on the living room floor, and I never felt as if I could tell you because even with you being Dianne's brother, I didn't know if you'd be disgusted" — he shook his head — "or puerile and typically male about the idea of me with a another woman, when it was very much *not* about you." She finally ran out of breath and lay panting beneath him, eyes still wide.

"Uh," Trey said, mostly to let her know she didn't need to keep talking. "Probably a good choice." Lara and his Jeanne?

Wow. Even in the moment it struck Trey as funny that where it had never occurred to him to get off on the idea of Lara with any other girl, the idea of Lara with his *wife....!*

He needed tell her about himself and Lara. But not now. Now he had something else that he needed to say to Jeanne. He looked down at her — eyes wide, mouth small, face flushed — and sighed. "Want to know *my* fantasy?" he asked. Before she could start speaking again, he continued, "It's the same one I've had since I met you. It involves a smart-mouthed brainiac with light brown hair lying on the bed we share, her legs around my back, both of us moaning each other's names, naked as the day we were born."

And with a pinch of finger and thumb, he finally popped the front clasp to her bra, freeing those glorious, thick-nippled breasts, to her delight and his.

"There's the naked bit," he said, and she gasped as his thumbs circled either nipple. He pressed his whole body against her, his cock working its way past the band of his boxers and onto her belly. She reached between them, pulled her panties to one side and guided him in — not gently, like she usually did, but firm and rough, and they both screamed.

"Th-there's the calling the names bit," she moaned, and then they didn't speak for a while.

The first time Trey and Jeanne fucked it had been her honest-to-goodness First Time, and he'd been terrified of hurting her. He wanted it to be perfect. It was the fall after his graduation — her junior year — and they'd been emailing and texting and calling, and he was in town for a job interview, and after, he'd gone to the library, and she'd swept down the stacks toward him, her eyes bright... They hadn't expected it, either of them: they'd smacked together like a pair of cannon balls, and all of the students had giggled, and the pair of old librarians — what were their names? — had whisked them up the stairs at the back to the stacks to a small office, and they had found themselves on the couch, gasping and panting, clothes disappearing as if by magic, and all Trey could think of was that it should be wonderful for her. Trey had kissed Jeanne and licked her every way he knew how. He'd kept pulling back from actually penetrating her until she'd finally screamed, "*Fuck it, Trey, just FUCK ME, PLEASE!*"

And he had. And it had been fucking fantastic.

And of course, Dianne had just happened to be at the bottom of the stairs. So when Trey and Jeanne finally came down, it was to a room full of very amused looking college students, a *very* amused looking Dianne, and a movable whiteboard reading FUCK IT, TREY, JUST FUCK ME, PLEASE!

Jeanne hadn't been able to show her face in the library for weeks after.

Their lovemaking had never been quiet, and it wasn't now.

When they finally came, howling and bellowing, to a halt, they were tangled, sweaty, panting.

Shreds of Jeanne's lovely panties were somehow tangled in her hair and Trey's toes.

"So," Jeanne said, breathlessly, "something like?"

"Huh?"

"Your fantasy?"

"Oh, yeah," he said, taking her earlobe between his teeth, causing her to shudder in such a way that he nearly came again. "Fuck *yeah!*" When their bodies had stopped exploding for a moment, he whispered into her ear, "Great thing 'bout my fantasy, I get to live it all the time. Not always as often as I'd like, mind, but plenty. "

She laughed, her cunt squeezing him tight. "Like Lara."

"Yeah."

"How often *would* you like, you ingrate?"

"Dunno that my body could actually survive that. But I wouldn't mind finding out." He squeezed her ass.

"Silly boy," she said in the special exasperated tone she saved just for him, and wriggled out from beneath him, trotting off to the toilet as she always did after a good fuck.

Trey flopped onto his back, his cock still lifting exultantly into the air.

Jeannie, may I fuck your husband? You've always said how nice his cock is.

Trey shuddered, his balls contracting.

What he was thinking of, it surprised him to find, wasn't an image of Lara and Jeanne kissing or fucking or whatever it was that two women did. It was of Jeanne's face. Jeanne's voice.

"Starting again without me?" that voice called through the mist of his burgeoning fantasy. To his surprise he found that he was stroking himself. *Did Jeanne puff her cheeks out and bite her lip when she came? What was it like?*

Shithead. He'd just seen what it was like.

He rolled on his side, still stroking away. "Was thinking about what you look like when you're excited."

"Mmm." She dropped the bathrobe she'd tossed on and lay down, facing him. "You get to see that all the time."

"Lucky me."

"Well, lucky me too!" She kissed his nose.

He ran his fingertips lightly over the hair of her arm, along the pinky, up the hip and around the fuzz of her ass. She shivered. She was always incredibly sensitive after they'd fucked. "You didn't just now, though, did you?"

"What?" Her eyes were closed; she looked like a very content cat. "Have an orgasm?"

"Yeah. We kind of went straight for the main event."

"I have no complaint."

He ran his fingers up her ribs, counting them. "Maybe, but it doesn't seem fair. And you know me and fair."

"Too true. I should never have gone and fallen in love with a *nice* boy." She grinned as she said this and shivered again; an army of goose pimples charged across her chest.

"Like you had any choice in the matter."

She raised an eyebrow, but remained silent.

"So," he said, pinching her earlobe lightly, "what's yours?"

"What?" she said, her voice deep and sounding very much as if she'd just been fucked really well, and was about to be again. "My... fantasy?"

"Uh-huh," Trey said, trailing a finger along the line of her chin. He loved her chin. "I mean, you got to hear a couple of mine for the price of one." *Actually, you gave me one I didn't realize I had*, he thought, but didn't say. "So what about yours?"

She grinned and arched as his finger — barely touching her skin — drew a line down the front of her throat. "Can't you guess?"

"Huh." Trey spread his hand so that thumb and fingers brushed along her collarbones. "Anything to do with academic robes?" She loved wearing them whenever the occasion warranted, which was almost never. He loved her in them because they made her happy.

She giggled, shuddering, so that her breasts bounced deliciously just below his hand. "Sounds more like one of yours."

"I prefer you *out* of robes, academic or otherwise." With his palm close enough to feel the heat rising from her skin, he skimmed the side of one perfect breast. "So, okay.... Something to do with the library?" As his palm left the breast behind, he allowed one fingernail to scratch lightly along the soft, pale flesh.

"N'guh."

"I beg your pardon, Mrs. Sayers, please speak clearly." With his thumb pad he began to count the bumps on her areola. "Did I get it?"

"Um." She arched again, and he could smell her excitement and the scent of their recent fuck rising again. "Not... quite. Closer."

"That so?" His hand moved on from the hypersensitive flesh of her breast and she gave a gasp of disappointment. His fingers trailed down her belly, circled her belly button and slithered their way into the tangle of hair below. "Getting closer, am I?"

Just as his finger was about to brush along the frilly cowl around her clit, she growled and pushed him onto his back. Surprised, he pulled his hand away, but she barked, "No!" and pulled his fingers back to her cunt.

Trey hadn't fallen in love with Jeanne because he minded being told what to do, now and then.

As he went back to caressing her cunt lips, she reached behind her to the nightstand. "Here," she grunted. Onto his chest thunked a heavy book.

"Uh?"

"Read it."

"Read…?"

Her face darkened and her eyes closed. "Read it. To me."

Perplexed, he reached up with both hands to grab the book, but once again she barked, "*No!*" and pulled his right hand back between her legs.

With his left hand, he picked up the book. *Paradise Lost.* New edition. Of fucking course. "You want me to…?"

"Read. It." She rolled her pelvis against his hand; without thinking, he stroked her, and she hissed.

He was about to apply himself entirely to diddling her to a screaming orgasm when she pushed the book back up, blocking his view, and opened it.

"If you insist, my dear," he said.

"I do."

With a quick breath for luck, trying to keep the fingers in his right hand playing across her pussy while his left hand kept the book still, he read. "*Of Man's First Disobedience, and the Fruit/Of that Forbidden Tree, whose mortal taste…*"

He read. He diddled. It wasn't exactly easy; his hands weren't Trey's preferred tools for getting Jeanne off, and doing it one-handed while simultaneously trying to focus on reading out loud from the least interesting book Trey had ever opened reminded Trey of sneaking with Dianne up into the attic with stolen cookies. The cookies tasted just as delicious, but the attic was every bit as nasty, and it was an even guess whether delicious or nasty would win out.

"…*and transgress his Will/For one restraint…* *Hey, you want me to read the footnotes?*"

Jeanne choked out something that sounded like *please*, and went back to helping press Trey's hand against her labia.

"*Here we go: one restraint.* That is, the single injunction against eating from the tree of the knowledge of good and evil (Genesis 2:17). *Damn. When he started talking about* restraint, *I kind of hoped —* "

"Trey." Jeanne sounded as if she were being diddled, and as if she were playing with her tits, which she was, but she also sounded as if she were getting annoyed.

Slipping his middle finger in to her wet, sticky cunt, he looked for his place on the page. "Right. Let's see. Uh. Right. *…and transgress his Will/For one restraint, Lords of the World besides?/Who first seduc'd them to that foul revolt?*"

He brought his right thumb to bear and was rewarded by a not-quite-stifled squeal of pleasure.

This might turn out to be fun after all, *he decided.*

As Trey read on and on about the fall of Lucifer — who sounded much more interesting than anyone else in the poem — his wife began to make unmistakable sounds of arousal. In Jeanne's case, this meant that she began swearing under her breath: "Shit. Oh, shit. Fuck. Oh."

He had just reached the climax of the first book — Satan coming before the assembled demons of Hell — when he felt a light touch just above his hip that made him nearly drop the book. Jeanne was running the rounded end of her favorite pen across his skin. "Jeanne? What…?"

"Taking... (Oh, fuck, fuck, shit, cunt) ...notes... Read. (Fuck…)"

On he read. On he diddled. On her pen flicked, here and there across his hip and belly.

When he reached the moment when Satan flew off toward the gates of Hell, Jeanne gave a shout and pushed Trey's hand away. Before he could ask what had happened, she lifted the book slightly to give herself room, threw her leg across Trey's waist and sank down onto his cock, causing both of them to swear almost in unison.

"*Read*," gasped Jeanne, and began to rock her pelvis against Trey. To drive the point home, she started "taking notes" again, doodling on his chest and belly with the soft side of the pen. This actually made it really, really *hard* to do what she asked, but he tried, lifting the book in both hands — enough to read from, but not so much that he couldn't see her half-closed eyes and open mouth, the sheen of sweat across her forehead.

"Satan with thoughts inflam'd of highest design,/Puts on swift wings, and towards the Gates of Hell …"

He read on, his hands trembling as his pelvis began to match Jeanne's rhythm. He reached out with his left hand, which Jeanne pulled against an unseen, bouncing breast.

"…But glad that now his Sea should find a shore,/With fresh alacritie and force renew'd/Springs upward like a Pyramid of fire/Into the wilde expanse …" *Trey's hips were slapping hard against the insides of Jeanne's thighs as he thrust up into her, as she slammed down onto him.* Springs upward like a Pyramid of fire…!

"*SHIT!*" screamed Jeanne, dropping her pen to the bed, note-taking forgotten. "*FUCK IT, FUCK ME, TREY, FUCK!*" Her knees squeezed against his ribs and her cunt pulsed *hard* around his cock, lighting his own fuse so that he thrust only once more, lifting her off of the bed and exploding into her, wet fire erasing the borders between them, and they both collapsed panting once again onto the bed.

When the stars cleared from his vision, Trey looked down. Jeanne's face was slack, resting on the still-open copy of *Paradise Lost* on his shoulder.

"Well," he gasped, "that… was certainly educational. Didn't you think?" There wasn't any fantasy about this, he thought. About the smooth heat of her around and against him. About the slowing drumbeat of her heart against his chest and the fan of her breath across his throat. This wasn't fantasy — it was fucking *real*, and it was fucking amazing. "Jeanne?"

"Fantastic," she said. She lifted her head, a loose, wicked grin on her face. And then she picked up the book. "Keep reading."

Sapphic Fairytales

The Sapphic Fairytales *series, of which the following stories are the first two titles, explore what happens when you look at classic stories through a lesbian lens.*

As K.D. West put it, "The Brothers Grimm, Perrault and Disney didn't show us any stories where the heroine got the princess; we'll just have to write them for ourselves!"

These stories are non-sexual.

Two Candles

*O*nce upon a time, in the north, where the rolling plains begin to rise into the mountains, there was a girl with hair as black as coal, and eyes as bright as diamonds, and she was called Brilliante. Her father was a merchant in the town, and her hand was promised in marriage to Georges, the brewer's son.

Now Georges was handsome and rich and pleasant enough, but whenever Brilliante looked at him, her heart was leaden, and when, on the occasions that he walked out with her, he happened to kiss her, her mouth was filled with the taste of ashes.

So it came to pass that, on the morning of her long-anticipated wedding, Brilliante walked out of her parents' house dressed in the crimson gown traditional for brides in that region, and passed north along the great river that flowed out of the heart of the mountains.

At first she had intended merely to clear her head on the way to the church. Yet as morning gave way to afternoon, she was still walking north, past the last farms and into the wild countryside of the mountain foothills.

She came to a place where the river blocked her path, and white water frothed around black rocks, and for the first time she considered turning around, for she had heard of this place, as had any child of her town. It was said to be inhabited by the Lorelei, *ondines*, who would lure men to their deaths in the swirling water–and there they where, white haired and fey beneath the water, singing for her to cross to them. At first she was terrified, thinking they meant to destroy her, but she could not ignore their song. Yet when she stepped out into the flood, she found that she was not borne under the waves, but rather walked across as if the river had frozen solid.

When she had crossed to the far shore, she turned around to see five white arms waving in farewell before disappearing into the foam.

Now she was in the great birch forest that blanketed the land above the river. Before she had time to wonder where she should go from here, bright copper hair flashed at the edge of her vision, and she thought she saw another white arm beckoning her even deeper into the wood.

Now, Brilliante was a well-read and intelligent young woman, and knew that following nymphs into the forest was courting trouble, yet she could not help but accept the invitation. Deeper and deeper into the wood she wandered, and every time she thought she was lost and forsaken, red hair would flicker and a white hand summon her further on. Whether it was a single mortal woman or a host of dryads, Brilliante could not tell, but she could no more ignore them than she had the river maidens.

Soon, the forest became wrapped in dusk, and Brilliante was no longer sure that she could distinguish the white arms from the bark of the trees, or red hair from the gold and crimson of the autumnal leaves. For the first time, fear truly gripped her.

Just as the night was truly about to set, Brilliante stumbled into a small farm. There was a tiny barn, a yard with several chickens, and a snug cottage with smoke curling deliciously from the chimney. Two candles burned in one of the windows — one bright red and one stark white. She went to knock on the door as the first stars twinkled overhead, but was surprised when, even after several minutes of knocking, no answer came from inside the house. The only response was a whiney from a startling white horse that had suddenly appeared outside the house.

Brilliante was growing cold there in the mountain night air, and she had not eaten all day–she had been too nervous to break her fast that morning. From inside the house she could smell fresh baked bread, rich stew, and the sharp scent of a pine fire on the hearth. She will be forgiven if, after some minutes of knocking and calling, she found she could wait no longer, and entered the cottage.

The sight inside made her breath catch. It was a lovely home, with merry fire with dinner bubbling in a heavy cauldron, a table set for two, a white, fluffy bed and–what most caught her eye–shelves full of leather-bound books.

At first, Brilliante promised herself she would wait to eat until the owner of the house arrived. She took down a book and was delighted to find that it contained one of her favorite stories, *La Belle et La Bête*, beautifully illustrated. Several times as she read through the familiar tale, she thought she heard someone at the threshold, and looked up. Yet each time she saw only the white horse, peering though its long eyelashes into the room.

Finally, she could stand it no longer. Thinking that she should not let good supper go to waste, and more hungry than she had ever been, she served herself a small portion of the stew and ate.

Once she had finished, she found that she could not keep her eyes open. *I'll just take a quick nap as I wait for the person who lives here*, she thought, and slipped under the heavy white eiderdown quilt beneath the protective gaze of the white mare. Before she had time to notice the smell of cedar and lavender in the pillow, she was fast asleep.

When she awoke, the sun had risen. Brilliante was stunned to find that the fire was still going and the smell of rich stew had given way to the scent of nutty porridge and honey. Again she was seized by hunger, and without considering the fact that she was taking a second meal without asking, Brilliante served out a healthy portion of the cereal and broke her fast.

In the window, two tapers stood in the candlesticks — once more, one red and one white, but now unlit, and full.

Once her belly too was full once more, the erstwhile bride weighed what she should do next. Thinking perhaps that her host must be working out in the barn, she opened the door.

She was stunned to find, not the beautiful white mare, but a woman. Like Brilliante herself, she was clad for a wedding — not in red, but the stark white traditional to the strange folk of the mountain north. Her hair was bronze, her eyes the blue of the winter sky, but her lashes were as long and elegant as a horse's. Looking at her, Brilliante's heart leapt with a flame as steady as midwinter candles.

White. And red.

"Good morning," said Brilliante.

"Good morning," said the beautiful young woman.

"Thank you for your wonderful hospitality," said Brilliante.

"Thank you for gracing this farm with your presence," said the woman, and Brilliante found herself blushing. Then the woman's brow furrowed slightly. "You are dressed," she said, "for a wedding. Are you married?"

"No," replied Brilliante, and she quickly told the stranger her story. "Are *you* married?" she asked, when she was done.

The woman shook her head.

"Is this your home?" asked Brilliante.

The woman nodded.

"Are you awaiting your beloved?" asked Brilliante.

"No longer," said the woman, and her eyes flashed so brightly that the flame in Brilliante's heart flared up.

They stood in silence, the morning sunshine flashing off of motes of dust drifting through the yard.

"May I tell you a tale?" said the young woman.

Now it was Brilliante's turn to nod.

"My name," the woman said, "is Kerzen. I was born on this farm, and have lived here my whole life, but I may not possess it yet. Let me tell you why.

"My mother died when I was born. She lay her dying kiss here." Very seriously, the woman touched a finger to her left check. "My father, wanting me to grow up in a woman's care, looked for another wife, grief-stricken as he was. We are two days from the closest village here, unless we go through the Haunted Woods, and so his search went in vain for some years, and so he was shocked when, one day, a woman came and said that she wished to marry him. She was fair-seeming and soft-spoken, cooked well, and knew the ways of a farm, and so my father agreed. They were wed on the day they met, and she became my stepmother.

"You seem well-spoken and well-read yourself, Brilliante, and so you will perhaps guess what happened. Alas, my stepmother was a witch. And by witch I do not mean merely that she was shrill and cruel, though she was that, nor that she was a follower of the old ways. Rather I mean it in the most literal sense: she was a caster of spells and a great brewer of potions and poisons. She enchanted the house so that it cooks and cleans itself, which seemed delightful at first. She set wards around this stead so that none may find it but who were meant to be here.

Kerzen paused and gazed at Brilliante for a long moment, then continued. "In the beginning, she treated me well, and this farm prospered and we were happy, though I never liked the way she ordered my father about. Then, when I reached my first womanhood, she began to become suspicious and resentful, jealous of my father's love of me. She banished me from the house, and made me do the most menial tasks around the farm. When this did not break my spirit, nor my father's love, she became bitter. She could not kill me, because of the protection of my mother's kiss. So she decided to kill my father and bewitch me." A tear leaked from Kerzen's pale blue eye.

"My father dearly loved mushroom pie. She prepared his dinner one night by hand, adding Death Caps to the pie. He died in agony that night, bestowing his dying kiss here." Very seriously, she touched her right cheek.

"When he died," Kerzen continued, "my stepmother howled with laughter, and cursed me, transforming me into a white mare and binding me to this place as one of the cattle of *her* farm. 'Just *wait*,' she cried, 'just wait and see how long it actually takes for True Love's first kiss to come riding over the hill!' Now tears flowed freely down her cheeks. Brilliante, moved by pity, and by some other passion, reached out to comfort the young woman, who held her hand up. "Brilliante, as she cackled away, crowing her victory over me and my father, she licked her fingers. The deadly mushrooms' essence lingered there, and so, fittingly, she too died in agony."

Now Kerzen gave a long, wet sigh. "And so, for the past two years, I have been imprisoned on my own homestead. Every night I transform back into a horse, and sleep in the barn. I am still banished from the house. I am still waiting, in my wedding dress, for True Love's first kiss to set me free."

Suddenly, Kerzen's eyes, still wet, flared with determination. She closed them, lifted her chin, and presented her mouth.

Brilliante looked at the beautiful young woman, and the love that had kindled in her heart roared into full flame. Leaning in to her, so that she could detect the smell of straw and tears, she joyfully bestowed upon Kerzen the kiss that would set her free. And many more besides.

That evening the two brides married in the country way, by plighting their troth and leaping hand in hand thrice over the broom that had belonged to Kerzen's mother.

The witch's curses broken, the two lovely young women retired to the enchanted cottage, where they spent their days in joy, their nights in bliss, and lived happily ever after.

Rose & Lily

Rose, Rose, Rose Red
Will I ever see thee wed?
I will marry at my will, sire,
At my will.

S ir Roland was a rare thing: a lord and knight beloved of his tenants and respected by his peers. The people of his valley loved him because he enforced the law with honor and justice, and kept the peace with an even, fair hand, raising his sword to none who did not deserve it. The knights and barons of the kingdom respected him because he was a formidable warrior and a strong voice at court for reason and compassion.

His three children were his pride: his eldest, Erec, who would succeed him, and who was his squire; Evain, who was studying to serve as the valley's priest, and his youngest, Rose.

Sir Roland would never have said it, for he loved his sons dearly, but no one doubted that Rose was his favorite. She could out-fence and out-joust Erec on the training ground more often than not, she was better read than Evain, and she shared her father's loyalty and sense of justice. If she were taller, broader of shoulder, and ruddier of cheek than was accounted pretty in those days, no one dared say it in her father's hearing.

One day, a messenger came desperately riding, not from the court, but across the kingdom's border. The neighboring king's daughter had been kidnapped by the infamous and mysterious Black Knight, who had taken her to his castle in the wilderness that lay between the two kingdoms. Could Sir Roland help?

"I will," said he.

"But father," objected Erec, face pale, "it should be I, not you, for we cannot risk your loss. The *Black Knight!"*

"Harvest is near. You must stay here and safeguard the valley," Sir Roland sighed. "'Twas the Black Knight when I was a boy, and 'twas the Black Knight when my father was a boy. It cannot be the same man."

Erec frowned, but agreed to stay.

Evain gulped and spluttered, "If you will go, F-father, I shall come and minister to you."

"Nay, my boy. I would not take you from the flock that needs you."

Evain looked down, but nodded.

Helping her father strap on his red armor, away from the others, Rose asked, "And what shall I do, Father? For I would not have you go alone."

Sir Roland turned and kissed her upon the forehead. "As I would not lose you for all the world. Stay," he said, "and help you brothers." She began to object, but he stilled her. "And if... If I should not return, come and fetch me, for I would not have my body rot in that wilderness. Do you promise me, daughter?"

Rose did not want to agree, but she knew that she must, and so she said, "It is against my will, but yes, Father, I swear that I shall do as you ask."

And off he rode, cheered by his people, but loudest by his youngest child.

When three days had passed, Rose knew that something was wrong. She went to Erec and begged him to gather up the men of the village and to help her bring their father back.

"It is only three days," said Erec with a frown, "and the fields must be harvested. Surely we can wait a little while longer."

Holding down her anger, Rose turned to Evain, who also refused. "Father bade me stay with my flock, and so I shall do."

And so that night Rose left on an old grey horse that no one would miss. Not wanting to go unarmed, she had strapped on her father's oldest armor, the red faded until it was scarcely there, had taken his oldest, most nicked sword, and had hefted a spare lance.

It was a bright, moonlit night, and Rose knew the woods, and so she approached the edge of the forest, she felt no greater fear than anyone might feel, riding into dark, bandit-haunted woods at night. Yet she should be pardoned for crying out in surprise when a magpie flew out of the shadows and landed upon her mount's head. "Oh! What are you doing out so late, friend?"

The bird gazed at her for a moment, and then said, "Rose of name and rose of hue, come and pay your father's due."

"How do you know my name!" asked Rose, but the bird merely repeated, "Rose of name and rose of hue, come and pay your father's due," and then flitted off down one of the forest tracks.

Not knowing what else to do, Rose followed where it flew.

As the sun rose the next morning, she was still following it. The light was beginning to spill through the black branches of the trees when the magpie flew out into a clearing and landed on the lip of an old well.

Blinking at the sudden light, Rose rode her horse out into the glade. At the far end stood a forbidding castle, with moss-covered walls of black stone and a heavy gate of iron-bound black oak, and soaring above it a single, narrow tower. Scowling at it, she let her horse walk to the well, where it drank from a bucket. "Where have you brought me, friend?" she asked the magpie, which was staring up at her.

The bird answered, "Spill some water, heed my verse, to save thy father from his curse."

That caught Rose's attention. She leaned over and took some water in her hand, and splashed it onto the ground.

Before the drops had time to sink into the earth, the huge gate groaned open, a portcullis rose with a screech of metal on stone, and a huge, black charger galloped out of the castle bearing an equally enormous man in armor darker than a raven's wing.

The Black Knight.

With no time to think, Rose lowered the visor of her battered helm, swung the shield from her back to her arm, and lifted her lance. She charged the knight.

Rose knew that she was not as strong as the Black Knight. She knew that her armor was not as sturdy, nor her horse as fast. Yet she also knew that to turn her back or side to her foe would be to die, and she could not die: she had promised her father that she would bring him back.

Rose also knew this: that the bigger, stronger, better-armed fighter would eventually win, unless the smaller, more lightly-armed, quicker fighter struck first. And so as she watched the Black Knight settle his lance high, clearly looking to knock her off of her horse, she leaned forward on the mare's neck, angled her shield to deflect the Black Knight's lance, and drove her own lance tip under the knight's helm and through his throat, knocking him from his horse and tearing the lance from Rose's grasp.

Terrified, Rose turned her horse, fumbling for her sword, but the knight was down and did not move. She leapt from her saddle, stumbling under the weight of the armor, and walked toward to fallen man.

The magpie landed on her shoulder and tweeted in her ear, "The man who would the Black Knight slay, will be Black Knight for all his days."

Rose ignored the bird, since what it said made little sense. Legs weak, she approached the figure on the ground. She could see the splinter of her lance passing through the man's flesh. He would not be getting up again.

She knelt beside the knight, lifting his visor to see if she could offer the dying man any succor.

As she raised the visor, Rose could not help but gasp: the face that she beheld was her father's.

As Rose's eyes filled with tears, the bird landed upon her father's chest, and sang again, "The man who would the Black Knight slay, will be Black Knight for all his days."

Rose heard a choking sound and cleared her eyes.

Her father's eyes were open, and he was smiling. "Good thing you're not a man, Rosie."

"Father?" She grasped his gauntleted hand in hers.

"Ah, Rosie, I'm so sorry... I did not want to attack you. But... the armor made it so. It *is* the Black Knight. When I defeated the last poor man to wear this gear, I found that..." He gasped. "...that *I* was now the Black Knight, and must attack whoever spilled the water from the well."

"Oh, Father," wept Rose.

"You have done..." He gasped again. "...done well. Defeated... Black Knight. Proud of you, Rosie."

"Thank you, Father."

"Rescue... princess. Tower. Curse."

"I will, Father."

"P-promise...?"

"Yes, Father," she said, "and I will bring you home."

And with that, he smiled, and died.

When Rose had finished weeping, she stood, wiped her face, and walked into the empty castle.

She felt light and heavy at the same time. Her father's death weighed on her, yet the fact that she had freed him from the curse of the Black Knight left her content, if hardly happy.

She staggered her way to the high tower, pulling her way up the winding stair.

As she reached the top, breathless and sweating in her not-quite-red armor, she found a room not entirely unlike her own at home: beautiful tapestries on two curved wall, arms on the other two.

And in the middle, a large bed.

And on the bed, the most beautiful creature that Rose had ever seen.

Rose had spent her time with her father, with her brothers, and with the men of her father's manor. Oh, she knew the other girls and women, but since her mother's death when Rose was little, none had been her friend. She had always been Sir Roland's daughter to them: the young mistress. The young mistress who liked to play with swords and disdained dresses for all but feast days.

The women of the valley were working folk who wore home-spun clothes. She herself was as sturdily built as many of the older boys and favored trousers and tunics.

She'd never known any woman like the one who slept on the bed.

The princess — for this must be she — was tiny, where Rose was large, and pale, where Rose was ruddy. She wore a dress of flowing, white silk that shown in the dim morning light of the chamber. Her hair was like spun faery gold and her lips...

Rose blushed at the thoughts that those lips were sparking in her. They were thoughts that she'd heard the other women give voice to from time to time when they didn't think she was listening. But always the women had been talking about how the *men* made them feel. About what they — the women — wanted to do to those men.

Kiss her, said the thoughts.

No! she told them, shocked at herself. *Kiss her?*

A black-and-white shape flew in through one of the slit windows and landed on the pillow beside the princess's bed. The magpie nodded at her as if to say, *Yes! Go ahead!* and then chirped, "To end thy quest and reach thy bliss, thou must deliver true love's kiss."

Any resistance that Rose might have felt melted away. The bird had always spoken truth to her before.

And so she leaned down, and with the zeal of new belief, kissed the sleeping princess.

No sooner had she done so than she felt the body beneath her move, heard a gasp against her lips, and felt a sharp pressure against the edge of her throat.

"I have no sword, Sir Knight," said a high, musical voice against Rose's mouth "but my broach pin can kill you just as well."

"I meant no harm," Rose said, and she was surprised to find that she was filled, not with fear, but with shame. *What did I think — ?*

"Back up," the musical voice ordered. "Let me... see you."

As Rose sat back on the bed, the princess kept the broach pin at Rose's throat, but the princess's eyes widened from suspicion to astonishment.

"A... *pink* knight?"

"What?" asked Rose, and then caught sight of her worn red armor, which did indeed look rather pink in the morning light. "I am no knight, though a knight's daughter." And she told the lady briefly of her adventure. "And so," she said, finally, crying once more, "I had to... to *kill* my father, because — "

"The man who would the Black Knight slay, will be Black Knight for all his days." She said it almost exactly as the bird had. The princess's pale eyes had grown, if anything, wider, and she had lowered her weapon. "You freed him from the Black Knight's curse. You *broke* the curse!"

Rose nodded, sniffing. "And now we have broken *your* curse. You must want to return to your father's kingdom."

"Oh," said the princess, and now she was the one who looked embarrassed. "I see."

"Well, my father wasn't the Black Knight who kidnapped you, but — "

"Ah," said the lady, and looked up again. "I wasn't kidnapped. Not at first — not until the knight brought me up to this tower. No. I ran away."

"You... ran away?"

The princess looked down, and Rose realized that she looked, if anything, younger than Rose herself. "I... I didn't want to get married."

"Oh." One heard such stories — of kings and dukes forcing their daughters to marry against their will. Rose's father had never done any such thing. "Did your parents want you to marry a man you did not love?"

True love's kiss.

"Not just one," mumbled the princess, blushing now, her fingers worrying at the golden broach with which she'd threatened Rose. Even her mumbles sounded musical. "All of them."

"All?"

"All of the men that my mother and father trooped in to be my husband — to be the future king. Some of them were very nice." Her eyes flashed up now, their pale blueness all the more startling for the delicate pinkness of her skin. "Your king's son, for instance, seemed very pleasant. But..."

Rose found that her heart was beating fast, and she could not account for it — the fight and the climb were long done. "But you did not want to marry — a man?"

Those pale eyes searched Rose's, and the lady nodded. "And so I ran away. My younger brother will make a good king. So I am a princess without a kingdom." She gave a sad laugh. "Not so much a princess any more."

"You have a castle, your highness," said Rose with a grin, and indicated the Black Knight's keep. Then she took the princess's small, delicate hand in her large, metal-clad one. "And you have a knight — a *pink* knight — who will serve you in whatever way your highness wishes."

The princess stared at her for a moment. "Do you think...? Could we check to make sure that the curse is truly broken?"

"Check?"

"Kiss me, lady knight."

And Rose did. And continued to do so. For some time. And Rose discovered that she would indeed be willing to do most anything if she were allowed to keep kissing this beautiful lady.

When their lips finally parted, the princess gazed at Rose seriously. "My name," she said breathlessly, "is Lily."

"And mine Rose."

Now the smile returned to those small, red lips. The princess raised the broach pin, still in her hand, and tapped it first against one of Rose's cheeks and then the other. "Arise, Lady Rose, Knight-Protector of Castle Black."

Rose felt a lump in her throat and only after a moment realized that she wished that her father could have been there, knowing the pride that he would have felt. "Thank you, my..." She blinked. "My queen."

Lily's fair skin went from being as red as Rose's namesake flower to as pale as her own, and back again. "Do you think —? Would it be all right for a lady knight to kiss her queen?"

"If her majesty wished to be kissed." Rose found herself smiling.

Lily smiled back. "We wish it so." She removed Rose's helm and ran her fingers through Rose's hair. "And call me Lily, please."

*L*ily accompanied Rose on the sad trip to return Sir Roland's body to his valley. Erec, Evain, and the people of the valley were glad to see Rose safe returned, astonished to hear Lily tell the story of Rose's defeat of the Black Knight and rescue of Lily herself, and filled with sorrow at the death of their beloved Sir Roland. There was a three-day feast — part celebration, part wake, and part harvest festival — at which Lily was the guest of honor, with Rose always at her side.

Rose noticed that the older women looked askance at her — as they had always done, she realized — but that the younger women and the girls looked at her for the first time not with deference, but with respect.

After the feasting was done, and the solemn farewells to Sir Roland said, Erec offered to escort Lily back to her father, the king, but Lily shook her head. "I have left my father's kingdom," she said, in a voice that all could hear, "to found mine own. I have taken possession of Castle Black, with my lady knight's aid, and with her help will keep it as a safe haven in the wilderness between our two countries."

And so it was. In their tiny kingdom, they kept the peace. Bandits, cutthroats, and rogue knights that had used to haunt the ways between the two kingdoms soon learned to fear the Pink Knight, and to abide by the just, firm rule of Queen Lily.

And people began to come and make their homes there in the wilderness. It was mostly women at first, but men too followed and lived content in Lily's domain.

And Lily and Rose ruled together in joy beneath the banner of a magpie, joyous all of their days and nights, and they lived happily ever after.

Over the Top

In Over the Top, *the first book in this series about new-minted adults discovering just how far from the straight and narrow they are, Danny went up to the woods after high school graduation with his friends.*

It was supposed to be Danny's best friends, Jamie and his girlfriend Luz, and Danny and his girlfriend Suzie.

But after graduation, Danny had broken it off with Suzie, since they were going to be going to colleges on the opposite sides of the country. And so he got to listen to his friends fucking every night, feeling more and more stupid.

Luckily for them both, Suzie couldn't stay away.

Under the Covers

Her family's taking the long post-Christmas drive up to the snow as they have nearly every year for as long as she can remember. What Suzie can't understand is why it's making her so sad this year.

Well, she knows why: Danny's not coming.

It's just that getting all emotional about it is silly: her boyfriend's never come up to the mountains with her family. And *his* family decided to take advantage of his going to school on the East Coast by celebrating the holidays with family *there*. Even if her family were staying were staying home this week, she wouldn't see him. She'd still be moping around, going to the mall with Alice, hanging with Luz and Jamie. It would be just as depressing at home.

She saw him at Thanksgiving. She'll see him Spring Break.

But a part of her wishes she were on an airplane bound for New York instead of sitting next to her little sister, who's got her music cranked up so high that Suzie can hear what's pouring out of the earbuds, and who is singing one One Direction song after another under her breath.

Not that she doesn't love Liz. It's just…

It's just she really, really wants to see Danny. To touch him. To feel him inside of her…

Suzie shudders.

Not good things to be thinking about in your family's minivan with your family all around you.

This last, schizophrenic summer — him pulling the stupid *We-can't-be-together-we're-headed-off-to-different-schools* routine just after graduation, and then her finally breaking, driving up to see him at *his* family's cabin, followed by six weeks of sweet, sweet, sex-filled bliss… It was wonderful. Scary wonderful. Addictive wonderful.

And now they are going to different schools.

And she won't see him for another three months. Suzie isn't sure she can survive another three months.

Liz's dark eyes are focused on Suzie. Ear-buds still firmly in place, she has an obnoxious smirk that portends trouble. She mouths, *Missing Daaaaaaaanny?*

Suzie feels the heat of annoyance — embarrassment — pushing up, but before she can pay Liz back, their mother turns around, clearly having sensed something, and says, "License-plate bingo?"

Suzie takes the playing card. It gives her an excuse to stare out the window and think of...

The snow cheers Suzie a bit — that and Liz's excitement about it. There's lots this year — for the first time in years, the hills, the trees, the roofs are all thick with it. They navigate along roads with sheer walls of white taller than the minivan, through a maze of snow-bound streets toward the cabin they've been renting every year since Suzie was little. The roads seem magical, fantastical with so much snow burying any familiar landmarks.

This is going to be fun. Even without Danny. And there's always videochat. If the internet is working.

"The street signs are buried!" gushes Liz, bouncing in her seat more as if she were seven than twelve.

Suzie can't blame her. It's beautiful.

"I think I can still find the way," their father laughs. "Look. Here's Raven. Almost there."

I wish Danny were here. The thought thrums through Suzie for the eight hundred and sixty-fourth time since they got into the car this morning. The ache. She barely pays it any attention. Barely. It's always there. Well, she's been paying it enough attention to rub herself sore over the past few weeks. Months.

She's a Human Biology major, for fuck's sake. She knows about how our brain chemistry encourages reproductive behavior. Oxytocin. Seratonin. Dopamine. Even a rush of endorphin from a nibble or a pinch.

But she knows that her longing for Danny is more than chemical. Otherwise any boy would do. Hell, any girl. And it isn't that she hasn't looked. It's that she knows what she wants. Who she loves.

"Good thing we got up when we did," Mom says. "Look: it's starting to snow already." Impossibly small flakes are floating through the low afternoon sunlight.

"There it is!" squeals Liz, pointing at the green, steeply peaked roof as it appears above the wall of snow.

Suzie is feeling excited too — excited to see so much snow, excited to be here, excited to get out of the car. Dad turns into the plowed drive.

There's smoke wafting from the chimney. *What the fuck?* "It... looks like there's someone else here. Look at the chimney."

Dad chuckles as he shifts the car into park and sets the brake. "Who else would be here?"

Liz snickers. "Yeah, Zuzu, don't be stupid."

What the fuck?

They pull on coats and trundle out of the minivan, and the cold hits Suzie like a wall. Liz starts dancing next to the car, catching snowflakes on her tongue.

"Suzie," says Mom, "while your dad parks the car, maybe you could open up the house? Here's the key." She passes it back.

Her family is being weird — or too normal — but Suzie is too cold and too happy to be out of the car after the long ride to think about it too much. She stomps up the recently shoveled stairs to the covered breezeway between the garage and the front door. As her fingers fumble with the key, as she shivers, she fights down the thought of how nice it would be to have her boyfriend here to warm her up.

Finally she manages to turn the key and steps inside.

It's warm. Deliciously. The smell of the wood fire is familiar and wonderful and *Christmas.*

Wondering who could have lit the fire, she turns toward the stove and...

And there's Danny. Kneeling in front of the stove, poking at it. He closes the glass door and turns to her, standing, grinning. He's got a smudge of ash on his nose. "Merry Christmas, Su—"

Suzie slams into him, her lips finding his, though she has no awareness of having moved. One hand is tangled in his hair — he's grown it out — and the other is up under his shirt and he is *here.*

She is just about to lose herself entirely in the kiss, just about to push her hand down his jeans — she can feel him losing it too, glories in the feeling of self-controlled Danny slipping over the edge — when her family calls from behind her: "*SURPRISE!*"

It takes them a moment to break the kiss. Suzie turns to her family. Her parents are grinning. Liz is smirking. "You *knew!*" Suzie gasps.

"Yup!" Liz giggles, and their parents laugh.

Suzie turns to Danny, who is flushed, but looking very pleased. "I got up here about an hour ago." He kisses her again. "I couldn't stay away."

It sounds like Suzie's mom is sighing and her dad is chuckling, but Suzie doesn't care. She kisses her boyfriend, happy beyond words that he is here.

Liz groans, "*EW!*" and they all laugh, and begin to load everything in from the car.

As they make and eat their traditional first-night dinner — spaghetti Bolognese, which Liz drowns in Parmesan — Danny shares the story of how he convinced his parents and Suzie's to help set this up. The snow is coming down heavily now; they were indeed lucky to get in when they did. Even with chains, the minivan wouldn't have made it over the pass in this kind of blizzard.

Some part of Suzie is always in contact with Danny. Holding hands. Knees touching. Hips. Lips.

Oxytocin. Seratonin.

As they're cleaning the dinner away, Suzie's dad clears his throat. "So. Sleeping arrangements."

Oh. Suzie hasn't thought that far ahead. She's been lost in enjoying her boyfriend's presence.

Suzie's mother continues, "Girls, you two are in your usual bedrooms upstairs. And your father and I have decided that to be hospitible it's only fair that we let Danny sleep in the downstairs bedroom."

"We're going to sleep out here on the pull-out," Dad says. "Very romantic." He leans over and kisses his wife, but they both then turn to look at the two college students. The message is very clear: *No hanky-panky. We'll be on guard at the bottom of the stairs.*

Danny shoots her an embarrassed smirk.

Ah, well. Nothing's perfect. "Well," says Suzie, "since I'm heading up for the night soon, I'm going to smooch my boyfriend. You can all sit there and watch, or head into the kitchen and finish the dishes."

Liz is about to object, but her parents haul her into the other room, both of them smiling. There's no door, but at least Suzie and Danny are alone for a moment.

"Nice," Danny says. "I don't know that my parents would have taken the hint."

Suzie sits on his lap — not astride, as she'd like, but she can still feel him stiffening against her hip. "I don't know that it would even occur to your parents that we might get up to something."

"You're right," he says, pulling her to him. "Next Christmas, we're with my family."

"Deal." She rolls her bottom against him, and feels him swell beneath her — not just his cock, but all of him. He begins to growl, but Suzie giggles and murmurs into his lips, "Less talking. More smooching."

It doesn't take long before they are both breathing heavily. Her nipples are so hard they almost hurt at the way he won't *quite* touch them, and she can feel him holding back from thrusting his hard-on against her bottom. "Want you," she whispers against his lips.

"Want you so bad it hurts," he whispers back, glasses fogged, breath uneven, and his fingers slide up the inside of her jeans leg —

And just at the moment that she has been looking forward to — awake and asleep — for months, just as his fingers are about to slide against her crotch and bring her the relief that her own fingers somehow never can...

Lizzie bursts in from the kitchen. *"EWWW!"*

Suzie flips her sister off, but the moment is broken.

Danny kisses her on the cheek and helps her stand again. "See you in my dreams."

She is dreaming of Danny. Dreaming of him fucking her *so hard....*

Suzie's eyes flick open. For a moment she doesn't know where she is. Not her room at home. Not her dorm.

Thin pre-dawn light shows around the curtain, barely lightening the walls but giving a pale blue glow to everything from the almost-empty bookshelf to the tattered poster of a snowboarding dragon.

Something is off.

She hears a rustling sound.

For a moment, fear grips her, but then...

Danny...

She creeps out of bed, willing the floorboards not to creak. Holding her breath she opens the door a crack. As always, her upstairs rooms is positively steamy, in spite of the cold outside.

The corridor is dark and empty. She can hear Liz wheezing like a freight train as usual.

Another sound—a quiet-as-owl-wings scuffle. Coming from the other side of the room.

What the fuck?

Closing the door again, she tiptoes over to the window and pulls open the drapes.

Danny is standing in his pajamas and parka, shivering knee-deep in the snow that has piled up nearly to Suzie's second-floor window.

"Good morning, Danny," giggles Suzie as quietly as she can, and slides the window open to let him in.

"Uh," Danny whispers, shifting from foot to snow-buried foot. "Merry Christmas?"

"Yes! Now come inside so that I can unwrap my first present!"

He crawls in and stands there shivering as she closes the windows — and the drapes again — and a smile twitches on his lips. It always makes Suzie's heart flutter a bit to see him smile—to see him smile because of *her.* He never smiles enough, especially recently—she knows how anxious and lonely he's been, hell, how lonely *she* has been, and so the sight of that smile, of those eyes pinching the way that they do when he laughs, it all makes her feel... It makes her feel. There are no words.

"Cold," he says, kicking snow-covered sneakes off of his feet.

"Comes with standing in the snow before the sun comes up," she says, but unzips his parka and presses her bed-warm body to his. "So how the hell did you get up here?"

His parka drops to the floor and his arms wrap around her. "Window from my room. Right next to the front door. Used the downspout to climb up on top of the snow and..." He holds out his arms as if to say, *Here I am!*

"How'd you know this wasn't Lizzie's room?" She pokes him. "Or maybe that's what you were *hoping?*"

She can feel his shivers subsiding, even as he chuckles. "No thanks. She's not my type — by about six years. Besides, she snores like a rhino. That's how I could tell. *You* snore like a mountain lion."

"I don't snore!"

"Of course not. And even if you did, it's a beautiful sound."

"Mmm. That's more like it." She kisses him, and can feel both her temperature and his rising.

Quickly, he stops shivering, and she pulls his shirt up over his head and pushes his bottoms down to his feet. Breaking the kiss, she backs up and lies back on the bed. "There. My first present, unwrapped and ready to play with."

"Well," he says at last, stepping towards her with a rather dangerous look on his face, "I do have a present for you. But you haven't gotten it yet."

"Oh," she responds, and his widening grin makes an entirely different part of her anatomy flutter.

"Yes. This is a present I've been wanting to give you... for a very, very long time."

Suzie has gone from sleep to fear to amusement in a few short moments, but the sound of Danny's voice and the promise in his eye takes her someplace else entirely. She feels her cunt flower open. "Oh," she murmurs again.

He leans forward and kisses her. Kisses her fully, leaving Suzie feeling far more naked than even sex ever has. She feels transparent, utterly exposed, as if this kiss reveals everything to Danny: not only her body, inside and out, but every little fear, every ugly little secret, every time she has been angry with him, or angry with herself, every time she has looked at a boy at one of the parties this year and thought, *Why not?* It is exciting to expose herself to Danny, but it is terrifying as well.

He breaks the kiss and smiles, and Suzie feels herself breathe again. "Least *you* had a chance to brush your teeth," she burbles, arms crossed in front of her diamond-hard nipples.

He gives a soft laugh. "You taste fabulous, just like you snore," he says, leaning forward again. Not into a kiss this time—his lips brush along her cheek and back to her ear. He murmurs, puffs of warm desire, "I want to taste you, Suzie. Every bit of you. I want to devour you whole. That's your present."

"Okay," Suzie answers, her voice suddenly very high.

Danny's hands move under her t-shirt—his t-shirt actually. She feels his palm sliding up her spine as he lifts the fabric. Her arms are still crossed and she can't manage to uncross them, to reveal this too, to let him see how a kiss and a caress and a smile have evoked such desire in her.

"Going to let me take this off, or do I have to tear it?" he mutters, letting his tongue slide along the lobe. "Yum."

Trembling, Suzie grabs the battered Dr. Who shirt reading *Two hearts beat as one* and pulls it up. Danny is straddling her legs, his body pressed close to hers, and so as the shirt lifts, it exposes her body to his, which also naked. She knows that body intimately now, but it feels cool and alien against her bed-warm flesh. Her breasts bounce free, the nipples buzzing as they slide against his ribs.

His tongue continues to explore her ear, the side of her neck. She whimpers with disappointment when he backs away to allow her to lift the shirt above her head, but once the horrible, offending shirt is gone, he attacks the bottom of her chin and works slowly around to the other ear.

His tongue finds its way in and she gasps.

"Roll over on your belly," Danny says.

Suzie stiffens.

"Come on, Suzie. Don't make me *make* you." His tone is playful and light and so-so-so *sexy*, but what on earth…? "Trust me, Suzie."

Moving with arms and legs that seem to have gone boneless, she rolls beneath him, feeling his balls brushing along one hip and across her ass. "I t-trust you, Danny. With everything."

He sits silently across her backside for a moment, and she feels him shudder. Then she feels him brushing his fingers just over the surface of her back — not quite touching.

What…?

"God," he says, "I've wanted you so fucking much." He shifts forward and brushes her mane, still wild from sleep, off of her shoulders. "Last night," Danny murmurs (*Don't wake anyone!*)—as he leans further forward still, "lying in the big bed right below you, I dreamed about doing this. I had the most amazing, explicit, exciting dream of lying right on your bed, not this one, the one back at home, naked against your naked back, kissing my way across every… single… freckle." He is as good as his word. His lips touch at the back of her neck and begin slowly to meander down the line of one shoulder. A vibration passes from each point of contact down through Suzie's cunt to her toes, which flex against her sheets.

"And as I kissed each one," he says, continuing his sweet torture, "I tasted you." His tongue passes down the top of one shoulder blade. "And you tasted *so good*."

He kisses her spine and Suzie releases a breathy moan into her mattress. "I… d-did?"

"In the dream you tasted like cinnamon sugar and pumpkin pie…" *His favorites*, a part of Suzie's mind sighs, and she'd yell at herself, but *fuck*, what he's doing demands every bit of her attention. He licks and nibbles along. "But nowhere as good as you taste in reality."

Suzie knows where this is headed. Knows what her fucking Christmas present is. And a part of her wishes he'd get *on* with it, but a part of her... Oh, a part of her, most of her really, is so awash in sensation that the idea of doing anything but feel those lips, that tongue, those teeth slowly make their pilgrimage down her back is simply unimaginable.

At the point of each hip, he gives a gentle nibble—her bony fucking hips that she's always hated so fucking much, but *ohhhhh*...—and then, as he reaches the dimple at the base of her spine he gives a long, languorous lick that carries him back up to the ribs.

There is nothing muffled about the moan that Suzie gives this time. She arches back like a cobra, her breasts bouncing tautly, and gives a good, low growl.

Danny laughs, covering her mouth — the first time he's touched her with anything other than his lips — and kisses her on each shoulder and then running his hands back down her sides. "Shhhh.... I haven't shown you the whole dream yet..." He kisses his way back down her spine, more lightly again. "I tasted *all* of you, Suzie."

His mouth reaches that dimple again, and his hands rest on her buttocks and urge them apart.

She squeaks. For the first time in years and years, Suzie Williams squeaks, fighting him in spite of herself. "Oh, God, Danny..."

"Shhhh," he soothes, kissing gently down the inner edge of one buttock and up the other. "It's all right."

"It is. *Oh*, it so fucking *issss*...!"

He touches his tongue to a place about which Suzie has thought as little as possible—really, it's a nasty, purely functional part of her body, isn't it? But the feel of his tongue, of his breath against her wrinkled flesh causes a wet wave of warmth to explode through her pelvis and she presses back against him, writhing. The first small orgasm of the morning. "*God.*"

"Yeah," said Danny, his voice husky.

He's going to fuck me there, he's going to fuck my ass, oh...! Please, God... But Danny begins kissing and nibbling his way down her trembling thigh. Some other time, perhaps...

He continues to move slowly, deliberately, savoring her like a really good piece of chocolate. "That was the end of the dream," Danny says, his voice low and urgent. "Came all over my sheets. Haven't done *that* in years. Woke up thanking God your folks were fast asleep. And that they're not telepathic."

Of course, he says this just as he begins laving attention on the back of her knee and she starts to giggle. "Stop it!"

He snorts too. "Stop...? You want me to...?"

"*NO!*" she howls into her pillow. "Oh, God, NO! Please, God, Danny, don't stop, please, don't, *ohhh...*"

He begins kissing her feet.

Another part of her body that Suzie has never thought of as anything but utilitarian. He nibbles at her ankle, licks at the instep, sending sparks right back up to Suzie's center, and then sucks Suzie's big toe into that moist, hot mouth, triggering another roman candle in Suzie's pelvis. "*HNNNNH.*"

Cool air washes over the toe as he releases her, and once again she whimpers.

Once again he says, "Roll over."

This time she does not hesitate.

Danny sucks each of the toes on the other foot into his mouth in turn, and Suzie pushes up onto her elbows, staring at him, at this boy who was barely able to touch her last year, but *now...*

"S-Suzie," he mumbles, kissing his way at a steady, studied pace up her leg, "I, I wanted to do your whole front too before—"

"Later," Suzie urges, her own voice suddenly low with need.

He nods and works his way up the inside of her left thigh, trailing his tongue as he goes.

"AHH!" she screams into her palm. Suzie stares down into his eyes, and the light of dawn breaking through the window washes across his back and his ass and it feels as if the whole world is glowing.

Danny's mouth meets Suzie's cunt and suddenly she can't look anymore. She closes her eyes, and her leg curls of its own accord over his shoulder and her chin droops to her chest.

Seratonin. Oxytocin.

The sunlight is inside of her. The sunrise is at their union.

And it *flares...*

Suzie's eyes flicker open; the ceiling is golden-pink with the dawn. She is panting.

Danny kisses his way up her belly. He is getting the front after all.

At each breast, another small sunburst.

His mouth meets hers. She tastes the salt from her body—when did she start sweating?—along with the tang of her own cunt and the tiniest bit of his toothpaste.

"Merry Christmas, Suzie."

"Mmmmmmmmmm..."

His smile is full and broad and Suzie feels as if her own happiness is going to overflow her body and drown them both.

She pushes him back.

"Suzie?" Green eyes blink, suddenly concerned.

"Lie back," she says.

He gawks at her.

"Don't make me hit you, D'Angelo. This *is* my Christmas present, right?"

"Sure…" He flops back, his legs over hers. They stare at each other, each propped up on elbows.

His cock stands proudly, twitching to his heartbeat.

Suzie spins onto her belly, her feet up in the air, and begins to run the tip of her wand up the inside of his leg. He shivers.

What to do? What does she want?

His cock.

She sticks out her tongue, touches the tip to the base of his cock and licks slowly up its length. Danny lets out a strangled gasp.

Mmmmmmmm…

"Suzie," pants Danny, "you don't have to…"

"Shh," Suzie commands. She grasps his erection with one hand and studies it. "I've been wanting to give you this… for a very, very long time."

He gulps.

"I want to taste you, Danny. I want to swallow you. I want to devour you whole." Savoring his stunned expression, the golden light, the flavor of him, the feeling of him, the closeness of him, she leans forward and does just that.

They make love as quietly as they can for the next half hour. It's every bit as sweet as she remembers. Sweeter. Brain chemistry doesn't even begin to explain it. And then they lie there under the covers, wishing the world would go away and leave them the fuck alone.

But then they hear Suzie's parents beginning to move around in the kitchen, and Suzie helps Danny back out the window and watches him slide back down to the breezeway to where his own window awaits.

She is just worrying at how to obscure the footprints outside her window when a thick slab of snow slides off of the roof, obliterating any sign that he was ever there. Grinning, she pats the house, silently thanking it, and closes the window again.

By the time Suzie stumbles downstairs, Danny is already in the kitchen, scrambling eggs for Dad to cook. Danny waves and says "Good morning!" and it's almost as if the lovemaking session they've just had was a dream.

Except that Suzie can still taste Danny's cum in her mouth, can still feel him dribbling from her pussy. "Morning, Danny." She gives him a fairly chaste kiss and turns to the table. Mom's sitting with Liz, who's resting her head on the placemat. "Didn't you sleep well, Lizzie?"

"No," grunts Suzie's sister. "There was a noise. Woke me up. Thought it was a big bear or something coming to eat you."

"Eat *me?*" Suzie asks, turning to the coffee to hide the blush she knows is lighting up her fair skin. "Weren't you worried it was going to eat *you?*" *And if it tried, I'd have had to kill it.*

"Nah," Lizzie grumbles, lifting her head. "There's more of you to eat."

Suzie narrows her eyes at her brat of a little sister. "Well, you're probably right. You're all gristle and bone anyway."

Liz sticks out her tongue, but the proper balance between the sisters has been maintained.

"Anyway," Suzie says, "it was probably that big pile of snow sliding off the roof."

Liz frowns as her mother starts to brush out her hair. "Oh."

Pouring a mug of coffee for herself, Suzie turns to her boyfriend. "You sleep okay, Danny? No bears?"

"Nope." He grins at her and waggles his eyebrows minutely in a way that Suzie chooses to interpret as *And that bear came and ate you all up, didn't it?* "And you? You slept okay?"

"Like a dream," she sighs, staring deep into his eyes.

He leans down and kisses her and —

"EWWWWW!"

Out of the Bag

It's just the two of them. Though everyone said that they'd try to help with the move, Suzie's parents are on a college tour with her sister Liz, Alice, Suzie's roommate and BFF, went off in search of enlightenment at a week-long retreat at a Zen monastery, Jamie and Luz are on their fucking honeymoon…. Danny and Suzie could have asked some of their other friends — former schoolmates, the folks each of them worked with — but. . .

Just the two of them. Finally.

Danny's helped pack up Suzie's clothes as well as her share of the kitchen stuff — Alice's things are pretty easy to identify, decorated as they are with animals ranging from mythological to bizarre — and they're finishing up in Suzie's bedroom when she sneaks up next to him, nibbles on his ear, and whispers, "Got to go to the girls'. Can you keep going?"

Danny shivers and nods.

"Good boy," says Suzie with a hint of a giggle. She gives his ear a wet lick, her bra-free breasts bouncing against his arm, and departs with a laugh.

Fucking amazing! After two years of on-again-off-again dating since college, they're moving in together. Tonight, once they've gotten her stuff over to the apartment they've rented together, they'll have a late dinner. He is going to serve her the fabulous meal he prepared with all of her favorite dishes, roses and candles on the table, and then he is going to get down on one knee and give her the diamond ring he's been carrying in his pocket all day. Then they'll probably fuck through the rest of the night — no work tomorrow for either of them, no parents or siblings to hear, no roommates to walk in.

If Danny was being honest, it's terrifying, but he knows that they both want this, he knows she'll say yes, and so he knows he'll get over it.

Fucking amazing.

After packing the last of Suzie's books, he sits on the floor and takes stock. The old armchair is already in the rented van — the armchair they've taken turns licking each other silly in, the one she straddled him on just last night.

The shelves are built in. The nightstand is Alice's, with painted dragons, so that's staying. No need to take the bed!

What else needs to come in this room?

He slides down on his belly to look beneath the nondescript single bed they've shared so often — though never often enough, and always desperately trying not to make too much noise. Peering, he spots a pair of running shoes — she'll want those — and a softball bat — God knows why she has that. Once those are stowed, he takes one last peek, not thinking to see anything else. . . .

There's a dark shape barely visible back toward the wall. Reaching out, he touches a rough, soft lump, grabs it, and pulls it out.

It is a sack of black leather the size of a small book bag, tied at the top with a red leather cord and bulging with odd shapes that looks nothing like books. He's going to put it on top of the rest of her stuff in the crate, when curiosity gets the better of him.

Feeling the thrill of doing something he knows he really shouldn't, he fumbles with the cord and opens the bag.

At the top is a red-and-gold tie — her college's colors — and a peacock feather. School mementos? Not pausing to think, he reaches in to take the tie and feather and his fingers brush something vaguely familiar: long, silky. . . .

What?

Drawing out his hand, he sees that it's a length of red satin cord. He knows what *this* is. He and Suzie don't play with toys much — why bother when the best sex toy of all was your partner's body? But Daphne — the last of the girls he dated briefly before finally convincing himself and Suzie that there wasn't anyone else — she really, really liked to have Danny tie her up during the couple of months that they were seeing each other. Didn't do a damned thing for him, but it made the usually prim Daphne an absolute sex animal, so he went along with it. Mistress Coraline's Restraints for Romantics featured largely in their short-lived love life.

As did the next item he pulls from the bag: a rubber ball with kid leather straps. A. . . A ball gag. He drops the thing, trying hard not to imagine Suzie's lovely, small mouth stretched around it.

Against his better judgment, almost against his will, his fingers reach once more into the bag and touch something. Something smooth and long. Something very familiar.

Out of the black bag his fingers draw what looks like his own erect penis.

Not really his, obviously. But the same length and thickness, the same skin tone. Attached to the root, however, where *he* should have been, there is a collection of buckles and straps in the same black kid leather as on the gag.

What in fucking hell has Suzie — ?

"Danny!"

Suzie stands in the doorway, pale and blank-faced. Her mouth is closed but her eyes are wide.

Blinking, Danny stares down at the thing in his hand, at the sex toys at his knees. The satin rope is draped across his thigh in a manner that seems somehow vaguely obscene. He slaps it away. "Suzie, I. . ."

Her expression does not change, but she crosses her arms tightly. Her nostrils and eyelids are slitted, her lips thin and white. This isn't embarrassment. This is anger, a mood of Suzie's that Danny has learned to recognize and respect and that he always does his best to avoid. He stammers, "I. . . I'm sorry."

She purses her lips, looks away for a moment, and shrugs. A slight softening, thank God. Her tone is anything but soft, however: "Do you know why?"

"Why?"

"Do you know what you should be apologizing for?"

"I. . ." He frowns back down at the collection. Not shame — Suzie is hard to embarrass anyway, and she definitely has no shame at all about things sexual. It is one of many things that he loves deeply about her — that he can be his own, over-the-top, horny-ass, perverted self with her. So: not the sex. "I'm sorry that. . . I'm sorry that I pried."

She peers at him for a moment, then sighs and looks away again.

"Sue—"

"You're an only, and I know that sucks in some ways, but you could at least put things away and know no one was going to look at them. Dig through them. Not me." Her freckles stand out in stark relief. "I grew up with absolutely no privacy, Danny. No space that I could call my own. Never even had a room of my own, until this year. Everything I had, if I didn't *have* to share it with Liz, she'd go through it anyway. And my parents weren't a whole lot better."

Danny loves Suzie's parents — loves that they have been so welcoming to him, even if they still won't let him sleep with Suzie under their roof. But yes: they've always felt that they were entitled to know everything about anything that had to do with Suzie. "I know."

She turns back to him, her bright eyes dark. "Even in college — and since — I've always had roommates. Didn't even have my own bedroom until this apartment. And I love Alice, but personal space is not her strong suit. You've had your own place the past two years."

He starts to say something, to try to reassure her, but she holds up a hand. "If we're going to live together, if we're going to do this for real, not just for now but for the long run, I need to know that I have privacy. I need to have the ability to know that, if I — if *we're* working something out, that there are things. . . that I have a place that I can call my own, trusting that you're not going to push your way in. Prying."

"Absolutely," he whispers, terrified that he's somehow fucked everything up. Who cares about the fucking sex toys, who cares about what Suzie got up to when they weren't together — he will do *anything*. . .

"It's not those. . . things," she says, echoing his thoughts. "It's that you went into that—"

"Without asking. I know."

"Do you?" She cocks her head and looks at him, hard. She is still pale, but blotches of color have blossomed on her cheeks, her ears. Then she lets loose a soft grunt of a laugh and shakes her head. "I guess you do."

He tries smiling at her.

Her marble-faced scowl softens. "Danny, I promise, I don't want to keep any secrets from you. I *promise*. But I need you to promise—"

"I won't go through your things without asking. I promise. I swear."

She takes a step toward him, and then another. "Not just my things, Danny. I need to know that my thoughts and my feelings are mine. If I seem upset or annoyed or something and I don't want to talk about it, I need you to respect that."

Now it's Danny's turn to frown. "But. . . I get to ask. Right?"

She kneels opposite him. "Of course. Just, I get to say no until I'm ready, all right?"

"But. . ." He hears what she's saying, but she's asking for a lot of trust — trust she's more than earned, but it's still hard. When he's thought of what a marriage, of that kind of relationship, of what it's supposed to look like — you're supposed to share *everything*, right? But he knows that's not really possible, or even a good idea. "I get it. I promise. I promise. But. . . You'll be ready *eventually*. Right?"

Finally she smiles, though he's not joking, not at all. "Danny, I'm not going anywhere. So unless you shove me out the door or out the window because I'm driving you nuts, yeah, I'll be ready eventually." She leans forward and kisses him gently.

Overwhelmed with relief, he throws his arms around her and kisses her back with everything that he is worth — everything.

After a few minutes, just as things are about to get interesting, she pulls back from him. "So. Do you have something you want to ask me about?"

For a moment, he has absolutely no idea what she's talking about. And then he realizes that he's still holding the penis. . . thing in his hand. He holds it up. "Uh. This. What *is* this?" He finds that he doesn't know where to look. He can't look at the thing, can't look at her face. Sure as fuck can't look at her body.

"Danny," she says, the gentle tease in her voice almost worse than the cold anger from earlier, "I'm sure you know what *that* is."

"Well, yeah, but. . .." He shakes the straps. "*This.*"

"Ah." She reaches out and guides his chin so that he's looking at her after all. Her lips are parted in a slight, open smile; her eyes glisten evilly — Suzie at her sexiest, sultriest, most seductive. "Well, Danny. Would you like me to *show* you what that is, and. . ." — she leans forward and finishes, in a low, breathy growl right into his ear — "*how I use it?*"

Danny gulps. He has *no* idea where this is going. Is she going to use the thing to play with herself? *Holy. . . !*

He also recognizes, however, that this is, after a fashion, a test: *Do you trust me, Danny, or do you not?* Nodding feebly, he rasps, "I guess. Sure."

Now the slight smile spreads, and becomes truly evil. This is the Suzie who once made him watch her masturbate, talking about all of the dirty dreams she'd had about him, diddling herself for an hour and a half before she would let him touch her — or himself, which was almost as bad; this is the Suzie who once showed up at the office where he had just started working, wearing nothing but an overcoat — *his* overcoat; this is the Suzie who, for his most recent birthday, gave him the world's slowest blowjob — *hours* — keeping him just on the edge of explosion, but never letting him peak. That nearly killed him. When he finally came — a puff of air from her lips was all that it took in the end to set him off — he thought it had. What in God's name does she have in mind *now*?

"Clothes off," she says, standing.

"*What?*" he squeaks.

She begins peeling her t-shirt up until the hem is just above the very bottom of the breasts that he's been dying to nuzzle at all day. "I'll show you mine," she says, rocking her hips and lifting the shirt a fraction of an inch with each sway, "if you show me yours."

"Okay." The sound that escapes Danny's lips now can't even be called in good conscience a squeak. It's barely audible. He doesn't give a shit. He stands, tears off his t-shirt, and starts to fumble with his zipper, the phallus still in his hand bouncing against his hip as he tries to remove jeans, boxers, and shoes simultaneously.

"*Daaanny*," sings Suzie as the shirt finally lifts above her nipples.

"Huh?"

"I'll take *that*." Stripping her shirt off in a single pull, she tosses it on his head, and plucks the dick-and-straps contraption from his hand.

Blinded, hobbled by his pants, Danny stumbles back against the bed and falls backwards.

Suzie laughs.

"Cruel woman," grumbles Danny, still flailing.

"You love me just like this."

He grunts. It is true: that is the truly awful thing. He starts to pull her shirt off his head, but her voice stops him: "No. Let me undress you the rest of the way. And it's good that you can't see; I'll have a surprise for you."

That sounds both promising and absolutely fucking horrifying.

She pulls off his hi-tops. "Will you be patient like a good boy?"

He snorts. "Yes, Miss Suzie."

"Hmm." He hears her mutter and then she tugs off his jeans, though her shirt — with her scent still clinging to it — continues to cover his head. "I like the sound of that."

"Yes, Miss Suzie?"

"Yes. Now put your hands out in front of you."

Nervous and intrigued, he does, and is rewarded by the feather-light brush of her nipples against his fingertips. He tries to caress them, but as he stretches out toward her, she must step back; his fingers find nothing but air.

Something smooth and silky slides around Danny's wrists, binding them together, and, in spite of himself, in spite of his excitement, in spite of looking forward to whatever it was that Suzie has planned, he cries out in alarm.

"Just a little satin rope. Shh," she says, and lets her chest brush against his outstretched, bound hands once more, and he can't help but groan.

Is she trying to *kill* him? "God, Suzie, just—"

"Shh," she repeats. "Give me just a sec and the fun will really begin. All shall be revealed."

He hears her moving around, hears *her* jeans hitting the floor; he desperately wants to pull the shirt off so he can watch that miraculous, heart-stopping body. But. . . *All shall be revealed.* "You did promise."

"Yes, I did."

"Well, then." Though it's one of the most difficult things he's ever done, he takes a deep breath and lets his satin-bound hands fall into his lap, where he is not at all surprised to discover that a rather emphatic erection is growing.

He hears Suzie give a quick gasp and realizes that she too is probably nervous. That makes him want to hold her, to make her feel safe, even as it makes him feel very safe. He trusts Suzie.

"Okay, Danny. We're almost ready. I just want you to trust me a bit more. Can you get on your belly on the bed, without the t-shirt falling off?"

He nods and maneuvers himself so that he is lying facing down on the bed, his bound hands beneath him, where they feel that his heart is beating like a hummingbird's wings.

"One more thing, Danny." She takes another steadying breath. "Because you've been a, uh, bad boy today, we're going to play this game by my rules. All right?"

"Yeah."

"Okay. Good." Her bare footsteps approach the bed. "But. . . I think you're going to enjoy this, Danny."

"Yeah."

"If you're. . . If it's not. . . fun, just say 'stop' and we'll stop. Okay?"

"Okay." And then, because he can hear that it is what *she* needs to hear, he adds, "I trust you, Suzie. I'll try anything you want to try. If you think it's going to be fun, it's going to be fun."

"Thanks. Ready?"

He nods, very aware that his cock is doing its best to drill through the mattress beneath him.

She approaches the bed, and though he hopes she'll join him on it, she doesn't. Cruel. Cruel. "Voilà." She lifts t-shirt from his head, clearing his vision, revealing. . .

Revealing Suzie, fully, gloriously naked, skin flushed, nipples hard. And where usually there is nothing but her magnificently red patch of pubic hair, a cock — an erect cock — HIS erect cock strains upward, held in place by a network of leather. "It's called a strap-on," she says, voice low, and he has to tear his eyes away from the thing to look up into her face. She's smirking. "It was a present. From Alice."

"What do you. . . *do* with it?" He finds himself once more staring at the thing, unable to look away.

"All sorts of fun things." He can hear the laughter in her voice. "Alice got it for me senior year. I thought I was going to die, Danny, I really did, I missed you so much, and we emailed every day, but you're a lousy correspondent."

"I know."

"Yeah, well, I didn't care, because I had *that* much, anyway. But what I didn't have was *this*." She circles the erection with her thin, strong fingers and strokes it. "Recognize it?"

He nods. "Mine."

"Yup." Continuing to stroke it, she kneels on the mattress, so that it is just inches from his face. "Didn't want just *any* cock in me. Wanted *this* one."

"Hnh."

She lets the tip of the strap-on touch his lips lightly, and then runs it in a circle around his mouth. "Was whining about it to Alice. Apparently, I was whining in enough detail that she was able to get me *just* the right one. She thought it was *very nice*, by the way."

Danny's heard Alice use the phrase *very nice* to describe everything from a hot slice of pizza to a wild weekend of sexual abandon with one of her occasional boyfriends. Or girlfriends. So he isn't sure how to take that.

Without breaking contact, Danny gazes up at his Suzie. Her eyes are burning with a dark, familiar flame, but one that is also somehow new. Hopeful. Frightened as he has not seen her since they first fucked, up by the lake after high school.

He swallows and takes a deep breath, the movement of the incredibly fleshlike tip continuing lightly around his mouth.

Just like mine? he wonders. *Hmm.* Willing himself not to think about what he's doing, Danny leans toward her and kisses the head of the cock.

She gives a hiss, and her whole body trembles. As if she can feel it. *Just like mine...* "God. Danny."

In for a dime, in for a dollar. He opens his mouth and gives the head a lick, as he had the pleasure of having her do just the night before on this self-same tiny bed.

"*Damn!*" She hisses again, her fingers finding his hair. "So fucking *sexy...*"

"Yeah." Filled with a kind of pride at bringing her so far so quickly (Suzie never swears until she's either incredibly pissed off or incredibly turned on), Danny closes his eyes, opens his mouth further (*It's not a real cock, it's just a strap-on, it's just—*) and takes the head into his mouth. He can almost feel it swell, can imagine feeling the foreskin pulling back.

"God, Danny. . ." She presses it in — just a little, but he's never been so happy not to have been better endowed. He lets his tongue run as far down the length of the cock as he can. Her fingers convulse in his hair. "Looks so fucking *sexy. . ..*"

She gives a deep groan, but suddenly the cock is gone. Danny would reach out and grab it, but his hands are tied beneath his chest, and he just flails there for a second until, just as suddenly, Suzie is on the bed beside him, her body pressed against his, her leg thrown over his ass, the fake cock sliding against his hip.

She bites his earlobe gently and licks his ear, her breath loud. "Can you see why I like sucking cock so much?" she whispers like a roar. "Can you see why I like doing that to you?"

He nods, trembling.

"You'd be a great cocksucker, wouldn't you, sweetie? But I want to show you something else. And like we agreed, because you've been a bad boy, I get to say how we're going to play today. Okay?"

He nods again.

"I need you to say it, Danny."

"Okay," he says, heart thumping in his throat. "We play your way. Okay. *Please.*"

"Good," she purrs, kissing his ear again, and then his neck. "'Cause what I really, really want you to feel, Danny, is what it's like to have this wonderful cock fucking you." She bites gently at his shoulder.

Holy...! "Okay," he gasps.

She licks down his spine, between his shoulder blades, her diamond-hard nipples dragging along his back. "I want you to feel what it's like to have this cock open you up, make you scream, make you feel" — her tits flow over his ass as she kisses her way down his back — "naked on the inside as on the outside."

When she reaches the base of his spine, she reaches underneath and gives his cock a feather-light squeeze, gives his balls a swirl of her fingertips, and he arches his ass up, opening himself to her, but also hoping she'll touch him there again.

Not yet.

She mutters, reaching back to a box on her desk. Her body shifts back over his, she kisses one cheek and then the other. Then he hears a loud squishy sound. "Lube," she murmurs, and then squirts another dollop right into the crack of Danny's ass.

He gasps, expecting it to feel cold, but instead the sensitive flesh tingles and then warms.

"Want me to fuck you, Danny?" Her breath whispers against the flesh of his ass, but somehow he's still surprised when her tongue touches his asshole, and he groans, his balls contracting. "Want to feel what it's like to take a hot, hard cock into your body?"

He is crying. His glasses are gone — somewhere, he isn't sure where. He is trembling and crying and scared out of his fucking mind, but yes: he wants it. He wants *her.* Inside of him, the way that he's been inside of her so many times. He nods.

"Say it, Danny."

"I. . . I want it, Suzie, please—"

She kneels up behind him, her fingernails scratching up the backs of his legs. "Want what?"

"*FUCK!*" he cries. "Fuck. . . *Fuck. . .* Fuck me, please, God, Suzie, fuck me, cock inside me, *please!*"

"What a good boy," she says, reaching past his hip and giving his cock — the living one — a light tug. At the same time something presses up against his opening — not the cock, not yet, smaller, her finger. She runs it around his sensitive flesh, once, twice, then begins to press up against his opening. Another squirt of lubricant, and she works it *in,* making it slick, like her cunt when she is so ready to be fucked, and so, though his muscles want to fight to keep her out (in spite of his own desires), the tip of her finger slides through the ring of muscle and a shout bursts from him: "*Suzie!*"

"Right here, sweetie," she whispers, withdrawing her finger until just the tip is inside him, then pressing in again, deeper this time, and it doesn't hurt — *fuck,* it feels *good!* — but the new sensation, the sense of invasion is overwhelming. She withdraws her finger and presses it in again, and this time, he feels the first knuckle ripple past his sphincter, which he can't seem to get to relax. "Breathe, Danny. Just breathe."

He does, breathing in and out, and she stays there, her finger part of the way into him, until they both feel his bottom unclench a bit.

"There you go, there you go." Then she presses into him again, and this time she slides slowly but insistently all of the way home. "Shh. Shh."

He doesn't know why she's shushing him, until he realizes that he's moaning loudly into the mattress, starbursts blinding his vision, the sense of fullness, of heat, expanding from his ass up through his throat.

She begins to slide her finger out, and he starts to cry, to ask her not to, but just as the fingertip comes close to letting his gate squeeze shut again, she slides slowly back in.

Danny hasn't ever made the sounds he's making now. That much he is sure of.

He doesn't know how, when, but he's pulled knees beneath him and raised his ass up into the air

"Remember the first time, Danny?" Suzie says, her voice almost sleepy as she buggers him with her finger. "Up at your parents' cabin by the lake, you'd pulled the whole *long distance relationships don't work* bullshit. . . I wanted you so much, but I was so fucking scared, driving all of the way up there; you wanted me too, so bad, I could see it the minute I walked in, you there on the bed, cock dripping, and it all happened so fucking *fast.*." She slides her finger all of the way out (*"NO!"*), but she places her lips against the vibrating flesh and he is speechless. "Not this time. The first time we fuck this way, I think we need to take our time." And then he feels a second finger joining the first, both of them pressing in, opening him gently but insistently. . .

Naked inside as out.

"One of the reasons I'm glad we didn't always stay together, Danny, is that I know what a good lover you are. I know I've got the best. The other boys, most of them, they barely cared I was even there. Even the ones who did, mostly they were just pleased with what they could do to me, what they could get me to do."

They've never talked about their other lovers beyond acknowledging that they had them. A mosaic of images flashes through his head, of other hands on her, other mouths on her, other cocks in her, her moaning, screaming other men's names. . ..

"You. . ." he gasps, "ever. . . the other boys. . . do *this?*"

"What, fuck Alan or Duane with the strap-on?" she asks with a laugh. "Nope." Her fingers still inside him, she moves right up against his raised pelvis, so that the two twin phalluses slide together; she reaches around and strokes them both together, so that he groans, speechless again. "Just you, lucky boy."

"Meant. . . anal. . ." he manages to pant.

They talked about him fucking her this way a few months back; she said she'd think about it, and he hasn't wanted to ask again, hasn't wanted to press. To pry.

"Ah," she said. She thrusts the strap-on cock through her fist, against his own. "Yeah. Didn't like it much, till I learned how to use the lubricant, how to take time."

"Learned from . . . ?"

"Who do you think, Danny-boy?" She thrusts her cock along his again.

He gasps. "Alice?" Their air-headed and apparently filthy-minded friend. Who *took care* of Suzie before Danny finally bowed to the fabulous inevitable and welcomed Suzie into his bed. *Did they . . . ?*

"'Course," she answers with a bit of a snort. "Who else? You? You ever do anything like this?"

"Huh. Hell. . . no."

She's started moving fingers and cock in the same rhythm. With her free hand, she's pinching her nipples.

In spite of himself, he smiles. "Daphne. . . liked. . . being tied up. . ."

Suzie whistled. "Wow. Who knew Miss D had it in her?"

"Didn't want it in her," Danny moans, trying to stay relaxed while trying also to stay sane. "Wanted it in *you*."

"Yeah, Danny?"

"Y-yeah."

"Lucky me." She groans, and the strap-on twitches against his erection. "You want it in you, Danny?"

"FUCK YES!"

"Could you be a bit more definitive?" she giggles.

"FUCK, Suzie, PLEASE, *FUCK ME!*"

"Okay, baby. Here it comes." She withdraws her fingers (*When did the third one get in there?*) and leans over him, pressing down on his neck with her hand. The tip of the strap-on slides up the no-man's land between his balls and his asshole, and suddenly, he can't breathe.

"Shh," she says, calming him again, running the tip of the ersatz erection up against his puckered hole. He can feel that it's open, that he is open, that he — "Breathe," she groans, and begins to press into him. He feels the insistent hardness press against him, bend. . .

And then slide through.

Danny's cock isn't huge — he's seen Jamie's, which stretched halfway down his thigh when it wasn't even hard — and he knows that the strap-on is exactly the same size as his.

But right now it feels like a tree trunk. Splitting him open.

. . .as on the outside. . .

"Damn, damn, Danny," Suzie hisses, "*sssooo* tight. . . How did you even get. . . all of the way in me those first few times without just. . ." She releases a deep, shuddering groan, and he knows that she's just had a small orgasm.

"Almost did," he says, voice small, eyes blind, cock weeping.

"And of course Luz'd leant a friendly helping *mouth.* Took the edge off." Suzie presses in deeper, lifting her left leg up so that she has a better angle.

"Aaaah." Suzie's thighs press against his own as she leans forward, pressing down on his neck. Thrusting in until her belly pushes against his ass, and the cock inside of him presses against *something.*

"Ahh!" he cries, as she withdraws the dick halfway, then slides it in again, once more touching that *place* — it's almost like a pinch or a squeeze, the feeling, but it feels so *good....*

Slowly, insistently, she begins to move in and out of him, pressing the breath out of him with each stroke, and filling him with fire instead.

He's never felt this way — never felt so much like he was having sex with all of himself, even though his cock itself is barely erect — it's dripping with his excitement. His whole fucking body is a hard-on. "Fuck, fuck, fuck, fuck me, Suzie, *fuck me.*"

Her breath catches, and he feels her hips slapping his backside all the more urgently, is sure he feels the rod inside of him swelling, *expanding* — it feels as if it must be the size of the whole fucking universe. "Damn, Danny, fuck, damn, damn, GOD. . ."

Reaching back between his legs with his bound hands, bowing his back so that her breasts — one hand still working at the nipples — are bouncing against his spine, he finds her dripping cunt with his fingers. So often when he fucks her she finds just the right moment to squeeze his balls, sending him off like a rocket. As her pelvis slams up against him, sliding her vulva back and forth over his searching fingers, he runs his fingers along either side. . .

"*Danny! Ah! Damn, SOOO—!*" Her breathing is ragged. She bows down against him, still pistoning in and out, but not as smoothly now.

His cock bouncing between his forearms, his head pressed against the mattress, Danny slips his middle and forefinger between the straps running under her thighs and her lips and as they slide through his fingers, the clit now erupting from the front like a ship's figurehead, he gently, firmly presses them together.

Suzie stops, buried all of the way inside of him, frozen in mid-stroke, and then convulses against him, a stream of obscenity exploding from her open throat.

And then they both collapse.

As they lie there, panting, sweaty, tangled, Danny finds himself regretting that he wasn't able to feel the splash of come inside of him. He's never really thought about how that must feel, but now — now he sure as hell has.

"Danny, Danny, Danny," Suzie murmurs, still inside of him. "Love you. Love you."

"Love you too." Without disengaging, they roll on their sides.

They lie there for quite some time.

She reaches around to where his cock lurches, limp but pouring fluid. "Did you come?"

"Uh, no, but—"

Her fingers slide around him, and he is mute. "God, Danny." She presses up tight behind him, breasts against his back, mouth against the nape of his neck. Her face is moist, and not just with sweat.

She starts to pull out of him, but he stops her. "Want. . . Can you get me to come like this?"

She nods against his back, and he could feel the cock wiggle inside of him. She strokes his soft, wet flesh between her fingers.

"Suzie?"

"Hmm?"

"So, I get the cock thing, I can see why you might, uh, enjoy having that."

"Called a dildo."

"Oh, right. The dildo." To be honest, it's hard to think about anything by the feeling of her fingers around his cock, of her breasts against his back, but that's what he's trying hardest *not* to think about. "I can see that, when you were alone, that might be. . ." He grunted as he felt her fingers sliding up and down him — still not hard, but gaining length, and *oh. . .*

"Nice, yeah." The smile in her voice makes him smile.

"But, mmm, I guess I'm wondering. . ." That spot that the dildo had been pressing against pulses, a small spill of liquid slipping out of his cock as her fingers slowly tease him hard. "Fuck. . . Um, but, see, what I don't get is. . ." As his erection grows, he feels her beginning to thrust too, small ones, and the pressure makes his eyes cross.

"Yeah, Danny? What you don't get? 'Cause it seems to me you're getting absolutely everything today."

"Lucky fucking me."

"Oh, yeah." She's got him hard now — not rock hard, he doesn't think he could be with that thing, that dildo, that erection pressing up into him, but he feels pretty fucking fabulous with her stroking him.

"What I don't get is, why the straps?"

"The—?"

"Well, if you never, you know, fucked any of the other boys this way—"

"Oh." She stops stroking him, and he whimpers at the pause. After a moment she begins moving hips and hand again, and at length she speaks. "So, Danny. Think about what you just said."

"What? That you'd never fucked any of the others this—?"

"That's. . . not what you said."

"I. . ." He ponders — hard to do while receiving a first-class hand job while having a beautiful woman fuck you gently up the ass. "I said, you'd never fucked any of the other boys this way?"

"Right."

He ponders some more. Or tries to. "Don't get it. Sorry."

"Any of the *boys*, Danny."

"The. . .?" He turns as much as he can without dislodging the prick from his ass or the hand from his cock. "You mean, you fucked—?"

He can barely see her face without his glasses, but can still see her face, bright red. "I was sleeping with Alice, Danny, yeah, that whole last break while you were off tying up Little Miss Daphne."

Well, that is sure as hell an image. "You. . . fucked Alice? With *my* cock?"

That brought a laugh, a deep, low laugh that bounced the cock inside of him and made him groan. "No, Danny, as it happens, no, I wasn't fucking her with your cock. *She* was fucking *me* with your cock."

"Oh." Yeah, he was definitely fully hard now, and probably would be for the rest of his life with those images running through his head.

She gives him a squeeze. "And it wasn't about missing my *ex*-boyfriend, shithead — at least not just. Sometimes," she says wetly into his ear, "we didn't need the strap-on at all."

"*Ah.*"

"Sometimes, we would lie right here on this bed, diddling each other for *hours*." Stretching the word to the breaking point, she cups just the head of his cock in her fingers, running the very tips minutely up and back over the flare.

"*Aaah.*"

"She'd done that to me before. You know that. But do you know who taught me how to make a woman scream with just my fingers?" She runs one of those very fingers around his nipple.

"*N-noooo, aah!*" He is going to die this time, he knows it, and really, really, that's okay.

"Well, he's a bit of a jerk, but I've got one hand stroking his cock, which both he and I agree is a very nice cock, and the other hand is stroking his balls, which are getting nice and tight, and I've got a hard cock of my own up his backside. . ." She presses up into him to drive that point home, hitting that *spot* inside so that he sees stars again, even as she picks up the pace with her hands, even as her speech remains absolutely steady. "And he's been carrying a ring box around all day in his jeans, so I think he's going to ask me to marry him, and I'm sure as fuck going to say yes, and then you know what, Danny?"

"*Aaah?*"

"Because he's been a very, very good boy, he's going to get to fuck me, any way he wants to, now, and for the rest of our lives."

And with that, the pressure of her quick-sliding hand and the pressure of her thick dildo and the pressure building up inside of him shatters him, and it all pours out — joy and regret and pleasure and pain — and he knows that they have made the right choice: that they will be prying into each other for as long as they both shall live.

On the Table

Suzie still can't quite wrap her mind around it.

Not that Alice burst out of a cake wearing nothing but an outfit of linked wine corks. No — Suzie spent weeks helping her put the crazy thing together so that it would be titillating without being obscene as her friend stood there, undulating unselfconsciously while singing a breathy rendition of "Happy Birthday," chocolate frosting smeared across her alabaster skin. Not the reaction of the birthday boy — Danny was rendered properly speechless — nor the reactions of their friends: Luz aghast and Jamie red-faced, Bill laughing wildly, Heather Snow trying to keep scowling though her lips kept twitching up, Chris snapping pictures like crazy, and — most interestingly — wild-boy Bennet hiding his face in Sarah's neck while conservative Sarah stared up at the cork-and-frosting-covered Alice, her mouth wide open.

No, all of this was just what Suzie had hoped would happen. The party teetered on more and more giddily over the last couple of hours, as everyone — even Luz and Jamie, who showed up in a sleep-deprived haze — had a wonderful, whiskey-fueled blow-out like they hadn't had in years. Alice blithely kept her wildly risqué yet remarkably unrevealing costume on, serving as a constant source of diversion, and all the girls took turns dancing atop the dining room table with an increasingly sweaty, increasingly shadow-free Danny, until at last Jamie couldn't take it any more, leapt up and lead Danny in a spirited polka that nearly collapsed the table. Danny hadn't even complained that Jamie insisted on leading.

No, he won't forget this combined birthday party and stag bash any time soon.

But it's what happened after. That is what is keeping Suzie's eyes wide — though the snoring isn't helping.

As the party wound down — as people began to stumble off — Suzie snagged her lover for herself, dancing slowly (on the floor) to one of those warbly old swing tunes that her mom used to love. She felt his breath against her cheek, all but smelt the desire radiating from him, and it took the little bit of restraint that no one ever believes Suzie actually has not to rip his clothes off and jump him even as the stragglers said their goodbyes.

Bennet and Sarah finally tottered to the door, smirking at her and Danny in so lascivious a manner as to make it very clear that they knew just what she and Danny would do right there in the entry hall as soon as the door slammed shut behind them.

"'Night, Bennet. 'Night, Sarah," Danny mumbled even as his fingers traced the most amazing patterns down the back of her dress, across her ass.

"Ga'night, luggy berfday boy, you!" Bennet slurred as Sarah tugged her boyfriend out of the door and giggled. She'd been giggling at Suzie kissing Danny for years — let her giggle all she wanted. As long as she did it somewhere *else*.

The door finally thudded shut behind them, and Suzie gave a shudder as Danny's other hand, holding his fresh scotch on the rocks, slid down and joined the first and he pulled her up and against him, her feet leaving the ground. She threw her legs around his waist. Fuck cleaning up.

"Happy birthday, sweetie," Suzie moaned into his neck. "You going to unwrap your last present... mmmmm.... right here?"

"Don't think I can stand to make it back to the bedroom," grunted Danny around nibbles on the top of her ear. "Over the back of the — " He hissed as she bit his neck and ground her crotch against him. " — of the couch, yeah." He walked her over towards the sitting room, his erection stiffening as she bounced against it.

When they'd reached the couch, she slid down and stepped back, reveling in the sight of Danny's utter arousal. He put down his drink and grinned at her wolfishly as she walked around the back of the settee, swaying her hipless hips at him and slowly lifting the hem of her dress over her butt.

He was stalking her, his hands on his fly, when another *thud* announced the departure of one last party-goer from the bathroom. Danny looked as if he had just been kicked in the crotch; Suzie didn't blame him — she wanted him inside of her *now*. Whichever of their stupid friends had managed to miss all of the not-so-subtle signals that she and Danny were sending out, Suzie was sure that a punch in the nose and a quick shove through the door wouldn't do too much damage.

"Hullo, Danny. Hello, Suzie," Alice said as she glided into the room. She was still dressed in her cork negligee. *Negligent*. That was just the word for Alice.

"Uh, everyone's gone," Suzie managed to say, forcing her fingers to release the hem of her dress so that it once again covered her butt, which was far from pleased at being shut away so soon.

"Oh," said Alice. She sidled over to the couch and sat.

Danny pleaded with Suzie wordlessly; he was biting his cheeks so hard that Suzie wouldn't have been surprised to learn that he had drawn blood.

Suzie looked down at her oldest, best, *weirdest* friend and had to stifle the urge to throttle her. "Alice," she said, pretending to yawn, "we're headed up to sleep."

"Really?" Alice said, eyes wider even than normal. "You don't look at all sleepy, either of you. You look as if you're about to fuck. Don't let me stop you. You can go upstairs. Or I can go upstairs. Or I could just stay here, if you wouldn't mind. I think that would be quite lovely."

Suzie was about to snap back that Alice could just fucking leave when she glanced at Danny. He was slack-jawed, staring at Alice. At the crotch of Alice. Who was sitting there, taking a sip from Danny's scotch while her long legs spread wide, bouncing one knee obliviously against the cushions on the back of the couch. *Negligent.*

Of course, it only occurred to Suzie then that the one direction into Alice's outfit that they hadn't thought to worry about had been the view from below. And Alice, of course, never wore underwear. Quite an oversight.

And it was at that moment that Suzie had the idea. It was *her* idea — that is the thing she can't quite come to grips with. She was the one to make this happen.

She teetered slightly as she leaned down to her friend and kissed her on the lips, which were cool from the ice in Danny's drink.

When they broke apart after a moment, Alice said, "Well, that was very nice. It's been a long time since we did that."

Ignoring the incoherent gibbering from Danny, Suzie asked, "You feeling lonely tonight, A?"

Her friend's usually smooth brow creased. "Yes, as a matter of fact, Suzie, I am."

"Then, Alice, sweetie," Suzie said, astonishing herself, "I don't think you need to stay down here. Or watch. Join us." Was it the alcohol that had her heart racing?

Alice gazed at her for fifteen or twenty seconds before saying, "That sounds quite lovely. But I don't know that Danny would necessarily agree."

Suzie looked at her lover, his face a battlefield of lust and shock. Danny blinked twice and mumbled, "Kissed her? You—?"

"You know we did, Danny," Suzie muttered. She knew he knew — knew that it had turned that secretly perverted brain of his to goo. "Well, no one else seemed to want to do it, so we took care of it ourselves. Remember that strap-on? I would pretend that she was you and she would pretend that I was Jaime."

Danny blinked.

"Actually, Danny," Alice said, knee still bouncing, fingers dancing mindlessly along the insides of her thighs, "she would pretend that I was you.

Sometimes I pretended that she was Jaime or Bill. And sometimes I pretended that she was you, since she made fucking you sound so lovely. And sometimes I pretended that she was herself. Which was rather more confuffling than it sounds."

"I bet" was as much as the poor boy could manage. Suzie sympathized. She had spent a lifetime puzzling out Alice's statements, and understood her as well as anyone, and even she was thoroughly confused as often as not. And that was under normal circumstances. Bringing her pixilated friend into their bed would not constitute *normal circumstances.*

"Danny," Suzie said, her hand finding Alice's cheek, "what do you think of this as your last birthday present?"

Danny's mouth flopped open and closed. His face took on that serious-fucking-Danny-face that let her know that he was going to do something stupid again. "Suzie. You don't really want this."

"Danny," she said. But she knew him well enough to know that appealing to his reason — even when he was drunk and horny — would never get him past the do-the-right-thing thing. So she leaned over the couch and kissed Alice once again.

She anticipated Danny's response: a sharp intake of breath and a quiet groan. What surprised her was the way that Alice reacted. Her normally diffuse friend answered Suzie's kiss with a ferocity that Suzie would never have guessed her capable of. Alice's mouth searched hers hungrily, her long, thin fingers danced over the same territory that Danny had been exploring so recently — the sides of Suzie's breasts, her back, her butt — and Suzie found herself melting into that same state of arousal that Alice had doused just moments before. Those insistent, scintillating fingers pulled Suzie forward into the kiss until she was on tiptoe; they gathered the silk of her dress, exposing her now *very* pleased ass.

Another, more familiar set of fingers ran up the backs of Suzie's thighs, over her ass, meeting the first bunch. Together, four hands began yanking Suzie's panties down.

Danny had clearly gotten the message.

Cool air met the warmth of her sex, but only for a moment. Lips met her lips, Danny's ever-loving tongue warming her again, and Suzie groaned, only to find Alice's tongue in her mouth dampening the sound, but stoking the fire.

If there had been an image in Suzie's head when she had first kissed Alice it had been of pleasing *them*: of giving Danny a birthday present unlike any he had ever received, of giving lovely, lonely Alice some of the contact and pleasure she so clearly longed for. It hadn't looked anything like *this*.

Suzie's legs were getting wobbly, and so she was forced to rest her weight on the arms that she had thrown around Alice's shoulders. Alice didn't seem to mind. Her hands performed a thorough, spiraling examination of Suzie's breasts and danced along her belly, which quivered at the overwhelming combination of sensations. When they reached the exposed flesh just below her navel, Suzie gasped and then whined as Danny's marvelous mouth disengaged at the very moment when she felt the first flutters of orgasm beginning to gather. No need to whine, though. First one and then two long Alice fingers found the spot that Danny's tongue had been flicking, and pleasure once again begin to mount.

Mount.

Danny is not extraordinarily long — he's always been very quick to tell her that, though she has never been much cared about it one way or the other. But Jesus, he is wonderfully thick and just right for her, and the nerve endings in Suzie's cunt exploded when he pressed slowly, deliberately into her from behind, spreading her. Filling her. *Mounting* her. Pressing her pelvis against Alice's whirring fingers. What was she doing with those...? Pleasure pulsed from Suzie's core, the waves of heat of Danny's thrusts coursed through her and Suzie felt her middle bloom and sound poured out and Alice swallowed all her screams and Danny howled behind her, liquid fire exuding up into her. Ready *now*.

Suzie's legs gave way and she pitched onto Alice's shoulder. Her hips slipped forward, leaving Danny behind, and one or both of them wailed, and she fell.

She found herself gazing up from Alice's lap, starred vision clearing. "Jesus."

"You've got frosting on your chin," Alice said, leaning down to lick it away. "Didn't hurt your fingers?"

"Oh, no," her friend replied, raising and wriggling the two digits in an indistinct, obscene salute before she cleaned them too with her tongue and Suzie's center trembled at the sight. "You're very light, you know." She picked up the scotch and ran her tongue over an ice cube.

Danny climbed over the couch — or around the couch, or through the couch — and began to kiss Suzie fiercely, there in Alice's lap. As they melted into each other, Alice stroked their hair.

Once they had finally begun to catch their breath, Danny backed away from Suzie. "Fuck, Suzie."

She found herself giggling as she hadn't done in years. "Yeah. Fuck." Looking up past Alice's cork-spangled breasts, Suzie spluttered, "Alice, where the fuck did you learn to do that?" She wiggled her fingers as her friend had done.

"Oh, practice." Alice grinned vaguely. "Lots and lots of practice. And I have picked up some things down at the lab, you know."

Danny leaned back and gazed at Alice. "Alice — what in God's name are you *researching?*"

"Well," Alice said with a frown, "I'm not supposed to tell. Though I've always thought that one of the advantages of hiring me for a top-secret job was that no one believes most of what I say anyway." When this was greeted with silence, she continued, "Well, this has been quite nice. But I should probably head on home."

Suzie could feel Danny choke back a response. Of course, it had to be *her* to say it. "We don't want you to leave, Alice. Do you want to go?"

Those enormous pale blue eyes managed somehow to get even bigger. "No, not particularly." Alice glanced up at Danny. "I haven't... woken up next to someone in quite a while. May I? Spend the night?" she asked, voice small.

"Of course," both of them answered, and — after a quick peek for approval — Danny leaned forward and shared one of Alice's warm, all-embracing kisses.

They pulled Alice to her feet and removed her ridiculous outfit, revealing the long, alabaster legs and curvy, porcelain butt that freckle-faced Suzie had always envied — and that she now found herself running her hands over as she kissed her friend's neck. Danny's fingers explored Alice's breasts as his mouth continued to pull at her lips.

"You're so beautiful," Suzie murmured into Alice's ear. It was true — something she had always thought but never said. "I can't believe you can't have any man."

Alice gasped as Danny's teeth found her throat; her head fell back, her hair spilling over Suzie's shoulder. "Ahhhh. Love is a mystery after all. Mmmm. I can't seem to find one. A man. Or a woman. I've never cared much about the outside really. Just someone lovely and... *Ohhhh.*"

Suzie was suddenly aware of the fresh scent of Alice's excitement. After all of these years together, she was very familiar with the smell of her own juices and Danny's — the juices that were still spilling out of her. But this was something new, tarter and richer. Without thinking, Suzie reached around her friend's hip and investigated the texture of a very different thatch of hair, of broad and frilly lips spread wide, a stiff nub at the front to circle. Her hand had danced this dance so many times, and yet here she was, fondling another woman's cunt, and there was something both familiar and frightening about the feeling. "Alice," Suzie muttered, "do you think Danny is lovely?"

Alice whimpered before nodding. He had lowered his head to her high breasts.

"Would you like him to fuck you?" Suzie asked, and felt a spark of panic flow through both of her partners. Why did she have to have been the calm one?

When Alice answered, however, her voice managed to sound as elsewhere-occupied as ever. "Yes, actually. That would be quite nice."

And so they led her to the bed — their bed — trailing clothing as they went, and Alice finally put down Danny's scotch (mostly half-melted ice now) and helped Suzie kiss Danny's cock back from its half-slumber to wonderful solidity. She contemplated sucking him dry, but knew that he would last longer than her jaw, since he'd already come tonight. Once he was hard, Suzie pushed him onto his back and maneuvered Alice astride him, pleased to find that she was admiring the contrast between their skins — Alice smooth and pale, Danny muscled and dark — rather than feeling jealous. She gave them each a kiss and then stroked their nipples as Alice lowered herself onto him.

Alice's expression usually ran a fairly tight gamut from utter distraction to vague pleasure to abstracted concentration. As Danny's flesh pressed into her, Suzie saw her friend's face take on an ecstatic expression — neither happiness nor sorrow, but of a feeling that Alice's usual placid features couldn't encompass.

As Alice began to rock her hips against Danny, Suzie moved behind her, running her hands over Alice's front, licking at her ear. Alice was making very un-Alice-like sounds; when Suzie's fingers reached her clit where it slid along Danny's pubic bone, she let loose a growl that was two full octaves lower than Alice's normal voice.

"So, Alice," Suzie murmured, "what was that thing you did with your fingers?"

Alice's first response utterly lacked vowels. Clearly Suzie's own diddling wasn't entirely ineffective — especially when combined with Danny's rolling thrusts.

"Come on, Alice, it was really amazing. What was that?"

Alice's hands reached back and clutched at Suzie's hair. "Ah! Alpha-wave. Stimulation. Chaotic. Pattern. Feeds the nerves a rhythm. Can't anticipate."

Which made no sense to Suzie at all, though it did make her wonder just what Alice and her colleagues got up to down in their lair. It didn't seem to matter much. She kept up her stroking and pinching, working in time and then in syncopation with Alice and Danny's writhing.

As Alice began to come for the first time, Suzie embraced her from behind, peering over Alice's shoulder into her man's blank, sweaty face. As Alice howled toward the ceiling, Danny locked eyes with Suzie and mouthed *I love you*.

For some reason it was that, of all of the possible things, that snapped the spell for Suzie. She released Alice, who fell forward onto Danny's chest. When Danny began to slow, Alice screamed, "NO!" and slammed her pelvis against Danny's.

Suzie moved beside them as they fucked, touching them still, though her mind was losing contact. Cold, slippery shame began to course through her, a feeling she hadn't struggled with much recently, and she began to cry.

Neither of her lovers noticed. Danny had his sex scowl on, a look that Suzie was intimately acquainted with, while Alice's fuck face was as always placid, utterly at peace, even as her body rippled with one orgasm after another.

At last, Danny flipped Alice onto her back, thrust into her twice more, and growled.

That was a sound that Suzie had heard once or twice.

Danny slowly backed away from Alice, uncoupling with a slurp, kissing her sweat-bright face. Suzie sat there, knees curled into her chest, appreciating the beauty of what she was seeing and yet filled with shame and terror. Soon she could not see.

A kiss cooled her cheek — Alice's, by the lips' fullness. Suzie tried to blink away the tears, but could only manage to see a black-haired blur and a blonde one. *This is how Danny sees without his glasses*, Suzie realized, and she began to laugh wetly.

"Okay, Suzie?" Danny's voice sounded very far away.

She tried to dismiss her own display. "Fine. I'm just..." But she couldn't think what she just was, and sobs bubbled up and choked her.

Four arms laced themselves around her, rocking her. Her boy. Her best friend. Alice's breasts against her arm. Danny's damp, softening cock — damp with Alice and with Suzie herself — against her hip. She sobbed in their arms until she felt ridiculous, but she could not stop.

Eventually, Danny lowered her head into his lap and began to stroke her hair. The smell of their fuck brought on fresh waves of panic, but his fingers in her hair, Alice's smooth palms circling her belly calmed Suzie enough to breathe.

"I do love you," Danny whispered, which made it better and worse at the same time.

"I know," Suzie hiccuped. "But... What did I do?" Their whole life together was built around their shared belief that they were meant for each other, this wonderful symmetry that had sustained them through school, their dating-not dating stretch and years of... whatever this was. The Never-ending Engagement. They got teased — mostly by her sister Liz — about being the Perfect Couple.

And now Suzie had introduced a wobble into their balance. A crack in their façade.

She wasn't jealous. Not at all. She trusted Danny totally. She trusted Alice. Hell, she trusted them in some ways more than she trusted herself.

No, she wasn't jealous. She was terrified.

Alice's voice wafted up from the vicinity of Suzie's hip. "Suzie," she said, "I don't want to move in."

"What?"

"I like having my own apartment. I like singing the words from X-Men comic books out loud at three in the morning, I like eating chocolate-covered Natternuts for breakfast. Other than you in the apartment we shared — and my mother — I've never been able to live with anyone for longer than a week."

"Alice," Suzie said, "what are you talking about?"

A long finger traced a line from Suzie's kneecap to her hip and back again. "I don't think I'm going to be taking Danny away from you. Or you away from Danny. And I don't want to move in, though your apartment really is quite lovely, and this is a very comfy bed. You love Danny and he loves you, and I love you both, but nothing that you started tonight is going to change anything. Is it, Danny?"

"No," Danny answered. Suzie looked up into his eyes. Without his glasses they seemed darker, deeper. She had been falling into those eyes for most of her life.

"You don't..." Suzie found that the frisson of their fingers' caresses was angering her. She didn't want to melt into the pleasure of touch. Closing her eyes, she forced herself past the reblooming of her own desire. "Alice, I am frightened. Nobody but Danny has touched me in years. I hope the same is true for him."

"Since... Yes," Danny murmured. "Suzie..."

"Please, Danny. Everything we've got together is based on that. So what now? Do we just fuck whoever we want? And what about you, Alice? I feel like I... used you and hate myself for doing — "

"You know, Suzie," Alice said, "I don't feel at all used. At least, not in a way I don't like. I am rather lonely, it's true, but I'll be honest with you — I rather prefer to be alone. It's very nice. No one moves my research. No one wants to talk about football while I'm reading. No one eats my last bit of Coffee Toffee Crunch Ice Cream. Of course, no one brushes my hair or listens to my nightmares. And no one fucks me until I cry. Sex really is quite lovely." Alice's fingertips ran lightly along Suzie's labia, and Suzie found herself biting down a moan. "This is just something nice that you decided to do for Danny and for me." Long fingers tugged at the tangle of Suzie's pubic hair. "I would like to do something nice for you, Suzie. Would you like that? Would that be all right with you, Danny?"

Danny had his sincere face on — the one that told Suzie that he would follow her anywhere. Suzie considered all of the times that she had followed her impulses — kissing Danny behind the boys' gym, telling Luz that Jaime and Lisa had just broken up. Driving up to the lake straight from Alice's bed, crotch and nipples on fire, to find Danny in bed screaming her name, hard cock in his hand (the hard cock she'd never seen but had been visualizing for months). Showing up at the his office wearing his overcoat... and nothing else. Kissing Alice. And kissing Alice.

Suzie nodded to Danny. Danny smiled. "Yeah, Alice. It's fine with me." He leaned down but stopped just short of kissing Suzie. "Can I help?"

"Oh, that would be very pleasant." Alice said — Suzie couldn't speak. "Does she still have that bag, Danny?"

He nodded. "Beneath the bed. On this side."

Suzie shivered, knowing just what bag Alice meant, and knowing that Danny and Alice both knew too — both knew just what was in that bag. Her mind raced. *What does Alice —?*

Suzie found herself gasping into Danny's hungry mouth as she felt Alice's taut nipples drag across her belly — Alice reaching for the bag where Suzie had hidden it, ready for use. It hadn't been used much recently.

Danny's hands found Suzie's own breasts and began to tease them gloriously — Danny had learned a lot over the years, including several magically kinky techniques for getting Suzie off. For this, however, he needed only the most basic of magic: the magic of flesh, nerves and mind. And he knew that magic quite well.

All shame forgotten for the moment, Suzie began to melt into the heat of her man's touch. As warmth began to pool languidly in her center, she heard Alice whispering something to herself. Heard silk and leather, metal and plastic sliding against each other, against skin. Alice's hand flowed over Suzie's leg, not *quite* touching. A different heat flowed through and around Suzie's body, and then a relaxation so complete that it felt as if only her bones kept Suzie's body from flowing off of the bed and onto the floor. Still Alice had not touched her, and calm as Suzie was, she felt anticipation gnaw at her cunt, knowing that something would come.

Probably her.

Hopefully her.

"Close your eyes, Suzie, and stay completely relaxed," Alice ordered, her voice unusually firm. Suzie did her best to obey.

After a few moments Suzie felt the bed shift, felt Alice's fingers slide over her own — felt a loop of satin rope loop around her wrist, felt Alice knot it deftly and securely. In spite of herself Suzie tensed.

"Shhh," Danny soothed, his mouth still glued to hers but shifting. "It's okay."

A slithering sound — the rope being pulled through the bars of the headboard — and then Danny's larger fingers tying Suzie's other wrist no less securely over her head as Alice tied the silk scarf that Danny and Suzie sometimes used as a blindfold over Suzie's eyes. Suzie urged her body to stay relaxed, to trust them. She was at her lovers' mercy.

Two mouths touched Suzie's lightly, and she couldn't suppress the shudder and the gooseflesh that the feeling raised in her.

Suzie had always laughed at the shamed pleasure that Danny took in being tied up, in having all control taken away. Suzie had always enjoyed the *game* of it, but. . .

But now, blindfolded and bound, her two lovers kissing their very different ways to her cheeks, to her ears, to her neck, Suzie reveled in it — reveled in the freedom of not being able to *do* anything except lie there and accept their ministrations.

"God, Suzie," Danny hissed into one ear, "if you only knew what a fucking wet dream you look like right now." That was all it took — Suzie felt air flow over her inner lips as they flowered open again.

Danny took hold of Suzie's cheeks and he kissed her.

She was about to demand that his hands wander elsewhere when she felt Alice (still letting one set of long fingers flow over the down of Suzie's thighs, riffling through the tangle of Suzie's pubes) lean across, dragging her tits over Suzie's belly again — *something else from the bag? The ball gag? The strap-on?* Suzie's heart sped up.

But instead of the slither of leather from the leather bag, Suzie heard the *klink* of ice in a glass and a slurp — Danny's long-nursed, long-forgotten drink.

While Danny continued to kiss Suzie — gloriously, completely — the hand that Alice had been floating over Suzie's legs and belly drew a line down the crease between Suzie's left thigh and her pussy, and Suzie groaned into Danny's mouth, her legs spreading without any instruction from Suzie.

But the tip of Alice's fingers gave Suzie's singing clit a deliciously close miss and continued up the other side. Suzie felt her pelvis rock involuntarily to try to capture the retreating hand, pushing her shoulders upward, and she understood suddenly why Danny and Alice had tied her in place. Fucking hell. They were going to take their time with this. And Suzie wanted them to, really, she did… Mostly, however, she just *wanted*.

The magic fingers floated back down Suzie's thigh and across her knee and drifted slowly back up the inside, doing another close flyby of Suzie's cunt. Panting, trying to maintain her relaxation, Suzie pulled on the rope with both arms, arched her back, and then groaned as Danny's fingers finally began to travel slowly down along her collarbone and toward her breasts, toward her nipples, which were almost painfully hard.

Something touched the inside of Suzie's left thigh — she gasped at the *burn* of it, searing… *Cold?* She felt wide, wet, *cool* lips kiss the sensitive flesh and then move up her thigh and plant another hot-cold kiss that sent a shock the few inches to Suzie's clit and then up her spine, spreading until it was all over her body at once, and the hot-cool liquid sensation poured up around her breasts and Alice's cool lips reached her labia, setting Suzie shivering — more with anticipation than with cold — and then Danny's fingers found Suzie's nipples at the same moment that Alice's skinny tongue reached out and dabbed her clit. *FUCK.*

And then Alice pushed a slick piece of ice into Suzie's pussy — *FUCK!* — and began to alternate between licking her and sucking the ice in and out of Suzie until it finally melted away, and it was all too much. Suzie squeezed her thighs around Alice's head, anchoring herself in space as her back arched. She tried to breathe deeply, to keep still as they pleasured her, Danny pulling and pinching her nipples in a way that he knew drove her wild and Alice finding that same erratic rhythm with her icy tongue that had so mesmerized Suzie earlier that night when Alice had used it with her fingers. Suzie's body quivered, trying to balance the contrary impulses, before finally releasing into a kind of rolling undulation and her blind eyes filled with light.

When she and Alice had played years before — before she and Danny were fucking, and on a couple of occasions when Danny and she had theoretically split up — Suzie had always been on her hands and knees or her belly. Though they'd kissed a bit, until tonight Alice had always diddled Suzie with her fingers or used the strap-on from behind.

Suzie loved Alice, and she'd loved the way Alice could get her off, but Suzie really, really was about as *not* bi as a girl who had sex with another girl could possibly be. When Alice had played with her, Suzie had been thinking about Danny. Pathetic.

Alice on the other hand was the living definition of pansexuality. As she'd said, she really didn't care about the gender of her lovers. Alice was always happy with whatever she could do to help her friend, and always happy with whatever her friend could do for her, with dildo and fingers.

They'd never gone down on one another. It had never occurred to Suzie before.

In that moment, Suzie regretted never having felt Alice's flame-like tongue on her clit before. As much as she could regret anything.

Danny loved to eat her. Ate her very well. Had eaten her just last night on this very bed for what felt like *hours*, after they'd had a long conversation about being married....

And now.

And now Danny's mouth was on her breasts again; she could feel his teeth against her pulsing nipples. And Alice's cold-hot tongue fluttered and her fingers pushed into Suzie's folds, making the walls of her cunt howl and Suzie came and she screamed and whose name it was that she screamed she did not know, but the sound ripped through her and she felt as if she had been unstrung, as if the laces the bound her to herself had been cut and she collapsed.

When she came to herself again, it took her some time to realize that she could see — they had untied her and removed the blindfold. Two faces smiled down on her. She was on the bed, lying between them.

"Hello, Suzie," Alice said. *Why did she say that?*

Danny said nothing, but his eyes, naked of glasses, spoke to her, and she cried again. "Happy birthday," she managed to splutter.

Danny whispered into Suzie's ear, "So. The honeymoon. Is there anyone special you'd like to invite?"

Speechless, Suzie stared up at the dark-masked ceiling.

"Alice again? Bill? Jaime?" When she didn't answer, he continued aloud, "Since the day you brought me to life, up at the lake, I've known that nothing could come between us, Suzie. I'm yours forever. You're mine."

As silent tears flowed over Suzie's cheeks, Alice's hand cupped Suzie's breast comfortably and she said, "I love you too, Suzie. It really is very nice of you to let me be here."

Danny picked her up, and Alice lifted back the duvet, and the two of them arranged themselves around her and put out the lights.

"Thank you both," Alice sighed, her long fingers locking with Danny's over Suzie's still fluttering belly. "I look forward to waking up with you."

"Hmm," Suzie replied.

"Perhaps in the morning you wouldn't mind letting me see you fuck? I have always wanted to see the two of you fuck."

Danny murmured something into Suzie's neck. Suzie nodded, and her lovers both passed immediately into slumber.

Qualms.

Suzie is not generally given to having *qualms*, but she's feeling them now. She believes Danny. She believes Alice. She knows that this experience is something she cannot, would not wish undone.

And now?

She longs to let Alice love her. She longs to lick Alice to tears while Danny fucks her. She longs to wake up to Alice's silk-light caresses and Danny's morning passion. She hungers to watch Jaime and Danny swallow each other's cocks while Bill fucks Luz from behind, her heavy breasts swaying to his thrusts as Luz laps at Alice's cunt and Alice's mouth and fingers do their magic to Suzie and she wants it all *now*, tired as she is.

And it's just sex.

But there is love too, and where does one begin and the other end?

Danny's hand slides up over her breast. She does love him, God knows. And she does love Alice.

And everything is on the table now; this genie is out of its bottle, and let it bestow its blessings where it may.

Pulling her lover and her friend tight around her, Suzie lets out a long, damp breath and floats slowly off to sleep herself.

Continued in...

Across the Threshold

Here comes the bride....

*Finally. **FINALLY!** Danny and Suzie are married!*

Danny and Suzie are on their honeymoon; once they've settled into the bridal suite, Danny has nothing in mind but making love to his wife. Suzie, however, lets him know that she's got bigger plans when she pulls out her little bag of tricks.

(New adult MF erotic romance. Bondage, submission. Adult readers only.

Share what you thought

Dear Reader,

Thanks so much for taking the time to read **Wilder West**. If you enjoyed it, please consider telling telling your friends or posting a short, honest review. Word of mouth is an author's best friend. Whether it's on the site where you found this book, your blog, Twitter, Facebook, or Goodreads, your honest review would help your friends — and me.

If you'd like to share your comments with me directly, or you have any questions for me, you can email me at kdwest@stillpointdigital.com

Until next time!

K.D. West

You can follow K.D. West on

WordPress, Twitter, Facebook, Pinterest, or Tumblr.

@KDWestWrites

Preview: The Visitor Has Company

"Let me see," sighed Lea, licking the index finger of her right hand as she ran the left one up Sean's bicep and down Andy's. "However shall I choose which of you I should marry?"

Both men moaned. Lea giggled. She didn't giggle very often, but this called for it.

They were back to back, sitting, each handcuffed to the legs of the other's chair. Naked. Each sporting a dark red erection, the tip of which glistened with pre-cum.

"Oh, gentlemen, you can't hurry a lady. And after all," she said, letting both hands flow down over their chests, stopping *just* short of their very emphatic hard-ons, "you did ask for this."

Both men whimpered.

Well, they hadn't exactly asked for *this* — they'd asked her to decide which side of their triangle would be the one to become official. And gay marriage wasn't legal in Georgia yet (though it was clearly just a matter of time), and so it was up to Lea to choose: Andy or Sean?

Only Lea didn't want to choose. Didn't see why they had to choose. And so she'd agreed to consider it only if they made themselves completely available for her delight. Which they'd done.

And so, for the past two hours, she'd been slowly teasing them — with her fingers, with her mouth, with the strapon they each loved her to use on him. All while slowly discussing the relative merits of each choice.

Which really wasn't a choice. She wanted them both, always. When they'd originally proposed to her, back at the beginning of the summer, it had been a way to keep Andy's family from finding out just what the three of them were up to. Sean had gotten down on one knee and asked her to marry *Andy*, for fuck's sake. Andy had asked her to marry Sean. Or to wear the diamond ring as a sign of a promise between the two men.

But Andy's family had seen through the charade quickly enough. Lea could still barely talk to Andy's mom, Nadine, or to his sister Jessie.

The whole getting married thing — what was the point?

She got down on her own knees, letting her fingertips brush the insides of their thighs. Andy twitched; Sean moaned.

Lea's Tantra-loving, West Coast parents would probably be more concerned with the idea of Lea staying in Georgia than with the idea of her shacking up with two guys. Probably.

And Kirsten—Sean's sister already knew all about it. Well, most about it.

Lea's fingers traced lines up the insides of the far legs, evoking twin shivers.

Not Violet. Not Sean and Kirsten's mother, whose ring Lea was wearing on her left hand. Lea loved Violet; her disappointment was actually the thing that Lea was most afraid of — that the very proper, very traditional Atlanta kindergarten teacher would be disgusted by the choices that her son and his lovers had made. That Violet would blame the whole thing on Lea. Which struck Lea as not just terrifying but blatantly unfair. It wasn't like she'd *asked* for things to turn out the way that they had. Exactly.

Shitty-shit-shit.

Tilting her head to one side and then the other, Lea admired the two lovely penises that were at her beck and call. She let her fingers run over their balls, which jumped, and then, for the first time since she had closed the handcuffs on them two hours before, she circled the bases of those two lovely penises, squeezing every so slightly as she let her hands stroke up — "I'll tell you what, boys." — and down.

Sean sounded as if he were trying to say *What?*, while Andy simply gibbered.

"I'll tell you what," she said again — again with an upstroke. "The one of you who can keep from coming the longest is the one I'll marry."

They both gasped; both set their jaws in determination, closing their eyes.

Okay, thought Lea with grin, *this might be fun.* And she began to give them the lightest, slowest handjob that she could. She leaned forward to lick the crevice between their elbows and —

And the doorbell rang.

Shitty-shit-shit! *"Um. Hold on a minute! Be right there!"* Could it be Lorelle from downstairs, requesting that we be *less* quiet?

Lea stood, grabbing her silk robe from where she'd let it pool to the floor.

The bell rang again.

The two men — firemen, after all — had managed to uncuff themselves and were pulling jeans up over their still-dripping erections.

"Sorry, guys," she whispered, giving each cock a quick tug and then pulling her robe shut. *"Coming!"*

"I wish," one of the guys muttered, which unfortunately struck Lea as amusing, and so she was giggling again as she opened the door and —

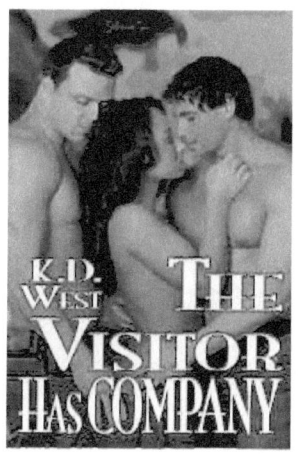

The Visitor Has Company: A Friendly MMF Ménage Tale
COMING JULY, 2015!

About K.D. West

The Amazon best-selling author of the *Erotic Tales: Letters to Allison* and *Juliet Takes Flight* story cycles as well as the up-coming novel *A Joy Forever: An Erotic Education*, **K.D. West** is a teacher, writer and performer living in a small suburb of a big city: "Not a huge amount to say — I'm an author of steamy stories who happens to be a teacher; these things don't mix well in public, so I tend to be fairly quiet about real life in my blogging. I am, however, interested in all sorts of things — books, writing, theater, mythology, and, obviously, erotica! I'm a huge reader of genre fiction — mostly mysteries and fantasy, but also science fiction and historical romance."

West is working on two intertwined series involving a young woman and her older lover (the *Juliet Takes Flight* and *Erotic Tales: Letters to Allison* stories), a series of stories about friends discovering that they can become much more (*Friendly Ménage Tales*), and a series of the kinds of fairytales that the Brothers Grimm might have written if they'd been interested in stories where the heroine got the princess (*Sapphic Fairytales*). Also on the way: *By the Numbers,* an erotic paranormal/urban fantasy novel involving a long-lost friend coming all-but-literally back from the dead, and showing a happily married couple just what they'd been missing.

You can follow K.D. West on
WordPress, Twitter, Facebook, Pinterest, or Tumblr.
@KDWestWrites

Stillpoint/Eros

Fine erotica and erotic romance

Ebook, print, and audiobook editions

Available at
StillpointEros.com

www.ingramcontent.com/pod-product-compliance
Lightning Source LLC
Chambersburg PA
CBHW020047180626
46812CB00006B/2228